Deadly Inheritance

by

Suzanne Rossi

This is a work of fiction. Names, characters, places, and incidents are either the product of the author's imagination or are used fictitiously, and any resemblance to actual persons living or dead, business establishments, events, or locales, is entirely coincidental.

Deadly Inheritance

Cover Art by *Debbie Taylor*

The Wild Rose Press, Inc.
PO Box 708
Adams Basin, NY 14410-0708
Visit us at www.thewildrosepress.com

Publishing History
First Crimson Rose Edition, 2013
Print ISBN 978-1-61217-799-1
Digital ISBN 978-1-61217-800-4

Published in the United States of America

"If I croak could the present will be contested again and revoked?"

"I'm not sure. I suppose someone could make a case that the exclusion of a death clause—against my advice—and the fact he wrote it himself, shows unsound mind."

I pulled the straw from my frappe and gulped the rest of the cold concoction, then licked the whipped cream from my lips. Stephen stared at me with a strange look on his face. I stopped to consider the whipped cream and my actions before tearing my mind away from prurient thoughts.

"Terrific. I feel like I have a target stamped on my forehead."

He finished his coffee, frowned, and then leaned forward, placing his hand on my arm. Warmth spread upward to my shoulder.

"Don't worry, Liza. I think Irene was relieved she didn't have to deal with the house and grounds. Her last divorce gave her a house on the south side of the island."

His hand slid down to mine and squeezed. A shot of adrenaline burst from the pit of my stomach. I had the strangest urge to leap across the tiny table and kiss him senseless.

"You feel safe, don't you?"

From the family—probably. From Stephen Albright—not a chance in hell. He was as dangerous as they come.

Praise for Suzanne Rossi

"I found [*ALONG CAME QUINN*] entertaining and a quick read. It's a fun road romance with a twist on the treasure that I think is different yet believable. And it just goes to show that sometimes you can't see what's right under your nose." ~*Dear Author*

"I couldn't wait to turn each page to see what would happen next. Suzanne Rossi has definitely been added to my must-read list. The terrific twist on the run of the mill mob story makes [*ALL IN THE FAMILY*] a definite keeper."

~*Theresa Joseph, The Romance Studio*

"[*A TANGLED WEB*] has to be THE BEST romantic/suspenseful/mystery novel that I have read to date. The love scenes were perfectly timed with the plot, the suspense kept me turning the pages, and the mystery was superbly developed. Once I started reading it, I could not stop."

~*Happily Ever After Reviews*

"[*NEARLY DEPARTED*] is the BEST ghost story I have read in a long time. The wacky cast of characters is so colorful and fun that they bring the story to life."

~*Night Owl Reviews*

"I really got a good laugh out of [*HEAR NO EVIL*] and enjoyed the plot immensely which draws you in from the beginning... This author has done an incredible job penning this amazing tale."

~*The Romance Studio*

Dedication

Several years ago, my husband and I vacationed on the Caribbean island of Barbados. The atmosphere was both bustling and laid back. The people were warm and friendly, always ready to smile and say hello.

~

When I needed a setting for this book, Barbados leaped into my mind. The estate, Bountiful, is based on a real home we toured while there. The dramatic views from the cliffs were taken directly from the views on the eastern coast of the island. Bridgetown and the fictional Port Elizabeth are similar. Even the cave is a small representation of the real Harrison's Cave.

~

So, here's to Barbados and Bajans. I love you all and hope to see you again soon.

Other books by Suzanne Rossi
available from The Wild Rose Press, Inc.

Along Came Quinn
All in the Family
A Tangled Web
Nearly Departed
Hear No Evil
The Reunion

Chapter One

"I've inherited a what, where?" I stared at family attorney, Adam Wyles, like he'd lost his mind.

He lowered the sheaf of papers and stared back over the rim of his glasses.

"You have inherited an estate on the Caribbean island of Grand Britannia from the late Sir Geoffrey Goodhue."

"Who the hell is Sir Geoffrey Goodhue, and why would he leave me anything?"

"According to this, he was a member of Parliament and former Governor of the island."

"Sir? As in a knight or something?"

"His knighthood was conveyed in nineteen-eighty-nine."

He redirected his gaze to a page held in his hand. "I, Geoffrey Goodhue, being of sound mind, do hereby bequeath my house and grounds to my great-granddaughter…" he paused "…Elizabeth Marie Channing."

I gasped as shock rolled through me. "Is this some kind of weird joke? My family names are Madison and Channing."

Adam sighed and dropped the paper onto his desk. "Liza, your mother was adopted as a baby."

"I know."

"This man is apparently your biological great-grandfather. His son was your grandfather, your mother's father."

"I understand the genealogy, but why me?"

He ignored my question. "He tracked down your mother some twenty years ago."

"Why wouldn't Mom tell me, or didn't she know?"

"She knew, but wanted nothing to do with the family."

"Why?"

"She didn't want to upset your grandparents and had no desire to meet the old man."

"So, he leaves this house to me instead? Why? Didn't he have any relatives left on this island?"

"Yes. Apparently, he has grandchildren, great-grandchildren, and other assorted relatives near the estate, Bountiful."

"It has a name? For God's sake, why not leave it to a grandchild or relative he knew?" I stopped to think. The word estate conjured up images of manor houses with loads of acreage. *And if it's got a name, then the house must be huge. And if the house is huge…* Dollar signs floated in front of my eyes. "How big is this place?"

Adam picked up another sheet of paper and scanned it. "The house is approximately ten thousand square feet with eight bedrooms, ten baths, a library, several sitting rooms, and all the rest. The grounds encompass fifty acres complete with a maze and sea views."

My jaw dropped. Jackpot! "No kidding? How much is this thing worth? If I can sell it…"

My attorney raised his hand. "Wait a minute,

there's a stipulation."

Crap. I hate stipulations. That's lawyerese for giving orders and setting boundaries.

"In order to inherit, you must take possession and live in the house for one year."

A year! I leaped to my feet. "What! That's insane. I'm an actress. I can't up and leave for a year. Forget it. Let a grandkid have it."

"According to the will, if you do not accept the terms, Geoffrey Goodhue's estate will be turned over to various charities. If you agree, then the other heirs will get their share." Adam cleared his throat. "There's apparently a lot of money involved, too."

"What do I care? I don't know these people." I resumed my seat and paused as his last sentence sank in. "How much money?"

"Quite a bit."

"Do I get some of that, too?"

"Yes. Liza, think about it. A year out of your life, then you can sell the place and live like a queen."

All that money, and potential money, sounded damned good. My career was in a massive slump. I hadn't nailed down anything other than a local TV commercial in four months. My out-of-work slush fund had withered, and I'd soon be forced back into waiting tables. Then ego overrode greed.

"What about my career? I can't abandon it now, especially for that length of time. My agent will drop me, and producers will forget I exist. Living like a queen won't buy me name recognition. Adam, I just can't do this."

"Liza, I don't know what this is all about, but other people's lives, their futures, are in the balance."

"So I make the sacrifice? That sucks."

"Look, you have until the end of the month to make a decision. Go home, think about it, and let me know. However, I strongly urge you not to pass on this opportunity."

I glared at Adam, torn by indecision. The island of Grand Britannia was a major tourist destination, and now, if I accepted, fifty acres of it was mine. That represented a large chunk of real estate—very expensive real estate.

"Does my mother know about this?"

"Yes, I informed her yesterday. She's also mentioned in the will."

"And what was her reaction?"

"She was surprised and not all together pleased with the old man's manipulations."

"Yeah, I can imagine." My mother was like me in that respect. She didn't like anyone telling her what to do either. It explained why she'd had five husbands.

Adam's desk phone buzzed. He handed me an envelope. "Here this is for you," he said before answering. "Yes… Have him wait. I'm just finishing up in here. Another couple of minutes. Oh, and give Mr. Mason a call about…"

I tuned Adam out, opened the envelope, and read the single sheet of paper with the embossed heading of Albright, Albright, and Swisher.

Miss Channing, my name is Stephen Albright and I represent the estate of the late Sir Geoffrey Goodhue. The terms, as I'm sure your attorney has delineated, are simple. While you are required to live in the house for a year, you are also given time to return to Los Angeles to conduct any business you may have in the

States. However, you must not spend any more than two weeks away from the estate, and those absences can only be redeemed once every three months. I understand this entire proceeding must be a shock to you, but please be aware of the consequences to others if you decline. Sincerely, Stephen G. Albright.

The message was to the point and slightly intimidating. His firm, legible signature along with the wording suggested he was in command at all times. *Not to mention arrogant, too.*

Well, I didn't intimidate easily and could hold my own with commanding, arrogant directors. What made Stephen Albright any different?

Adam hung up and turned to me, rising. "I have another client, Liza. Think it over."

"Hold it. Not so fast. What's this about me having only two weeks every three months to return? I can't audition for anything. Directors and producers take forever to make up their minds—even for a simple thirty-second TV spot. My career will be in the toilet."

He sighed. "Liza, only contestants on *Survivor* are cut off from the rest of the world. Keep in touch through social media. Start a blog of your experiences on Grand Britannia. I have a client who owns a small newspaper in the San Fernando Valley. With a little persuasion, he might pick up your musings as a weekly column. You'll be connected." He checked his watch. "Talk to your mother. However, I recommend you do this."

I left his office mulling over his advice and glanced at my watch—eleven forty-five. "Talk to my mother, huh?" I muttered to myself in the elevator. "Damned right I'm gonna talk to her."

I wanted answers, and I wanted them now.

****

"Darling, I'm sorry, but I just don't know what to tell you." My mother sipped from her wine glass, no doubt to avoid meeting my gaze.

I'd called her from the car. She hadn't been surprised and agreed to meet for lunch at Rue de la Paix, a very trendy bistro just off Rodeo Drive.

"You could start with this great-grandfather thing. How come you never mentioned him to me?"

"You were ten years old. What was I going to say? Besides, your father and I were going through the divorce. I had other things on my mind."

"But why didn't you want to meet him?"

She drained her drink and held the glass aloft for the waiter to see. He nodded, disappearing toward the bar.

"Mother, answer me. I need guidance here. What should I do? If I go, I could screw up my career. If I don't, I lose out on a butt-load of money."

"You'll inherit a decent estate from me, so why bother with relatives you've never met? Don't mess up your career now. Besides, Goodhues probably marry well, so don't worry that they'll end up on the street corner selling pencils or something." She ran a hand through her short sandy hair.

Sometimes, looking at Mother was like looking in a mirror. We both had blonde hair—mine longer, slightly lighter, and with more dramatic highlights— blue eyes, and even features. We were even the same height, five-seven. And each of us claimed artistic talent. Hers was painting. People paid dearly for a Janelle Madison landscape or still life. Unfortunately, we were also both good at avoiding unpleasant subjects. I'd be damned if I let her off the hook.

"You still haven't answered my question. Why did you refuse to see him? Did he come here?"

She snorted. "Hell, no. He demanded my presence in Grand Britannia. Demanded! When I declined the royal summons, he had the nerve to say that even though illegitimate, I was still a Goodhue and family belonged together. He'd take care of me until finding me a good husband. Can you imagine?"

No, I couldn't. Ordering my independent, free-spirited mother to do anything was courting death. I didn't want to go into the husband part.

"So he was an overbearing jerk. What did you say?"

"Told him to drop dead, of course. What else?"

What else, indeed.

Her drink arrived, and she shifted in her seat, her gaze lowering to the Pinot Grigio in the glass. As an actress I know all about body language, and my mother was still in deep avoidance.

"Was that the end of it, or did you hear from him again?"

She set her glass on the table, fished in the over-sized tote bag that accompanies her everywhere, removed a large manila envelope, and then said with a frown, "He wrote off and on for two or three years. I never answered. Can't imagine why I kept the damned things." She gulped half of her wine and muttered, "I just knew you were going to accept this bizarre arrangement."

I extracted a dozen or so letters. The handwriting on the envelopes was bold, written with an old-fashioned fountain pen telling me the old boy was used to getting his way. The script reminded me of Stephen Albright's signature.

"I haven't said yes yet," I reminded her, flipping through the packets. The last five remained unopened. "You didn't read all of them?"

"Roger and I were an item at that time. I couldn't be bothered." She sipped her wine and settled back in her chair with a petulant expression.

Roger Lathrop, eventually husband number three, had lasted six years. He'd been all right as far as step-fathers went, taking me to the zoo and other kid-oriented places. I'd been sorry to see him go.

"Yet you *did* read the first letters."

My mother fixed me with a stern stare and then shrugged. "I was curious."

"And maybe a little tempted?"

"Never." She set the glass down. "Are we going to eat or what?"

I returned the letters to the envelope and picked up the menu. "We'll eat."

"Are you going to do this?"

It was my turn to employ avoidance. "The Chicken Royale Salad looks good."

Knowing when she'd been out-maneuvered, my mother went with the flow. "It is. I've had it before."

****

I had just arrived home from lunch with Mother when my agent called. He'd set up three auditions in four days, two TV commercials and one pilot for a new sitcom. That was two weeks ago. I washed out on all of them. In a foul mood, I'd brooded on my lack of employment. Naturally, I Googled my late, great-grandfather. During his prime, he'd been a major league mover and shaker on Grand Britannia. I found his obituary in the local island newspaper online. The last sentence made my eyes pop.

The police are investigating the possibility of foul play.

I got on the horn immediately to Adam. "What the hell does that mean?" I demanded.

"I don't know, Liza. This is the first I've heard of it. Let me e-mail this Albright fellow and ask."

It took two days to get an answer. "According to Mr. Albright, there was never any suspicion of foul play. Since the Goodhue family is so prominent in island society, he thinks it was just some reporter trying to stir up trouble."

"Swell, a tabloid mentality. Just what I needed."

"He also asked if you were going to accept the terms."

"Tell him I'm still thinking about it."

One night, for want of anything better to do, I poured a glass of wine and picked up the manila envelope from the desk where I'd tossed it. I settled into the plush comfort of the sofa, scattering the contents on the cushion next to me, and then sorted them by date. Taking a sip of wine to fortify my courage, I slid the pages from the first envelope.

Two hours later, I slipped the last letter back. At first, Geoffrey Goodhue had taken the demanding tone my mother had described sometimes accompanied by bribery, but as time passed, the demands turned to pleas. The last letter, dated almost seventeen years ago suggested the old man had been ill. I also discovered my grandfather's name was Mercer Goodhue. Refilling my wine glass, I assumed the first missives showed the true personality of the sender—a tough old bird who not only got his own way, but demanded unquestioning allegiance from his family.

I'll bet he was hell on wheels in Parliament and as the Governor.

The letters had piqued my interest. I'd never met a great-grandfather before—mine or anyone else's. Taking a sip, I contemplated my immediate future. With acting being an on-again, off-again profession, I'd never followed the path of spend it while you can. I saved half of everything I made. Mother had given me the down payment on the condo, and the mortgage was reasonable. I could afford to take time off, provided Mother lent me some money, and like Adam said, I could always stay connected via the internet.

No reason not to have the best of both worlds.

With my decision made, I rose and called Adam at home.

"Adam, contact this attorney for Geoffrey Goodhue. Tell him I accept the terms of the will. I need a couple of weeks to take care of business, but see no reason why I can't be in Grand Britannia by the end of the month."

"I'll call first thing in the morning, Liza. According to another letter accompanying the will, you'll be met by Stephen Albright."

I hung up and resettled on the sofa, then drained my glass. Being met by this guy Albright? Terrific. I didn't have much use for lawyers. Mother with her numerous divorces had seen to that. The whole set-up sounded strange, but I had to give it a shot. I could be hell on wheels, too.

The police are investigating the possibility of foul play.

In spite of the reassurances from this Albright fellow, the words concerned me. Was I doing the right thing?

I shook off my qualms. *Why not? Claim your inheritance and meet relatives you never knew existed. What could possibly go wrong?*

A sudden shiver slithered down my spine.

Chapter Two

"Miss Channing?"

I turned from the stack of luggage on the sidewalk outside the Grand Britannia Air Terminal and faced a tall man with light brown hair. His striking good looks suggested he could probably have any woman he wanted.

Terrific. Good-looking and a lawyer. Not the best of beginnings.

"Yes."

"My name is Stephen Albright. I'm here to escort you to the house."

His strong voice evoked an image of a man who commanded the courtroom. I visualized Perry Mason. Instinctively, I knew this guy didn't like to lose.

He didn't offer to shake hands and his cool, impervious accent—a cross between British and island patois—along with a composed, unsmiling face was intimidating—just like his letter.

Refusing to show trepidation, I stuck out my hand. "Oh yes, my attorney in Los Angeles mentioned you."

He accepted the handshake and nodded his head. If I hadn't been so hot and tired, I might have ignored the funny little flutter in the pit of my stomach at his touch.

"Is this your luggage?"

"That's it." I eyed the half dozen bags that had cost

a fortune in baggage fees. "A year is a long time."

The barest trace of a smile curved his lips. Without answering, he turned and nodded. A dark-skinned man wearing a chauffeur's uniform and standing beside a limo leaped forward.

"If you'll come with me, I'll take you to the house."

I had no choice but to follow. He'd cupped his hand around my elbow, steering me to the back door. The flutter returned. I slid inside like riding in a limo was an everyday occurrence. A moment later, he opened the opposite door and did the same. The faint scent of his aftershave, a crisp, clean aroma reminding me of the outdoors, wafted to my nose. I took an extra deep breath, resisting the urge to lean closer. Handsome and smelling even better might override my dislike for lawyers.

Down girl. You're just tired, that's all.

"I take it you had a pleasant flight, Miss Channing."

"Long, but pleasant." Uncomfortable in the Caribbean heat and humidity, I was grateful when the driver returned from his task and started the car. The rear seat air conditioning kicked in giving me a much needed blast of cool air. Late September heralded autumn in Los Angeles. I turned my attention back to the man who met me. "So, you are the attorney of record regarding this nonsense."

He turned a penetrating gaze my way, and I almost gasped at the intensity of his sea green eyes.

"If you find it nonsense, then why accept?"

"Apparently, a lot of people lose out if I don't."

"I wouldn't say a lot. Just immediate family."

13

"Why did my great-grandfather do this? It sounds so Victorian. Why bring me in to the equation? Didn't he like the rest of his family?"

"Sir Geoffrey had his ups and downs with the family. His children are all dead. The people I mentioned are his grandchildren—not counting your mother, of course."

"You still haven't answered my question. Why?"

"He was a cantankerous old man, who struck fear into those daring to oppose his wishes. Your mother marched to the top of his 'bend and break list' twenty years ago. He bided his time. This is his way of winning."

"Mom tells him to take a hike, and I end up as the deal breaker for the rest of the family? Couldn't he have used one of his other great-grandchildren as a pawn?"

He rubbed a hand over his chin. "I tried to talk him out of it, but he refused. At ninety-five, he was still calling the shots."

"Ninety-five? Was he competent to call the shots? If I got stiffed like this, I'd question whether he was of sound mind."

"They did, he was, and that's the end of it. They all breathed a sigh of relief when you accepted the terms."

"Yeah, I'll just bet." Then I remembered the old boy's last letter. "Wait a minute—ninety-five? He said in a letter to Mother he was in poor health, and that was over fifteen years ago."

"He lied."

That figured. If he was a master manipulator, then of course he was a liar in the bargain. Reminded me of a few producers and directors I'd known—and lawyers.

During our conversation, the chauffeur had driven

through the streets of Port Elizabeth. I wasn't overly impressed. It looked like any other Caribbean capitol that had grown too fast with tourist money.

We soon left the city and wound through lush vegetation, while climbing higher into the hills. My nerves tightened and my heart rate accelerated. Would my relatives greet me with distain or show gratitude that my presence guaranteed their inheritance? If it was me, I'd make sure I felt welcomed and fulfilled the agreement.

I shot a glance at Albright who was reading some papers he'd taken from his briefcase. I'd also Googled him. He was highly respected and the third Albright generation with the firm that did everything from wills and estates to criminal cases. Personal data, however, was lacking.

"So, will anybody be at this house to say hi?" I asked, hoping my interruption irritated him.

He looked up with a frown. "I'm sure Richard and Mary Ellen will be available since they live on the estate. No doubt by the weekend, the rest of the crowd will come to check you out."

"What fun. Who are Richard and Mary Ellen and why do they live on the estate?"

"Richard is Richard Goodhue, Sir Geoffrey's youngest grandson. Mary Ellen is his wife. They live on the estate because Richard is the estate manager. The original Goodhue, Jonathon, established a shipping line. At one time the family owned thousands of Grand Britannia acres growing sugar cane, which naturally led to the operation of a distillery. Goodhue Rum is known throughout the Caribbean as one of the best."

"And the family still owns all of this?"

"Yes, plus other businesses and real estate in Port Elizabeth."

I'd hit the mother lode. "No wonder the family is glad to see me. I imagine there's a bit of resentment about the will since they challenged it in court."

"The shock has worn off, but I wouldn't go playing lady of the manor. Richard's sister, Irene is top dog for social events and might not adjust to a new hostess."

His sister? Not his wife? That was interesting. Well, good old Irene could cram it. On the other hand, why antagonize a possible ally? I'd play it by ear and assert my opinions once I got to know everybody. I had a year to learn.

"I don't think Irene has anything to worry about, Mr. Albright."

"Call me Stephen. I live on the adjoining estate. I'm sure we'll be seeing a lot of each other. The families get together often."

He smiled. My breath caught in my throat. He was damned good-looking. I'd never seen eyes that color before. They made me think of the sea on a sunlit day. The light streaming through the car window glanced off golden highlights in his hair. I swallowed to suppress that recurring flutter in my stomach and wished the driver would turn up the air conditioning a notch.

I tore my gaze away and focused on the scenery sliding past the window. Good-looking or not, I had no intention of pursuing anything other than a working relationship with the man.

The car continued its climb through the trees and I caught glimpses of the blue-green ocean, the sunlight sparkling off the swells with diamond bright pinpricks. It brought my mind back to Stephen Albright's eyes. I took a deep breath and exhaled heavily. *Definitely gonna be a long year.*

A large stone wall loomed beside the road blocking my view of the water.

"Wow, someone sure likes their privacy," I commented.

"Geoffrey Goodhue hated trespassers," Stephen said without looking up from the file in his hand.

While the wall didn't have razor wire on top, it still reminded me of a prison. Apprehension sat like a lump in my stomach. Had I made a major mistake in coming here?

The limo turned into a driveway and glided to a stop next to a guard house. Ahead stood two massive wrought iron gates each emblazoned with a curly-cued "G." A small, guard house stood off to the side. A man inside nodded to the chauffeur.

Is he employed to keep the riff-raff out or the inmates in? Doubts about this adventure resurfaced.

Our driver pressed a button on a remote clipped to the visor. The gates slid open, and we passed through.

The driveway wound through a dense forest of hardwood trees. Thick undergrowth discouraged a casual walk. The sun didn't shine so brightly here.

"Well, this is gloomy enough," I said.

"As I said, Sir Geoffrey hated trespassers. Not many people want to battle all that vegetation on foot. You'll find the main part of the property is well-maintained." He stared and skewered me with those incredible eyes. "Miss Channing…"

"Call me Liza."

"Very well, Liza. If you find this whole experience so distasteful why *did* you agree to the terms? What's it to you if the rest of the family loses an inheritance?"

I shrugged. "Curiosity mostly. Plus, my career has rather stalled. It seemed like a good time for a change."

"That's right, you're an actress." He frowned. "Forgive me, but I imagine the money plays a part, too."

Couldn't get much blunter than that. I'd expected more subtlety from him.

"Who can't use money?"

"Nothing is yours until you fulfill the contract of living here for one year."

I didn't like his challenging tone and sensed his resentment. Why? Because my great-grandfather had ignored his advice?

"I'm aware of the terms, *Mr. Albright*," I replied in a frosty voice.

A contrite expression crossed his face. "My apologies. I didn't mean to upset you. I'm here to make your transition as smooth as possible. I don't want you to think of me as the enemy."

I wasn't sure he was a friend either.

The car exited the woods back into the sunlight. Bountiful stood before me. I couldn't suppress a gasp of delight. Long and rectangular, it reminded me a bit of an old Southern plantation house. Three stories high, the painted white clapboard shone in a dazzling display. Black shutters created a pleasing contrast. Fluted columns every ten, or so, feet supported the roof and the second story of the wrap around veranda. Above that a series of dormers made up the third floor architecture. Manicured lawns dotted with palm trees swaying in the breeze stretched forever. Lush flowerbeds complimented the house.

"Holy crap!"

"Lovely, isn't it?" He spoke in a soft, almost reverent tone and leaned forward as though seeing the house for the first time.

"It's gorgeous. I don't know what I was expecting, but this wasn't it."

He turned to me and smiled. "The original builder had a taste for the good life and a land grant from the crown."

"Well, he certainly made the most of it."

The car stopped in front of the porch steps. The chauffeur got out and came around to open my door. I exited looking up at the soaring magnificence of the place. Not usually impressed with opulence, Bountiful was the exception. Thoughts of selling the place diminished. I visualized myself living here in a manner I could become accustomed to in no time.

Stephen said nothing, but stood next to me. I'm not short, but his six-foot-two-inch height made me feel like a Munchkin. I looked into his eyes, and our gazes locked. For a moment I felt as though I was being drawn into those blue-green depths. He breathed in a ragged breath, and I wondered if he also experienced recurring flutters.

"Shall we?" Once again cupping my elbow in his hand, he guided me up the steps. The ornate door opened. A plump, unsmiling black woman stared before stepping back and motioning us inside.

"Good afternoon, Beatrice," Stephen said.

"Good afternoon, Mr. Albright." She nodded, and then cast her neutral gaze on me. I sensed neither welcome nor resentment.

"Beatrice, this is Elizabeth Channing, Sir

Geoffrey's great-granddaughter. Liza, this is Beatrice. She's been the Goodhue housekeeper for close to thirty years."

I thrust my hand out. "I'm so pleased to meet you."

Her eyebrows rose a fraction and the corners of her mouth curved upward ever so slightly as she accepted the gesture.

"My pleasure, Miss Channing. If there's anything I can do for you, please let me know." Her voice had the soft tonal lilt indigenous to the islands.

I took a moment to inspect the entry hall. The thing was enormous, a good twenty-five feet square with a soaring ceiling. A chandelier hung over a massive round table in the center of the room. Pocket doors opened off opposite sides. I caught a glimpse of a dining room to the right. The door on the left was closed. A light breeze tickled my bare arms.

As impressive as the foyer was, the focus of attention was a magnificent staircase that rose from the left to curve gracefully upwards. My gaze followed the lines as far as the ten foot Palladian window at the apex of the curve.

"Are Mr. and Mrs. Goodhue around?" Stephen asked.

"In the drawing room, sir." An elderly black man entered the foyer from a hallway leading toward the back of the house. "Willie, this is Miss Channing, Sir Geoffrey's great-granddaughter. Please take her bags up to the master bedroom."

Willie bowed and moved toward the front door. Were they serious? This old man was expected to cart six suitcases up that enormous staircase?

"Willie, please don't bother. I can get them later."

He stared at me in surprise, his expression bordering on outrage. I had made my first *faux pas* as the owner of an estate.

"Myron, the chauffeur, will help," Stephen said.

"Yes, of course," I murmured.

Beatrice stared. I sensed disapproval.

"Perhaps, Miss Channing would like to freshen up," Stephen suggested, bridging the awkward moment.

"Yes, I'd like that."

"Please follow me, miss," she said.

Stephen walked toward the closed doors, opened them, and entered, re-closing them behind him. I followed the housekeeper. Portraits of past Goodhues lined the wall to my left—at least that's what the name plates on the frames said. The eyes glared as I ascended. The higher I climbed the further back in time the manner of dress traveled. The last one showed an aristocratic woman with dark hair and an impervious expression as though resentful of my presence. I wouldn't be surprised if she knew about the current state of affairs.

Beatrice didn't speak until we reached an ornately carved door.

"This is the master suite," she said opening the door with a flourish.

I entered a bedroom almost as large as my condo in Los Angeles. Gleaming dark hardwood floors covered with beautifully woven throw rugs contrasted with the stark white walls. A huge fireplace graced one wall. Over it hung the portrait of a lovely redheaded woman dressed in a '50s style evening gown. Situated opposite between two French doors stood an enormous four-poster bed, its wood dark with age. Two more sets of

French doors opened onto the upper front veranda. Velvet drapes, now open, hung at the windows and doors. The rest of the furniture was antique. With the exception of the window coverings, the room was bright and airy.

"I hope you will be comfortable here, Miss," Beatrice commented, tweaking one of the draperies an inch further open. The underlying sheers bulged slightly in the breeze.

"The house isn't air conditioned?" I asked.

"No, miss. We're on the cliffs overlooking Hidden Cove. I think you'll find the sea breeze adequate and refreshing. Is there anything I can get for you?"

"I may have to pole vault into bed," I said eyeing the high mattress.

A genuine smile lit the woman's face, and she pointed to a set of steps at the side of the monstrosity.

"Steps, miss. I understand your great-grandmother, Evangeline, used to say it made her feel like a queen."

"Evangeline? What a lovely name."

"I'm told she was a lovely woman," she said nodding toward the portrait.

So that's my great-grandmother. And she married Sir Geoffrey? I refrained from asking. *See how deep the pool is before leaping off the high dive.*

Willie and Myron entered with my luggage. Before I could thank them, Beatrice indicated a corner of the room.

"Put them over there out of the way." They complied and left. "I'll have one of the maids unpack for you."

"That won't be necessary. I can do it myself."

Her eyebrows rose. I had once again apparently

broached some kind of estate owner etiquette. I wasn't comfortable with others performing tasks I was capable of doing.

"Very well, miss. The bathroom is right through that door," she said showing me with a wave of her hand. "As soon as you freshen up, please come downstairs. Mr. Richard and Miss Mary Ellen are awaiting your presence in the drawing room. It's the door on the right at the foot of the stairs."

Awaiting my presence in the drawing room? That sounded grandiose. So the drawing room was behind door number two—the one Stephen had entered. I wondered what he was telling the occupants.

"Thank you, Beatrice. And my name is Liza. I'm not a formal person. 'Miss' makes me sound like someone I'm not."

The housekeeper nodded and left the room. I headed for the bathroom and discovered, not to my surprise, opulent fixtures—all marble and brass. I washed my hands and face, brushed my hair, and reapplied a light layer of make-up. My jeans and polo shirt were too casual for a first meeting with unknown relatives, so I scrounged a pair of tan slacks and a bright green top—only slightly wrinkled—from my suitcase. I also found a pair of low-heeled sandals.

I stared at my reflection in a cheval mirror. From the corner of my eye, I caught a movement. I whirled. The sheer curtain on the far window billowed slightly as though someone had just exited the room. Silly, of course. I was alone. Still, I couldn't shake the feeling I was being watched. Then, from outside, I heard the slightest of creaks.

I swallowed and turned back to the mirror refusing

to give in to my fantasies. The wind had moved the curtain and this was an old house. Naturally, it creaked. Or maybe the house was haunted. *Don't even go there, Channing.*

Since my arrival I had not impressed either Stephen Albright or the servants.

I opened the door and lifted my chin. *Time to unimpress Mr. Richard and Miss Mary Ellen, too.*

Chapter Three

I stood in front of the closed drawing room doors listening to the murmur of voices from behind it. Casting a careful glance around the foyer, I put my ear to the wood. The doors were thick and well-built. Nothing distinguishable came through.

Straightening, I wiped damp palms down the sides of my slacks. My heart thudded in slow, heavy beats. What was the proper etiquette? Did I knock or just go in? This was almost as bad as the first stage entrance on opening night. I stiffened my spine, lifted my chin, called upon years of acting classes, grasped the handles, and slid the doors open.

All conversation ceased as three sets of eyes focused on my entrance. Stephen Albright sat in a large wingback chair in front of another enormous fireplace, a glass of amber-colored liquid in his hand. A slender woman, her brown hair coifed in a style that hadn't been seen in fifteen years, sat on the edge of a loveseat. She held a glass of white wine in shaky fingers. Another man, tall, blond and also holding a glass of amber liquid stood off to the side, his sharp blue gaze staring me down.

Stephen rose in a smooth motion. "Ah, Liza, I was just telling Richard and Mary Ellen about our ride in."

I approached the threesome.

The tall man smiled and closed the distance between us. "Miss Channing, I'm Richard Goodhue, your cousin. Welcome to Bountiful."

I took his proffered hand and shook it. "I'm delighted to meet you."

Acting 101—lady meeting stranger under tense circumstances. Boy, did the shoe ever fit.

Richard turned to the woman on the loveseat. "And this is my wife, Mary Ellen."

She licked her lips and sipped from her glass before answering in a tense tone, "How do you do? I hope you enjoy your stay with us."

Stay? She made it sound like I was a weekend guest.

"I'm sure I will. And please, everybody call me Liza."

Richard seemed pleasant enough, while his wife's body language and vocal tone resonated with resentment.

"Then Liza it is," he said. "We're Richard and Mary Ellen. Stephen, get the girl a drink. What would you like?"

"Oh, I'm not really sure…"

"Let me mix you a rum punch," Stephen interrupted with a smile. "Kind of a welcome to Grand Britannia. It's the unofficial cocktail of the island."

"Thank you. That would be lovely, but make it light. It's been a long day and too much rum might send me into dreamland."

Both Stephen and Richard laughed as the former crossed the room to a bar cart along the wall. The corners of Mary Ellen's mouth curved upwards slightly. This time when she raised the glass to her lips, she didn't sip, but gulped.

"Please, have a seat, Liza," Richard said.

I chose the opposite end of the loveseat from Mary Ellen. She didn't make eye contact.

The large room was dominated by the fireplace. The dark, ornately carved wood contrasted with the soft yellow of the walls. My gaze was drawn to the portrait over the mantel. A man in 17th century clothing stared down at me. Blond hair was pulled back into the nape of his neck. His hand rested on a sword at his side while his lips curved in the faintest of smiles as though he knew a secret.

Stephen brought my drink. Our fingers brushed as he handed it to me. Warmth settled in the pit of my stomach. He smiled and resumed his seat.

I sipped the fruity concoction appreciating the taste of the rum while at the same time trying to ignore the already cooling warmth from his touch.

"How do you like it," he asked, his smile widening.

"It's wonderful. Family owned rum, I take it."

Richard nodded. "Goodhue Rum is the best in the world. Don't let those rascals in Puerto Rico or Barbados tell you differently."

I sipped again as an uncomfortable silence descended. To break the mood, I switched my gaze to the portrait.

"And who is that?"

"That is our ancestor and original owner of Bountiful, Jonathon Goodhue," Richard said, pride in his voice.

"My goodness, he certainly was handsome."

"The portrait at the head of the staircase is his wife, Isabelle," Mary Ellen said.

Ah, the supercilious one.

"I noticed her on my way upstairs. How come she's not down here with him?"

"She died young, and Jonathon was so heartbroken he never remarried," Richard said.

"Nonsense. Legend has it he had a wide array of mistresses in Port Elizabeth and West End," his wife said.

Richard smiled at me. "I prefer to think of him as heartbroken. Much more romantic."

Richard didn't strike me as the romantic type.

Mary Ellen emptied her glass in a single swallow. She held it out to Stephen who rose, took it, and headed for the bar.

"Well, I'm all for romance," I said.

Stephen handed the refilled glass back to the woman.

"Better go easy on that, dear, or you'll nap through supper," Richard told her.

She smiled. "I'm fine. And supper will be at seven tonight. I thought perhaps Liza might want to retire early. I find traveling very tiring, don't you?"

"Yes, especially from the West Coast. It's three o'clock here, but my stomach is telling me it's only lunchtime at home, so an early dinner will be welcome."

"And speaking of welcome," she continued. "Irene has arranged a little soiree for you Friday night. Nothing extravagant. Just family."

"Friday?" Stephen said with raised eyebrows. "I'd have thought even Irene would have allowed Liza to settle in longer."

Mary Ellen shrugged. "She said she wanted to meet

our newest cousin."

"And who is Irene?" I asked.

Stephen's facial expression and the term "even Irene" suggested more than just wanting to meet me.

"Irene is my sister," Richard said. "She owns a small beachfront home in Cutlass Bay on the Southwest side of the island."

Mary Ellen gulped her wine. "Small? I wouldn't call a ten room house small."

Richard ignored her and glanced at his watch. "I'm sorry to cut this short, but I have a few things I need to do. An estate manager's work is never done. Mary, I suggest you go up and catch a nap before supper."

Up? Did that mean they lived in the house?

She drained the rest of the wine. "I'm not tired."

Richard removed the glass from her fingers. "Of course, you are. Mustn't overdue things."

Mary Ellen glared for a moment and then turned to me with a smile.

"So nice to have met you, Liza. I'll see you here in the drawing room at six-thirty for cocktails."

She rose, steadied herself, and walked with a careful stride out of the room. I wondered how many glasses of wine she'd had before I'd come down.

I also finished my rum punch. A nap didn't sound half bad.

"Please forgive Mary Ellen. She doesn't have a strong constitution. I have to keep my eyes on her to make sure she gets her proper rest."

"There's nothing to forgive." I set my glass on the end table and rose. "I think I'll follow her example. By the way, do we dress for dinner?"

"No, this is the Caribbean. Casual is a state of

mind."

I left, but didn't close the door all the way. Pausing just out of eye shot, I listened.

After a brief moment, Richard said, "Well, she doesn't seem too bad. Think she'll stick out the year?"

"She wants the money as much as everybody else. I don't see her leaving any time soon. Now, why is Irene really coming down so fast?"

"Your guess is as good as mine, but I'd wager she needs money again. She may try an end run."

"Won't work. Liza doesn't have a thing to say about the money. She receives a monthly allowance, but that's all. By the way…"

An allowance? Nobody had said anything about an allowance from the estate. I assumed I'd have to make do with my own finances or what I could borrow from Mother.

The conversation from the drawing room continued.

"I don't like this whole set-up," Stephen said. "She's already seen that damned newspaper article about foul play."

"That was total nonsense written by a disgruntled reporter Sir Geoffrey had once thrown off the estate." Richard paused. "Yet she still came."

"I think we're making a big mistake by not telling her about…"

"We've been through that. She doesn't need to know at this point in time. Besides, who's going to tell her?"

"I still don't like it."

The by-play intrigued me. What weren't they telling me? What didn't I need to know? They went on to discuss the distillery. My eavesdropping had ceased being useful.

I tiptoed to the foot of the stairs when my gaze was drawn to a large open French door toward the back of the long hallway. Walking in the middle of an antique runner to muffle my footsteps, I investigated.

A gasp of pure delight burst from my throat. I crossed the threshold to a large terrace running the entire width of the house and close to twenty feet deep. The roof of the second floor veranda partially shaded it. A waist high stone parapet surrounded the patio.

I walked across the flagstones to the steps leading to a lush garden. I descended and stared at the array of roses of all colors and varieties, their heady scents filling my nostrils with an intoxicating aroma. Who needed rum when this was available?

Graveled paths led to the left and the right. I chose the left one and wandered down it, stopping occasionally to sniff an individual bloom in appreciation.

The narrow trails wound through the bushes in a maze-like fashion. Rather than take the chance of getting lost, I retraced my steps to the terrace where I turned. The lawn sloped toward a cliff, and beyond, the sea beckoned. I breathed the salt air, drawing it deeply into my lungs.

Stunning. Absolutely stunning. Already part of Bountiful had clutched my heart.

Mom, you blew it. You should have come here. Just think of the paintings you could have produced.

I resumed my steps into the house and entered my bedroom to find a young woman hanging my clothes in one of three large, antique armoires. Beatrice had obviously paid no attention to my statement of doing things for myself.

The woman paused with a pair of slacks and a couple of tops draped over her arm, smiled, and bowed her head slightly as she half-curtsied. Blonde curls peeked out from under a maid's cap.

"Good afternoon, miss. My name is Violet and I've been assigned to tend your needs."

Tend my needs? "Thank you, but I'm perfectly capable of hanging up my own clothes, Violet."

She looked confused. "You don't like me?"

"No, no, that isn't the case. I just feel a bit odd having someone—ah, tend to me."

"Oh, but I enjoy it, miss." She turned and placed the tops and slacks on hangers in the converted armoires. "This is an advancement for me. I've always wanted to be a lady's maid."

"What did you do before?"

"I'm a server, miss. Been doing that for almost two years now. Before that, I washed the dishes."

A scullery maid and server? Well, who was I to stand in the way of promotion? If I ever got a part as a maid, I'd have the role down pat.

"Does Mrs. Goodhue also have a personal maid?"

"Oh, yes, miss. Gladys does for her when she isn't busy elsewhere. She's our laundress."

"Well, carry on, I guess."

"Yes, miss. I'm almost finished. Would you like me to draw you a bath? You must be tired from your journey."

"Sure, why not? And my name is Liza."

Her eyes opened wide. "Oh, I couldn't do that. It wouldn't be proper."

"Right. Proper." And what the hell did I do while she finished unpacking and drew a bath? I had a lot to learn about the upper crust of society—especially island society.

Not wanting to twiddle my thumbs in front of Violet, I stepped through one of the open French doors leading to the front veranda. Earlier my attention had been focused on the house, but now I saw that the front lawn rivaled that of the back. Neat and manicured, the grass ran to the edge of the woods. In the middle of the looping circular drive, a large square fountain bubbled water. Once again flowers bloomed everywhere. Someone enjoyed gardening. Mary Ellen? Then it dawned on me a gardener probably dealt with the upkeep.

Below and to my right the limo that had brought me to Bountiful remained parked. Stephen Albright must still be here.

I didn't know what to make of him. Good-looking and slightly arrogant, he reminded me of several actors I knew, although if I was casting him in a part, lawyer would be it. A couple of times in the drawing room, I'd caught him staring at me as though taking my measure. Perhaps he speculated on how long I'd last. I speculated on how much he stood to make if I didn't. I liked to think he stared because he was interested.

As I surveyed the lawn, the chauffeur exited the house and opened the rear door of the limo. Stephen followed a moment later. Before entering the car, he looked up in my direction, smiled, and nodded. I returned the gesture. He slid into the seat. Myron closed the door, took his place behind the wheel, and drove away.

I inhaled a shaky breath. Even from this distance, that smile worked wonders on a girl's imagination.

"Your bath is ready, miss."

I returned inside. "Thank you, Violet."

"There's a towel on the stool next to the tub and a robe hanging on the hook behind the door. If you'll tell me what you'd like to wear tonight, I'll press and lay out the clothing for you."

I knew exactly what I wanted to wear. "I'll wear the sapphire slacks along with the long-sleeved white tunic and the silver ballet slippers."

"Would you like me to help you dress?"

"No, thank you. I can manage." Some things would just take time.

She nodded as I sailed into the bathroom and closed the door. Steam, along with the scent of lavender, rose from the huge Romanesque tub. I dumped my clothes in a pile and tested the heat with my big toe. Hot, but not scalding. I slid in resting my head on the tub rim, and for the first time since boarding the plane early this morning, relaxed.

I could get used to this.

****

An hour later I emerged from the bathroom in the fluffiest, most comfortable robe I'd ever donned. I didn't quite float across the room, but came close. My clothes for the evening were laid out on the bed, but I couldn't bring myself to part with the robe just yet.

Instead, I removed my laptop from its carrying case and set it up on the desk in the corner. I'd splurged for international calling on my cell, but preferred e-mail for keeping in touch.

I sat down and logged in. I had fifteen messages—

one from Adam Wylie, one from Mother, one from my agent, and the rest from friends. I'd deal with friends later. I opened my agent's first, informing me he'd be on the French Riviera for three weeks.

Good for him. I'd paid for at least a portion of his trip.

Adam's was brief and to the point. His client with the newspaper liked the idea of me blogging about my experiences and would pay twenty-five dollars per blog. It was chicken feed, but better than waiting tables. I followed the link to the guy's e-mail and accepted, promising a short column in a day or two.

Mother's message was longer. She was still upset that I'd agreed to do this, but at the same time wanted running commentary on damned near everything.

I e-mailed her back with a positive attitude and the promise of complete descriptions of people, places, and things.

When I'd finished with the messages, I logged onto Facebook for a while. Done with that, I had only fifteen minutes to dress and put on a decent layer of make-up before dinner.

As I opened the bedroom door a gong sounded from below scaring me half out of my silver ballet slippers. I leaned over the balustrade and looked into the foyer. A Chinese-type gong stood on a side table. Willie walked toward the back of the house.

I straightened my shoulders and descended the grand staircase with what I hoped was a Greta Garbo-like haughtiness.

I had been summoned.

Chapter Four

This time the drawing room doors stood open. I entered with my chin up. Richard and Mary Ellen had already arrived and sat in the two chairs by the fireplace. Both held drinks in their hands.

"Liza, what can I get you from the bar?" he said, rising.

I glanced at Mary Ellen's wine glass. "White wine is fine. What the hell was that God-awful noise a moment ago?"

Mary Ellen sipped. "That was the gong announcing the cocktail hour has begun."

I perched on the loveseat. "Well, it scared the stuffing out of me."

Richard handed me a glass of chilled Chardonnay. "I'm afraid that was one of Grandfather's little peccadilloes. He loathed people who were late to anything, so he initiated the gong to tell family and guests their presence was required in the drawing room immediately. Woe be it to anyone who came in even five minutes after the appointed hour. I should have warned you. Sorry."

"Poor Willie is a creature of habit," his wife said. "He'll continue banging the bloody thing until he's told to stop."

"Consider him told. It sounds like a royal

summons," I stated, sipping from my glass. The cool liquid slid down my throat. The Goodhues knew fine wine when they saw it.

"I'll inform him," Richard replied.

"I hate that gong," Mary Ellen said, gulping half the contents of her glass.

"It's an arrogant way to tell guests cocktails are being served," I observed.

"I remember when one of our sons had a houseguest who strolled into the room twenty minutes late. Rather a dramatic young lady who loved making an entrance."

I wondered if she'd just taken a shot at me, but ignored the obvious allusion to acting.

Richard nodded. "Grandfather refused to serve her. Said if she couldn't be on time, she didn't need a drink."

"Sounds like he was an autocratic old bird."

"He was," Mary Ellen said shortly. She finished her wine, rose, and walked to the bar where she grabbed the bottle from the ice bucket and refilled her glass.

"Grandfather loved being in control," Richard said.

I sipped again. "I'll bet my mother refusing to come and see him must have been a shock."

"He was enraged," Mary Ellen said, resuming her seat with a look on her face that indicated the idea of her husband's grandfather being thwarted at anything was pleasant. "Actually, your mother came as a shock. Nobody had any idea Uncle Mercer had a daughter."

"It came as a bit of a shock to Mother, too."

"I can understand," Richard said. "Still, I do wish she'd come for a visit. We'd all like to get to know her."

"Any clue as to how my biological grandfather met my biological grandmother?"

"Sir Geoffrey never even divulged he'd tracked her down," Mary Ellen said. "I'm sure Stephen can enlighten you."

"I'll ask him. I'm sure my mother would like to know."

I was sure Mother didn't give a crap and *I* wasn't sure a tête-à-tête with Stephen Albright was a good idea. The less seen of him the better. Part of me was highly attracted to the man. Another part didn't trust him. After what I'd overheard earlier, I sensed he had secrets, but then, didn't we all?

"Speaking of Stephen, he asked me to inform you he'll be glad to discuss provisions of the will at your convenience. And on behalf of the entire family, thank you for accepting the terms."

Mary Ellen finished the wine. "Yes, thank you. I'm not sure what we would have done if you'd refused."

I also finished my wine. It was about time they said it. "I imagine you would have made do and gone on with your lives."

"Dinner is served," intoned a voice from the doorway.

I turned. Willie bowed and walked across the foyer toward the dining room with a regal step. The rest of us followed.

The dining room—a place set aside for the purpose of eating. I was used to small, intimate rooms. This dining room was the antithesis.

Three places had been set at a table that could easily have seated twenty. Two huge crystal chandeliers hung over it. A snow white tablecloth covered the area where we'd dine. Light bounced off the silverware and refracted through the crystal glasses. The upper walls were papered in an intricate white pattern set against a sage green background. The wainscoting and the rest of the woodwork were dark. A fireplace boasted the same surround and mantel as in the drawing room. Four sets of French doors—two in front and two in back were open allowing the refreshing breeze to enter.

Richard held first my chair, then his wife's before taking his. Mary Ellen shook a small bell beside her plate. A moment later, Willie appeared in full butler array carrying a bottle of wine. He poured for Richard, who tasted and nodded.

While Willie filled our glasses, Mary Ellen smiled at me and said, "I took the liberty of ordering a simple meal for tonight. Vichyssoise, Chicken Française with Duchess Potatoes, asparagus with Hollandaise, a mixed greens salad with vinaigrette, and apple tart for dessert."

Was she kidding? Simple? My idea of simple was stuffing a meatloaf-with-mashed-potatoes-and-gravy frozen dinner into the microwave.

I returned to the Greta Garbo act and intoned as if this was an everyday meal, "Sounds marvelous. I'm looking forward to the soup. Vichyssoise is tricky. My last experience with it was less than successful at a five star Beverly Hills restaurant. I had to send it back." It was a lie, but how would they know?

"I can guarantee you won't be sending back Georgette's soup or anything else from her kitchen," Richard replied with a smile. He raised his glass. "Here's to Liza. May you have a wonderful year getting to know us."

Mary Ellen raised hers with a strained smile.

I sipped from my glass. "Thank you. I'm sure I'll enjoy my time here."

Violet entered from the rear of the room with a tray. Placing it on a sideboard, she served the soup.

I hate Vichyssoise. What could be more disgusting than cold potato and onion soup? I ate it anyway. The salad course was better.

We progressed to the excellent chicken and potatoes with small talk about air travel and time zones. Eventually, that line of conversation ran out.

"I saw the rose garden out back earlier," I said. "It's lovely."

"That's my wife's domain."

Mary Ellen brightened. "Thank you so much. I love gardening, especially roses. The garden is a maze, you know. At the very center is a replica of an artifact dating from Jonathon Goodhue's day. If you'd like, I'll show you tomorrow."

"Thank you, I'd love to see it. I'd hate to get lost in the maze though."

She laughed. "I don't believe we've lost anyone yet."

"We have a full time gardener, but Mary Ellen insists on doing most of the work herself," Richard said. "Before we came to live here, the garden was just a run of the mill thing."

"Yes, for once Sir Geoffrey allowed me full control."

"The house is also quite amazing," I said forking perfectly seasoned potatoes into my mouth. "Hope I don't get lost here, too."

"Tomorrow morning after breakfast I'll give you a

full tour of the place," Richard said.

"Thank you, I'd appreciate that." I nibbled on the chicken, savoring the tasty sauce. "I was impressed by all the portraits lining the staircase."

"I find it strange. It's rather like having the family watching your every move," Mary Ellen said. "I think my favorite is young Sarah Woodruff Goodhue. She's the one in the middle. One of the Goodhues took a trip to England and returned with her as his bride. She died in childbirth and is rumored to still walk the hallways searching for her child."

I choked slightly on my wine recalling my sense of being watched. "Bountiful is haunted?"

"Of course not," Richard said, giving his wife an exasperated glance.

"Yes, it is," she insisted. "I myself have felt her presence on several occasions. Just a brief glimpse of a fluttering white dress in the distance."

Mary Ellen didn't strike me as the ghost hunting type. Was this her way of trying to scare me off? "Well, I don't believe in ghosts, so I doubt Miss Sarah will put in an appearance for me."

One of the maids removed the dishes from in front of us and served the dessert. Sweet with a hint of cinnamon and a flaky buttery crust, I enjoyed every last bite. If this meal was simple in Mary Ellen's mind, I'd soon weigh two hundred pounds.

Back in the drawing room, Richard poured us each an after dinner Drambuie. I settled in one of the chairs and stared at the portrait of the family founder. He had a dashing look about him and his green eyes held a hint of humor. I had the feeling we'd have hit it off.

I sipped the sweet scotch-based drink and said, "I

don't understand why this house has so many fireplaces. This is Grand Britannia in the middle of the Caribbean. Who needs heat?"

Richard laughed. "Occasionally, it can get chilly, even here, what with the wind blowing in from the sea. It's a holdover from our British roots. Can't have an English manor house without a fireplace or two."

"Or three or four or more," Mary Ellen murmured, finishing her drink.

"When the house was converted to central heating, the upper fireplaces were deactivated with the exception of Sir Geoffrey's. The ones downstairs were left intact."

I sipped again as Richard refilled his wife's glass. "I take it the two of you live in the house."

She looked at me with a sharp gaze. "Yes. We used to live in West End, but moved here at Sir Geoffrey's request about ten years ago. I hope you don't mind sharing."

"Not at all. Having others in this huge house is comforting. I'm afraid I'd be bored to tears on my own."

"You could be bored to tears anyway," Richard replied in a dry tone.

A knock sounded on the door. A moment later, Beatrice entered.

"Good evening, Mr. Richard, Miss Mary Ellen, Miss Channing. Was dinner to your satisfaction?"

"It was fine," Richard told her.

I considered fine insulting to the cook. "It was fabulous."

She nodded. "I'll convey your compliments to Georgette. Do you find Violet adequate for your needs?"

I wanted to say I didn't need a maid, but let it pass.

"Violet will do nicely. Thank you."

"If I am no longer needed, then I'll retire. Miss Channing, will you be having your breakfast in bed?"

"Certainly not. I'll eat in the dining room or wherever it's served."

"Very well, miss." She left the room and closed the door behind her.

"Are you one of those early risers who do all sorts of energetic things at the crack of dawn?" Mary Ellen asked in a tone suggesting such activity was plebian.

"No, but I consider breakfast in bed a sign of laziness."

Her eyebrows rose. "I always breakfast in bed."

Oops. Major mistake. "I'm sorry. I didn't mean to insinuate…"

She waved my apology aside. "No harm. Things are different in the islands. I'm sure you'll adjust."

Somewhere a clock struck the hour of nine. I'd had enough of making small talk with these two. Although too early for sleep, perhaps I could read in my room for another couple of hours. I finished my drink and, rising, set the tiny glass on the table beside me.

"Will you excuse me? It's been an incredibly long day and that excellent meal along with the superb wine is catching up to me. I think I'll call it a night."

Richard also stood. "Of course not. We understand. Breakfast is served in the dining room from seven until nine. I'll keep you company, and then we can tour the house."

"Sounds like a plan to me," I said injecting enthusiasm into my voice.

"And perhaps after luncheon, you'd like to accompany me to the garden," Mary Ellen said.

"I'd like that very much. As for now, I'll just say goodnight."

"Good evening," they both said at once.

I exited the room, and then paused at the foot of the stairs. Eavesdropping had worked earlier. Why not now?

"Get me another drink," Mary Ellen said. "Wine this time."

"Go easy on that."

"I want her gone—permanently. That bloody old man had no business doing what he did."

"You seem to forget that if she goes, so do we," Richard said.

"I still say we can break the will. I can't believe your grandfather had already changed it. At luncheon he'd merely said he was thinking about it. And then the accident…"

"Don't dwell on it, dear. And Stephen says…"

"Oh bother Stephen! He's got a stake in this, too." Her voice had steadily risen.

"Keep your voice down. Do you want someone to hear?"

No one said anything for a few seconds. Then Mary Ellen ordered, "Get me another wine."

Good grief, had she finished off the last one already?

"You have got to lay off the wine and cocktails. Liquor loosens the tongue. I don't want you saying something you shouldn't."

"Oh, shut up and just get me the damned drink!"

I had no desire to listen to an argument. A noise

from the dining room told me it was time to go. As before, this conversation suggested things were not quite right with this deal.

The urge to pack my bags and head home was strong. I could understand the resentment, but Mary Ellen's tone had been furious, and her allusion to wanting me gone permanently gave me the shivers. On the other hand, maybe my over-active imagination and the long trip today were playing with my mind. Perhaps I'd feel better tomorrow.

I climbed the stairs past all those Goodhue's, stopping for a moment in front of the portrait labeled, Sarah Woodruff Goodhue. Blonde, petite, and dressed in the fashion of the 1920s, she looked no more than sixteen.

I continued on to my room. Violet was there turning down the bed. Overhead two ceiling fans spun helping to circulate the air drifting in the open windows.

"Oh, you're up here early, miss. Is there anything I can do for you?"

"No, not really. I think I'll read for a while."

She nodded, finished with the bed, and proceeded to remove a white silk nightgown from the dresser drawer. A gift from Mother, it sported spaghetti straps, the skirt skimming the tops of my knees. Violet laid it on the foot of the bed and turned to leave.

"Will you be taking breakfast in your room, miss?"

"No."

"Very well. Have a good night, miss, and oh, if you need anything, the house phone is on the nightstand."

She left and I inspected the house phone. I had a casual knowledge of them having once played the part of an aristocratic nincompoop in a play. This one had several buttons, all labeled in strong handwriting I recognized from the letters to Mother.

For want of anything better to do, I brushed my teeth, donned the nightie, turned off the overhead light, picked up the thriller I'd been reading on the flight, and mounting the steps next to the bed, slid beneath the cool, crisp sheets. The bedside lamp emitted enough light to read.

The breeze coming in the windows coupled with that of the ceiling fans made the room comfortable. The fifteen foot high ceiling helped dissipate most of the heat from the day.

I read until a huge yawn had me glancing at the bedside clock. Ten-thirty. Still early for me, but given my day, not unreasonable. I closed the book, turned off the light, and fluffing the pillows settled in for my first night as almost-mistress of Bountiful.

****

A loud boom jerked me from a sound sleep. I sat up, clutching the sheet under my chin. A moment later, the room lit brilliantly with a flash of lightning. Five seconds later, another boom reverberated and rumbled. The sheer curtains at all four French doors billowed and flapped as the wind swept in.

I scrambled from the bed and, forgetting the exaggerated height, fell face first onto the floor with a thump. Feeling like a fool, I picked myself up and rushed to the nearest door, swinging first one half, and then the other closed.

I smelled rain on the wind.

Hurrying around the bed, I did the same with that door. Lightning flashed and thunder pealed in quickening succession. The storm would break in a matter of seconds. I fumbled the third door closed, and turned for the last one.

Another brilliant flash illuminated the room. The almost immediate crash of thunder drowned out my startled cry.

A woman wearing a short white dress stood in the corner of the room.

Chapter Five

I froze. For one brief instant, I wondered if I had met Sarah Woodruff Goodhue. I also wondered if I'd scared her as much as she had me.

I sucked in a deep breath and advanced toward that corner with a slow step. I didn't believe in ghosts, so there had to be a reasonable explanation. Maybe I'd seen a piece of statuary, although I couldn't recall one there earlier.

The lightning flashed again. The image remained. I clapped my handover my mouth to stifle a scream. Then another flash with accompanying thunder made me gasp—this time with laughter.

It was me. I was seeing my reflection in the large cheval mirror.

I relaxed, sputtering with mirth. The dinner conversation must have had more of an effect on me than I thought.

Amid more lightning and thunder, the storm broke. Rain didn't slowly patter and build to a crescendo. It exploded from the sky striking the veranda roof like a waterfall. The wind screamed, and I had to battle the curtains standing almost straight out to find the doors. Rain sluiced across the veranda floor and into the bedroom. Pushing against the wind, I finally accomplished my mission and closed the doors.

I stopped in the bathroom to dry my wet legs and returned to bed. The storm raged and each flash of lightning sent my gaze toward the mirror. I chuckled as I settled back into the bed.

The savagery of the storm lasted a brief fifteen minutes before moving on. Mother Nature had welcomed me to Grand Britannia.

As I nestled my head into the pillows, a noise, like that of a footstep, from outside my door made me pause. I hadn't thought to lock myself in. With my heart pounding, I got up, crossed the room, and opened the door. A dim light illuminated the hallway, and from the far end, thought I saw movement as someone turned the corner.

Probably a maid checking on the windows what with the storm and all, and then deciding not to disturb me after all.

At least, that's what I told myself.

****

I descended the stairs the next morning at the absurd hour of seven-thirty. My sleep after the storm had been broken, and I could have slept in, but I didn't want to pass up Richard's offer on a tour of the house. As the nominal owner, it sounded like a good idea. I figured ten thousand square feet had a lot of nooks and crannies.

In the dining room, the sideboard was set with several chafing dishes. I peeked under the lid of one and found sausages the size of a small bratwurst. Another raised lid revealed bacon. I eased on down the line—scrambled eggs, hash browns, pancakes, tropical fruit, and finally a lid I slammed back immediately. Tiny fish for breakfast was not on my menu. Hot water was in a pot at the end of the buffet along with another of coffee and a pitcher of orange juice. A stack of toast sat next to small containers of butter and jams. A box of tea bags was on the end.

"Ah, good morning, Liza. Checking out our breakfast offerings?"

I turned to find Richard in the entryway, a smile on his face.

"You certainly put on a big spread."

He laughed, advanced to the sideboard, grabbed a plate from the stack at the end, and proceeded to fill it from the various bins.

"Have to keep up the English tradition of lots of carbohydrates and calories. Come on, fill up. What do you fancy?"

I picked up a plate and followed him down the line.

"Well, certainly not fish."

He laughed again. "Kippers. Smoked herring. My wife loves them."

"This seems like a lot of food for three people," I commented, taking one sausage just for taste.

"When we're finished, the food goes back to the kitchen for the servants."

"And how many servants are here?"I moved on to the eggs, hash browns, and fruit, shuddering when Richard filled his plate with numerous little fish.

"At last count, ten." He added toast, butter, and jam to his plate, and then headed to the table.

I followed him. "Wow, for only two people in residence?"

"It's a big house. Someone has to clean it and maintain the grounds," he said returning for a cup of hot water and a tea bag. "Mary Ellen was born to money in England. The only time she's ever in the kitchen is to discuss something with the cook. I know this must look like an extravagance. Americans aren't as tradition bound as we colonials who stayed attached to the mother country, but we enjoy keeping some of the strings uncut. Grand Britannia didn't receive full independence until nineteen-ninety."

Mother country? Hadn't Goodhues been here for four hundred years? He forked a portion of the disgusting kippers into his mouth.

"That wasn't a criticism. I was just curious. Will I be meeting them or is that not considered proper?"

"Sooner or later, I imagine."

Shrugging, I cut into my first English sausage. It may have looked like a brat, but that was where the resemblance ended. Inside, the thing was mealy and heavy. If shorter in length, I could substitute it for a shotgun shell and do damage. It was also bland. I moved on to the bacon and eggs.

"So, Liza, do you normally eat breakfast in the States? I understand coffee is the main source of sustenance in the morning."

"That's true for many, but I try to eat some cereal with fruit. Big breakfasts like this are usually reserved for Sundays. See, we still pay homage to the mother country, too."

We ate the rest of the meal with small talk about the similarities between Britain and the U.S. He finished his tea at the same time I did my coffee.

"Well, are you ready for your tour?"

I laid my napkin beside my plate and rose. "Absolutely. I'm looking forward to it."

"Wonderful. Shall we begin upstairs and work our

way down?"

I followed him from the dining room and up the stairs.

We began on the third floor.

"These were once the servants' quarters," he explained. "The larger rooms toward the end of the hall housed the nursery and where older children took instruction from tutors. As you can see, no one's been up here in a long while. I believe the bathrooms are kept presentable, however."

I counted a total of eight cell-like rooms with two bathrooms on opposite ends of the corridor. In the larger nursery areas, a couple of doors led into smaller chambers.

"What were these used for? They certainly are tiny."

"Cots and cribs were set up for nap times during the day."

"So, Mommy stuffed the kidlets up here. Out of sight, out of mind?"

"In a sense. For many well-to-do English families that was the norm. Children did not join their parents for meals until they were able to display correct manners. Fortunately, that's a thing of the past. Lack of money in the 1930s brought about change."

I didn't reply. It sounded cold, but then I was an American who, in spite of having to deal with the Daddy of the moment, had contact with my mother on a regular basis.

"Lack of money brings about a lot of things," I murmured, then wondered about the Goodhue's personal finances. Some people with pots of money often owed big time.

I peeked into one of the baths. The floors were done in small white mosaic tiles with black accent pieces, all in a hexagon pattern. The pedestal sink didn't look much different from those of today, while the claw foot tub would fit in any modern bathroom. The toilet was a true antique with the tank elevated several feet up the wall. The room was spacious, but not overly so. After all, these were the servants' quarters.

"I take it the present day staff lives off property," I said.

"Yes, with the exception of Willie, Georgette, Myron, and Beatrice. Georgette and Myron, the chauffeur, are married and live in a suite of rooms over the garage. Willie also lives in a smaller apartment there. Beatrice lives in a cottage at the edge of the woods near the drive. Perhaps you saw it when you arrived."

I hadn't. I'd been busy talking with Stephen Albright and gazing at Bountiful.

"It's very quiet up here, isn't it?" I asked.

"After all it was the servants' quarters. It was supposed to be isolated."

His words reminded me that I was in a portion of the house not frequented by anyone with a man I barely knew. A wave of uneasiness rolled through me. Then I brought myself up short. *Of course, you're safe, dummy. One of these days eavesdropping will get you into serious trouble.* Still I couldn't get what I'd overheard out of my mind.

"I think I've seen enough up here. Shall we move on?"

The second floor revealed larger bedrooms connected with what we called in the States, a Jack and

Jill bath—one bathroom servicing two bedrooms via connecting doors.

Richard paused in front of one of the bedroom doors. "This is where Mary Ellen and I live. We take up two rooms. One's been turned into a sitting area. Grandfather was getting on in years and thought it best if a family member was in the house. It sounded like a sensible solution."

In other words, the old boy demanded and Richard jumped.

"I'm sure he must have appreciated the company."

Richard laughed. "He had a routine and rarely deviated. After breakfast he worked from nine until five, took a bath, honored cocktail hour by sipping one small glass of rum…"

"Goodhue, of course," I interrupted.

"Of course," Richard said with a grin. "After dinner he returned to the drawing room for another drink and conversation before retiring."

Sounded like the ultimate in boredom to me. No wonder Mary Ellen sucked down too much wine.

In addition to the drawing and dining rooms, the ground floor housed a library and a study along with a couple of smaller rooms that appeared to have no special use.

Richard obviously used the study as his office. An oversized butler's pantry—complete with a rope pulley dumbwaiter—opened off the dining room. A set of stairs led to the kitchen below. We descended the narrow spiral staircase.

Large and airy, the kitchen had the latest in modern appliances. The flagstone floor must have been hard on the feet, but the windows over the sink and part of the counter let in abundant light. The view of the garage wasn't anything to write home about, but this area wasn't meant for gazing at dazzling vistas. A door to the outside was located in the mud room. In the States we'd call this a daylight basement.

I met Georgette and two of the maids. After thanking her for a lovely meal the night before, I turned to leave when my gaze settled on a mammoth door in the corner. It looked like something from a castle with horizontal iron strips, huge hinges, and a lock the size of Delaware.

"What on earth is that?"

Richard laughed. "That's the wine cellar. Would you like to see it?"

Of course, I would. He removed a large key from a hook beside the door, opened it, and flipped a switch at the top of another spiral staircase. I followed him down the dimly lit steps, clinging to the railing. Did I dare suggest higher wattage light bulbs in the sconces along the wall? At the bottom, he flipped another switch. Modern light fixtures blazed.

I gaped at what stood before me. Row after row of bottles nestled in wooden wine racks eight feet tall.

"Holy crap! That's a lot of wine."

Richard laughed again. It sounded forced and grated on my nerves.

"The Goodhues like fine wine. Grandfather would consult every evening with Willie about which wine to serve with dinner. Willie is not only a butler, but an excellent sommelier."

I shivered in the cool atmosphere.

"Chilly?" he asked.

I rubbed my arms not sure if it was the

temperature, the atmosphere, or Richard's laugh. "A bit. But then, that's the way a wine cellar should be, isn't it?"

He nodded and we retraced our steps.

Back in the foyer, Beatrice awaited.

"Miss Channing, Mr. Stephen called asking that if it wouldn't be too much of an inconvenience, could he stop by around ten o'clock?"

"Ah, that's right, Stephen did say something about seeing you today," Richard said.

"Thank you," I replied. Like with Violet, I gave up on her using my given name.

Richard glanced at his watch as she disappeared down the hallway. "I hope you don't mind being left on your own for a while. Estate business is waiting. I'll see you at luncheon."

I drifted into the drawing room. It wasn't the most attractive of rooms. The furniture placement struck me as haphazard. The only area I'd call cozy was in front of the fireplace. Other random seating was located in corners and at intervals along the walls and between the French doors.

I was mentally rearranging the room when a car drove up. Stephen Albright emerged and a few seconds later the doorbell rang. Beatrice answered and ushered him in to see me.

A seed of heat germinated in my stomach. I swallowed to prevent further growth.

"Liza, so good of you to see me on such short notice," he greeted.

Today he wore a light gray suit with a pale blue silk shirt. The suit had impeccable tailoring and had probably cost a fortune. He looked every inch an attorney—or barrister, or solicitor, or whatever they called it in the islands—and carried a slim black leather briefcase.

His neatly combed hair begged for my fingers to tunnel through it. I clenched my fists for a moment before releasing them again.

Perhaps it was a trick of the morning light streaming in the windows, but his eyes gleamed more blue than green. I blinked, looked away, heaved a small breath, and cleared my throat.

"No problem. It's not like I have a whole lot to do."

He smiled, his wide mobile mouth becoming another focal point.

For the love of God, Channing, get a grip. I took another cleansing breath and gestured toward the sofa.

"Have a seat. Would you like a cup of coffee? Or are you a tea person?"

The smile widened. "I'm strictly a coffee man. Don't tell anybody, but I hate tea."

I had to laugh. A quasi-Englishman who hated tea?

"Good heavens, call the police. A crime has been committed."

He laughed along before glancing at his watch, a thin, expensive make. "Do you mind if we get started? I have several clients this morning and have to be in court this afternoon."

"Of course not." I gestured again toward the sofa. "Exactly what is it you want to discuss?"

He hesitated. "Could we use the library? It's more private."

"Of course."

I followed him through the foyer and down the hall

into the library. The room more than lived up to its name. Two of the walls were floor to ceiling bookcases. Dark paneling should have made it resemble a cave, but the light from two sets of French doors cut through the gloom. A fireplace graced one wall. A leather sofa and two accompanying chairs were grouped in front of it along with a coffee table.

Stephen strode to the sofa, placed his case on the table, sat, and opened it. I plunked my fanny next to him. Like yesterday, the scent of his cologne reminded me of a fresh breeze just prior to a rain. I liked it. Clean, but not heavy.

He removed a file from the case, and handed it to me.

"This is a copy of the will. I assume you must have read it, but this is for you should you have any questions."

I accepted the folder, but didn't open it. I hadn't bothered to read the will even though Adam Wylie had given me a copy. The language of lawyers confused and irritated me.

"Actually, I do have a question or two. If I fulfill my part of the deal, exactly how much will I inherit? I mean the distillery must be worth quite a bit and what real estate holdings are there?"

His face wore an inscrutable expression and his eyes darkened. Emeralds stared back at me.

"I can see you haven't read the will." He rubbed the bridge of his nose. "Sir Geoffrey divided the majority of his estate years ago. Each grandchild received stock in the distillery. Giles Harrison's oldest son runs the business."

"And who is Giles Harrison?"

"Sir Geoffrey's only daughter's son."

"I see." I'd figure out the lineage later.

Stephen continued. "Many of the real estate holdings were liquidated, and the proceeds set aside in trusts for his grandchildren, including your mother. The remaining real estate is in the form of apartment buildings in West End and Port Elizabeth. Very profitable."

"I don't want to sound greedy about this, but exactly what do I inherit?"

"You inherit Bountiful and everything in it along with the grounds. You also will receive a share of the income from the apartments. It's quite a sizable sum. The house and grounds are worth quite a bit. Of course, real estate values have fallen dramatically in the last couple of years. The apartment income remains fairly steady."

"And what happens if I decide this is for the birds and go home?"

"The Grand Britannia Historical and Preservation Society will take over the house and grounds. The apartment buildings are slated to go to The Mariner's Trust."

"What's that?"

"It's an organization that sees to the needs of widows and orphans of mariners. It's based in Port Elizabeth, but has offices in Bristol on the west side of the island."

I fingered the folder in my lap. I still didn't like this set up.

"Seems to me the Historical Society and this Mariner's thing would like to see me hightail it back to the States. What about other great-grandkids or am I the only one on display?"

"No other great-grandchildren are mentioned." His gaze was steady on my face making me squirm inside. I had no idea what he was thinking.

"So, my contemporaries are dependent on Mommy and Daddy inheriting?"

"They all have legitimate jobs, of course, but put that way—yes."

"And if I don't comply, what about the trusts?"

He took a deep breath. "A large portion would be revoked and the money turned over to the Historical Society. Bountiful is not an inexpensive property to maintain."

A snippet of conversation I'd overheard yesterday came back.

"Has any money been set aside for me while I'm in residence? I may want to shop on occasion."

He stared and smiled as though knowing I'd eavesdropped. Then he frowned as if wondering how much I'd overheard. I tried to keep an inquisitive look on my face.

The smile returned. "Yes, you have an allowance of a thousand dollars a month."

"And just where would I spend that much money per month?" When he didn't answer, I moved on. "Let's say I do stick it out. What happens then?"

"The trusts become irrevocable and Bountiful becomes yours and yours alone. No strings or conditions."

"Mine alone, huh? Does that also include the high maintenance price tag?"

"I'm afraid so."

I needed to think on this. And if I did inherit, what

would happen to Richard? Exactly what was his job? I had no idea what an estate manager did. As far as I could see, the property had no sustainable income, so why did Bountiful need a manager?

Stephen set aside several folders and snapped his case closed.

"Is there anything else?" he asked, a hint of impatience in his tone.

"Actually, there is. What can you tell me about my grandparents? How and where did they meet? Do you know? What sent Sir Geoffrey on the quest to find his long-lost granddaughter twenty years ago?"

"I know some of the story, but haven't as yet been through all his personal papers and correspondence." He glanced at his watch. "I have to be in the office. Perhaps we can discuss this later." He rose.

I had no choice but to stand also. "Of course. It's waited almost sixty years. Another few days won't kill me."

I saw him to the door, lingering in the doorway until he'd slipped behind the wheel of a BMW sports car and left.

With the folders in my hand, I wandered back into the drawing room, sat in one of the chairs and stared at the antique fireplace screen.

I'd walked into a mess. Unable to manipulate my mother, Geoffrey Goodhue had manipulated me—from the grave. If I stayed and inherited, changes would be made. The house was enormous—much too big for just one or two people. Perhaps a deal could be struck with the Historical Society in which they could hold tours provided they paid some of the costs of running Bountiful.

Or maybe the house could pay its own way. With all those bedrooms, a bed and breakfast might be possible. Add a swimming pool and tennis courts, and the whole thing could be packaged for tourists. It was something to think about.

I sighed and headed upstairs where I set the folders on the desk. I had a couple of hours before lunch after which Mary Ellen would traipse me around the grounds. I'd keep an eye open for pool and court sites.

In the meantime, I fired up my computer and blogged about my experiences so far. I'd ask more questions later. And then, there was that damned party tomorrow night.

I was sure to meet more resentful, but needy relatives.

Chapter Six

Lunch consisted of another cold soup, cucumber this time, a salad, and some kind of lamb curry. I wasn't a fan of either lamb or curry. If I wanted any type of American food, I'd have to talk to Georgette.

Richard had little to say during the meal, merely stating he was busy. I wondered with what, but held my tongue. I'd get into that later.

"Well, are you ready for your grounds tour?" Mary Ellen asked as the last of the dishes were whisked away.

"I'm looking forward to it. Richard showed me around this morning. It's a big house. I even saw the wine cellar."

"I can remember when everyone came and stayed for Christmas. Our children loved all the nooks and crannies." She sighed. "That doesn't happen often anymore."

"Time moves on. People have different priorities."

"Yes, I suppose so." She rose from her chair. "Shall we go?"

Richard also stood. "Have a nice tour. I'll see you at seven-thirty for cocktails."

In the foyer, he turned toward the back of the house. Mary Ellen turned to me.

"Let's begin out here." She opened the front door.

"You should have seen the place before I came. I was appalled and asked Sir Geoffrey if I could replant. When he said yes, I dug right in—literally. The old boy employed a gardener, but his main task was to see the lawns were mowed."

She led me from flowerbed to flowerbed, pointing out the various species of whatever grew in the well-mulched areas. Los Angeles condo living didn't inspire the nature lover in me. The less I had to do the better. Still, I made all the appropriate remarks regarding beauty and tasteful landscaping. It was true. Mary Ellen had the knack.

We moved on to the enormous fountain in the center of the circular drive. The base covered a good twelve-by-twelve foot area and the concrete pineapple on top soared several feet above my head. The water burbled from the fixture into a smaller bowl before falling into the main pool. Koi swam.

We crossed the lawn to the woods.

"If you ever feel like just walking, there are several pathways you might enjoy," Mary Ellen said.

"I thought the whole idea of overgrown woods was to discourage trespassers."

"Oh, it was, but the trails aren't close to the road."

She led me back around the side of the house. I glanced up at my little corner of paradise. A figure stepped away from one of the French doors.

I stopped and stared. *Who the hell is in my room?*

"Is something wrong?"

"I thought I saw someone standing in the window."

She spared the upper veranda a fleeting glance. "It's probably Violet. Or perhaps Beatrice checking to make sure Violet has done everything properly. Let me show you the rose garden and the maze."

I tore my gaze away from the upper balcony and followed her. I'd only seen a small portion of the rose garden yesterday, but viewing it now proved stunning. Here, Mary Ellen bloomed as beautifully as the flowers. And the maze wasn't as complicated as it first appeared. We wound our way through until emerging into a large circular space. At the center stood an inlaid compass rose.

"How lovely," I said.

"Rumor has it the original was an honest-to-God compass from one of the Goodhue ships. An ancestor built the maze using hedges. They were fifteen feet high and gave me claustrophobia. I had them ripped out and put in the roses."

She led the way to a gap in the bushes near the rear of the maze and onto the back lawn.

"I know some people find it a bit daunting to have to go through the maze to get to the cove, but it really is quite simple and I like it."

I did, too. It was different and who wouldn't love the heady aroma of those roses mixed with the scent of the sea?

A brief walk brought us to the edge of the cliff and down a short flight of steps, to a large wooden deck overlooking the rock strewn beach sixty feet below. The occasional palm tree hugged the base of the precipice. A set of stairs zigzagged down the embankment.

The view was breathtaking. The cove was smooth as glass with little wave action. To my left, a finger of land protruded, the cliff falling straight to meet the sea. A small cabin-like structure nestled against the rocks not far from the water's edge, and the remains of an old pier jutted out. In the distance, twin headlands encircled the cove like a loving pair of arms.

"What's that?" I asked, pointing to the structures.

"A jetty and a small storage house for boat equipment. It hasn't housed any in a long time. Your grandfather was fond of sailing. And I seem to recall my father-in-law having a speedboat at some point in time."

From what I could see, the narrow beach continued around the cove until meeting the same cliffs on the opposite side. I placed my hands on the wooden railing. It moved. I quickly stepped back.

"Whoa! Needs a little repair."

She turned her light blue gaze on me. "No one really uses the overlook anymore, so I guess it's not unexpected. Best be careful. Wouldn't want to lose you." She looked back to the cove. "But the view is lovely."

Couldn't argue with her there, but the words concerning not losing me rang false. I remembered her comments from the night before, and took another step back as the uneasiness I'd experienced earlier with Richard returned.

I shook off the feeling and gazed over the water. Through the trees a house gleamed white in the sunlight.

"Goodness, this is impressive. Who lives over there?" I asked pointing again.

"The house on the other side is being rented to a man by the name of Collier. He's some kind of photographer, I believe."

"Is the house as large as Bountiful?"

"Not at all. It's more of a villa. He's been there two years or so. There's still more to see. Shall we go?"

The rest of the tour was short. The driveway branched off along the servants' entrance and culminated at the eight bay garage.

"Do you have that many cars?"

"Not any more. We have the limo, but it's small. Richard has a Jaguar and I drive a Mercedes—when I drive. The roads are quite narrow with sharp curves and the island drivers dreadful. If I go anywhere, I have Myron take me."

We had come full circle back to the front. Inside, she smiled and headed for the drawing room.

"Would you like a glass of wine?"

It was four o'clock in the afternoon. "No, thank you. If you don't mind, I think I'll go upstairs, catch up on some e-mails, and have a bath." I turned to leave, then turned back. "Oh, by the way, what is the dress for tomorrow night's affair? I didn't think to bring anything formal."

"Nothing is formal on Grand Britannia. A simple cocktail dress will do."

I thanked her again and climbed the stairs. I hadn't thought to pack a cocktail dress either. I only had one, and it was close to ten years old. I needed a quick trip to the nearest boutique.

Back in my room, I stood at the French doors where I thought I'd seen someone earlier. The sheer curtain billowed in the breeze. I could have been mistaken. Maybe I'd seen the curtain moving.

I turned, walked over to the desk, and reached for my laptop. As I did, my gaze fell onto the folders Stephen had given me. They had been moved. I opened the topmost. It contained Sir Geoffrey's will. Since he'd given me that one first, it had been on the bottom.

Someone had snooped. But who?

****

After e-mailing Mother with a glowing daily report, I drew my own bath. Soaking, I wondered who had read Sir Geoffrey's will. Mary Ellen was in the clear since she'd been with me. Richard? Why would he want to read it? He already knew the contents. Violet? Why should she care? Ditto for Beatrice.

I finally came to the conclusion that the culprit was Violet who succumbed to curiosity. *She probably got scared when she saw me looking at the windows. And did I actually have that particular file on the bottom?* I couldn't remember.

Dinner was intensely boring. Nobody had much to say. The food was its saving grace. I had no idea what Richard and Mary Ellen were thinking, but my mind was occupied with what I'd seen on my tours.

Bountiful was beautiful and, according to Stephen, cost a fortune to maintain. The taxes alone must have been horrendous. I still had to question Richard about his job, but assumed the house and grounds were part of it. Somehow, the estate had to pay its fair share, which brought my mind back to the bed and breakfast theme.

A small, intimate resort might be the ticket.

Some rearrangement on the third floor would provide a few more rooms by knocking out a wall here and there. Additional bathrooms could also be added. The lawn area near the servants' entrance would do for a pool and tennis courts.

And the beach was perfect. The palm trees randomly dotting the sand would provide respite from the unrelenting sun.

It's something to think about. I'd keep my plans quiet for a while until I could do research.

Back in the drawing room, Richard sat in one of the chairs while Mary Ellen and I chose the sofa. She'd managed two martinis during cocktail hour, three glasses of wine at dinner, and now sat taking generous sips of Drambuie.

The silence stretched my nerves. To break it I asked about the party. "So, who is going to be at this shindig tomorrow night?"

Richard winced at my terminology. Mary Ellen drained her glass.

"Most of the family left on the island," she replied. "Some will stay overnight."

"Good grief, guess I'd better buy one killer dress," I said trying to lighten the mood.

"Irene is a bitch," Mary Ellen said, slightly slurring the words.

"My dear, I think you've had enough to drink," her husband said. His tone may have sounded mild, but his eyes were hard.

"Well, it's true. She only wants to see if she can pry money out of Liza."

"That'll be a tough sell. Stephen told me this morning that I'm on an allowance."

"She'll try anyway. She spends it fast." She rose and walked to the bar where she refilled her glass.

"Irene is your sister, right, Richard?"

"Yes, she's five years younger."

"Does she have a job or anything?"

"She works for the Grand Britannia Historical Society on occasion."

Interesting. Richard's sister worked for the entity that stood to gain by my premature departure.

"What does she do for them?"

Mary Ellen resumed her seat. "Genealogies mostly."

"Oh, really?" I sipped my Drambuie.

Richard uncrossed, and then re-crossed his legs. "Yes, she loves delving into the past. Researching has become much easier, what with online sites to help. Many of the old families on the island are requesting information. She did the Goodhue family tree."

"I'd like to see that some time. It would be nice to learn more about my grandfather."

Mary Ellen drained her glass in one gulp. "From what I understand, he got randy while on an extended business trip to the States."

Richard rose and pried the glass from his wife's fingers. "That was uncalled for. Mercer was my uncle, and I was fond of him. Plus you've just insulted Liza. It's time for you to retire."

She glared at him for a moment, and then rose. "I apologize for my choice of words, Liza. I meant no disrespect. I'll see you in the morning."

Mary Ellen exited the room with the precise walk of someone who'd had too much to drink. I'd done it myself upon occasion, both on and off stage.

Richard turned to me. "My sincerest apologies, too. The past few months have been very stressful for the family. Mary Ellen tends to isolate herself at Bountiful. Perhaps now that you're here, she'll have someone to talk to again. If you'll excuse me, I'd better make sure she's all right. I'll see you in the morning."

He left, closing the door behind him. I finished my

drink, walked across the room, and through the open French doors. The breeze ruffled my hair, and I inhaled the refreshing scent of the sea. Dim lights illuminated the fountain.

I had no idea of the Goodhue family dynamics. Maybe the party would shed some light on things. I'd play the part of a spy, chatting politely while observing actions and reactions. It could be my most challenging role to date.

Returning inside, I climbed the stairs. If nothing else, I'd see what Google could find on the rest of the Goodhues.

Two hours later, I shut down the computer. Not much information was available. My new-found family members were pros at the privacy game. I'd also done a preliminary search on Facebook and Twitter, but came up dry. Not surprising. I didn't see Richard or Mary Ellen coming forth with snippets of information on how they'd spent the day in a hundred-forty characters or less.

I brushed my teeth, donned my nightie from where Violet had placed it on the foot of the bed, and climbed the steps to the mammoth mattress. Pulling the sheets up, my gaze fell on a radio/CD player sitting on the nightstand to my left. Reaching over, I opened the drawer. CDs of several classical artists were arranged neatly inside. I chose Vivaldi's *Four Seasons*, slipped it into the machine, set the timer, then turned out the light. The French doors were open to their fullest again, but the breeze barely rippled the curtains. The overhead fans provided comfort.

I stared at the ceiling letting the lilting notes of the first movement relax me. To stave off total boredom,

I'd need to get out once in a while. A car would be nice, although adjusting to the right hand drive might take a while. I'd have to get an international driver's license or something. Perhaps Stephen could help with that.

I'd blocked the handsome lawyer from my mind most of the day, but now my imagination knew no bounds. Tall, good-looking, and even though wearing suits, I had no problem discerning he possessed a damned fine body. And while I wasn't sure if I trusted him, he expelled a sex appeal that called to my baser instincts. Maybe his aloofness was a device to keep things professional. I wouldn't mind cracking that icy shell.

I rolled over and punched my pillows into another shape as Vivaldi's *Spring* gave way to *Summer*.

Get a grip. He looks to be at least thirty-five. Probably married with a passel of kids. Now, go to sleep.

I inhaled a couple of deep cleansing breaths and closed my eyes, then focused my brain into calming thoughts and visuals to go along with the music, a trick I'd learned from an acting coach years ago.

I was finally relaxed when the creaking of one of the veranda floorboards made me roll over. The faint glow of the fountain lights backlit a shadow outside my French door.

Startled, I gasped, sat up, and blinked. The shadow was gone.

"Is anyone there?" I called out in a breathy voice.

No one answered. The floorboard creaked again. Then all was silent.

I lay back down and pulled the sheet up to my chin with trembling fingers.

Don't be an idiot. It was probably Richard or Mary Ellen getting a breath of air. Or maybe no one was there. The shadow was a palm frond blowing in the breeze. This is an old house. It's going to make weird noises.

I closed my eyes when an unwelcome thought sprang into my mind. *What the hell happens with the conditions of the will if I die?*

Chapter Seven

Sleep turned elusive after the incident on the veranda and my silly question. Sunlight flooding the room had awakened me at eight. After breakfast Myron drove me into West End, waiting on a side street while I shopped. I stared into the window of a small boutique. The dresses displayed weren't semi-formal status. I moved on.

A dress on a mannequin in the next store caught my eye. I entered for a closer look.

Midnight blue silk, dark as a tropical night, begged my fingers to stroke its soft, cool folds. Sleeveless with a scoop neckline, the gathered skirt fell in graceful knee-length swirls from a fitted bodice. A two inch band of crystal beading gave definition to the waist. I thought of 1950s *haute couture*—timeless and elegant.

"Isn't it a wonderful creation?" a voice said from behind.

"It certainly is," I replied, caressing the soft fabric again.

"Would you like to try it on?"

"Of course." She whisked me into a tiny changing room. Five minutes later, I stood in front of a three-way mirror admiring the effect. *Fabulous*. I had to have it.

"It was made for you, miss," the sales lady insisted.

"Can't argue with you there. How much is it?"

"Five hundred and ninety-five dollars."

Ouch. Quite a dent in my allowance. And since I had no clue how to ask for any of the money that meant the sale would have to scorch my MasterCard. I turned to admire the back of the dress.

No way was I leaving the store empty-handed. "Lady, you've just made a sale."

Her smile became genuine. I'd probably made her day with an enormous commission.

"Wonderful. Will you be taking it with you or shall I have it delivered to your hotel?"

"I'll take it with me." No need to advertise I was at Bountiful. I imagined the island grapevine had already registered my presence. A tinkling bell told me the shop door had opened and closed. I ignored it and preened, turning from side to side to view all angles again in the mirror.

"You'll need shoes, of course, to go with it. May I suggest Antoine's down the street? They have an excellent selection. Now, how about a clutch? I have a marvelous little bag for only a hundred and twenty dollars."

"Sounds like a bargain to me," a man's voice said.

Startled, I turned. Stephen leaned against the glass counter near the cash register, a smile on his face. His gaze roamed up and down my figure. I hoped he liked what he saw.

I tried to ignore the surge of heat flooding my body and all those enticing flutters. "I don't want to blow the allowance I don't have yet, on frivolous things."

He laughed. "You're all set up at the bank. Just go in, show your identification, sign a few papers, and you're in business."

"Oh, Mr. Albright, I was going to call you," the sales lady said in a purring tone. "The item you ordered is here. Let me write this lady up and I'll be right with you. Will you be taking the clutch, too, miss? It matches the dress."

I had no use for a clutch, but unable to tear my gaze away from Stephen Albright, nodded. Feeling like a numbskull for gawking, I broke eye contact and returned to the fitting room.

When I reentered the salon, Stephen still stood at the counter while the clerk wrapped the dress in tissue paper and settled it in a box. I had never seen anything in a box outside of Christmas gifts. Bags from TJ Maxx were the norm for me. I handed her my credit card.

Stephen waved it away. "No need. When I'm finished, we'll go to the bank and activate your account. Leave it here until you're ready to return home. Then just have Myron pull up out front, and you can pay for it."

The sales lady sealed the box with an elaborate ribbon. "I'll be happy to keep it for you, Miss Channing. You are Miss Channing, aren't you? The lady who inherited Bountiful."

"Guilty as charged."

"I hope you enjoy the dress. Please come back again. Now, Mr. Albright, let me get that handbag."

Handbag? He was in here for a purse? Guess that nailed down his marital status. My heart plummeted to my toes, and an overwhelming sense of loss replaced that giddy excitement his voice had evoked. *Just my luck. Tall, good-looking, and married. Well, damn!*

The woman returned from the back of the shop with a square box. She set it on the counter, opened the lid, and removed a deep russet colored Coach shoulder bag. It probably cost more than my dress.

"Here it is, Mr. Albright. Isn't it lovely?"

He shrugged and took a thin reptile skin wallet from the inside pocket of his suit coat.

"It's a handbag. I'm sure Madeleine will love it." He handed over a credit card. "Wrap it in something cheerful and send it along to the office this afternoon."

With the transaction finished, he turned to me. "After stopping at the bank, may I treat you to a cup of coffee?"

Married or not, I couldn't say no.

The bank procedure took ten minutes, and I left secure in the knowledge I had funds that weren't connected to my personal account in Los Angeles.

He steered me toward a sidewalk patio in front of a local coffee house.

Taking a seat, I couldn't help saying, "That was a gorgeous purse. I hope your wife likes it."

He sat across from me and smiled. The action crinkled the corners of his eyes and deepened the grooves in his face. Oddly enough, they didn't make him look old, but heightened his character, as though he enjoyed outdoor life and didn't care. I'd been around actors who flinched at the mere mention of sun.

"I'm not married. It's a gift for my sister. She lives in Miami with her husband and three children. Her birthday's next month and they'll all be here to celebrate the big four-oh."

A weight lifted from my shoulders and my heart returned to its rightful place in my chest. No wife.

A waiter stopped by the table. I ordered a caramel frappe, while Stephen kept it simple with black coffee.

"So, are you ready for tonight's party?" he asked.

"I suppose. I guess I have to meet the rest of the clan sooner or later. Will you be there?"

"Oh, yes. It's been a while since so much of the family has gotten together, I believe. How are you getting along? Are Richard and Mary Ellen showing you around?"

I told him about the tours, but said nothing of my possible plans for making Bountiful pay its own way. Instead, I broached the subject that had kept me awake half the night.

"Stephen, what would happen to Bountiful and the conditions of the will if I were to die?"

The waiter bringing our drinks snuffed the look of astonishment from his face.

"What on earth brought this on?" he asked when the man left.

I sucked some of the caramel frappe through the straw and for once avoided looking into those blue-green eyes. I had no intention of revealing someone had snooped at the folders he'd given me or the strange creaking sounds from the veranda and outside my door.

"Nothing. Just one of those aggravating questions that pop into my head when I can't sleep. I mean, if I get run over by a bus five minutes from now, will that be construed as me not fulfilling the contract?"

He sipped from the cup. "You still haven't read the will?"

"I hate legal jargon."

"The terms state that if you return to the United States for longer than a two week period, then the inheritance is forfeited. It says nothing about death."

"You didn't consider the possibility when you

wrote the will?" I asked pulling more frappe through the straw.

"I always consider the unexpected—or try to. In this case Sir Geoffrey wrote the will himself. I brought up a death clause, but he refused to include it."

"Why?"

"I don't know. Said you were young and not likely to die anytime soon. He was a cantankerous old man who thought he knew it all."

Stephen's voice had an irritated quality in it. I suspected he and Sir Geoffrey had gone round and round on a lot of items over the course of time.

"So, if this hypothetical bus and I meet then it's a free for all as to who inherits Bountiful?"

"Unless you make a will. Do you have one?"

"Thirty-year-olds don't think of death, and most don't have an estate. And can I even leave an inheritance that isn't mine yet to someone?"

"It brings up an interesting possibility. I wonder if a will could be treated like a divorce decree discussing potential income in a settlement. If nothing else, the situation would keep the whole mess in court for years."

I want her gone—permanently. The words rose before I could stop them.

"How did my great-grandfather distribute the wealth before this will?"

"Equal shares of businesses and money to his grandchildren with the exception of Bountiful. It went to Irene, Richard's sister."

My head snapped up. Irene? The woman so anxious to meet me she was throwing a welcome party tonight?

"When did he change his will?"

"About two months before he died."

"If I croak could the present will be contested again and revoked?"

"I'm not sure. I suppose someone could make a case that the exclusion of a death clause—against my advice—and the fact he wrote it himself, shows unsound mind."

I pulled the straw from my frappe and gulped the rest of the cold concoction, then licked the whipped cream from my lips. Stephen stared at me with a strange look on his face. I stopped to consider the whipped cream and my actions before tearing my mind away from prurient thoughts.

"Terrific. I feel like I have a target stamped on my forehead."

He finished his coffee, frowned, and then leaned forward, placing his hand on my arm. Warmth spread upward to my shoulder.

"Don't worry, Liza. I think Irene was relieved she didn't have to deal with the house and grounds. Her last divorce gave her a house on the south side of the island."

His hand slid down to mine and squeezed. A shot of adrenaline burst from the pit of my stomach. I had the strangest urge to leap across the tiny table and kiss him senseless.

"You feel safe, don't you?"

From the family—probably. From Stephen Albright—not a chance in hell. He was as dangerous as they come.

"Yes. I didn't mean to suggest otherwise. It was just one of those silly, random thoughts people think of when they can't control their brains." I reluctantly pulled my hand free and glanced at my watch. When I looked up again, he stared at my hand as if sorry I'd broken contact. "If I want shoes to go with my dress, I'd better get on with it. I don't want to miss lunch either."

"And I have a client due in another few minutes." He rose and tossed some bills on the table, then smiled. "I'll see you tonight."

I couldn't keep my gaze off of him as he walked away. Commanding, determined, and confident were three words that popped into my head. He had great stage presence.

Sighing, I turned and headed for the shoe store.

****

I twisted my head around to view the back of my new dress in the cheval mirror. The silver stiletto sandals with the rhinestone straps also looked great. Sterling dangle earrings and a cuff bracelet completed the ensemble.

Downstairs, most of the family awaited my arrival. After lunch, I'd stayed out of the way in my room blogging, e-mailing, and catching up on Facebook. That didn't prevent me from hearing the cars crunch up the driveway or the activity of suitcases being brought upstairs. No one consulted me about the overnight guests.

A final glance in the mirror convinced me I looked terrific. That stupid gong sounded again. Either Willie didn't like giving up tradition or Richard hadn't told him to knock it off.

I sucked in a deep breath and dawdled a few minutes longer. Cocktails followed by dinner, all arranged by Irene but implemented by Mary Ellen. Holding my head high, I descended the staircase pausing on the last step. The drawing room doors were open and the conversation spilled into the foyer.

"For Pete's sake, don't ask her for money, Irene." I recognized Mary Ellen's voice.

"Why not? She's grandfather's relative of choice to inherit. She might as well write a check."

"Because Grandfather set her up with an allowance less than you get," Richard replied.

"Miserable old coot," the person I assumed was Irene answered.

Eavesdropping had its uses until one of the maids walked in from the dining room with a tray full of canapés. I nodded and made my entrance, stage right.

All conversation ceased as I stood in the doorway. Richard immediately came forward.

"Ah, there you are, Liza. Please let me introduce you." With his hand in the small of my back, he guided me toward a tall, slender, redhead. "This is my sister, Irene."

She flicked a stray lock of hair over her shoulder, smiled, and held out a hand.

"Liza, I'm so glad to make your acquaintance."

The smile looked genuine, but her eyes held speculation. I took the proffered hand.

"Irene, I've heard a lot about you."

"Do I need to defend myself, Mary Ellen?" she asked.

Mary Ellen's lips curved into a tight smile as she sipped a martini.

Richard moved on to a couple sitting on the sofa.

"This is my cousin, Giles Harrison, and his wife,

Evelyn."

The woman leaped to her feet and embraced me. "Liza, it's so good to meet you at last. I can't tell you how happy I am you're here. What a gorgeous dress." She burbled like a swiftly moving stream.

"How do you do, Liza," Giles said in a placid tone.

"How do you like Bountiful so far?" Evelyn asked. She reached down to pick up a cocktail glass from the end table. "Don't you find it magnificent? I always loved coming here for the holidays. I do hope the tradition continues."

"Uh, I haven't given it much thought. Christmas is still a ways off."

"Mary Ellen said she showed you the gardens. She's such a marvelous landscaper. I wish I had her talent. Of course, she has the time to spend on it. Now that the children are grown, I help Giles with the auctions and in the shop. It keeps me busy and I…"

Richard interrupted. "Would you like a drink, Liza?"

I glanced at the others in the room. Most held cocktail glasses. "A rum punch would be nice."

"Excellent. Excuse us for a moment."

With a nod at the Harrisons, he steered me toward the bar cart and introduced me to the man standing next to it.

"This is Giles and Evelyn's youngest son, Roger. Could you mix up a rum punch for Liza?"

"One rum punch for the new owner of Bountiful," he said with a smile.

In his mid-twenties, Roger quickly made the drink and presented it to me. His smile was infectious and his eyes held a hint of humor.

"So, Cousin Richard is making you run the gauntlet. Think you'll survive?"

I sipped the fruity concoction and laughed lightly. "Let's hope so. I'm sure I won't remember all the names or who goes with who."

"If you have any problems, just call on me. I sell insurance and have no axe to grind with our mutual great-grandfather."

Richard and I moved on meeting more relatives. I hadn't lied. I needed a scorecard.

Eventually, I found myself sitting on the sofa next to Evelyn. Irene lounged in a chair, her sharp blue gaze measuring me. Mary Ellen sat on the loveseat facing me and drinking another martini. She drained the glass and a man I remembered as being her oldest son took it from her fingers.

"So, how are you getting along?" Stephen's voice asked from over my shoulder.

I turned my head happy to see him. He held a glass of amber liquid. "Fine. It's fun meeting relatives you didn't know you had."

"Provided the relatives are bearable," Irene drawled.

"Oh, Irene, I think we're quite bearable," Evelyn said. "It's just so awkward. I mean none of us knew Uncle Mercer had a daughter, let alone a granddaughter. I suppose we're as much a shock to Liza as she was to us."

"That's putting it mildly," I replied. Polite laughter followed my statement.

Stephen's hand descended to my shoulder where he squeezed, and then leaned down to whisper in my ear. "They won't eat you."

His warm breath on my ear sent a shiver of delight up my spine. The cocktail party wore on. More people arrived with Richard making introductions.

Then Mary Ellen, who said little, but drank three martinis, straightened and stared over my shoulder.

"What the devil is *he* doing here?" she blurted.

Irene rose with a smile on her face. "I invited him. After all, he is a neighbor—and a friend."

I gazed toward the entryway. A dark-haired man of medium height stood, his eyes scanning the room. He broke into a smile as Irene approached. They kissed each others' cheeks, then Irene looped her arm through his and headed back toward the fireplace.

"Liza, this is Benjamin Collier. He lives in the villa on the other side of the cove. Ben, this is Liza Channing, the new owner of Bountiful."

He smiled and took my offered hand. "Liza, it's a pleasure to meet you. I'm sorry I'm late, but I couldn't tear myself away from the scenery over on Wellington Cay. Got some great shots."

His accent was pure American. A compatriot at last.

"That's right; Mary Ellen mentioned something about a photographer living across the cove when she showed me around yesterday."

"That would be me." His smile widened into a grin.

Irene shifted her gaze between the two of us before flagging down a nearby family member.

"Wesley, be an angel and get Ben a cocktail, would you? What'll you have, dear?"

Ben's scrutiny of me and his smile never wavered. "What are you having, Liza?"

"Rum punch."

"Then rum punch it is."

His continued stare was both flattering and unnerving at the same time. I finally looked away to drink the remainder of my cocktail. His fixated gaze made me uncomfortable, especially since it was obvious he and Irene were close.

"I wondered if you'd put in an appearance," Stephen said.

Both his expression and tone were neutral. I sensed the men didn't like each other yet were determined to be polite. I'd often seen this game played in Hollywood.

"When Irene calls with an invitation to a party, who am I to refuse?"

"Of course, you couldn't," Irene said with a smile as Wesley handed Ben a tall glass.

He took a sip and looked at Mary Ellen. "Good evening, Mary Ellen. How nice to see your smiling face again."

I cast a glance at Mary Ellen. She simply stared at Ben with ill-concealed distaste.

Giles drifted up to the group. "Hello, Collier. Still taking photos of all the fish life?"

"Was out on the reef all day. Got some spectacular shots."

"Dinner is served," Willie intoned from the doorway.

Stephen extended his hand. "Allow me to escort you, Liza."

Ben turned away with Irene, an amused expression on his face.

I was grateful to see the cocktail hour end. I counted eighteen of us marching toward the dining room where we took our assigned seats. Now if only I could make it through dinner.

Stephen sat to my right while the place card to my left read James. Across the table to my right was Irene with Ben by her side. I could put names to some of the faces, but for the most part was clueless.

The man to my left introduced himself as Richard and Mary Ellen's youngest son, James. He worked in an art gallery and painted. Referencing Mother, I made a comment about artistic talent running in the family.

To my right, Stephen said in a low tone, "Surviving the onslaught of relatives?"

"More or less."

He smiled. "Have I told you how lovely you look? That dress looks even better here than at the shop."

"Thank you. It put a sizable dent in my allowance. I hope the executor of the estate will be understanding."

The smile widened. "He will."

Evelyn, across the table to my left, leaned forward. "And how are your parents, Stephen? Why aren't they here tonight?"

"Mother and Dad are touring the Orient for the next month, or so. They've already done Japan and Korea. I believe they're in Singapore at the moment. Hong Kong and China are next on the list."

"Oh, how exciting! Have you traveled much, Liza?" she asked.

"This is my first time out of the States, but I've managed to see some of my own country."

The soup course was served followed by the salad, and then some kind of white fish with an almandine sauce and asparagus. Willie was kept busy pouring the appropriate wines.

Conversation flowed, mostly about the weather and business. I listened with no comments and learned Giles was the owner of a high-end auction house in Port Elizabeth. According to him, due to the recession, business was good. Also, however, due to the recession, items weren't bringing the high sales prices of a few years ago.

Richard sat at the head of the table. Mary Ellen graced the other end speaking softly with those near her and downing glass after glass of wine. At this rate, she'd need assistance getting up the stairs.

The meat course arrived—prime rib *au jus* with roasted potatoes and glazed carrots. It smelled delicious, but I wondered if I'd have room to eat it. Was Mary Ellen trying to impress me? Then I remembered Irene was the official hostess at large events. I cast a glance at both women.

Mary Ellen picked at her food, her face a mask. Botox? Irene ate with gusto and wasn't afraid to lower the level of the wine bottle either. She just handled it better.

I sensed curiosity, resentment, dislike, and a myriad of other emotions—not all directed at me. They made for an uncomfortable party, and I wished the night would end.

Irene had talked a blue streak during much of the meal, mostly discussing people and places I didn't know. Occasionally, she talked sotto voice with Ben who would wink at her and smile. Finally, he turned his attention toward me and asked several questions about my life.

"I understand you're an actress. Movies? TV? Stage?"

"I've had a few television roles in things like *CSI* and *Law and Order, SVU*. Nothing big. Only a line or two. And I was an extra in several movies with big name stars. I also was the first victim in a slasher flick. My line was, 'No, no, don't!' Then I screamed. That got me a role in another film."

"So, I guess coming here has put a crimp in your career," Ben said as he cut his meat.

"Things are on hold at the moment." I also cut a piece of prime rib and popped it into my mouth. Tender and juicy, just the way it should be.

"We're so glad you came," Evelyn said. "I'm surprised you agreed to the deal, considering everything."

"Finding out I had a great-grandfather who bequeathed me an estate was too intriguing to pass up."

"Oh, I didn't mean that," she said lifting her wine glass. "I meant I'd have refused simply because Sir Geoffrey was murdered."

Chapter Eight

Talk about a conversation stopper.

I froze with my fork halfway to my mouth and stared. A choking sound made me look toward Mary Ellen as she hastily lowered her wine glass and covered her mouth with her napkin. Irene banged her knife and fork onto the table. Beside me, Stephen groaned. On my other side, James muttered something under his breath.

I knew Hollywood directors who would kill for the reactions displayed before me.

"Evelyn, really!" Mary Ellen said with a gasp as she glared down the table.

"God dammit, Evelyn, the old boy tripped and fell down the freaking stairs!" Irene said between clenched teeth.

Giles tried to intercede. "Dear, perhaps now is not…"

His wife ignored him. "And maybe someone pushed him."

"Why would someone push him down the stairs?" James asked.

"Because he hinted he was going to change his will at lunch. Remember?"

I finally came out of my shock. With the stress of the last couple of days and this evening's entertainment, I'd almost forgotten about the newspaper article.

"I read where the subject of foul play was suggested by a reporter, but was assured nothing of the kind occurred."

Irene waved her hand in the air. "Of course, it didn't. Ridiculous accusation."

Richard glared at Evelyn before turning his gaze toward me. "Liza, over the years, the Goodhue's have been on the receiving end of accusations and innuendos by rival politicians and ambitious reporters. That particular reporter is no longer on the island. It was nothing more than idle speculation."

"Exactly when did all this happen?"

"New Year's Eve," Stephen said. "Take my word for it, he was not murdered. Evelyn, you can't go around saying these things."

Clearing my throat, I said, "New Year's Eve?"

Richard sipped his wine. "Yes. The house was almost full. We were all upstairs changing for cocktails when we heard Mary Ellen scream. There was nothing we could do, of course."

His wife nodded. "I had just finished dressing when I heard him fall. I was the first one to the top of the stairs. I looked down and there he was, crumbled at the bottom."

"Mother, I think perhaps you should keep your opinions to yourself. What will Liza think of us?" Roger said.

"That maybe one of us is a murderer?" Evelyn replied.

"That's enough!" Mary Ellen said. "Evelyn, why do you so enjoy stirring up controversy where none exists?"

"Maybe because this family needs a little stirring

up."

I laid my fork on my plate. "I have the feeling I've just been punked."

"Punked?" James asked.

"Put on. On the receiving end of a joke. Somebody says or does something outrageous to produce a reaction. Usually, such things are videoed and released on YouTube."

Mary Ellen relaxed. "Well, Evelyn, if that was the intention, it fell flat. What a silly thing to say."

For once I agreed with Mary Ellen, but doubts nagged. I let my gaze wander around the table until finally making contact with Ben's. He smiled, shrugged lightly, and sipped from his wine glass. Had he been included in the family gathering that night?

Evelyn's right eyebrow rose a fraction and she resumed eating. I followed her example, but suddenly the food didn't taste as good as it had a few minutes earlier. The only sound in the room was the clink of silverware on fine china.

I stepped in to break the awkward silence. "Irene, I understand you work for the Historical Society. That must be fascinating."

"It can be."

"Someone said you did a genealogy of the family."

She smiled and took a long drink from her wine glass. "It was a lot of work, but not as much if I'd done it twenty years ago. Luckily, our family is good at keeping records and the online services are a tremendous help."

"I imagine living on an island helped consolidate the records."

"It did, although I managed to trace our ancestor

Jonathon Goodhue's roots back to Hampshire in the south of England."

"Wasn't he a pirate?" one of the wives asked.

Irene frowned. "Good heavens, silly statements must run in the family. No he was not a pirate, but a privateer."

"He robbed Spanish galleons, set the crews adrift in lifeboats, and sank the ships, didn't he? Sounds like a pirate thing to me," James said.

"He had permission in writing from the crown to do so," Irene explained.

"So, that made it cool?" I asked.

"Of course. During those times, Spain was the sworn enemy of England and anybody who could disrupt their commerce was considered a hero. The captain who stopped and successfully plundered the ship was allowed to keep some of the cargo."

"Which, of course, included doubloons, pieces of eight, gold, silver, and precious gems the Spanish had already plundered from Central and South America," Ben added, speaking for the first time in a while. "How else do you think the Goodhue's got so rich? The old boy socked away a lot of ill-gotten gains."

"That is an old rumor," Mary Ellen said in a frosty tone. "Liza, don't listen to them. Jonathon Goodhue received a land grant for three thousand acres on Grand Britannia from King Charles II in sixteen seventy-one."

"And privateers didn't keep all they plundered. A large portion went to the Crown. Whatever money he had was used to build a shipping empire. He also grew sugar cane and built a distillery," Richard said.

"Still, it's quite an accomplishment," I said. "Genealogy might be an interesting business to start. I know people in the States who'd pay someone to research their family trees."

"Funny you should bring that up," Irene answered. "I had a request from a relative of Jonathon Goodhue's first mate, Elijah Taylor, asking to do a genealogy of his family."

"There, you see, Irene, start a business and you won't be so hard up," Evelyn said with a malicious smile.

Irene's eyes widened and her nostrils flared. Before she could retort, Willie and one of the maids entered with trays.

The main course dishes were cleared away and the dessert served. I was stuffed, but determined to enjoy the trifle placed before me.

Finally, Mary Ellen rose. "Shall we have coffee and after dinner drinks in the drawing room?"

I was glad to get up and move around. Two hours for a dinner made my butt tired.

"So, how did you like your first formal dinner as an official Goodhue?" Stephen asked in a low tone.

"It was exhausting and long. I've never seen so much food. Does this occur on a regular basis?"

"Heavens, no. I can't decide whether Irene was honoring you or sizing you up. Probably both. Has she asked for any money yet?"

"No, but it won't do her any good."

We entered the drawing room. Mary Ellen, Richard, Irene, Ben, and I gravitated to the seats near the fireplace. The others broke off into smaller groups.

"Would you care for a Drambuie?" Stephen asked.

"That would be fine."

Richard and Ben followed Stephen to the bar. Irene

sat next to me on the sofa and crossed her elegant legs.

"So, Liza, do you find us tedious?"

"I'd say she probably found us officious," Mary Ellen said.

Irene waved her hand. "Pay no mind to Evelyn. She often says outlandish things to get a reaction. She loves to needle me because I'm divorced and independent. She'd love to be in my shoes. Giles comes close to being the most boring man on the face of the earth."

"Well, throwing out that Sir Geoffrey was murdered certainly got a reaction," I said.

"Total nonsense," Mary Ellen replied with a frown. "Damn that reporter. That's the kind of talk that leads to unpleasant rumors. My sons and sons-in-law have to live and work on the island. Who would invest with someone accused of being a killer?"

"She didn't actually accuse anyone," I pointed out.

"Doesn't matter. Once the word is spoken, there's no putting it back in one's mouth."

The men returned with drinks for themselves and the rest of us. Stephen settled on the arm of the sofa next to me while Ben did the same next to Irene.

I sipped and let my gaze wander to the portrait of Jonathon Goodhue.

"You know, he does look like a pirate—er, excuse me—a privateer what with that sword and all. Why did he quit sacking Spanish galleons?"

"The British signed a treaty with the Spanish and all privateering stopped. Old Jonathon was out of a job. Any hijackings after that were considered piracy and illegal. If caught the pirates were hanged. As for our ancestor, his ship sank in a hurricane in sixteen seventy," Irene replied. "According to legend, he and his men had just raided a galleon, hidden the treasure, and were on their way to Port Elizabeth when the storm hit. Only he and the first mate survived."

"And he and the first mate split the treasure?" I asked.

She shrugged. "No one knows for sure. Island records show an E. Taylor as dying in a barroom brawl in Port Elizabeth three years later. He's buried in an old section of Evergreen Cemetery."

"And you say one of his descendents has asked you to do research?" Stephen said.

"I doubt if there's much of a record substantiating that. Marriage records are sketchy at best, and a lot of mariners had women in every port of call," Mary Ellen added.

"Which means there was probably no marriage at all," Ben concluded.

"Beatrice has excellent documentation dating from the mid-seventeen-hundreds. I'm sure I can trace the line back further," Irene said.

Richard's eyebrows rose. "Beatrice! I had no idea she was descended from the first mate. When did she decide to do this?"

"About two months ago."

Mary Ellen shifted in her chair and lowered her eyes. I glanced at Stephen. He stared into his brandy, his forehead furrowed. I wondered what had brought about the scowl. The subject matter of pirates? Murder? He glanced down at me, then replaced the frown with a smile, and sipped from his glass.

Ben gulped his liquor and set the empty glass on the table. "How on earth will you trace anything with no records?"

"Oh, there are ways. And the term 'no records' isn't accurate. Death certificates were written in those days, even on Grand Britannia, and many of the families left journals, letters, and such with the Historical Society over the years. It might take a while, but eventually it can be found."

I finished my Drambuie and blinked my eyes. The room was warm and the gigantic meal plus the liquor made me sleepy.

Stephen touched my arm. "Would you like to step out onto the veranda for a breath of air?"

I nodded gratefully. "I sure would."

We rose and headed for the French doors to the side of the house. The warm, humid night air didn't help much until a small breeze wafted past. I lifted my hair from my neck and fanned it out before letting it fall back. Stephen walked me around the corner to the flagstone terrace above the maze where the breeze blew stronger in off the sea.

"They can be a bit much," he said.

"Boy, I'll say. The topic of murder sure stopped the conversation."

He waved a hand. "Pay no attention to Evelyn. Richard and I complained to the paper about unsubstantiated rumors. When the police confirmed no foul play was suspected, the reporter was fired."

"There were lots of undercurrents I didn't understand. But I'll learn. I still don't know who some of these people are."

He chuckled. "And not everyone is here tonight."

"Damn, I *do* need a scorecard."

"They'll put in an appearance sooner or later. Sir

Geoffrey liked having his family—all of them—dancing attendance on him. The house used to be full of relatives on the holidays."

I heaved a deep sigh drinking in the heavy scent of roses drifting up from the maze.

"How come no one seems to like Ben Collier?"

He turned to face the house and leaned against the stone parapet. "Ben came to Grand Britannia about three years ago. One day he showed up at a family function with Irene. I have no idea how or where they met, but from their actions, it was obvious they were having an affair. Shortly afterward, he rented the villa across the cove."

"She did seem a little clingy."

"The affair is over now, but they're still friends."

His voice held a tone of reserve.

"You haven't answered my question. How come nobody likes him?"

He shrugged. "Personally, I just never liked the man. The way he danced attendance on Irene reminded me of a gigolo. I know she paid the first year's rent on the villa."

"Sounds like a gigolo to me. And what was Sir Geoffrey's reaction to that?" Somehow, I couldn't see the old boy approving of his granddaughter paying a man's expenses.

"Oddly enough, they got along." Stephen crossed his arms over his chest. "I think that's what irritated Mary Ellen so much. According to her, Collier was often at the house asking questions and buttering up the old boy."

"What kind of questions?"

"Family things. He seemed fascinated by the

portraits and had an idea for some kind of project that involved family members dressing up in costumes mirroring the paintings. Then he'd take their photos and assemble a book of some sort."

"You mean like, the Goodhues now and then?"

His eyebrows rose. "I suppose. You'd have to ask Mary Ellen. She and Richard opposed the idea."

"And Sir Geoffrey?"

"Don't know. The whole thing died when Irene said no to his marriage proposal."

Marriage proposal? So Ben had been rejected, yet they still see each other? I could see why some of the family didn't like him. He was an American, an interloper like me. Snobbery was alive and well in the islands.

I drew another deep breath. "Does Evelyn toss out murder as dinner conversation often?"

He uncrossed his arms and pushed away from the parapet. "As I said, don't pay any attention to her. She reads too many mysteries and speaks before she thinks."

Did she? Mary Ellen was right. Once the word is spoken, it hangs in the air forever. I shivered.

He glanced at me and smiled. "Cold?"

"Just a bit."

He placed his hands on my arms and rubbed them up and down with a light touch. Heat gushed from the pit of my stomach to the tips of my toes.

"There, that better?"

"Yes, thank you," I replied a trifle breathless. Much to my dismay, he removed his hands, but the warmth lingered. Warmth? My skin felt scorched.

"Would you like to go to dinner tomorrow night in

Port Elizabeth? I find it ironic your name and the town's are the same."

His invitation both surprised and delighted me. An evening on the town with Stephen Albright? The prospect stirred my imagination toward candlelight, champagne, and an intimate dance floor. I shivered at the thought of those arms pulling me close to his broad chest. I shivered again at what could happen after the dance ended before slamming a mental door on those speculations. I had to get these images out of my mind.

"Thank you. I'd like that."

"Excellent. Suppose I pick you up around two? We'll drive down, see a few of the sights, and then have dinner. I promise to get you home at a decent hour."

"What a disappointment," I replied in a teasing tone.

He laughed. "I suppose you must find life on an island a bore after the bright lights of Hollywood."

"The lifestyle of actors and actresses partying every night is hooey. We have to be up early, on the set with our lines memorized, and prepared to put in long hours."

He placed his hands lightly on my shoulders. Like two magnets, we drifted toward each other. My head tilted back to accept the kiss I was sure to come. Then he stepped back.

"Guess we'd better go in."

It was too dark to see his facial expression, but his voice sounded slightly hoarse.

"Yes, I suppose we should."

Back inside, Stephen stopped to speak with Giles while I ambled back to the fireplace. Some of the guests were heading toward the foyer. A few came up and wished me a goodnight, saying how glad they were to meet me. I thanked them even though the cynic in me thought they had no other choice.

Ben cupped my elbow and led me away from the group. He stopped near the doorway and smiled.

"You must be feeling like a fish out of water with this bunch of stiffs. How about dinner tomorrow night? We Americans have to stick together."

Suddenly, I was the homecoming queen. "Thank you, but I already have plans."

His gaze shifted to Stephen, and then back to me. "I'm not surprised. Perhaps later in the week then. May I call you?"

"Of course."

I didn't really want to go out with him, but he had a point about Americans sticking together. I wasn't sure how long my free spirit could stand Richard and Mary Ellen. And I hoped Giles and Evelyn weren't frequent visitors. She indulged in enough drama to make any actress envious.

Ben leaned down, kissed both of my cheeks and winked.

I backed up, not liking the familiarity. Out of the corner of my eye, I saw Irene watching with an amused expression. She said no to his proposal. Did that mean I was next on his list of rich women to sponge off?

"Good night, Liza." He left the room.

I turned and gazed around the room while wiping my cheeks where Ben's lips had briefly rested. Stephen stared at the empty doorway with a frown. Mary Ellen did the same, but with a very well-bred sneer on her lips. Irene's mouth drew up into a half smile, the amusement still there.

Stephen walked over to me. "It's time I should be going, too. I'll see you tomorrow."

He leaned down and kissed my cheeks like Ben. This time I enjoyed the action. Then he also departed. The exodus continued until only Giles, Evelyn, Irene, and a few others remained along with Richard, Mary Ellen and me.

Giles cleared his throat. "I hope you didn't find us too boring, Liza."

"No, it was a very entertaining dinner." What else could I say?

"Indeed it was," Irene drawled with a glance toward Evelyn.

Evelyn said nothing, but smiled. Her gaze shot to Mary Ellen who frowned.

"Can I get anyone another nightcap?" Richard asked.

A man rose from his seat in the corner of the room. "No thanks, Dad. I think I'll turn in. We need to get an early start in the morning."

A woman joined him. "Yes, we're having guests tomorrow night. It was lovely meeting you, Liza."

I murmured the proper response as they left the room.

"I'll take you up on that drink," Roger said.

"If you don't mind, I think I'll turn in, too," Mary Ellen said. She rose and headed for the bar where she poured another glass of wine before following the others.

"Would you like another drink, dear?" Giles asked Evelyn.

"No thank you. It's been a long day, and I'm tired." She also rose from her seat near the fireplace and rubbed her forehead. "I feel a headache coming on. Better go take something for it before it grows. Nice to have met you, Liza."

She left the room, still massaging her brow.

"In that case, I'll also pack it in," Giles said with a smile.

"I hope Evelyn feels better tomorrow."

"She suffers from migraines, but as long as she can get to the medication in time, she'll be fine." He nodded and followed his wife.

Only Roger, Richard, Irene, and I were left. Evelyn was right. It had been a long day, and I was exhausted.

"Please excuse me, but I think I'll follow the leaders on this. Goodnight. See you in the morning."

Irene quaffed what was left in her glass. "Me, too. Goodnight."

We climbed the stairs side by side.

"So, did Ben ask you out?" she inquired.

I wondered if some kind of jealous fit was coming.

"As a matter of fact, he did."

She shot me an amused glance. "And I'll bet good, old Stephen got in first."

"You would be correct."

"Ben'll ask you again."

"Are you all right with that? The two of you seemed close."

Her lips curved upward as though she knew Stephen had told me their story.

"I'm fine. Just keep in mind; he's on the prowl for women with money."

We reached the top of the steps and paused. I couldn't decide if her words were malicious or merely helpful. "No problem there, I don't have any yet."

"And I'd be careful with Stephen Albright, too. He's not without ulterior motives."

I assumed she referred to his position as executor of Sir Geoffrey's estate, but didn't ask. It was late and I'd had enough for tonight.

"It's simply a dinner in Port Elizabeth. He thought I might enjoy seeing the sights."

She turned to the left, and then looked back over her shoulder. "Just don't trust him too much, dear."

She sauntered down the hallway to the last door on the right, opened it, and waved before sliding through.

I stood and stared contemplating her enigmatic words.

Chapter Nine

I came downstairs the following morning wondering if my new relatives were early risers. I didn't consider eight o'clock early, but admitted to curiosity. To my surprise the only occupant was Irene.

"Good morning," I murmured heading toward the coffee pot set up on the sideboard.

"Well, another early bird," she replied. "Did you sleep well?"

"Like a baby." I kept my tone cheerful and poured a cup of coffee, then set it on the dining table across from her. "How about you?"

"Oh, I always sleep well."

I turned, walked back to the sideboard, grabbed a plate and made my selections of bacon, scrambled eggs, fruit, and toast before taking a seat.

Irene sipped what I assumed was hot tea and stared at me over the rim. I could almost see the gears meshing in her mind.

"I want to apologize for Evelyn last night. She had no business bringing up such a ridiculous subject."

"You mean suggesting Sir Geoffrey was murdered? Have to admit, she had me going for a moment." I spread strawberry jam on my toast, took a bite, and made eye contact.

"Evelyn often has strange ideas. And Mary Ellen's

not above a few oddities of her own," she said while sipping her tea.

"She told me about some ghost that's supposed to wander the halls."

Irene rolled her eyes. "Sarah Woodruff Goodhue? You'll soon discover that underneath all that proper British posture, Mary Ellen is a very unhappy woman. She's bored living at Bountiful and drinks to compensate. The ghost business probably arose out of an inferior bottle of Chardonnay. Pay it no mind."

"I did notice she liked her wine. Why doesn't she do more around the place? The gardens are lovely."

I tackled a slice of bacon and forked the fluffy eggs into my mouth.

"I'll give her that. She does have a talent for flowers and shrubs. Grandfather flatly refused to have her act as hostess for large parties. Preferred me, which infuriated her—in a well-bred way, of course."

"So, I take it she and the old boy didn't get along?"

Irene rose and refilled her cup. "Not really. She wanted to make changes, bring Bountiful up to date with furnishings and such. Grandfather didn't like change. I think she expected to be queen of the manor and hold court with her town friends. When that didn't happen, resentment built."

"And now he's dead. I guess she assumed she'd be in charge. My inheriting must have come as a hell of a shock."

She resumed her seat. "It did to all of us."

I put my fork down. "Somebody mentioned a lot of guests the night he fell down the stairs."

"We were all here for the holidays at Christmas. He sprang the will changing thing on us during lunch.

Mary Ellen was mad enough to chew nails. Richard was stunned. Evelyn looked like she wanted to cry, and even stuffy old Giles came out of his silence to protest."

"And what did you think?"

She blew on her tea and sipped. "About the will change? Didn't surprise me in the least. Sir Geoffrey was a controlling bastard. I just didn't expect the change to be you. None of us knew about your mother. Am I sorry not to be the mistress of Bountiful? No. If you stick it out, you'll find this place costs a fortune to maintain." She set her cup down. "Which brings me to a rather delicate matter."

I took a deep breath. *Here it comes.*

"I find myself a bit low on funds at the moment. I have this unfortunate tendency to overspend my budget. I was wondering if you could lend me some cash. A thousand should do it."

Well, I had been warned. I just hadn't expected to be nailed over breakfast.

"Honey, if I had that kind of money, I wouldn't be here. I'm short myself. Sir Geoffrey gave me an allowance that won't buy anything other than the necessities."

She sighed. "Oh well, it was worth a try. No offense."

"None taken. I thought all the grandkids were included a few years ago when the trusts were set up."

"We were. The old boy didn't approve of my third husband, Ian, so I received less than the others. He warned me not to marry him. Called Ian a scoundrel. He was right and, when I filed for divorce, took great glee in telling me so."

Voices in the stairwell outside the room told me

others were up and about to join us. A moment later, Giles and Evelyn entered.

"Good morning," Giles said in a hearty tone making his way to the buffet. He lifted the lid of a chafing dish and sniffed, then closed it again. "Kippers. I can't understand why fish is served for breakfast."

"Because Richard and the Queen of England upstairs like them," Evelyn said, pouring a cup of tea.

Irene grinned and lowered her cup. "If you all will excuse me, I have several errands to run in West End, and then have to spend some time researching Elijah Taylor. I'll see you later."

"Are you staying the entire weekend?" I asked.

"Yes. I'll leave for home Monday morning."

"We're staying, too," Giles said, filling a plate with a mountain of bacon, sausages, and eggs. "There's an estate sale in Landover this afternoon. I'd like to see what it has to offer for the shop and possible resell at auction."

"Would you like to come with us, Liza?" Evelyn inquired. "We could stop and have dinner on the way back."

"I'm sorry, but I have dinner plans tonight."

"Indeed? Ben's a fast worker." She shot a smug smile toward Irene.

Irene smiled back. "Ben's a social creature, but her dinner partner will be Stephen," she informed the others. "Now, if you'll excuse me."

Evelyn's gaze returned to her cup of tea as Irene left the room.

"How's your headache?" I asked.

She smiled. "Gone. I caught it in time."

"I have a friend in Los Angles who has migraines

all the time. She can get laid up for days with one."

"That's true, but I have some wonderful meds if I need them. Sometimes a simple aspirin will nip it in the bud."

Giles had taken a seat across from me where he attacked his food with gusto shoveling large chunks of the heavy sausage into his mouth. Luckily, it prevented him from talking. Not so his wife.

"So, Stephen Albright is taking you to dinner. I'm surprised he thought to move that fast," she said sipping her tea.

I didn't like her tone and had no intention of discussing Stephen at the breakfast table. Irene was right—Evelyn enjoyed stirring up trouble.

"Why don't you like Irene?" I asked.

"I like her, but she's spoiled rotten. Always has been. She's never accepted an ounce of responsibility for anything. The woman's had three husbands, and managed to snag large settlements from each of them, yet always needs a loan from someone. Has she hit on you yet?"

"Shortly before you came in, but I haven't got a sou."

"How did she take it?"

"Philosophically."

I could see similarities between my mother and Irene as far as the husbands and large settlements went, but thank God Mother had money sense.

Giles polished off his plate of goodies, then rose and headed to the sideboard for more.

"Aren't you eating, dear?"

Evelyn joined him while I finished last of my now cold eggs. Pushing the plate aside I waited until she returned with miniscule amounts of just about everything.

"You don't seem to like Mary Ellen much either."

She nibbled on a piece of toast. "Mary Ellen is a snob. She was born to money and looks down on the entire family. She hates me because my father owned a haberdashery in Port Elizabeth. I clerked for him."

"She doesn't hate you, dear," Giles said. He'd rejoined us with another large helping. "She's very aloof, reserved."

"Nonsense. She hates me. That's why I like elevating her blood pressure."

"Is that why you brought up murder at the dinner table last night?"

Evelyn smiled. "More or less, although I wouldn't be surprised if it were true."

"Why?"

She laid her fork on the side of her plate. "Sir Geoffrey dropped a bomb on the entire family that afternoon when he announced he was changing his will. Everyone was upset. Year after year of kowtowing to the old bastard only to learn all your hard work was for nothing. One of the family sees him at the head of the stairs and a sharp push does it."

Her eyes held a spark of supreme pleasure at the thought of someone bumping off my great-grandfather.

I remembered the conversation from the night before. "Are you suggesting Mary Ellen shoved the old boy into his grave?"

"I was the second person on the scene and she was already there."

Giles finally ceased his obsession with food and heaved a heavy sigh.

"Evelyn, stop it. Mary Ellen did not kill Grandfather. He undoubtedly tripped and fell down the stairs breaking his neck in the process."

His wife shrugged and resumed eating.

I had had enough of both food and the conversation. I laid my napkin on the table and rose.

"If you'll excuse me, I think I'll go upstairs for a while. I'm sure I have e-mail to answer."

Neither offered a reply as I walked from the room. On the whole, my new-found relatives were a pain in the ass. At the head of the stairs, I met a maid carrying a tray of half-eaten food. Violet was just finishing making the bed when I entered my room.

"I'll be finished in a moment, miss."

"That's all right." I wandered onto the veranda. I still felt uncomfortable around servants, especially one who was close to my age. Out front the fountain bubbled with a muted tone. Birds sang in the trees, and a light breeze rustled the palm fronds creating a sound not unlike rushing water.

The air smelled clean and of the sea. I breathed deeply and strolled down the veranda, stopping abruptly when a board creaked under my foot. It reminded me of the sound I'd heard the other night. Richard and Mary Ellen's rooms lay ahead on the opposite corner of the house. The French doors were open, and when I caught the murmur of voices, tiptoed closer to listen.

"I'm telling you, Richard, I cannot take another full day of Irene or Evelyn. Tell everyone I'm indisposed. I'll stay here until they're gone."

"Hiding won't make them stop talking, you know."

"I don't care. Irene is the hostess. Let her host. I can't believe she published a genealogy of the family and revealed your ancestor was a pirate. It's scurrilous, humiliating."

"Privateer, Mary. He was a privateer."

"Pirate, privateer, what does it matter? They did the same thing." Her voice rose. "And Evelyn is unbalanced if you ask me. Imagine! Throwing out that Sir Geoffrey was murdered, and at the dinner table, of all places. *And* in front of Liza, of all *people*! Oh, damn your grandfather to hell! How could he leave Bountiful to some illegitimate American relative? And an actress, no less. A classless upstart. I cannot understand why the courts didn't declare him of unsound mind."

"Calm down. I'll inform Beatrice to send your meals up today. When they're gone, why don't you spend a couple of days in West End with Colin and Elaine? See your friends. Do a little shopping."

"Yes, I suppose that might help. Did Colin and Elaine get off this morning?"

"Yes. Beatrice said they ate a quick breakfast and left immediately. I wish they'd stayed longer. I needed to talk to..."

I backed away from the vicinity of the door slowly, avoiding the creaky board. *Guess I know where I stand in Mary Ellen's estimation.* A classless upstart, huh? I shouldn't have been surprised, yet hearing the words hurt. The least she could have done was given me the benefit of the doubt.

I reentered my room as Violet emerged from the bath with one of those Swiffer mops in her hand along with a plastic bag. She clutched several used towels to her chest with her free arm.

"I'm finished now, miss."

When she left, I checked my e-mail—not much,

and then moved on to my Facebook and Twitter sites. I made a few comments on both and shut down. It was only ten o'clock. What the hell was I going to do with the rest of my day?

From out front came the murmur of voices through the French doors. I stepped onto the veranda and peeked over the railing. Giles and Evelyn were getting into a car, no doubt on their way to the estate sale. And with Mary Ellen holed up like a burrowing owl that left only Irene, and she had stated she was going to do genealogy research.

Genealogy—Goodhue genealogy to be precise—leaped into my mind. Mary Ellen had called it scurrilous and last night someone had mentioned a copy here at the house.

I hurried downstairs to find Beatrice. I hadn't seen much of the woman since arriving. She flitted about like a black ghost, and I wondered how much she heard and observed. I found her in the butler's pantry counting napkins.

"Good morning, Beatrice."

She looked up and nodded. "Good morning, Miss Channing. May I help you with something?"

"Yes. Last night someone mentioned a Goodhue family record. Would you know where it is? I'd like to read it."

She put the napkins in a drawer. "I believe you'll find it in the library. It has a red binding with the name Goodhue in gold on the spine. I'm not sure which bookcase or shelf."

"That's all right. I'll find it. Thank you."

"My pleasure. Are you interested in genealogy, miss?"

I shrugged. "Never thought much about it. But given the circumstances of me being here, I'm curious. I'd like to know more about my grandfather and the family in general. Did you know my grandfather?"

"Not well, miss. He died shortly after I came. Is there anything else you need?"

"I was wondering about lunch. I have an engagement tonight with Mr. Albright and don't want to spoil my dinner with a large mid-day meal."

"Saturday luncheons are always a buffet of cold cuts and a variety of salads."

"Excellent."

She stared at me as though expecting me to say or do something. Then it dawned on me that as mistress of the house, I was supposed to end the conversation. I nodded and left.

As I made my way to the library, I decided Beatrice was as much a snob as Mary Ellen, but more neutral. She had nothing to lose or gain by my presence. I don't think she disliked me. It was more of a "she's here, let's make the best of it" attitude.

Finding a red bound book amongst the sea of black and brown spines didn't take long. I found it in the second bookcase in the middle of the third shelf.

"*The Goodhue Family*," I read out loud. Not a terribly original title, but then this said it all. I had a feeling some family members could recite the generations straight through without pausing for breath.

The large club chair near the window looked inviting, so I plunked my fanny into its supple leather and opened the book riffling the pages. Photos held a special place in the center.

I read for two hours. The object of the drawing

room portrait had indeed plundered Spanish shipping all over the Caribbean. Little mention was made of the sinking of his ship, *The Marauder* or of the survivors, but several pages were devoted to his land grant from the Crown and the establishment of Goodhue Shipping. The building of Bountiful and estate operations was also glossed over. The narrative dealt more with genealogy than substance.

The author had kept the information in chronological order and stayed to the facts. I wondered if Irene had written the book or if she'd had someone else do it. I was about to skip ahead to my grandfather, Mercer Goodhue when a quick glance at my watch spurred me out of the comfortable chair and to my feet. Closing the book, I tucked it under my arm and climbed the stairs. Lunch was in another hour and Stephen was picking me up at two. I needed to shower and dress.

Lunch consisted of me, Irene, and Richard. Mary Ellen was still in hiding. The excuse was a severe headache. I forked some leftover roast beef and a slice of ham onto my plate. A salad and roll followed.

"Hope you don't mind the informality of cold cuts," Richard said.

"Not at all. I don't usually eat large lunches." I turned to Irene. "How is your research coming?"

"Not bad. At present I'm online with the Historical Society's archives. I think I found the death certificate for Elijah Taylor. It's dated sixteen seventy-four and says he was stabbed in a fight, which is basically what the legend had to say. I'm going through marriage certificates this afternoon. Oh, by the way, Richard, I won't be in for dinner this evening. I have an engagement."

She didn't elucidate, but I wondered if her engagement was with Ben. I ate quickly and then headed upstairs to change. Since I had no idea where we would dine or what to expect, I chose white slacks and a red silk top. A pair of simple white flats and my trusty silver jewelry finished the outfit. I figured if we were sightseeing before eating, then the attire wouldn't be too fancy.

I brushed my hair and lifted my chin. The expression staring back at me in the mirror reflected a slightly haughty look. I moved a few facial muscles. Now, I appeared downright snooty. Maybe I should perfect this and use it on the family.

I touched my lips with a neutral lipstick and glanced at my watch. Stephen would be here soon. I wanted to go downstairs, then decided to stay in my room.

Can't have him thinking I'm too anxious.

I sat at the desk and picked up the genealogy, flipping through the pages, but not really reading. The excitement of spending the afternoon and evening with Stephen built. I had no idea what to expect.

A few minutes later, the crunch of tires on gravel announced his arrival. I counted to fifty before someone knocked on my door. Waiting another few seconds, I opened up.

"Mr. Albright is here, Miss Channing."

"Thank you, Violet. Please tell him I'll be right down."

She nodded and left, while I picked up a small purse and slung the silver chain strap over my shoulder. Taking a deep breath, I descended the staircase.

Stephen stood in the foyer gazing into the drawing

room. He turned as I approached and smiled.

"Hello, you look lovely."

"Thank you. You look pretty good yourself."

I didn't lie. He wore navy blue slacks, the creases sharp. His light blue-green shirt, open from the neck by several buttons, did wicked things to those green eyes. My brain kicked into high gear, and I wondered if chest hair lurked just out of sight—just enough to run my fingers through. I inhaled a deep breath to steady my thoughts.

"I hope this is all right. I wasn't sure how fancy the restaurant was."

The smile broadened. "You're in the islands. It never gets too fancy. Shall we go?"

As we drove away, I had this funny feeling we were being watched. I turned to stare at the upper story. A curtain in Mary Ellen's room twitched.

First someone in my room and now Mary Ellen. I didn't like being watched. An unpleasant shiver roamed up my spine causing goose bumps to pop out on my arms.

Chapter Ten

"I think you'll like Port Elizabeth," Stephen said. "Some of the old town is still standing, but much of it was destroyed during a hurricane in seventeen sixty-two. Historians think a category five came right up the harbor with a storm surge of close to thirty feet."

I jerked my attention away from the twitching curtain and rubbed the bumps from my arms. I wondered if Mary Ellen's maid, Gladys, could have snooped in the files at her mistress's bidding.

Shaking my head to clear it of speculation, I answered. "Being from California, I can relate to earthquakes and the Richter scale, but I have no idea what a category five or a storm surge is."

"A category five is the strongest and most deadly hurricane. Storm surge is the water the wind pushes toward land. Imagine standing on the beach and seeing a thirty foot wall of water coming at you."

"So, it's kinda like a tsunami?"

"Similar. How are things at the house this morning?"

I spent most of the ride to the capitol telling him about the strange conversations.

"I'm not surprised Irene asked for a loan, which by the way, she'd not likely have paid back. Her father and Sir Geoffrey were always nagging her about spending. I imagine her husbands did, too."

"She took my rejection in good grace."

"Irene rolls with the punches."

"Evelyn seems stuck on Sir Geoffrey being murdered."

He sighed. "Evelyn needs a hobby."

"Does an over-active imagination meet the criteria?"

Stephen laughed. The pleasant sound erased my earlier concerns about who might be watching me.

We entered the outskirts of Port Elizabeth. I still wasn't overly impressed. The city had grown in sections with the architecture dating the growth. I saw nothing unique, but as Stephen wound the car through ever-narrowing streets, my interest was piqued. Finally, some character.

"Is this the old section?" I asked.

"This part of town was constructed around eighteen-hundred. In a few blocks, you'll see older buildings. Some are leftovers from prior to the hurricane."

He negotiated the streets before finding a parking space. As I exited the car, my gaze was drawn to a soaring structure a couple of blocks away.

"I see you noticed the lighthouse." He looked at me and grinned. "There are exactly two hundred seventy-two steps from bottom to top. The view is spectacular. Are you game?"

"This place is full of spectacular views. Who am I to pass one up?"

I climbed with Stephen right behind me. By the time we reached the top, my legs burned and my breathing had intensified. Obviously, I needed more exercise. However, the view was everything promised. The dark blue of the harbor met the turquoise of the sea at the entrance. Behind me, the city rose on terraced hills, the homes clinging to the sides like barnacles.

"This is spectacular."

Stephen smiled. "Thought you'd like it. I'll take a good view any day of the week."

My ego hoped he referred to my backside as we'd climbed. My practical side said he meant the words exactly as spoken. I shot a quick glance his direction.

He widened the smile and let his gaze roam for a brief moment to my hips. "I'm glad I suggested this. Living here sometimes makes me forget how beautiful Grand Britannia is. Shall we go or do you want to soak up more?"

"I'll have a year to soak." I turned and headed for the steps. The trip down proved easier, though not nearly as viewable for him as the one up.

The old city had taken on a new atmosphere with tourist money. Shops lined narrow cobblestone streets and deals could be found on everything from leather goods to jewelry. I made a mental note to return soon. Mother would go crazy at some of the necklaces and earrings displayed in the windows. He showed me the current houses of parliament, a mixture of modern and mid-eighteenth century buildings.

"Sir Geoffrey held court while Governor in that corner office on the top floor," he said pointing. "He liked the view. After his term, when he was reelected to the legislature, he bullied the sitting governor into giving it up to him."

"Sounds like the old boy. How long was he Governor of the island?"

"Twenty years. He served in the legislature both before and after his governorship."

He steered me toward a grassy park. Hardwood and palm trees shaded cobblestone pathways dotted with benches every few feet. Picnic tables occupied an area close to the street. Flowers bloomed in numerous perfectly kept beds. I walked slowly admiring the multicolored parrots and other birds flitting from tree to tree until we came to a statue in the center of the complex.

A bronze man gazed toward the harbor with a haughty expression. He held the Bible in one hand and pointed a finger to the sky with the other.

"Sir Geoffrey Goodhue, Governor nineteen-seventy to nineteen-ninety," I read from the plaque on the base of the statue. "Can't have been too bad a governor if they erected a statue to him."

Stephen leaned down and whispered, "He put up the funds."

"So, he built a statue to himself."

He chuckled. "Sir Geoffrey never passed up an opportunity for self-promotion. In his eyes, he was the best governor the island of Grand Britannia ever had."

As we spoke, a pigeon landed on my great-grandfather's bronze head and immediately relieved itself.

I laughed. "Serves the old boy right."

He laughed along with me. We continued on to the harbor. Three cruise ships anchored in the deeper water, while cargo vessels unloaded materials at the port on the other side of the large bay. Sailboats and yachts bobbed side-by-side in the nearby marina. In spite of its proximity to industrial endeavors, the water remained unsullied. I sighed. Not only was the view peaceful, but Stephen held my hand making my heart beat accelerate and my imagination soar throughout our tour.

Eventually, we retraced our steps. Back in the car, he made several turns until we once again drove on a wide road out of town.

"So, where are we going?"

"To a restaurant called Gentleman Jack's."

I shot him a glance. "Isn't that what the first Goodhue was called in his pirate days?"

He grinned. "Please, privateer, and yes, the place is named after him. They have some of the best jerk pork and chicken on the island. Better than Jamaica."

"Jerk?"

The grin turned into a laugh. "You'll see."

Fifteen minutes later we turned into a parking lot. I gaped at the scene before me. A galleon complete with three masts, rose from the surrounding forest. "Are you kidding me?"

He laughed. "Surprising find in the middle of nowhere, isn't it? Actually, the ship design is a fraud. Real pirates...er, privateers...preferred ships with more maneuverability, shallower drafts, and sleek lines."

Stephen pulled up under a royal purple canopy in front of the entrance. A doorman helped me from the car. My escort opened the door and I entered a whole new world.

Wooden floors along with brass lanterns hanging from the beams above made me feel all was authentic. Multiple levels of dining gave the place charm. A waiter dressed in pirate garb walked past carrying a tray of pewter-colored mugs. From somewhere out of sight, a ship's bell clanged. We stopped at a podium set off to the left.

"Good evening, Mr. Albright," the maitre d' greeted. "How nice to see you again. Table for two?"

So, Stephen was known here. But then why not? I was on an island. Not that many places to dine.

"Yes, thank you, Robert."

The man checked a layout and smiled. "I have a nice table on the rear level near the railing. You and the lady will have a lovely view."

We followed the maitre d' down an aisle, then up a flight of stairs to a table. He held my chair and when we were seated, handed us menus.

"Please enjoy your meal." With a bow he vanished only to be replaced with someone filling our water glasses.

A few moments later another man in full pirate array appeared to take our drink orders—a rum punch for me and scotch for Stephen.

"Well, I must say, this is not what I expected," I said. "Is it a real ship?"

"No, the cost of actually trekking one over the hills was prohibitive. The owner built it from scratch, although I believe the masts did come from a real vessel."

I looked down on the crowded scene below. "Lots of people here, but then it is Saturday."

"It's a popular place, especially for tourists. The cruise ships stay overnight. Quite a few passengers end up here for dinner." He opened his menu. "I recommend anything, but may I suggest jerk chicken?"

"Exactly what is jerk?"

"It's a paste of scotch bonnets and other spices rubbed on meat that is then grilled. It's usually served with rice."

"Scotch bonnets? Isn't that a very spicy pepper of some sort?"

"Very spicy says it all." He grinned. "All jerk recipes are different, but it's a common item throughout the Caribbean. Jamaica claims to be the king of jerk, but Grand Britannia has its champions. Are you interested?"

"Game on. Why don't you order for me? I promise to hold up my end and at least sample anything put before me."

The pirate clad waiter arrived with our drinks. "Would you like more time or are you ready to order?" he asked.

"Check back in ten or fifteen minutes," Stephen said.

The man nodded and moved off.

Stephen fastened his gaze on me, sipped his scotch, and smiled. A tremor rippled from the pit of stomach outward. Just his smile left me a trifle breathless and I was conscious of the dim intimacy of the restaurant.

"So, tell me about Liza Channing. What was your childhood like?" he asked.

I took a long drink of rum punch to steady my nerves. "There's not much to tell. It had its highs and lows like any childhood."

I spent the next twenty minutes describing my mother, her husbands, their effect on me growing up, and my interest in acting. The narrative was often prompted by questions from him. During my discourse, he ordered another round of drinks. My first had gone down like water.

When they arrived, he ordered jerk chicken for

both of us along with a bottle of wine.

"If you had been here longer, I'd have ordered the pepper pot soup, but don't want to strain your taste buds."

I chuckled. "I guess we'll just have to do this again sometime in the future."

"Indeed, we will."

He reached across the table and squeezed my hand. My hormones went ape shit. I inhaled a deep breath and gulped half of my new rum punch. This was crazy. I barely knew the man and thanks to Irene's warning the night before, didn't completely trust him either. Although it could have been her way of sowing trouble. I had the feeling she and Evelyn had a lot in common on that front.

"Enough about me. I spilled my guts, now it's your turn. I want to know more about Stephen Albright."

He smiled and sipped his drink. "I've led a very ordinary life. My father was a lawyer, as was my grandfather. The firm picked up a lot of business in the early seventies when Grand Britannia modified its banking laws. We now rival the Caymans as a friendly offshore banking country."

"Ah, so you help Americans hide the loot, huh? Does that make you a modern day Gentleman Jack Goodhue?"

He chuckled. "It's a large chunk of our economy. Many of my clients have bought or built homes down here."

He went on to describe other lawyer type duties, but avoided mentioning his personal life. I wanted to probe, but wasn't sure I'd like the answers. In the end, my curiosity got the better of me.

"So, you aren't married. Anyone special lurking on the horizon?"

"Not at the moment." He made the statement with a small smile, which made me wonder if he meant it. And was I the object of his mindset?

The waiter returned with a wine stand containing a bottle of French Chardonnay. He uncorked it, poured, and handed Stephen the glass. He sipped and nodded. The glass was refilled and another poured for me. I finished my rum punch just as a food runner brought our dinner.

The sizzling plate was set in front of me. The delicious aroma made my stomach grumble. The browned chicken was surrounded by a concoction of rice, red kidney beans, scallions, and from the smell, wonderful seasoning. A side dish of cooked greens completed the meal.

Stephen smiled and sipped his wine. "Here's to your first taste of jerk."

I cut into the meat and popped a morsel into my mouth. Now, I'm from Los Angeles and have had my fair share of spicy Mexican cuisine. Plus, the food at a Vietnamese restaurant down the street from my condo had once caused my neck to sweat, but one bite of jerk chicken made my eyes water and my nose run. I grabbed my wine glass and gulped, then switched to the water goblet.

"Holy crap!" I exclaimed when I could talk again. Grabbing tissue from my purse, I daubed at my eyes and discreetly wiped my nose.

"That's the expression most non-islanders say at their first taste." He laughed. "May I suggest smaller bites?"

"You sadist. You could have warned me."

"What, and miss all the fun?"

For the rest of the meal I ate small bits at a time, often chasing them with wine and water. The rice and side dishes were seasoned, but not taste-bud destroying so. When I finished, the fire in my mouth had been reduced to a pleasant glow.

Stephen paid the bill. I thanked the waiter and stopped at the podium to do the same to the maitre d'.

He bowed to both of us. "Thank you for dining at Gentleman Jack's."

I yawned as I settled into the car. Two rum punches and all that wine, not to mention the delicious, if spicy, food had put me in a mellow mood.

During dinner, darkness had fallen. The dashboard clock read nine-thirty. I was tired, but not exhausted. Maybe it had something to do with the company. Stephen Albright was an enigma—one I'd like to solve. Good-looking, commanding presence and I suspected he was more than adequate in the lovemaking department. Nothing to go on, of course. Just a gut instinct.

"Still awake?" he asked.

"Barely. Thank you for taking me to see the sights. And the dinner was wonderful."

"I'm glad you enjoyed it. I have a busy schedule this coming week, but perhaps we can do this again next weekend. There's a lovely beach on the southwest side of the island. It's touristy, but lined with small restaurants. You might enjoy it."

I had to wait a whole week? "Sounds like fun. Give me a call when you can."

We pulled into the drive at Bountiful and glided to

a stop in front of the steps. Light streamed through the open French doors and across the veranda.

Stephen helped me from the car and guided me up the steps, but stopped by the front door.

"If you don't mind, I'd rather say good night here. I'm not in the mood to put up with the rest of the family tonight."

He turned to face me and placed his hands on my shoulders. "Damn, I didn't expect this," he murmured. He pulled me close and lowered his lips to mine.

His lips were soft, yet firm and sent my nerves into overdrive. Without stopping to think, I wrapped my arms around his neck and kissed him back. Our tongues twined together. Ripples of delight and desire spread from the pit of my stomach to the tips of my fingers and toes. My heart hammered and my ears buzzed. His body, lean and hard, radiated heat. He gathered me closer. His hands roamed up and down my back. A delightful hardening nestled against my abdomen.

As a goodnight kiss, it knocked my socks off.

Eventually, he stepped back. In the filtered light from the drawing room, his expression showed surprise and something akin to fear.

He smiled and kissed the tip of my nose. "Goodnight, Liza. I'll be in touch soon."

I couldn't speak, but nodded as he turned, retraced his way down the steps, got into the car, and drove off.

Oh boy. I inhaled several deep breaths, opened the door and went inside.

"Liza! Come join us," Evelyn said from the doorway to the drawing room.

Richard, standing by the liquor cart, poured a small glass of something and handed it to me. Drambuie. On top of the rum punches and wine, I'd be asleep in about fifteen minutes.

"Tell us about your day with Stephen," Evelyn said, settling onto the sofa.

"I take it he took you to the usual sights in Port Elizabeth," Giles offered.

Still in turmoil from the best goodnight kiss I'd had in years, I gave them the *Reader's Digest* version of the tour and dinner.

"So, he took you to Gentleman Jack's," Richard said with a smile. "Not surprising. His family owns it."

I sipped my Drambuie to hide my astonishment. "No wonder the maitre d' greeted him by name. I thought he just dined there a lot."

"He does," Giles added. "His grandfather on his mother's side built the place. Quite good food."

"Yes, it was very good. Where's Irene tonight?"

Evelyn shrugged. "I have no idea. Probably out buying that gigolo, Collier, dinner, and then indulging in some after dinner exercise."

"Evelyn!" her husband protested. "That's not very nice, and who are we to criticize Irene's actions?"

"I don't like him. He's a parasite sponging off women."

"I'm not fond of him either, but Irene is a big girl. She can take care of herself," Richard commented.

I noted Mary Ellen was still absent.

"I think your sister needs to be more discriminating in her choice of men. Look at the last husband. What a disaster," Evelyn said turning toward me. "Ian was Irene's third husband. He not only ran around with other women, but tried to finagle money out of friends by calling himself an investment banker. Turns out he didn't invest in anything other than himself. When Irene found out, she divorced him. How he avoided prison is beyond me. Sir Geoffrey unmasked the scheme."

I sipped more of my drink and listened. With Evelyn around, I wouldn't need to eavesdrop anymore.

"And then she took up with Ben. They used Ben's villa, once Irene paid for it, of course." Evelyn smiled like a well-fed cat. "I'll bet that's who she's with tonight."

I didn't want to hear about Irene and Ben, or what they did. Draining my glass, I placed it on the table and rose.

"It's been a long day. If you all will excuse me, I think I'll call it a night."

A chorus of goodnights followed me as I left. I closed the door to my bedroom and leaned against it. The trio would probably stay up until Irene returned. No doubt questioning her about her activities. I wondered if Irene would tell them where to stuff it.

My bed had been turned down and my nightie laid out. I was getting used to this servant business. After brushing my teeth, I fluffed the pillows, climbed into bed, and turned off the light on the nightstand. Moonlight illuminated the room with a soft glow.

I sighed. Try as I might, I couldn't keep my mind off that kiss Stephen had planted on me. My racing hormones wanted more, but my practical side said, go easy—take it slow. I didn't want to go easy or take it slow. I wanted his happy ass in bed with me.

Liza, you've only known him a couple of days. I was picky about who I spent the night with and found this confusing. While I didn't know that much about him, he met the criteria on my list of serious relationship material—intelligent, a good sense of humor, even if it was slightly reserved in the British sense, and of course, sexy as hell. The good kissing part didn't hurt.

I rolled over and burrowed my head in the pillow. *Calm down. Listen to your practical side. It's all hormones right now.*

With a tiny nudge from him, I wouldn't have a hard time falling for this guy.

I tossed and turned for close to an hour before the liquor I'd consumed over the evening finally caught up to me. I was drifting into the twilight zone where the last thread of consciousness hung on. Already visions of Stephen and me were taking on erotic form.

Then a distant scream brought me back to reality.

Chapter Eleven

I sat up and shook my head to clear the image of a naked Stephen Albright and listened. Had I heard something or had my mind, on the cusp of solid sleep, imagined it? All was silent. The clock on the nightstand read twelve-fifteen. So late? Perhaps I'd been asleep after all.

I slid out of bed. No investigation meant no getting back to my erotic dream. Padding to the open French doors, I stepped onto the front balcony. An almost full moon dappled the landscape with brighter than normal light. It glistened off the softly burbling fountain waters and threw the woods beyond into deep shadows. The usual insects chirped and buzzed.

A quick glance down the balcony revealed no light coming from Richard and Mary Ellen's room. I turned the corner and walked a few steps toward Irene's also dark room. Either she was still out or asleep. I tiptoed past her room and gazed in the direction of the cove. The water glistened in the moonlight, its surface smooth. In the distance, I thought I detected the sound of a motorboat, but saw nothing. Total silence made me wonder if I'd heard anything at all, including a scream.

Then from somewhere within the maze came the yowls of two warring cats. I relaxed and heaved a deep sigh.

"Damned cats," I muttered. They'd torn me out of a perfectly good x-rated dream.

I re-entered my room and climbed back into bed. Fluffing the pillows, I pulled the sheet over me and settled in for the night.

If I don't recover that dream, there's going to be a few less cats at Bountiful.

****

I descended the staircase the next morning in a grumpy mood. In spite of thinking sexy thoughts of Stephen and me on a secluded beach, the naked Stephen dream had not returned. Voices from the dining room told me my morning coffee would not be drunk alone.

Sure enough, the same bunch from last night had relocated. Mary Ellen was still "indisposed." I imagined she'd have a miraculous recovery as soon as Giles and Evelyn's car cleared the driveway. Irene was also a no-show.

"Oh, good morning, Liza. Did you sleep well?" Evelyn asked in a cheery tone.

"Morning. I slept well, thank you." I kept my answer short. I wasn't in the mood for Evelyn before my coffee.

I poured a cup and sat next to Giles. As usual, his plate was piled with enough cholesterol and carbs to kill ten men. Richard had the disgusting kippers again. At least Evelyn opted for simple bacon and scrambled eggs.

"What? Not eating?" Giles asked through a mouthful of those heavy sausages.

"I need my coffee first. Perhaps in a while."

"I wonder what time Irene got in," Evelyn said. "Did you hear her?"

"No, can't say that I did." I didn't want to start my morning off with another discussion about Irene's love life, so I turned to Giles. "How did your estate sale go yesterday?"

"Jolly good. Got some nice pieces."

"I still say we didn't need three dressing tables," his wife said.

"One was a Victorian with an undamaged marble top. Another was made here on the island in the early nineteenth century, and the last is pure Art Deco. All will turn a profit," he replied.

"What else did you find?" I sipped my coffee and contemplated a simple breakfast of fruit and toast.

Giles continued to describe the other items he and Evelyn had bought in detail. Listening to Giles drone on was preferable to hearing Evelyn babble.

"So, when are you leaving?" I asked when he paused for breath.

"Before lunch. Richard and I have some family business to discuss, but it shouldn't take too long."

Richard pushed his plate away, and drank the last of his tea. "I suggest we talk as soon as possible then. I've got a busy day lined up."

Doing what? It's Sunday. I still had no idea what an estate manager did. It was on my list of things to check out.

"Then, let's get started." Giles glanced at his watch. "It's almost nine. I'd like to be on the road by ten."

He finished shoveling in the last of his waffle and sausages then rose.

"Have you finished packing yet, dear?"

Evelyn sighed. "Not yet. I suppose I'd better get it

done." She brightened and smiled. "Maybe I'll stop in and say goodbye to Irene."

"I wouldn't wake her if I were you. She likes sleeping in after a night out," Richard said. "Are you ready, Giles?"

The two men left the room, but Evelyn lingered sipping the last of her tea.

"I've enjoyed meeting you, Liza. Of course, this isn't all of the family, but I imagine you'll meet the others soon enough."

"I'm sure I will." I rose, helped myself to the promised light meal, freshened my coffee, and resumed my seat while Evelyn talked.

"Giles has two sisters. Portia lives with her family in Trinidad, while Denise calls Bermuda home. We see them once or twice a year."

Sounded like Portia and Denise had the right idea. They didn't have to put up with Evelyn. I speared a piece of pineapple and ate it. My remaining breakfast companion rambled on.

"And then, there's Irene's offspring. Wyatt flatly refuses to come to Bountiful. At least he did when Sir Geoffrey was alive."

"Is that so," I murmured. Sounded like Wyatt had his head screwed on right too.

"Now, the daughter is a chip off the old block, so to speak. Married some Puerto Rican—I can't remember his name—and lives in Port Elizabeth. To the best of my knowledge, they sponge off her mother."

I finished several strawberries before attacking a piece of toast. The family-according-to-Evelyn narrative was wearing thin.

She halted and shot me a glance. "So, how do you

like Stephen? I always found him attractive, but dull."

"I didn't find him dull at all. He was a wonderful guide. Probably told me a side of Grand Britannia history I'd have never heard otherwise. And the dinner was superb, if a bit spicy."

"Ah, yes. Gentleman Jack's. I take it you had jerk something or other."

"Yes. Once I got used to the heat level, I enjoyed it." I finished my toast and the last of my coffee. Evelyn's chatter was giving me a headache. I needed to get out of there.

"So, Stephen didn't tell you his family owned the place?"

"No, but then maybe he thought it would be superfluous bragging."

She laughed. "Stephen Albright doesn't brag. In fact, he keeps a lot of things to himself." Still smiling, she leaned forward. "You do know that he's…"

"Good grief, Evelyn. Are you still here?" Giles interrupted from the doorway. "I need to catalogue what we bought when it's brought in. Your stuff upstairs is strewn all over the room. It'll take an hour to pack."

She rolled her eyes. "Oh, don't fuss so, Giles. All I have to do is toss it into a suitcase. It'll take fifteen minutes."

I pushed back my chair and rose. "If I don't see you before you leave, have a safe journey home. It was nice meeting you both, and I hope to see you again." I made my way toward the door.

"Goodbye, Liza," Giles said. "Evelyn, hurry up."

"Come visit soon," his wife called out.

After listening to the non-stop babble from Evelyn,

I needed a walk in the air. The rose garden beckoned and I wandered onto the terrace. The scent of roses mingling with the sea air was refreshing. The memory of my go-to-sleep fantasy of Stephen and me on a secluded beach resurfaced. That was the one place I hadn't as yet explored, and wondered if the water felt as good as it looked. I had worn shorts today, so maybe getting my feet wet was an option. I liked to swim and since this cove was available, it seemed wasteful not to use it.

I strolled across the downward sloping lawn to the overlook steps and descended to the deck. A casual glance to my right made me freeze in my tracks and gasp. An entire section of railing was gone. I walked cautiously over the decking and without touching the remaining banister, looked down. I cried out and clapped a hand over my mouth.

Irene's body was sprawled on the rocks and sand below like a rag doll, her long red hair fanned out. A dark stain under her head told me she was dead.

I backed away in horror until the rough stone of the cliff halted my progress. A sob broke from my throat and my legs trembled. I stumbled from the overlook up the steps onto solid ground, collapsed to my knees, and threw up.

Oh, my God! How had this happened? Then I remembered the scream I thought I'd heard last night. It hadn't been a dream or cats after all. I had listened to Irene Goodhue's death cry.

I pushed myself back to my feet and ran for the house.

****

"Here, drink this," Stephen said, handing me a

glass of amber liquid.

I wrapped my still shaking hands around the crystal tumbler and sniffed. Scotch. I sipped. Warmth slid down my throat. I took another, larger drink. The warmth intensified.

The island equivalent of cops and paramedics swarmed over Bountiful. The family and servants had been sequestered in different areas of the house. I sat on the loveseat in the drawing room. Stephen stood facing a man wearing the uniform of the local constabulary.

He introduced himself as Constable Wainwright, flipped out a notebook and asked, "Miss Channing, could you please tell me how you found Ms. Goodhue's body?"

I inhaled a deep, if somewhat shaky, breath and told him.

"And then what did you do?"

"I ran back to the house. Richard, Giles, and Evelyn were in the foyer. Giles and Evelyn had been here for the weekend and were about to leave. When I told them about Irene we all ran back to the overlook. The men went down to the beach while Evelyn and I stayed above. I didn't want an up close and personal view. They returned and confirmed she was dead. Richard called you."

I didn't add that I'd also insisted he call Stephen. As Sir Geoffrey's lawyer, he had every right to be here. Irene's death could have affected the old boy's will. I assumed I'd done the right thing since nobody objected.

"And when did you last see Ms. Goodhue?"

"Lunch on Saturday. We both had separate engagements for dinner."

"Do you know who she was dining with?"

"No. She didn't say."

"Constable Wainwright, may I suggest you talk to Ben Collier? It's entirely possible he was her escort last night," Stephen said.

"Collier? Oh yes, that photographer chap. He lives just across the cove doesn't he?" He made a notation in the notebook.

I drank the rest of the scotch. "I feel wretched. I knew the railing was loose, but I didn't think it dangerous."

"How loose was it and when did you notice?" the constable asked.

I told him about my tour of the grounds with Mary Ellen. "It just wobbled a bit, and she said a lot of things needed repair around Bountiful, but since no one ever used the overlook anymore it had been relegated to the bottom of the to do list." I rubbed a hand across by forehead. "I should have investigated the cry I heard last night further."

Constable Wainwright's gaze sharpened. "What cry and when?"

I gave him the lowdown on my nocturnal activities. "I just assumed it was cats or that I'd dreamed it. Guess I was wrong. I should have checked more."

"Nothing you could have done," Stephen said. "She probably died on impact."

The policeman closed his notebook. "Thank you, Miss Channing. If you would, please remain here for a few minutes while I continue with my interviews."

He left, and Stephen took the glass from my hand. "More?"

"No, thanks. Why would Irene be on the overlook

at midnight?"

He sat in the chair next to me. "I have no idea. Irene had seen the view hundreds of times. She certainly didn't need to gaze at the cove in the moonlight."

"Could she have been meeting someone?"

"Who? If she wanted to talk to a family member, she'd have done it in the house."

"Maybe they wanted to keep the discussion private or not disturb the rest of the household," I suggested.

"The overlook at midnight still doesn't make sense."

"What about Ben? Could she have been meeting him?"

Stephen shrugged. "Why? My guess is she'd just been out with him. And you heard nothing that sounded like a car leaving, did you?"

"Actually, I did," I said slowly remembering the sound of a motor.

"What? Why didn't you tell Constable Wainwright?"

"Because I just now remembered it."

"He needs to know. I'll be right back."

Stephen hurried from the room. I rose and walked to the front windows. The driveway was clogged with emergency vehicles. Officers stood talking or walked near the fountain.

Poor Irene. In spite of hitting me up for money, I liked her. Perhaps, we could have become friends over time. I suspected she and my mother would have gotten along, too.

Stephen returned with Constable Wainwright.

"Mr. Albright says you have something to add,

Miss Channing?"

I told him what I thought I'd heard.

"And when was this?"

"Shortly after I heard the cry. I was on the back corner of the upper veranda, near Irene's room. I could see a portion of the cove, but nothing disturbed the water, at least at that time. That's when I heard the cats fighting and went back inside."

He wrote quickly, and then pinned me with a look. "And you're sure you heard a motorboat?"

I shook my head. "No, I'm not sure. The sound could have come from the road, a car or a motorbike maybe. You know how sounds ricochet off things, especially around water. I wish I could be more help."

He smiled and closed the notebook. "You've been very helpful, Miss Channing."

"Are you about finished?" Stephen asked.

"Yes, I interviewed Mr. and Mrs. Harrison and Mr. and Mrs. Goodhue before Miss Channing. The servants are next. I won't be but a few more minutes. Chief Inspector Bradshaw is seeing to the removal of Ms. Goodhue's body. He'll be back presently."

Stephen turned to me as the officer left.

"So, it is possible Irene met someone. But who?"

"We don't even know who she was dining with," I reminded him.

"My money's on Collier."

I continued to stare out the window, but saw little of what was in front of me. Instead my mind flashed back to the view while standing with a shocked Evelyn. Several railing supports hung from the deck, the wood jagged and torn, the nails bent as Irene's weight had cantilevered over space. The rest had broken free scattering over the beach and rocks below.

I shivered. Stephen came up from behind and turned me into his chest, his arms holding me close.

"I'm so sorry you had to be the one to find her," he whispered, kissing the top of my head.

If Irene had met someone, then why didn't they sound the alarm immediately? Did she have help falling over that railing?

That thought chilled me even further. Maybe it was an accident, and the person she was with had panicked and run.

Stephen released me as Giles and Evelyn entered the drawing room. Mary Ellen, down from her ivory tower, followed them. She headed immediately for the bar cart and poured a glass of scotch. Giles did the same for him and Evelyn.

"Good God, what a mess," he said.

"I can't believe it," Evelyn replied.

"The railing was loose, but not that loose," I commented.

Evelyn shot a glance toward Mary Ellen. "The railing was loose? Did you know?"

Mary Ellen popped the shot down her throat and poured another. "Yes, but repair wasn't a priority."

"Bet Irene wouldn't agree with that," Evelyn said.

Before an argument erupted from Evelyn's snide remark, I jumped in. "Where's Richard?"

Diverted, Mary Ellen sipped this time. "Making arrangements. Shame the family plot here at Bountiful is full."

"There's a family cemetery on the property?"

"Yes. It's through the woods toward the west. Most of the early Goodhue's are buried there. Will there be an inquest, Stephen?" she asked.

"Definitely. I see Doctor Margate's car out front. He's most likely down on the beach with the Chief Inspector."

Beatrice entered the room. Her face bore the usual neutral expression, but her red, puffy eyes had known tears.

"Georgette wants to know about lunch."

Mary Ellen appeared not to have heard and emptied her glass again.

I stepped in. "Please tell the cook to keep it simple. Set up a buffet of hot soup, salad, and some sandwiches. I doubt many of us will have an appetite."

Beatrice glanced at Mary Ellen for confirmation. She in turn stared at me with ill-concealed irritation. I'd treaded into her territory. I lifted my chin and stared back. An elaborate meal now sounded absurd.

She backed down. "Yes, a buffet will work. Tell Georgette."

"And dinner tonight?" Beatrice asked.

Once again, I answered first. "Still a simple meal. A salad, main course, and dessert will be fine."

Mary Ellen opened her mouth as though to contradict my order, and then closed it again. Beatrice nodded and left.

"Was Beatrice close to Irene?" I asked concerned nobody had said anything to the housekeeper.

"Not particularly," Mary Ellen said.

"I imagine she's as shocked as any of us," Evelyn replied.

"Did anybody wait up for Irene after I went to bed?"

"Not I," Giles contended. "Evelyn and I turned in

shortly after you."

"I have no idea when Richard came up," Mary Ellen said. "I was sound asleep."

I turned to Stephen. "Will you stay for lunch?"

"Yes, thank you. Perhaps I should help Richard with the arrangements. Please, excuse me."

He turned to leave when Richard and a man I'd not yet seen entered.

Richard walked to the bar cart, his face ashen and set in grim lines. Without a word to anybody, he poured a large neat scotch and gulped half of it.

The other man spoke. "I'm Chief Inspector Bradshaw. My condolences to all of you. I'm sure this has been an awful shock."

"Indeed it has," Giles said.

The Chief Inspector held up a plastic bag containing the remains of a green bottle.

"Can any of you identify this? We found it at the base of the cliff."

"Looks like a champagne bottle to me," Stephen replied.

"So the label claims. Chateau de Rothschild, nineteen ninety-one. Any idea how it came to be with the body?"

Richard winced and finished his scotch. "Chief Inspector, could you please refer to my sister by her name?"

"I apologize."

"And the champagne may have come from our cellar. I remember when Sir Geoffrey laid in several bottles last year. Are you trying to tell me my sister was drunk when she fell?"

"The doctor hasn't determined that yet."

"So, Irene came in from her dinner, grabbed a bottle of champagne from the cellar, and then drank it on the overlook?" Giles said.

"And in a drunken state, leaned too hard on a loose railing thereby falling to her death," Evelyn added.

"We also found the shattered remains of a glass." The Chief Inspector gazed at us with an unreadable expression, but his eyes held questions.

I shook my head. "So, she decided to indulge, perhaps got dizzy from the combination of alcohol and height, then fell. What a horrible accident."

"You're Miss Channing, are you not?"

"Yes. I arrived from the States the other day."

"So I heard. I'm sorry, but you're wrong about this being an accident. Irene Goodhue was murdered."

Chapter Twelve

The Chief Inspector's statement froze everyone like statues, except for Mary Ellen who drained her glass and Richard who didn't seem all that surprised. The policeman must have notified him before entering the drawing room.

Then the paralysis wore off. Giles's jaw dropped. Evelyn's eyes widened and she place a hand over her mouth. I wondered if her silly nonsense the other night had given someone ideas.

"How do you know that?" Stephen asked. Being a lawyer, he kept calm façade.

The head honcho didn't answer but looked at me. "Miss Channing, in your statement a while ago you commented about a loose railing. Exactly where on the overlook were you standing?"

"Good grief, I don't know. I followed Mary Ellen onto the deck, admired the view, and then leaned on it to look down the cove. It moved and I stepped back."

"Was it near where you saw the missing section this morning?"

I licked my lips and thought. "No, that was further along. I don't think I was any more than a few feet from the steps."

"Yes, that's right," Mary Ellen confirmed. "I was in the middle of the overlook. Of course, more than one section of railing may have been in need of repair."

"The railing had little to do with Ms. Goodhue's death. The doctor discovered a deep laceration on the back of her head embedded with several shards of dark green glass."

"You mean she was hit with the champagne bottle?" I said, horrified.

"Certainly looks that way."

"Someone was with her," Evelyn whispered. "But who?"

"And why?" Stephen replied.

"That's precisely what I want to know."

"Is that what killed her? The blow to the head?" I asked.

"We don't know yet," the Chief Inspector answered. "Her body was found among the rocks."

"Couldn't she have dropped the bottle over the railing in a drunken stupor first, then leaned over and fallen on top of it?" Giles questioned.

Inspector Bradshaw frowned. "We also found a few tiny pieces of green glass stuck in the cracks between the boards of the decking on the overlook. The assailant struck her, and either pushed her against the railing or threw her over before kicking it down to make it look like an accident."

"But who on earth would want to kill Irene?" Evelyn blurted.

"That's what I'm going to find out."

Before any of us could form a reply a car raced up the drive and screeched to a halt. The door slammed and footsteps hurried across the veranda. Without a by-your-leave the front door opened, and then slammed shut. Ben appeared in the threshold of the drawing room.

"Is it true? Irene's dead?" he demanded between panting breaths, his eyes wide with shock.

"Yes, I'm afraid it's true," I said.

He ran a hand through his dark unruly hair causing the thick curls to stand up.

"How? I mean was it an automobile accident?"

"No, she fell from the overlook. A part of the railing collapsed. I found the body a while ago."

"Exactly who are you?" Chief Inspector Bradshaw asked.

Stephen's sharp gaze sliced at Ben. "This is Ben Collier," he said, his lips set in a grim line. "He lives across the cove. Perhaps he can help narrow the time frame. What time did you drop Irene off?"

"What are you talking about?"

"When did you bring Irene home from dinner?" Stephen's tone also sharpened.

"What dinner? I wasn't having dinner or anything else with her."

"So, you were not the lady's dining companion last evening?" Bradshaw asked.

"No, I wasn't. I spent the evening at home preparing for a photo shoot." He directed his distraught gaze to me. "What the hell was she doing on the overlook?"

"We don't know," I answered.

"When did it happen?"

"Somewhere around midnight, we think," Bradshaw said. He pulled his cell phone from the clip around his belt and dialed before moving off to the side.

"Midnight! That doesn't make any sense."

"How did you find out about it?" Mary Ellen said,

sending Ben a malicious look.

"At the marina. It's the main topic of conversation. I was going to take the boat out. When I got there, one of the security people said he saw a bunch of emergency vehicles turning into Bountiful. The rumor was Irene had had some kind of accident and was dead. I jumped back into the car and came over."

Bradshaw ended his conversation and returned. "Mr. Collier, we need to talk to you further. You can, of course, verify your whereabouts last evening."

"Verify? As in a witness? No, I told you. I was preparing for a shoot. I had dinner in, made sure my equipment was in order, watched a little TV, read for a while, and then went to bed."

"So, you never saw or talked to Irene?" Stephen asked.

"How many times do I have to tell you no, Albright?"

The Chief Inspector stepped forward. "Mr. Collier, Constable Wainwright will be here in a moment to take your statement. Please wait in the study."

Ben nodded and moved toward the doorway where he paused and looked at all of us. "This wasn't an accident, was it?"

"No, sir, I'm afraid not. The lady was murdered."

"Who the hell would want to kill Irene?" Ben's gaze swept over us again. "Come to think of it, I can probably supply a name, or two."

On that cryptic note, he marched from the room.

"Well! Of all the nerve!" Giles said sputtering with indignation.

Mary Ellen waved a hand. "It's his way of getting in his digs at me. He knows I don't like him."

Constable Wainwright appeared in the doorway.

"Another statement to be taken in the study, Wainwright. Man by the name of Collier."

The officer nodded and left. Bradshaw turned back to us. "By the way, this is all preliminary. You'll need to come into the department for a formal statement later. And no one should plan on leaving the island. I'll be in touch."

He left and a moment later the front door closed.

During all of this, Richard stood in silence, his face pale, but his composure in place.

"Richard, I'm so sorry about Irene. I know I just met her, but she seemed pleasant. Please accept my condolences," I said.

"Yes, if there's anything I can do, please don't hesitate to let me know," Stephen added.

Richard nodded. "Thank you. I've already called her solicitor in Cutlass Bay."

"Do Wyatt and Isabelle know?" Giles asked.

"Yes. I notified them first. If you'll excuse me, I have to give them this latest information. Mary Ellen, inform Beatrice both will be staying here. The funeral will take place in West End. She'll be buried in the family crypt there."

He left without another word. Mary Ellen followed.

"Should we stay here or go home?" Evelyn asked her husband.

"I vote we stay until after the funeral." Giles rose from his seat. "I'll get the bags out of the car."

"I'll need to go into town for something to wear. I don't have anything appropriate for a funeral," Evelyn commented.

The two drifted out of the room leaving me alone

with Stephen.

"Well, this is certainly a new twist. I found the dinner conversation the other night bizarre. I wonder if Evelyn told the cops about her theory that Sir Geoffrey was murdered."

Stephen heaved a deep breath. "Probably not, but I'm sure someone brought it up."

"Like Mary Ellen?"

"Or Collier right now. I know Bradshaw. He'll mull over the initial statements, and then come back for more."

"There's nothing more I can tell him," I protested.

"He'll still be back." He looked at me with a worried expression. "Liza, yesterday you asked a question about what happens if you die. When I asked why, you brushed it aside. Something must have prompted it. What?"

I gave him the lowdown on how I suspected someone had discreetly searched the folders he'd given me, someone at my bedroom door that first night, the creaking boards on the veranda, and my eerie feeling of being watched.

"And when we left yesterday, I'm sure Mary Ellen spied from her window." I pulled on my earlobe. "I don't know. I could have been mistaken about the folders being out of sequence, and there's no reason why either Richard or Mary Ellen shouldn't take some fresh air on the veranda. For all I know a servant was in the hallway. And nervousness at meeting new relatives could have amped my imagination."

He frowned. "I'm not sure I like…"

Giles and Evelyn returned to the foyer and dropped their luggage in the middle of the floor. Mary Ellen chose that moment to also appear.

"What's this? I thought you were going home?"

"What's the use of going home, just to come back again in a few days for the funeral?" Evelyn replied.

"Well, you'll have to take them up yourselves. Willie is busy at the moment."

Without another word, she whirled and returned to the drawing room, sinking into the sofa as Giles and Evelyn made their way upstairs.

"God, what a morning. Do you think Chief Inspector Bradshaw is right about Irene's death being murder, Stephen?"

"He's the professional. He should know."

She patted her hair. "And I don't believe that Collier man for a moment. I think he and Irene were together last night, perhaps dining at his place. We only have his word he was alone."

"Shredding my reputation again?" Ben asked from the doorway.

He entered and went straight for the liquor cart, poured a generous shot of scotch, and then raised the bottle in Mary Ellen's direction.

"May I get you a drink, Mary Ellen? I know scotch isn't your usual preference, but in a pinch I'm sure anything will do. It usually does."

I found his words insulting, and I didn't like the way he made himself at home indulging in Goodhue booze.

The object of Ben's derision breathed heavily through flared nostrils. "A small scotch will be fine. It's been a very upsetting day. And you don't need me to shred your reputation. You do a good job of that on your own."

Ben laughed, poured her a drink and handed it off. "Anyone else?"

Stephen and I shook our heads. Giles and Evelyn entered the room.

"So, how did your interview go?" Giles asked Ben.

"Quickly. I told him the truth…" he shot an amused glance toward Mary Ellen who took a long sip of her drink… "And that was the end of it. What reason would I have to kill Irene?"

"Well, she did refuse your marriage proposal," Evelyn murmured.

He laughed. "Good God, that was over a year ago. If I wanted to off her, I'd have done it then. By the way, am I invited to lunch?"

"Certainly not!" Mary Ellen snapped.

"Is it really up to you, my dear? Bountiful has a new mistress now." He turned his snidely smiling face to me. "How about it, Liza? Will you break bread with me or am I *persona non grata* at the dinner table?"

If I didn't get out of this room soon there'd be another murder. I didn't want to invite Ben, but saw no graceful way out of it.

"Oh, sure, what the hell? The more the merrier. I'll go inform Beatrice to set another place. If you'll excuse me, I'm going upstairs until lunch is served. This has been a very stressful morning and I have a headache."

I didn't wait around for an answer, but swept from the room in a regal fashion as once requested by a director when I played an aristocrat.

I found Beatrice in the butler's pantry, told her there'd be one more for lunch, and expressed my condolences.

"Thank you, Miss Channing. Ms. Goodhue was

always nice to me."

As I walked upstairs, the murmur of voices drifted from the drawing room. I ignored them. In my room, I closed the door, ran a hot bath, and downed a couple of aspirin. By the time I'd soaked all the heat from the water, I was back to normal.

Dressed again, I blogged about the wonderful sights I'd seen in Port Elizabeth the day before. I also didn't tell Mother about the tragedy when I sent my daily e-mail. Why upset her? Instead I gave a description of jerk chicken and my impression of our newly extended family—complimentary, of course.

I stood and stretched when someone knocked on my door.

"Come in."

Violet entered. "They sent me to tell you luncheon is being served, miss."

Oh, goody. "Thank you, Violet. I'll be down in a moment."

I stalled by refreshing my lipstick, combing my hair, and washing my hands. Unable to delay longer, I descended the staircase. Stephen met me at the bottom.

"Had about all you can take of relatives today?" he asked.

"That and then some. Are the police still here?"

"No. They left about half an hour ago."

"Funny they didn't ask about Evelyn's accusation of murder the other night."

"Could be nobody mentioned it. Kind of a self-preservation thing." He paused heaving a small sigh. "I have an idea. Why don't you come to my place for dinner tonight? You can relax and not have to put up with the family."

A boulder lifted from my shoulders. "I'd love to. And don't think you are the date of last resort. I much prefer your company."

Honest to God, the blue-green of his eyes intensified to turquoise. I wanted to dive into them like the sea they resembled.

"I'm glad," he said softly. "Now, shall we eat?"

I preceded him into the dining room. The cook had gotten the word about my request for a simple meal. A tureen of cream of mushroom soup sat on the sideboard along with three plates of sandwiches. A large salad bowl sat toward the other end. Two urns, one with coffee and one with hot water for tea were also present.

Everyone else had already entered with the exception of Mary Ellen and Richard. I asked about them.

"Mary Ellen *also* declared she had a headache and excused herself," Evelyn said.

"And Richard was talking to the funeral home when I last saw him," Giles added. "I doubt he'll be in."

Confirming that statement, Willie entered with a tray. He filled a bowl with soup, a plate with salad, and another plate with sandwiches, then poured a cup of hot water and tucked a tea bag under the saucer. He left without a word.

The rest of us filled our plates and found seats.

"Rather casual dining for the Goodhue family, isn't it?" Ben asked.

"It was my idea. An elaborate lunch in view of Irene's death seemed inappropriate," I replied.

"Ah, flexing your mistress of the manor muscles are you? What was her Highness's reaction to that?"

I didn't like his insinuation. "If you're referring to

Mary Ellen, I don't think she minded too much. And I've really had enough of the snide comments from everyone. Let's discuss something else. Exactly where is this family cemetery located?"

"There's a pathway near the garage that leads to it," Giles said. "Most of the early Goodhue family is buried there. Also has the original crypt."

"Didn't Irene live on another part of the island?"

"Cutlass Bay," Evelyn told me. "It's about forty miles from here."

"Cutlass Bay. Sounds very piratey," I said spooning some incredibly creamy thick mushroom soup into my mouth.

"Legend has it the last pirates on the island fought with the authorities on the beach. They lost and were never seen again," Giles informed us.

"Of course, Grand Britannia is full of legends—some true, some not," Stephen replied.

"Like the legend of Jonathon Goodhue and his treasure," I added.

Ben took a large bite out of a sandwich. "My guess is old Jonathon's treasure wasn't nearly as large as it sounds. Over time, the amount grows."

"That's true. Time does have a way of magnifying things. He probably spent it all on this house," I said.

Giles spooned soup into his mouth. "I can remember as kids we used to believe he'd hidden it in the maze. My sisters and I once dug huge holes in the flower beds. The gardener of the moment chased us with a shovel. Stephen, I believe your father was with us."

"He told me about it. The gardener was from Haiti and yelled in Creole. Dad said he'd never been so scared. Thought the man was going to chop off everyone's head and use it in some voodoo ritual," Stephen said.

"Stephen's father was a playmate?" I asked.

Stephen waved a hand in dismissal. "It's an island. Everyone knows everyone else after a while. Besides, our house is next door, so to speak."

Ben stared at Stephen with a smirk. Evelyn's gaze darted from me to Stephen, and then down to her plate. Giles munched on a sandwich. I had the feeling something wasn't being said. I'd heard voodoo was practiced in some parts of the Caribbean. Could a cult be on Grand Britannia?

I wanted to ask, but decided to do research first. Instead, I commented, "I'm surprised you didn't dig up the basement or something."

Giles wiped his mouth with a napkin. "Bountiful doesn't really have a basement. It was converted into the wine cellar sometime in the 1920s. Seems I recall Sir Geoffrey saying it wasn't ever used for much before that. Too damp. And I think the house is mostly built on the bedrock of the cliffs with very little digging beyond the foundations."

"Really? How interesting," I commented. "I wonder if the original plans are still around. Might be fun to have a look. Maybe we'd discover a hidden door leading to a lair of gold and silver."

"And precious gems. Have to have precious gems in the bargain," Ben added with a chuckle.

I found his jocularity rather odd for someone who'd barged in and invited himself to lunch. He showed no real grief at Irene's death. As a former lover, I'd have expected to see more emotion.

"Rumor also has it Jonathon Goodhue kept a diary," Giles said.

"A diary?" Ben intoned. "Now that might be fun. Wonder if he used it to log every item stolen from the Spanish."

"Are the original plans still around?" Evelyn asked.

"I doubt it," her husband said. "Once the place was built, why bother to keep them?"

"They might have come in handy for any future additions," I replied.

"I don't think any were ever added," Stephen said.

"My bet is the plans exist somewhere in this house," Ben maintained. "Probably the library. In fact, from what I've gleaned about Jonathon Goodhue, he was a wily old fox. It wouldn't surprise me in the least to discover one or more hidden rooms in this monstrosity."

"And that's where we find the gold, silver, and precious gems," Evelyn remarked.

"Along with the diary," Ben said.

The rest of the meal conversation was along the same lines of pirates, pirate treasure, and Grand Britannia's place in the folklore.

As we rose from the table, Evelyn said, "Giles, can you run me into town? I need something suitable for a funeral."

"I want to talk to Richard for a moment. Be right back." He disappeared toward the study while his wife headed upstairs.

Ben placed a hand on my arm detaining me. His eyes held an intense look and his smile seemed out of place. "Liza, would have dinner with me tonight? I'd like to hear more about what went on here over the weekend."

I removed my arm from his grasp not seeing where it was any of his business, but decided not to be mean. "I'm sorry Ben, but I have plans. Perhaps some other time."

His lips tightened as he cast a glance at Stephen who stood in the foyer. "I won't ask with whom. Just be aware that not everything is as it seems. I'll call later."

What the hell did that mean? I didn't ask.

Ben left and I joined Stephen in the drawing room. "I have several things to do this afternoon. I'll pick you up about six if that's all right," he said.

"Six is fine."

He hesitated. "Liza, please be careful. I don't like that you feel someone is watching you. Maybe Irene was the wrong person on that overlook."

"What?"

"Maybe someone was counting on *you* to…" he didn't finish.

"What? Die? But how would that help anyone?"

"You brought it up. Sir Geoffrey's will doesn't specify the estate's distribution if you were to die. In fact, the whole business could become null and void. I think you need to make a will. Let's discuss it tonight.

He leaned down and kissed me hard on the mouth. He departed leaving me with a warm glow from head to foot. Then a knot of fear tightened in my stomach.

Chapter Thirteen

I spent much of the afternoon in quiet isolation. Stephen's parting words disturbed me, even though I'd first thought about Sir Geoffrey's will days ago. To take my mind off the unsettling assumption, I sat in the library with the family history.

Jonathon Goodhue had made for interesting reading, but along about the middle of the 19th century I grew bored. The Goodhues had become one of the established leaders of the island in both commerce and politics. They raked in cash like autumn leaves enabling them to buy seats on city councils and magistrates on various courts. Naturally, the magistrates and lawmakers saw to it no Goodhue paid too many taxes. The writing style sounded ordinary as though the writer was also bored.

I gave in to temptation and flipped ahead to the 20th century. Sir Geoffrey was prominently mentioned, especially the years during his Governorship and his stint in Parliament. I also noted his brother, Edgar, had been appointed Chief Magistrate of the island around the same time.

Keeping it in the family. Oh well, nepotism isn't unusual in the islands.

I flipped on further, but didn't find much on my grandfather, Mercer. Apparently, he'd been involved in a bit of a social scandal in the 1950s when he abruptly broke off his engagement to a local debutant whose father just happened to be governor.

Wonder what old Geoffrey thought about that. Probably not happy his son had screwed any family ambitions with the match. *And did my grandmother play a part in it?*

Further along, a brief mention was made of Mercer's death in a boating accident. He'd never married.

And less than a year later, Mother received the first letter. Interesting. How did the old boy know about her? I wasn't likely to find the answer in the family history.

I closed the book and stared at the bookcases. The conversation from lunch concerning house plans swirled in my head. Rising, I made my way across the room and inspected the shelves, pulling out books here and there. Nothing entitled *The Building of Bountiful* appeared. I didn't expect it to, but Ben's suggestion of hidden spaces intrigued me. I finally returned to my room. Violet was in the bathroom changing the towels again. I guess one use and they were considered dirty. More like a hotel than a home.

"Oh, miss, may I say how sorry I am about Ms. Goodhue?" she said.

"Thank you, Violet. It was quite a shock."

"I wouldn't have known what to do if I'd found her."

"Not the most pleasant thing in the world."

"The constable questioned all of us. Made me very nervous."

"Yes, I can imagine. Having to answer questions

from the authorities even when you're innocent is scary." I changed the subject. "I'll be dining out tonight. Please inform Beatrice or the cook or whoever you inform."

"Yes, miss. I'll tell Georgette. Would you like me to lay out your clothing?"

"That won't be necessary."

She nodded and left the room. I had no desire to play dress-up tonight, so settled on an aqua skirt and a simple white tank top. I slipped on the silver ballet flats and kept the jewelry to a minimum. I glanced at my watch. Stephen would be here soon. I grabbed my purse and headed downstairs. I needed a drink.

I waited in the drawing room with a glass of sherry. Stephen arrived precisely at six o'clock. Willie answered the door and showed him in.

"Good evening, Liza. You look quite cool and island perfect in that outfit."

"Thank you. Would you care for something to drink?"

"What are you having? Sherry?"

I nodded as he poured a glass. I hadn't pegged him as a sherry kind of guy, but then I was beginning to realize Stephen Albright defied conventional assumptions.

He was also dressed casually tonight. Navy blue slacks and a light blue polo shirt brought out his best feature—those fabulous eyes. I wondered if he knew that.

He rejoined me and took a seat in one of the chairs. "I hope what I said when I left this afternoon didn't upset you too much."

"Not upset so much as aware. With sudden wealth

comes the need for a will. I should have done it before leaving the States."

"My offices are in West End. Have Myron bring you around tomorrow morning, say tenish? We can draw up something simple and have you sign it."

"Sounds good."

Richard entered the room and made for the liquor cart. "Hullo, Stephen. Didn't know you were coming for dinner."

"I'm not. Liza's dining with me at Land's End this evening."

Land's End? So Stephen's place had a name, too.

"How's Mary Ellen?" I asked.

"Much better. She'll be down shortly along with Evelyn."

"And Giles?"

"As soon as they returned from shopping, he received a phone call and had to run over to Bristol. Something about some of the merchandise he bought at the sale the other day not being picked up. He won't be in until late."

"Where's Bristol?" I asked.

"Not far from Cutlass Bay," Stephen said, and then looked at Richard. "Are the arrangements complete?"

"More or less. As soon as the autopsy is finished, Irene's body will be released. Time hasn't been set yet, but I imagine the funeral will be Tuesday or Wednesday with a private burial afterward. Wyatt and Isabelle will be arriving sometime tomorrow."

Stephen and I finished our sherry at the same time.

"Are you ready?" he asked.

I rose and set my glass on the end table. "Yes. Have a pleasant dinner, Richard. I don't know when I'll be in."

He sat in the chair Stephen had vacated, stared at the portrait of Jonathon Goodhue, but said nothing.

The drive to Stephen's took only a few minutes along a twisting road before he pulled into a driveway not unlike that of Bountiful. We emerged from the privacy woods and I got my first look at Land's End.

Smaller than Bountiful, it had been built in the Georgian style. The landscaping was perfect.

"How lovely!"

"Thank you. It's been the family home since the early nineteen-hundreds." He stopped near the front steps.

"And you live here alone?"

"I don't live here at all anymore. My parents do. I have a townhouse in West End. When they're gone on an extended trip, I stay here to keep an eye on the place."

He helped me from the car, up the porch steps and into the house where he led me into a small front room. "Would you like another glass of sherry?"

"Yes, thank you."

He smiled, poured sherry for me, and a small scotch for himself. No servants appeared.

I took a sip. "So, what's for dinner?"

"I thought maybe you'd like something American. I've got two New York strips. I'll grill them on the back patio."

"You're cooking?"

"I take exception to that tone. I'm very self-sufficient. When my father retired, most of the staff was let go. My parents travel a lot and thought the extra expense unnecessary. When they come home, Mother does most of the cooking unless guests are expected, then she hires a local woman. A gardener comes out once a week to cut the grass and tend the flowerbeds."

Taking our drinks, he led me through the house to the back terrace. A swimming pool graced the lawn off to the left.

"How extravagant. A pool and the cove," I said with a chuckle.

"Mother hated the steps down to the cove. That tiny headland jutting out between the properties makes the beach very private, but she prefers fresh to salt water."

A table with a three branch candelabra and full place settings graced one end of the terrace. It had romance written all over it.

He fired up the gas grill. "I've taken the liberty of already tossing a salad. I also have an assortment of fresh fruit and whipped cream for dessert."

"Wow, I'm impressed. You have been busy this afternoon, haven't you?"

He chuckled. "The whipped cream is in a can and the fruit pre-made from the grocery. I did, however, make the salad. Would you like to see the view from the cliff?"

Cliffs weren't high on my list at the moment, but a stroll across the lawn with Stephen was, so I accepted. He held my hand the entire distance.

Land's End also had an overlook, but the decking and rails looked new. To the right, the small headland between here and Bountiful gave the needed privacy to both estates. The Albright's also had built a small boathouse at its base. To my left the cliff curved in a graceful arc toward the headland doing the same from the opposite side of the cove. Beyond the narrow entrance, the open waters of the Caribbean gleamed in the waning sunlight.

"This is lovely." I shaded my eyes with my free hand. "I don't see too many other beaches along the cove."

"No, the cliffs are almost continuous. A few grains of sand at the apex of the cove and more over by Collier's place are all."

"How many homes are along the cliffs?"

"At one time Jonathon Goodhue owned the entire cove. Over the years, the family has sold off the majority. Only a few houses were built. Some of them were destroyed during a hurricane in nineteen sixty-four. I'm not sure who owns the land now."

We walked back. He didn't relinquish my hand until we were on the patio. My heart thumped and I finished the last of my sherry to steady my nerves.

Stephen fiddled with the grills control knobs. *Does he have romance on his mind or is he just a fast worker?*

I had no idea, but wouldn't mind a chance to find out.

"Grill's ready," he called out, and then made his way inside.

I followed and stood by the doorway while he uncorked the Cabernet Sauvignon.

"Here, put this on the table so it can breathe," he said, handing me the bottle. "I'll get the steaks. How do you like yours cooked?"

"Medium rare."

He smiled. "Ah, a woman of taste."

The sizzle of cold meat hitting the hot grill and the

accompanying aroma set my stomach to grumbling. As Stephen attended to the cooking, I brought out the salad and fruit platter, then lit the candles. Popping a grape into my mouth, I decided romance sounded like a damned fine idea. I visualized me lying naked on a chaise with an equally naked Stephen feeding me whipped cream laden slices of fruit. Then I imagined those lips caressing most of my anatomy. My imagination steamed onward until I had to flap the front of my top to cool off.

He chose that moment to look at me. "Too hot for you out here? We could move inside if you prefer."

Yeah, it was too hot, but the weather had nothing to do with it. I inhaled a deep breath and removed my mind from fantasyland.

"No, I'm fine. Must be the sherry."

With the steaks done, he held my chair as I sat, and then forked a perfectly grilled New York strip onto my plate. I cut off a small bite and tasted. Ahhh. No condiments need apply. The salad, a mixture of garden greens, scallions, and tomatoes with a light vinaigrette dressing hit the spot. I couldn't wait for the fruit and whipped cream—the reality based items, that is.

Stephen poured wine into my glass. The flickering candlelight bounced off the crystal in shards of yellow and white while turning the wine within shades from maroon to blood red. I sipped. It was perfect, too.

"How's the steak?" he asked.

"Wonderful. So's the wine. You set a very romantic table, Mr. Albright."

"I do?" His eyelids dropped a fraction to hood that sea green gaze. The effect was drop dead sexy, and I resisted the urge to leap across the table. Maybe there'd be time for that later.

He smiled and resumed eating. "What did you do all afternoon?"

"Read some of the family history. Jonathon Goodhue is an interesting read, but about six generations along the family is downright boring."

"By then they were established and putting up a façade of British gentility."

I ate another bite of salad and sipped more wine. "Stephen, have you found out any more about my grandfather and grandmother?"

He shook his head. "Haven't had much time to look. I'll ask my father when they get back. He was the family solicitor when your grandfather died."

"I'm curious as to why Sir Geoffrey suddenly made contact with Mother after all those years."

He shrugged. "His oldest and favorite son had died. Maybe he was curious."

"But how did he know about her? I'm sure my grandmother must have contacted somebody when she found out she was pregnant. I can only assume nobody cared until my grandfather died."

"That's an interesting question. He must have known something. Why else make contact? And how did he make contact? I wonder if my father initiated a search at the old boy's request."

"How did my grandfather die?"

"He drowned in a sailboat accident. A storm blew up and, before he could make the safety of the cove, the boat capsized. What about your grandmother? Know anything about her?"

"No, Mother was adopted as a baby. As far as I know, her birth mother was never revealed." I leaned back in my chair. "I wonder if she's still alive. Mother would kill me, but I might see what I can find out. I mean, Mother was born in New Orleans and we have the date. It's not much to go on. Hospitals keep records, and a birth certificate would have been filed."

"I'm afraid I can't help you much there. I don't know American law."

"Mother has a good lawyer. I'll ask Adam to look into it."

We finished our meal, including the fruit and whipped cream, and then took our wine glasses poolside.

"Have a seat," he said indicating the heavily padded chaise lounges. "Moon's lovely tonight."

He settled in a chair next to me. We sat in silence. A light breeze ruffled the palm fronds. Beyond the cliffs, moonlight danced on the water.

I finished my wine, set the glass on the pavers, and turned my head to ask, "A penny for them."

"What?"

"A penny for your thoughts."

He sighed. "I was just thinking about Irene."

"In what way?"

"What the hell was she doing on the overlook? And who was with her? There's no lighting and she wouldn't wander out there without a reason."

I shivered before murmuring, "Murder."

"I want you in the office at ten sharp tomorrow morning. Any idea how you plan to distribute the estate?"

"None whatsoever. I'll sleep on it." Not wanting to talk about Irene or her horrible death any longer, I rose and walked to pool's edge staring into the rippling depths. The muted underwater lights cast a dim glow. A crest of some sort had been painted on the bottom. I wondered how long the Albrights had been on Grand Britannia.

Stephen walked up behind me and placed his arms around my waist gently turning me around. I slid my arms around his neck as he lowered his head.

Those soft, yet firm, lips teased mine, his tongue tracing my lips. A tremor quaked from the pit of my stomach to the tips of my toes. His arms tightened and his mouth demanded I respond. I had no problem doing that.

The kiss went on forever. The heat built until I feared spontaneous combustion would end our lives. Not a bad way to die, but I wanted what comes in between first. His hands roamed up and down my back until finding my derriere. He squeezed and pulled my hips against his. I had no trouble feeling his excitement. It pressed heavy and hard on my lower abdomen.

He raised his head. "I want you, Liza."

The moonlight combined with the underwater lights of the pool carved his face into strong lines of light and shadow. I couldn't see his eyes clearly, but imagined the blue-green had intensified.

"I want you, too." I stepped back and fell into space. I clutched at Stephen's arms, but it was too late. We fell into the pool. The cool water on my overheated body shocked me out of all romantic thought. I surfaced, sputtering with laughter and swam for the side. My skirt hampered the movement. His arm encircled my waist and helped me along.

"Oh my God, I can't believe I did that!"

He laughed, too. "I totally forgot where we were."

Stephen heaved himself out of the water, and then helped me up beside him. I pulled the soaking skirt from around my legs wringing as much water out of it as possible.

"I say we need to get inside and find a couple of towels," he said, still laughing. He took my hand and led me into the house. My ballet slippers squished with every step. At least they weren't at the bottom of the pool.

I followed him upstairs and into a large bedroom. A bath led off to the right.

"Towels are in there. I'll see if I can find you a bathrobe while I dump our clothes in the dryer."

"Looks like we'll be getting naked after all."

He shot me a glance, then hooded those eyes again, and smiled.

"Yes, I guess we will."

The slow sexy voice turned my insides to mush. How long would I remain in that bathrobe?

Chapter Fourteen

I tossed my sopping clothes into the tub, then wrapped my body in a thick, fluffy towel. I used another to dry my hair. I felt like a complete idiot. A wonderful, romantic moment had ended up as a fully clothed, chlorine-infused midnight swim.

Stephen knocked on the door and called out, "Are you decent?"

"I'm not sure about decent, but I am covered. Come on in."

He poked his head through the opening and handed me a wad of bronze-colored silk.

"There's a hair dryer in the left hand drawer if you need it. When you're finished come join me in my sitting room. It's down the hall, third door on the right. Hand me your clothes and I'll take them to the laundry."

He left carrying my things, including the ballet slippers, which may or may not survive the process.

I found the blow dryer and made quick work of my hair. Done, I whipped off the towel and slipped into the robe. It was huge. The bottom puddled a good six inches around my feet and the sleeves hung well past my fingertips. The belt tied closer to my hips than waist.

Rolling up the sleeves, I wondered if this was

Stephen's robe or his father's. I hitched the lapels as close together as possible before tying the belt in a tight bow.

I found the sitting room with no problem and through the open French doors spied Stephen sitting on the balcony.

"Ah, there you are. Come on out," he said, rising.

I walked through the room. A small leather sofa along with a couple of matching chairs and a coffee table sat on a dark red, tan, and black oriental rug in the middle of the floor. A large bookcase stood against one of the walls. Next to it was a liquor cart. An oversized armoire graced another, and an ornate roll-top desk complete with an antique swivel chair filled the last. It was a man's room, even to the faint scent of aftershave or cologne. I passed a door leading to a bedroom.

"I thought you didn't live here?"

"I don't. This is the guest suite. Here, have a seat." He handed me a snifter as I settled into a wicker chair. "Brandy. To ward off any evil germs."

I accepted the offering and sipped. The fiery liquid burned all the way down my throat. Any chill I felt disappeared."I'm so sorry for all of this," I said. "I swear I'm not usually a klutz."

He laughed, took my hand, and raised it to his lips.

"I found the experience enlightening."

"Enlightening?"

"Those wet clothes clinging to your body left little to the imagination."

Non-brandy induced heat swept me from head to toe. I was right. I *wouldn't* be in this robe long and we *would* get naked. I eyed his attire, not dissimilar from mine only deep claret red.

I sipped some more and tried to think of clever conversation. Nothing came to mind. Here I was wearing a silk robe, my nipples clearly visible through the thin material, sitting next to an incredibly sexy man on the balcony of his bedroom, and I couldn't come up with one decent morsel of repartee. All I'd learned from my Improvisation course at drama school remained buried in my mind. Then Stephen chuckled.

"What's so funny?"

"Us. We were on the brink of a romantic interlude, took an unexpected dip in the pool, and are now sitting here unable to make casual conversation."

"Strange, but I was just thinking the same. We're quite the pair."

He took my hand again and stroked the palm with his thumb before replacing it with his lips. Instant heat churned in my stomach.

"Couldn't have said it better myself."

The light cascading from the room beyond lit this small slice of the balcony. I couldn't see his eyes clearly, but his smile was the slow sexy one of earlier in the evening. I set my snifter on the floor.

Oh, yeah. Definitely getting naked.

He leaned over and pulled me from the chair into his lap. I twined my arms around his neck and let my lips play up and down his cheek. His grasp tightened. Then his hand slid from my waist, traveled to the gapping labels of my robe, and then hesitated before plunging inside.

The warmth of his hand sizzled against my skin. It covered my breast and caressed with a feather light touch. His other hand tangled in my hair. He tugged gently pulling my head back until his lips met mine.

My hormones spiked sending nerve endings into terminal overload. Desire gushed from the pit of my stomach to the rest of my body. Our tongues twined and explored. I think I moaned. It was a humdinger of a kiss.

Meanwhile, his hand in the robe had not been idle. His fingers squeezed and manipulated my erect nipples until I wanted to scream. I squirmed on his lap and felt the familiar hardness growing harder and larger, the silk coverings not hiding a thing.

Stephen broke off the kiss, and slid his lips down my throat to that, oh so sensitive, pulse point. I gasped. My arms automatically gripped his neck forcefully.

He said nothing, just removed his hands from all wonderful places, slid his arms under my knees and across my back, and then stood carrying me inside while I nibbled his neck like a vampire. He set me on my feet next to the bed. Nimble fingers untied the bow at my waist and within seconds the silky robe lay at my feet like a pool of melted chocolate.

Never one to be passive, I returned the favor, and then stepped back to admire my first real view of Stephen Albright. His smooth chest rippled with toned muscles. My hands touched and stroked before moving down to his narrow waist and hips. My fingers encircled his erection. I caressed with a light touch.

Stephen closed his eyes and groaned.

"Oh God, Liza," he said in a breathless tone. Without another word, he pushed me onto the bed. This very reserved man was anything but between the sheets. We went at each other like animals in heat—scratching, moaning, and thrashing around. First with him on top, then me, a never ending battle of dominance.

I won.

I straddled his hips and let my lips travel from his chest to his navel, scooting down his body as I went until reaching that hot shaft. Using my tongue to tickle for a moment, I then took him into my mouth. He gasped and groaned. If he actually said anything I didn't hear it. He pumped his hips a few times before I let go and allowed my lips to retrace their journey until I reached his chest again.

With the speed of a tiger pouncing, he flipped me onto my back. He was now in control. I didn't care.

He kissed his way down my neck to my breasts where he nibbled and laved first one erect center then the other. His hand glided down my torso to the apex of my thighs. His thumb found the right spot and massaged. Then his mouth replaced the thumb.

I couldn't stop my hips from undulating. I gasped and may have called out his name. I'm not sure. I had no coherent thought—just raw, burning, basic need. The flames within threatened to consume me. I wanted to be consumed. Now. That knot of desire tightened to the point of painful. Pleasure and pain—a powerful combination. I squirmed for release from the torture and the thrill.

Stephen kissed his way back up my body. I opened my eyes as he reached over to the nightstand, opened the drawer and withdrew a foil packet. I writhed as he sheathed himself.

"Now," I pleaded. "I need you now."

"I know," he whispered. "I want you, too. Now!" He plunged in.

I cried out as the shock wave ricocheted throughout my body. A deep throb told me I wasn't far away from that ultimate pleasure. I locked my legs around his waist and matched him thrust for thrust. The knot tightened further until finally I came in strong, sharp spasms that nearly tore me apart. I thrust and bucked like a wild mare and still the contractions continued. Could it last forever?

Then with a hoarse shout, Stephen also reached the peak. He lunged deeply and shouted not words, but noise, the kind that comes from the gut. We ground our hips together trying to wring that last bit of pleasure from our bodies. Finally, he collapsed and rolled away.

I lay there panting, the ripples of sex still sliding through my insides. The throbbing gradually subsided.

"Oh, wow," I said when I could speak again.

He grasped my hand and brought it to his lips.

"You can say that again."

"Oh, wow."

He smiled against my skin. "I didn't really plan on this tonight."

"Neither did I, but I can't say I'm disappointed."

"Definitely not the word I'd use."

I slithered over close to him. His arm slid under my head and pulled it to his shoulder. We laid in silence, satiated. I marveled at the change of events. In less than a week, he'd gone from being an arrogant enemy, to a possible ally, to a lover.

I'd had boyfriends over the years, some serious. But the relationships had progressed in a time honored fashion and took months to develop. I didn't just leap into bed with any attractive guy.

Yet here I was cuddled up to a man I barely knew. I had no idea what it signified. All I knew was I enjoyed it. *Is this love?* I didn't have an answer.

****

We slept for a short while before waking to make love again, this time slow and sweet. The results were the same.

The bedside clock showed it to be almost one. I needed to get home.

"You're welcome to stay, you know," Stephen said.

"I know, but considering the situation I think it might look better if I left."

He rose, grabbed one of the robes and exited, returning a few minutes later with my clothes.

I dressed quickly. Most of the wrinkles had been ironed out by the dryer, so I didn't look too disheveled. The ballet slippers weren't as lucky. They still bore signs of dampness and the supple leather had hardened. Stephen dressed in a pair of slacks and a pullover.

As we descended the staircase, I realized I'd not thought about the consequences of our actions. Now that we had broken the sexual ice, what was next? *Of course, I'm assuming he is thinking long term. For all I know, this is a one night stand.*

I had the beginnings of a relationship in mind. But did he?

I still mulled those thoughts around in my mind as Stephen turned out of his driveway and headed toward Bountiful.

After a minute he glanced in my direction. "You're awfully quiet. Is anything wrong?"

"No, I'm just thinking."

"About what?"

No way did I intend to divulge the truth. "Oh, just how wonderful tonight was."

He laughed lightly. "Dinner wasn't bad, either."

I chuckled with him, and then sobered. The road before us twisted and curved. We'd be at Bountiful in a few minutes. Perhaps I could probe his thoughts.

"Stephen, I don't want you to think…"

We rounded a sharp curve and my words were choked off. A car raced up behind us, headlights on high beam. The driver pulled out to pass. He edged us toward the ditch. With an oath, Stephen jerked the wheel to the left. I screamed. The car missed us by inches. The left side tires dropped off the pavement onto the soft, narrow shoulder. He twisted the wheel back to the right, but the vehicle continued to slide toward the ditch. In front of me a small tree materialized.

"Hang on!" Stephen said with a gasp.

I grasped the armrest, closed my eyes, and raised an arm to shield my face. A second later, we impacted.

Chapter Fifteen

The airbag deployed and my forward motion stopped abruptly thanks to the seat and shoulder belts.

"Goddamned lunatic!" Stephen cursed.

I opened my eyes and stared through a cracked windshield at the tree a mere five feet from my face. My heart pounded and my breaths came in gasps.

"Are you all right?" he asked.

"I…I think so." I swallowed the lump of fear still stuck in my throat. "How about you?"

"I'm fine." Stephen wrenched the door open and exited. The night was silent save for the chirp of insects and the hissing steam escaping the radiator.

"Is the car badly damaged?" I called out.

"Bad enough to need a tow. Dammit, the guy didn't even have the decency to stop."

"Must have been drunk."

I fumbled to open my door and stepped out only to tumble into the ditch.

Stephen came around to help me to my feet. "Be careful. Maybe it would be better if you waited back a bit. We're in a precarious situation."

I saw what he meant. The headlights revealed we were at the apex of the curve. Another driver rounding the bend could hit us. I eased my way several yards beyond the ditch.

Stephen called the police from his cell while I shivered in the warm night air. A light breeze rattled through the woods. In the distance, an owl hooted. He finished his call and joined me.

"Are you sure you're all right?" he asked placing and arm around my shoulders and hugging me close.

"Yeah. Reaction, I guess. And these woods are creepy."

He pulled me into an embrace and kissed the top of my head.

"The constable is on his way along with a tow truck. Do you want to call Bountiful and tell them what happened?"

I shook my head. "Not really. It's after one and everybody will be asleep. Besides, I'm not hurt."

The wait for the authorities stretched forever. Finally, a patrol car arrived and stopped on the berm. Two men emerged. One lit flares placing them alongside the road. The other approached us.

"Are you all right?"

"Yes, we're fine," Stephen answered.

"What happened?"

I didn't recognize this constable, but Stephen seemed to know him, so I let him handle the explanation.

The second officer joined us. "I always said this road is a deathtrap. Too many curves and too many cars."

"Add alcohol to the mix and tragedy can't be far away," the first man said. "I don't suppose you can identify the car or driver, can you?"

Stephen shook his head. "No, it was dark and it happened too fast. Once second he was there, the next he was gone. Sorry."

"I think it was a light color—white, tan, maybe gray. I kept staring out the window as the car moved closer," I added.

The tow truck arrived and had the car on the hook in less than thirty minutes. Stephen and I slid into the back seat of a patrol car. We drove through the open gate and pulled up to Bountiful at two-thirty in the morning.

"I'm sorry the evening ended so badly," he said escorting me to the front door.

"No one was hurt. That's what counts. Hope your car isn't too badly damaged."

"Me, too." He leaned down and kissed me hard and deeply. "I'll see you tomorrow morning."

As Stephen left, I entered a dimly lit foyer and made my way upstairs. All was quiet. I undressed and slid between the sheets. Exhaustion would prove better than any sleeping pill. Hovering on the edge of unconsciousness, I heard the veranda floorboard creak.

****

I rushed into the dining room a few minutes before nine the next morning. Only Richard and Evelyn were present. Conversation ceased as I entered.

"Good morning," I said. "Am I too late for breakfast?"

"Of course not," Richard said finishing his tea and glancing at his watch. "Help yourself. I'm afraid I have to leave you two ladies. I need to contact the authorities as to when Irene's autopsy will be over and make the final arrangements."

"Is there anything I can do?" I asked. For a grief stricken brother he seemed remarkably cool—almost unemotional. I stared in his direction. Come to think of it, Richard always put himself on a tight leash.

"No thank you, Liza. Wyatt and Isabelle will be arriving later. I'm sure you, Evelyn, and Mary Ellen can fill them in on the details as you know them."

He headed for the foyer when I remembered my promise to Stephen.

"Oh, I need to go into West End this morning on business. Is Myron available to drive me?"

He paused and looked back. "Business?"

I had no intention of telling him I planned on making a will. "Yes," I replied in a cool tone. "It shouldn't take but an hour or so."

He stared for a moment, and then nodded. "I'm sure Myron is available. Just use the house phone to ring through to his quarters. Now, if you'll excuse me."

When he left, I made my way to the sideboard and poured a cup of coffee. The accident last night hadn't left me too banged up, thank God. I was sore and might have a bruise or two, but other than that no physical evidence manifested itself.

I lifted the cover of a chafing dish. The scrambled eggs look dry. I decided on toast and fruit.

Evelyn eyed me over the rim of her coffee cup as I resumed my seat. Her scrutiny got on my nerves.

"Where's Giles this morning?"

"Still in Bristol, I imagine. He called around ten last night and said he needed to go to Port Elizabeth today. Half the furniture we bought didn't get delivered to the auction house."

"What a shame. I'm so sorry he had to make the trip. Is it far?"

"Not terribly." She paused and sipped. "So, how

was your date last night with Stephen?"

I kept it sweet and simple. "Very nice, although some drunk ran us off the road on the way home."

Her eyes widened. "Good heavens! No one was hurt were they?"

"No, no. Both Stephen and I are fine, but the car hit a small tree and has some damage."

"Honestly, the roads on this island get more dangerous every day. Too many people don't know how to drive properly, and I don't know where the government spends its money. Certainly not for road repair."

"We have the same complaint in the States."

"Are you sure it was an accident?" Her eyes gleamed with speculation.

"Of course. What else?"

"Oh, I don't know, but it seems odd that a car would choose that time of night to run you off the road."

"Late at night is when the drunks come out."

One of the maids entered from the butler's pantry and stopped when she saw us.

"Oh, I'm sorry. I thought you were finished."

I waved a hand toward the sideboard. "I am. Not too hungry this morning."

Evelyn set her cup down. "Same here."

The maid nodded and removed one of the chafing dishes.

Evelyn rose. "Well, I guess I'd better find something to do for a while until Irene's kids get here. I'll talk to you later."

Damn Evelyn. Now she had me thinking. *Was it an accident? Oh, of course it was. Still…*

I finished breakfast quickly. It was almost ten and I needed to get to Stephen's office. I found a phone in the butler's pantry, a list of numbers attached to the wall next to it. Myron was number 6. I pressed it and waited. He answered on the third ring.

I made my request and hung up, then dashed upstairs for a fast shower before scrambling into a pair of slacks and a blouse.

Myron waited beside the limo. "Please take me to Stephen Albright's law office in West End," I said as he held the door for me.

In the limo I resisted the urge to look over my shoulder at the house. If Mary Ellen watched, I didn't want to know.

We entered the woods and Bountiful was soon out of sight. A few yards down the driveway, I spied a narrow track running deeper into the trees. Through the foliage, a splash of white caught my eye as we drove by.

"Myron, what was that house off in the woods?"

"Beatrice lives there, Miss. It's an old caretaker's cottage. Sir Geoffrey had it renovated several years ago when she requested private accommodations."

"I see. Thank you."

Beatrice perplexed me. Cool to the point of cold, she rarely smiled or spoke to the family. Well, at least not to me. I assumed she had frequent contact with Richard and Mary Ellen. I knew she mourned Irene.

Perhaps I'll pay a visit and offer my condolences in person. Maybe I could pry some information regarding my grandfather from her. Even though not at Bountiful during that time, she could have talked with other servants.

Myron dropped me off and I entered the law offices of Albright, Albright, and Swisher. A receptionist sat behind a large mahogany desk.

"Hello, I'm here to see Stephen Albright. My name is Elizabeth Channing."

She quickly scrolled down a schedule on the computer. "I'm sorry. I don't see your name listed. What time was your appointment?"

She didn't sound sorry—just efficient.

"The appointment was made last evening with Mr. Albright. He said to come in around ten. I may be a little late."

"I see. One moment, please." She lifted the receiver of her desk phone and dialed in a number. "Mr. Albright, I have a lady at the desk named Channing who says she made an appointment with you last night…Very well." She hung up and indicated a waiting area with plush chairs and sofas off to the right. "Please have a seat. Mr. Albright will be here in a moment. May I get you something to drink? Coffee? Tea? A bottle of water?"

"No, thank you." I chose a chair and waited.

Ten minutes later, Stephen entered from a hallway. "Liza, sorry to keep you waiting, but I was on the phone with my auto mechanic. Please, come on back."

I followed him back down the corridor. "Was the car badly damaged?"

"It needs a new radiator and windshield along with some body work. I was going to trade it in anyway."

He opened a door into an anteroom complete with chairs and another desk.

"My secretary has stepped out for a moment. Come on in."

I entered the inner sanctum. I don't know what I expected, but this wasn't it. No antiques or heavy mahogany here. Light streamed in the windows revealing modern furniture with lots of smoked glass and linear curves. He indicated a chair and I sat. Stephen did the same behind the desk.

"How are you feeling this morning? Not too sore, I hope."

"Uh, no, I'm fine." I found his cool tone daunting.

"I doubt the constable will find the guy who did it. Did Janice offer you something to drink?"

"Janice? Oh, the woman out front? Yes. I don't need anything."

A knock sounded on the open door. I turned and saw a man standing on the threshold.

"Hullo, Stephen. Hope I haven't kept you waiting."

"Not at all, Pete." He rose. "Liza, this is Peter Swanson. He's a solicitor with the firm and handles wills. You'll be working with him. I'm afraid I have a client due in half an hour. Pete, this is Liza Channing, Sir Geoffrey's great-granddaughter."

"A pleasure, Miss Channing."

"I'll bring her along in a moment," Stephen said.

The man nodded, turned and closed the door behind him. Stephen walked from behind his desk. I rose. He placed his hands on my shoulders and gave me a quick kiss.

"Wanted to do that in the lobby, but there were too many eyes," he said with a smile. "Do you have any idea how you're going to distribute your property?"

I sighed. The Stephen I knew was back. The cool professional had been intimidating.

I stood on tiptoe, placed my hand at the back of his

head and lowered his face to mine giving him a kiss in return.

"I think so. I want the Historical Society to have Bountiful and the Mariner's Home the income from the rentals. Anything left over will go to my mother."

His eyebrows rose. "That's interesting. I'd have thought your mother was the natural choice to inherit."

"Mom has plenty of money. She inherited quite a bit from her parents, and charges a fortune for her paintings. Besides, this will is only in effect for a year. When I take full title to the house and all the rest, I'll make a new one."

He grinned. "Now you're thinking! Come on, let's get this over with."

He led me down a hallway to Peter's office, and then left, saying, "I'll drop by tonight on my way home."

"What are you driving?"

"My father's Bentley. I'd better not wreck that. It's his baby, and he'd have a fit."

I laughed while Peter nodded toward a chair in front of his desk. I sat and for the next hour hammered out the details of my last will and testament.

I arrived back at Bountiful just in time for lunch and to meet Irene's children. I paused in the foyer and heard a man's voice come through the open drawing room doors.

"So, where is this American relative who shafted Mother out of her inheritance?"

At least he was blunt and to the point. No fancy, schmancy beating around the bush like the rest of the family. This I could deal with. I strode to the doorway.

"I'm right here."

A tall, well-built man turned. Shock rolled through me. I stared at Jonathon Goodhue. The portrait had come to life.

"Way to go, Wyatt," drawled a dark haired woman sitting on the sofa next to Mary Ellen. "Nothing like insulting someone before introductions are even made."

Wyatt had the grace to blush. "Sorry. Subtlety and tact aren't my strong suits. I meant no offense."

"None taken," I replied. "My condolences on your mother's death."

Wyatt's face turned grim while the woman blinked and bit her lip.

"In case you haven't guessed, these are Irene's children, Wyatt Harding and Isabelle Ramirez. Wyatt, Isabelle, the *new* owner of Bountiful, Liza Channing," Mary Ellen said.

"Pleased to meet you," Isabelle said with a nod, not bothering to rise from her seat.

Wyatt offered his hand. I accepted it and glanced at the portrait.

"The resemblance is amazing," I commented.

That was an understatement. His hair was on the long side and given another month or two, he'd be able to pull it back into a ponytail further heightening the likeness.

"Guess I'm just a throwback," he said.

"I suppose there are just so many genes to go around. And I didn't shaft your mother out of anything. This is all the doing of our great-grandfather."

Isabelle waved a hand. "Don't worry about it. Wyatt was just being a pain in the rump. Besides, I don't think Mother cared much one way or the other."

"And Sir Geoffrey loved meddling in other

people's affairs," Wyatt said. "It's the main reason why I rarely came to Bountiful."

I took a seat in one of the chairs. "Yes, from everything I heard, he liked being in control."

Isabelle rolled her eyes. "That's putting it mildly. He cut me out of the will when I married Carlos. Didn't approve of a Goodhue marrying a Puerto Rican."

"Is your husband here?"

She leaned back and crossed her legs. "No. We separated a few months ago. He's back in San Juan."

I turned to Wyatt. "And what about you? Are you married?"

He smiled and winked. "Not at the moment."

Evelyn breezed into the room. "Hello, am I late?"

"You still have a few minutes," Mary Ellen answered.

"Wyatt, Isabelle, I'm so sorry about your mother. It must have been a horrible shock."

Wyatt ceased smiling and frowned. Isabelle blinked rapidly to clear suddenly clouded eyes.

"Yes, Evelyn, it was a shock," Wyatt said.

I couldn't tell if he was sincere or mocking her. Of course, it was a shock. But then, perhaps I was being harsh. What else could she say?

Willie appeared in the doorway to announce luncheon was ready. While walking to the dining room, I decided neither of Irene's children displayed much grief. Before I could ask any questions, Richard entered and took his place.

"Sorry I'm late, but I was on the phone. The autopsy is over, and Irene's been released for burial. I thought maybe day after tomorrow for the funeral. Is that all right with you, Wyatt, Isabelle?"

"Fine," her son answered. "Any results yet?"

"No, much too early."

"And what on earth was she doing on the overlook at that time of night?" Wyatt replied.

"We've all asked those questions. Shame the railing was so unsafe," Evelyn said.

"That's silly," Mary Ellen declared. "It was simply loose."

Evelyn smiled. "Seems a lot of things are in disrepair at Bountiful."

Richard shot her a nasty look, while Mary Ellen glared. I caught the insinuation that perhaps the estate manager hadn't been doing his job.

Luckily, one of the servers entered with a tray of soup bowls defusing the situation. When the soup was placed before me, I suppressed a shudder. Some kind of jellied consommé stared back at me. What was it with these people and cold soups?

I took a small spoonful. The stuff slithered down my throat like edible slime. I put the spoon down and gazed at Isabelle.

"And do you live in Cutlass Bay, too?"

"I live in Port Elizabeth. When Carlos and I split, Mother let me use her apartment there."

"Do you have a job?"

"I was a real estate agent before my marriage. As soon as I'm back on my feet, I'll go back to it."

"And what about you?" I asked Wyatt.

"I live in Bristol and do as little as possible. Which reminds me, where is Giles, Evelyn? How late did he get back last night?"

Evelyn stopped spooning consommé into her mouth and stared.

"Giles didn't come here last night. When I last talked to him, he said he would stay overnight in Bristol, and then head for Port Elizabeth first thing in the morning. When did you see him?"

"I didn't actually. When I got home around three in the morning, I found a note stuck on the door of my apartment. It was from Giles. He'd planned on staying with me, but when I wasn't home he said he'd carry on and see me here at Bountiful."

Evelyn sighed. "I hope he went to a hotel or something and didn't attempt the drive. These roads are horrible after dark. Why just last night Liza and Stephen were run into a ditch by some drunk."

"What's this?" Richard said with raised eyebrows.

I gave them an abbreviated version of the adventure. "I'm sure the other driver doesn't even remember the incident."

Mary Ellen shook her head. "People have no sense of personal responsibility anymore. They drink and drive, overspend credit cards, and…" she cast a quick eye toward Wyatt and Isabelle…"live a life they can't afford."

Isabelle pushed the half-eaten consommé away and stared at Mary Ellen with a raised eyebrow. Wyatt looked like he didn't give a damn about the words. I could believe that. He struck me as the kind who didn't care what others thought of him.

As usual, this meal was deteriorating into a verbal jousting match. I ate the rest of lunch in silence. If I had any sense, I'd take a day off tomorrow and spend it in West End.

Evelyn was also remarkably quiet. Her forehead furrowed as though in deep thought. Deep thought wasn't one of her character traits. Perhaps she was concerned about her husband. She obviously hadn't talked to him today.

I hoped he hadn't had an accident.

Chapter Sixteen

I declined to accompany Irene's children on a trip to the scene of her death. I'd already seen enough.

Instead, I closeted myself in the library with the Goodhue genealogy. Bored, I finally tossed the book aside. Not coming from a close-knit family, the accomplishments of past generations didn't stoke my interest. This tome was so heavy on Sir Geoffrey's achievements I wondered if he'd written it.

Curiosity about those building plans for Bountiful and a diary written by Jonathon still tickled my mind. *If I was going to hide something, where would it be?*

I let my gaze wander around the room. Under the rug? No, rugs get changed. In a hidden floorboard? Possibly, but it would have to be accessible.

"And why hide anything at all?" I said out loud. What if a great-great someone decided an old family secret could damage *their* reputation?

I rose, walked over to the dark paneling near the fireplace, and then rapped gently with my knuckles. No ominous hollow sound echoed back to me. The wall was as solid as the cliffs surrounding the cove.

I left the library and walked toward the front door. Fresh air and exercise sounded better than rapping on wood paneling looking for non-existent hidey-holes.

I ambled further up the driveway toward the garage

intent upon finding the family cemetery. A path angled into the woods.

Vegetation brushed my arms proving it hadn't been used in a while. I kept my eyes focused down to avoid tripping over vines and roots. The twisting passage must have made for one arduous funeral procession.

Eventually, I spied a wrought iron fence gate. Ahead of me stood a large stone edifice with sturdy columns and a wooden door. Headstones poked through the weeds. I pushed the gate open on protesting hinges. Rust gritted under my fingers. Stooping, I pulled the weeds away from one of the markers.

Carolina Rothwell Goodhue
January 4, 1774
February 20, 1802

About my age. How had she died? In an epidemic? In childbirth? I continued my exploration. Some of the names I remembered from the genealogy. Others were unknown. All in all, perhaps twenty graves dotted the little cemetery.

They lived, they died, and now they were forgotten.

I turned my attention to the crypt. The ornate carving indicated whoever was interred there intended on being remembered. Old Jonathon no doubt, although my great-grandfather probably tried to figure out a way in.

Making my way to the door, I grasped the metal handle, pushed the latch with my thumb and pulled. Screeching metal echoed off the surrounding woods silencing chirping insects and sending birds into hurried flight. Feeble light drifted in from two tiny back windows. The glass had long since disappeared leaving only the iron panes. Vines had begun the insidious process of invasion.

Two sarcophagi stood before me. I stepped to the side of one and blowing the dust from the ornately carved lid depicting a woman, her hands held in prayer over her breast. A rosary and crucifix twined through the fingers.

Isabelle DeSantos Goodhue
Beloved Wife and Mother
September 17, 1648
April 30, 1684
RIP

"Not big on sentiment were you, Jonathon?" My words bounced off the walls.

DeSantos? Spanish? What irony. My ancestor made his fortune from blundering Spanish galleons and ended up marrying a woman of Spanish descent.

I moved to the other sarcophagus and wiped the dirt away.

Jonathon Goodhue
November 2, 1640
June 23, 1705
"A Man of Integrity
A Man of Strength
A Man for the Ages"

Who thought that one up? I shook my head. Integrity? I guess even pirates must have had an ethics code.

Outside, the breeze rustled the leaves in the trees. It occurred to me that no one knew where I'd gone and that I was in a very secluded part of the estate.

With Evelyn's question still hovering in my mind, I straightened and whirled to face the door. Nothing, yet I

196

had the impression I wasn't alone. I remembered Stephen's warning. I needed to go back to the house. Rushing through the door, I pushed it shut and hurried along the path, not stopping until I reached the garage. All was quiet.

I felt like a fool for my panicked retreat. Of course, no one had followed me. I'd heard the wind or some animal scurrying through the underbrush.

"Liza, you are one paranoid fruitcake," I muttered.

I slowed my pace and sauntered back to the house. Evelyn sat on one of the veranda chairs fanning her flushed face.

"Hi, Liza. Where have you been?"

"Oh, just walking. What about you? You look hot."

She made a face. "I went down to the beach. Those steps are steep."

"The beach? What were you doing down there?"

She shrugged. "I wanted to see where Irene died. Most of the mess is gone."

I found her ghoulish interest disturbing. On my part, I had no intention of seeing that strip of sand until after the next hard rain.

Evelyn rose. "I don't know about you, but I could use something cold to drink."

I moved toward the door. "Is Giles back yet?"

"No, but I talked to him earlier. He drove straight through to Port Elizabeth last night. He said he got things straightened out and will be here in time for dinner."

Evelyn headed for the drawing room while I climbed the stairs to my room. I needed to wash up from the dust and grime of the crypt.

Finished with my task, I stood near the desk

undecided about whether to join Evelyn. I stepped through the French doors and strolled down the veranda toward the back of the house, pausing by Irene's room. Curious, I opened the French door and entered. I supposed the police searched it, but a jacket carelessly tossed on a chair told me no one had bothered to pack anything.

The room was a good size with a double bed, a dresser, two nightstands, and a small desk in the corner. Through an open door, I spotted a bath. The armoire door stood ajar. I gave into temptation and peeked inside. Irene's clothes hung on hangers as if expecting their owner to select them. Her shoes were neatly lined up—two high heels and four pairs of flat sandals.

I wandered over to the desk. Her laptop sat closed, a stack of file folders on top of it. I opened the first one—a genealogy of some family named Corrigan. The fourth folder contained a large folded sheet of paper. I unfolded it and gasped.

I stared at a copy of the original floor plans of Bountiful.

Where and when had Irene obtained them? Good heavens! Did she also have the diary? And if so, why hadn't she mentioned it the other night when we discussed how many island families kept diaries?

I tossed the folder on the bed and searched. The dresser held only underwear and an interesting sex toy. I reexamined the armoire, but found nothing. I was about to give up when my gaze fell on the suitcase in the corner.

Moving swiftly, I unzipped it. Empty. I was about to close the lid when I spotted a lump in the top compartment. I opened it and voila, pulled out a leather bound journal the size of a laptop.

The brown leather was cracked with age and smelled musty. I lifted the cover and read: *Log of The Marauder, Captain Jonathon Goodhue, Master.*

"Holy crap!" I exclaimed out loud. The original log? Jonathon must have had time to save it before abandoning ship. I fingered the pages. They were stiff and brittle. Too much handling would send the entire missive into dust. I gently closed the journal, gathered the folder, and returned to my room via the veranda. I had no intention of telling anyone I had either it or the plans to Bountiful.

The problem was—where to hide things? The folder could go in with the other folders Stephen had given me on my desk. The ship's log was another story. With Violet in and out on a daily basis, the dresser and armoire didn't work. The nightstand? Violet would have no reason to look there. And if someone *had* searched my room, then what would be the purpose of snooping here again?

I opened the drawer and dropped the book in. A knock on the door startled me. Drawing a shaky breath, I moved to the desk and called out, "Come in."

Violet entered. "Oh, Miss Channing, Mr. Albright is here and wonders if you could see him for a moment."

"Yes, of course. I'll be right down."

"He's in the drawing room with Mrs. Harrison." Violet dipped her knees in a small curtsey and left.

I smoothed my hair and checked my make-up before descending the stairs. Stephen rose from his chair as I entered. Evelyn smiled and sipped from an almost empty glass.

"Would you mind if I had a few moments alone with Liza, Evelyn?"

Her eyebrows shot up, but she stood. "Not at all. I need more iced tea anyway. I'll be in the kitchen."

Alone, Stephen kissed me soundly before opening his briefcase. He extracted a folded packet and hand it to me.

"Here's a copy of your will. Please read it over and if you need to make any changes, let my office know immediately. Unfortunately, I'll be flying over to Santo Domingo tomorrow. I should be back in time for the funeral." He kissed me again. "Wish you could come with me, but it's going to be a full work day."

I stroked his face. "Ah well, absence makes the heart grow fonder, or some such nonsense."

He kissed me a third time, and then pulled away when the front door slammed. Richard, Wyatt, and Isabelle walked into the room.

"Hullo, Stephen," Wyatt said. "Good to see you."

"Hello, Wyatt, Isabelle. I'm sorry about Irene," he replied.

Isabelle nodded and sank onto the loveseat, pulling a tissue from her pocket. "I can't believe she's gone," she said wiping her eyes. "Mother loved life so much and to die like that…"

"It's ironic that the new mistress of the house finds the body of the former mistress," Wyatt commented.

"Nothing odd about it," I said. "I was going to explore the beach when I noticed the railing was missing. I looked down and saw her. It was awful."

"Of course, it was," Richard added. "Please don't go making insinuations, Wyatt. You're as bad as Evelyn."

"How am I bad?" Evelyn asked from the doorway. She entered and resumed her seat in a chair.

"All that nonsense the other night about Sir Geoffrey being murdered."

"Murdered!" Isabelle said with a gasp.

"I just said, what if," Evelyn defended.

"Well, it was a damned stupid thing to say!" Wyatt declared.

"I don't see why. The police say your mother was murdered, too."

Richard glared at Evelyn. "Have a little tact."

"To the best of my knowledge, she hadn't pissed anyone off lately," Wyatt said.

"Other than that gigolo across the cove," Isabelle responded.

"That's right. He was upset when she turned down his proposal, but that was ages ago. A long wait to exact revenge," her brother answered.

"Revenge on whom?" Mary Ellen said, entering. "What are you talking about?"

"Ben," I informed her.

"And his motive for perhaps killing Irene," Evelyn added.

Mary Ellen sniffed. "My money's on him. Can't imagine what kind of story he spun for the police."

"For once I agree with Mary Ellen," Evelyn said. "I'll bet the police will find out it was Ben Irene had dinner with that evening."

If this continued throughout dinner, I was in for a long night. At the moment, I was pissed off at the insensitivity being tossed around the conversation.

"Are the funeral arrangements finished?" I asked.

"Yes. We'll have a brief ceremony at the church in

West End, and then burial in the family section of the cemetery day after tomorrow. I think a memorial service held in Cutlass Bay next week would be nice," Richard said.

I shot a quick glance toward Wyatt and Isabelle. Didn't they have some say in their mother's funeral? Or were they content to let Richard do everything?

Stephen nodded. "I have business on Santo Domingo tomorrow, but should be back. What time?"

"Noon. We'll also hold a reception here at Bountiful." Richard looked at me. "If that's all right with you, Liza."

"Very appropriate." *He's asking my permission now?* Being an afterthought didn't set well. I turned to Stephen. "Why don't you join us for dinner tonight?"

"Thank you, I'd like that."

"Excellent. Now, if you all will excuse me, I have a few things to do. I'll see you in a while."

Before I could leave, tires crunched on the gravel drive. A moment later the doorbell rang. Willie answered and led Chief Inspector Bradshaw into the room.

"Inspector Bradshaw, what brings you out here?" Richard asked.

"Thought I'd drop by and give you the preliminary results of some of the tests. Ms. Goodhue's blood alcohol level was .04, not enough to be impaired."

"Mother drank, but rarely got drunk," Wyatt said, his lips set in a grim line.

"But who would want to hurt Mother?" Isabelle wailed.

I revamped my earlier opinion about Wyatt and Isabelle not showing much grief. Wyatt's casual attitude masked deep feelings. Isabelle was softer, more prone to tearing up, but not ready to openly cry.

"It was Ben," Evelyn insisted. "Who else would she be meeting at midnight with a bottle of champagne? He brought her home after dinner, and enticed her onto the overlook. They argued, he hit her with the bottle, and, when she fell, ran like a coward."

"I agree!" Mary Ellen declared.

Mary Ellen and Evelyn being on the same side of anything gave me momentary lightheadedness.

Chief Inspector Bradshaw shook his head. "I'm afraid Mr. Collier is in the clear. Ms. Goodhue did not dine with him. She had dinner with Beatrice Hawthorne."

Mary Ellen stared with a look of total amazement.

Evelyn's jaw dropped. "Beatrice! For the love of God, why?"

"According to Ms. Hawthorne, Ms. Goodhue was doing research on a relative. They met to discuss the project."

"I remember she mentioned that the night of the party. Everyone seemed surprised Beatrice was an ancestor of Jonathon Goodhue's first mate," I said.

So Irene met with Beatrice. No doubt gathering as much information as possible before beginning her search. Then a thought hit me. Did Irene have more than just the ship's log in her possession? And if so, where was it now?

"I don't believe it," Mary Ellen said bringing me back into the conversation.

"What? That Ben might be telling the truth?" Isabelle challenged. "Look, I didn't like the guy much either, but I can't see him killing Mother."

"Isabelle's right," Wyatt interjected. "He may have been a gigolo, but why bother to kill this late after the fact? Doesn't make sense. And I'd like to suggest that both of you put a cork in it. Don't go stirring up trouble and innuendo where none exists. I'm here to bury my mother."

"An excellent suggestion, Wyatt," Richard said quietly. "I find all this speculation distasteful. After all, she was my sister."

The Chief Inspector looked like he wished he was anywhere except Bountiful. I didn't blame him. Mary Ellen's obvious loathing of Ben and Evelyn's snide insinuations didn't help anyone through this tragic time.

"I must be getting back to headquarters. If you have any questions, please feel free to ask." He touched his finger to his hat brim and fled.

"From a legal standpoint, accusations should not be bandied about in casual conversation, especially around non-family members. If word gets back to Collier, he could sue," Stephen said. "If you'll excuse me, I need to get home and change clothes before dinner."

Stephen walked with me into the foyer where he leaned down and kissed me lightly.

"I'm truly sorry you've stepped into this dynamic."

I shrugged. "I feel like I'm auditioning for a bizarre play—only the playwright keeps changing the script."

He laughed. "I see your point. I'll be back in a couple of hours. Dinner should be interesting."

"God, I hope not." I thought about the log book upstairs. "Oh, by the way, could you tell me where the Historical Society is located? I may want to see if I can find more about my grandfather."

"The main offices are in Port Elizabeth on Dunstan

Street."

"Yet, Irene lived in Cutlass Bay. Didn't you tell me that's on the opposite end of the island?"

"She worked from home a lot online. However, the Historical Society does have a small office in Bristol. I'm not sure where it's located, but shouldn't be hard to find."

"Thanks, Stephen. I'll see you in a while."

He kissed me again and exited. I headed upstairs for some much needed peace and quiet.

Besides, I couldn't wait to read the *Marauder's* log.

****

The *Marauder's* log was boring as hell. By the time I got through the faded text and bad penmanship, all I had was a ship's manifest. Ole Gentleman Jack had listed each item plundered from the Spanish in excruciating detail. Occasionally, he tossed in a few tidbits about life aboard a pirate ship. *Okay, privateer. It's still boring as hell.*

I descended the staircase at exactly seven-thirty. No gong had sounded, so I assumed Willie had finally gotten the message. The rest of the family was already sipping cocktails. Even Stephen had shown up. I accepted a rum punch and settled onto the sofa next to Evelyn. Giles stood by the fireplace.

"Glad to see you made it back, Giles. Did you get your problems solved?" I asked, taking a sip.

"Yes, finally. Island time is not necessarily the same to all people."

"I'm afraid you'll find that two days can stretch into a week or more," Evelyn added.

"Guess I'll have to get used to it."

Mary Ellen drained her wine glass. Richard promptly refilled it. Wyatt held a glass of amber liquid as did the rest of the men. Evelyn and Isabelle also indulged in the rum punch.

I shot a glance at Stephen who smiled. A warm glow spread from my stomach to my fingers and toes.

"So, you're going to another island tomorrow? Where is Santo Domingo?" I asked. Anything to keep my mind off sex and away from family matters.

"It's an hour's plane ride to the south. The island is part of the San Cristobal chain."

"Why are you going there?" Mary Ellen asked.

"An old and very wealthy client wants to make a new will. Normally, I'd send one of the solicitors, but he's insisting I do it. It's a pain, but the man is ninety years old and was my grandfather's client."

"Well, I hope you talk him out of leaving his fortune to a surprise relative," Evelyn said with a small laugh.

I was not amused. She may have laughed, but I caught the malicious look in her eyes. For two cents, I'd get up and dump rum punch on her head.

"Maybe it's becoming a trend in the islands to leave your estate to someone you don't know well as opposed to ungrateful relatives whom you do." I kept my voice cool.

Evelyn's eyes widened as though I'd jabbed her with a cattle prod. Mary Ellen hitched in a sharp breath, then let it out and gulped half her wine. Stephen's lips curved in a smile. Isabelle sipped from her glass. Richard and Giles said nothing, but stared at the floor.

Wyatt laughed out loud. "Good one, Liza! Guess that puts you in your place, Evelyn."

"I meant no disrespect," she replied stiffening her spine.

"I'm sure you didn't," I said. My tone indicated I wasn't sincere.

Violet appeared in the doorway. "Excuse me, Miss Channing, but you have a phone call."

I looked up in surprise. "Me?"

"Yes, miss."

"Who on earth would be calling Liza?" Mary Ellen said as I stood and left the room.

Who indeed? My first thought was Mother, and if it was, then something must be wrong at home.

Violet led me to the study where I picked up the old-fashioned corded receiver. As soon as the maid closed the door, I answered.

"Hello?"

"Liza, this is Ben. I was wondering if you'd like to go snorkeling with me tomorrow. I know several wonderful spots."

Even though not overly fond of Ben, Stephen would be gone and I had no desire to be cooped up with the rest of the family for the entire day. And while I'd love to go snorkeling, I had another mission in mind.

"Ben, that sounds great, but could we put it off until later? If you don't mind, I'd like to go to the Historical Society in Port Elizabeth."

"Of course. No problem."

"Thank you. I don't want to stay here tomorrow and I'm sure other family members will need Myron's services what with the upcoming funeral."

"I'll even buy lunch. Let's get an early start," he suggested. "I'll pick you up after breakfast. Maybe we could explore other parts of the island you haven't seen yet. Is nine o'clock too early?"

"No, it's perfect. I'll see you tomorrow."

Before hanging up, I heard a soft click. I returned to the drawing room. Everybody stopped talking and stared at me. Had one of the servants eavesdropped?

"Well?" Evelyn finally said.

I finished my rum punch. "It was Ben. He asked me out snorkeling tomorrow, but we decided to go to the Historical Society in Port Elizabeth."

"The Historical Society? Why there?" Isabelle said.

"Perhaps I can find more information on my grandfather. Maybe even mention of my grandmother. I still don't know her name."

Stephen frowned. "I'll be glad to take you when I get back. What's the hurry?"

"No hurry. I just need to get out, that's all."

"Afraid Ben will set his sights on Liza?" Evelyn asked, the malicious smile back in place.

Stephen smiled back. "I'm sure Liza can handle herself. And I'm not afraid of anything."

Willie appeared announcing dinner.

As Stephen held my chair, I hoped he was right. I didn't want to fend off subtle advances by a known gigolo.

On the other hand, anything was better than being stuck here with my family.

Chapter Seventeen

Dinner was subdued and I hoped to keep that mood. I walked with Stephen out to his car where he kissed me goodnight.

"I wish you'd rethink going anywhere with Collier. I don't trust him."

"I'll be fine. I need to get out, and this is the perfect time. Everyone will be dealing with funeral arrangements anyway."

He kissed me again, longer and harder. Just when my body heat rose to combustible levels, he pulled away.

"Promise me you'll be careful."

"I will, silly. What on earth could happen?"

"He doesn't like the family, so don't put too much stock in what he might say. Okay?"

I found it an odd comment, but agreed.

Back inside, I ignored the gathering in the drawing room. Bits of conversation drifted into the foyer, mostly from Mary Ellen and Evelyn. I didn't need this and headed upstairs where I caught up on my Facebook and Twitter pages, blogged about the differences between American English and British English, and e-mailed Mother a glowing report on nice relatives.

In bed, I opened the nightstand drawer and extracted the ship's log, carefully opened it, and re-read portions of it.

If nothing else, my ancestor was a meticulous thief. I wondered how much of the loot had made its way into the captain's pocket.

Can't blame him. If captured, the Spanish would hang him.

I finally turned out the light and snuggled in for the night looking forward to tomorrow. I was curious about Ben.

****

For the first time since arriving at Bountiful, I asked for breakfast in my room. I couldn't take any more of the silly rhetoric with my coffee. I informed Violet I would not be in for lunch.

Ben arrived at nine sharp. I didn't bother to say anything to the group in the dining room.

"You look good this morning," Ben said as he opened the door of a late model white Mercedes.

"Thank you."

I fingered the leather interior while he slid behind the wheel and wondered if Irene had also paid for this. I then smoothed a hand down my lime green slacks and hoped the shoulder belt didn't wrinkle the turquoise top.

"If nothing else, I'm tropical. I resemble a parrot."

He laughed and drove down the driveway. I didn't bother to look back to see if someone watched.

"Why the Historical Society?" he asked.

"I thought perhaps I could find some information about my grandparents."

"Irene probably could have helped you."

I wasn't sure I liked Ben. Okay, he might have been on the make with Irene, but that didn't brand him as untrustworthy. More of an opportunist. We all took advantage of situations from time to time. However, he was an American in a foreign country. That put us both in the same boat, so to speak.

"So, tell me, what makes Ben Collier, Ben Collier?"

"You want my life story?"

"Sure, why not?"

"I'm a very boring person."

"Few people lead wildly exciting lives."

He glanced at me and chuckled. "Okay, you asked for it. I was born in Des Moines. Never knew my father. He split right after I was born. When I was six my mother married my stepfather, and we moved to the thriving metropolis of Burlington, Kansas. Still awake?"

"Of course. Go on. What did you do in Burlington, Kansas?"

"My stepfather was a farmer."

"Did you like living on a farm?" I personally couldn't imagine getting up with the sun, gathering eggs, and doing chores that involved feeding live animals.

He shrugged. "It was all right. He was a nice guy, and we had most of what we wanted. Problem was I wanted more."

"How did you get from the farm to Grand Britannia?"

"My folks gave me a camera for my twelfth birthday. Whatever money I earned was quickly spent on film. As soon as I graduated high school, I headed for the Keys and never looked back. Sold some of my photos. Bought more expensive equipment. I never stayed any place too long."

"Yet you've been here for almost three years," I said.

"I like it here. I liked—loved—Irene. She was as free a spirit as me, but could never quite break the bonds of family and the money it produced. If the sheriff is looking for a killer, then he should take a gander at the family."

"You think one of them killed Irene?"

He shrugged. "Who else?"

"I'd hate to think someone hated her enough to kill."

"Your turn. What makes Liza Channing, Liza Channing?"

I regaled him with the misadventures of my life the rest of the way into Port Elizabeth. Most of the narrative was in generalities. My mind was on what I'd find at the Historical Society.

The Grand Britannia Historical Society was housed in an old home near the waterfront. The giant oak doors still retained the inlays of carved glass and opened into a huge reception foyer. The wainscoting was a burnished dark wood not unlike that at Bountiful. Subtle striped wallpaper ran up to the soaring ceiling. A woman with silver hair manned the massive mahogany desk.

She looked up as we approached. "Good morning, how may I help you?"

"Good morning. My name is Liza Channing and I…"

"Oh yes, Miss Channing, the new owner of Bountiful," she interrupted. "I'm Stephanie Wallace. Jean told me all about you. Welcome."

I had no idea who Jean was. "Uh, thank you. This is Ben Collier."

She glanced at my companion, and then back at me. "Yes, I know Mr. Collier."

I looked at him only to find a smile on his face as if he enjoyed the snub.

Before I could say anything, Ms. Wallace continued. "May I offer my condolences on Irene's death? So tragic. She was a valuable asset to the Society."

"Thank you. I didn't know her very well, but she seemed like a wonderful person."

"Oh, she was. And so dedicated, too. She loved doing research into the first families of Grand Britannia. Wrote one a few years ago on the Goodhue family."

"I found a copy at the house. But I was wondering if you might have more information on my grandfather, Mercer Goodhue. Perhaps something mentioning my grandmother, too. I understand many journals and diaries were bequeathed to the Historical Society."

"That's true," the woman said with a frown. "But Irene read all that we had on the Goodhues. I'm afraid your family was not as generous with material as others. Irene told me that Sir Geoffrey liked to keep things like that within the family."

Dirty linen wasn't about to be publicly aired. At least, not until it had been thoroughly washed and bleached.

"So, anything Irene had, she got from the old boy?" Ben asked.

"I would imagine. I know she mentioned several diaries of various Goodhues throughout the years, but nothing specific."

"Any idea where these diaries are now?" Ben persisted.

"None. I assume she returned them to Sir Geoffrey. If not, perhaps they're still in her house in Cutlass Bay. Irene frequently worked from there."

"I was told the Society has a small office in Bristol, too," I said.

"Yes, but that's more of a museum type of thing. It's on Canal Street."

"Well, thank you very much for your time."

"The pleasure was all mine. I hope you don't get too bored with us here in the tropics. Any plans for Bountiful?"

As in letting the Historical Society have it?

"No. It's too early." I looked around the foyer. "This house is magnificent."

She smiled. "It was built by Jonathon Goodhue's second son, Bradford. He ran the Goodhue Shipping Line."

Of course.

We thanked the lady and returned to the car.

"Do you feel like running to Irene's place in Cutlass Bay?" Ben asked.

"And do what?"

"Look to see if we can find those diaries."

"How will we get in?"

He smiled. "I still have a key."

Why didn't this surprise me? I should have said no, but curiosity pushed its way to the front of the line.

"Let's go to Cutlass Bay."

Ben drove along the southern coast of the island. The terrain was flatter and the road had fewer twists and curves. This was the area of tourist-filled resorts. To my left the water gleamed in shades of blue and green, the breaking waves adding a froth of white to the palette. Mother would have loved this.

As if reading my mind, Ben asked, "Tell me about your mother."

"Do you know you're the first person on Grand Britannia to ask about her?"

"The family could care less. They wouldn't care about you either if Sir Geoffrey hadn't screwed them."

He sounded like Wyatt yesterday.

"Mother is Mother. She's an artist. Mostly she paints still lifes and landscapes."

"Does she make a living at it?"

"A very good living. Janelle Madison works are very popular. She hasn't had a showing in almost two years. Likes to keep the work to a minimum."

"Which jacks up the price to the max," Ben said with a smile.

"Mother is not stupid."

"I was surprised to hear she ignored the old boy's command performance all those years ago."

"Mother was very close to her parents. She knew she was adopted from the start, so when Sir Geoffrey made his demand, she told him to go to hell. Wanted nothing to do with him or her long-lost family."

"Wasn't that a tad short-sighted considering the possible payoff?"

I squirmed at his question and at the interest he displayed in Mom. He needed a new money tree. If not me, then my mother? She and Irene were about the same age. *Or maybe he really is interested?*

I shoved the uncharitable thoughts from my mind.

"Mother didn't need money. My grandfather had a highly successful business. He owned a real estate company in Beverly Hills. Enough said. And of course, Mother prospered from her numerous divorces. Couple that with her income, and she didn't give a flip." I paused to look at the sea flashing by my window. "She would love this, however. Maybe I can convince her to come down—at least for a few weeks."

Ben laughed. "That should send Mary Ellen in anaphylactic shock."

I laughed with him. "It would certainly give Evelyn a new bone to chew."

"Good old Evelyn. God save me from bored housewives. On the other hand, she makes my day because she pisses off Mary Ellen."

"Still, I think barfing out that business about Sir Geoffrey being murdered was in bad taste."

He drew in and exhaled a deep breath. "From what Irene told me, the autopsy showed he died from a broken neck."

"So why bring it up?"

"To get Mary Ellen's goat."

We passed into the small town of Cutlass Bay. Here, the architecture remained in the Colonial style. Buildings were painted in cool pastels and the traffic flowed at a steady, but reasonable pace. Definitely a laid back atmosphere. I was surprised Irene preferred it to the bustling of the capital.

"Would you like to go on to Bristol before heading for Irene's? We could check out the museum and have lunch first."

The dashboard clock showed it to be almost noon. On cue, my stomach grumbled reminding me I'd eaten a light breakfast.

"I'd like that."

We drove the ten miles into Bristol. Smaller than Port Elizabeth, it still commanded a couple of cruise ships in a deep harbor.

The Historical Society Museum was located two blocks from the waterfront in a lovely pink building. We entered and approached the desk.

The woman manning it smiled. "Good afternoon. Welcome." She picked up a brochure from in front of her and handed it to me. "Would you like a tour or do you prefer to be on your own?"

"I think we can cover it on our own." I proceeded to ask about any diaries or ledgers that might refer to my grandfather.

"Not that I know of," the woman answered after offering condolences on Irene's death. "Irene stopped by occasionally, but not on a regular basis. New information and journals always go to the headquarters in Port Elizabeth."

I thanked the lady, and then we spent the next half an hour touring the museum. Most of the artifacts dealt with the maritime industry and the pirate trade, including a diorama of the Battle of Cutlass Bay. I left a twenty dollar donation in the jar as we left.

"Do you know, that's the first time I've seen the museum," Ben said as we returned to the car.

"It was interesting. I imagine it's something the tourists from the cruise ships take in while here. Where are we eating?"

"There's a place on the water called Harbor Inn. The menu's good and the view spectacular."

He parked the car and we strolled down the sloping

street to the piers. The restaurant sat nestled in the curve of the harbor with tables situated under an awning on the patio.

"Inside or out?" Ben asked.

The breeze lifted the hair from my forehead. "Outside. It's not too hot and the awning protects."

We were shown to a table in the corner with a clear view of the harbor. Hills rose on the opposite side of the water. The green vegetation contrasted with the deep blue of the sky and sea. Houses of all colors dotted the slopes. Tiny puffball clouds skimmed the distant tree tops.

"This is lovely."

"I was here several times with Irene. She liked it."

A waiter stopped by and we gave him our drink order—white wine for both of us. We spent the next few minutes looking over the menu. Salad and seafood along with the inevitable jerk seasoned meat dominated.

"Anything you would recommend?"

"The seafood is always fresh."

The waiter arrived with our drinks. We ordered; grilled grouper for him; crab salad for me. I sipped the refreshing wine and looked at Ben. He stared out over the harbor with a thoughtful expression.

Is he thinking about Irene? Did they sit at this very table? What did they talk about?

I wanted to know more about their relationship. So far, I only had the family's side of things.

"Ben, tell me about you and Irene."

He sighed and turned his gaze to me. "Irene was special. She didn't care what people thought. She did her own thing—kinda like me."

"How did you meet?"

"In a bar here in Bristol. The place was crowded with tourists and I bumped into her. Spilled her drink all over. I apologized and bought her another. We got to talking. I asked her out to dinner. She accepted, and it was as if fate had intervened."

Fate? Strange, Ben didn't strike me as the fateful type.

"At any rate, we hit it off and started seeing each other. She had a great sense of humor. Made me laugh. I'm going to miss her." He shook his head and drank half his wine.

Miss her so much you immediately ask me out? Once again I dismissed the thought.

"I'd think the family would be pleased she found a friend." That was my way of being nosy.

"Irene didn't speak much about anyone other than Wyatt, Isabelle, and her grandfather. Sometimes I think she was the only one who actually loved him. She knew how he was and accepted it—but not always obeying his dictates." He trained his gaze on me again. "What you really want to know is how much money she gave me."

"Why don't you tell me your side of it?"

"I was staying in a hostel on the outskirts of Bristol. Didn't have any privacy and I hated leaving my photo equipment lying around whenever I was out. Money was short, and when she offered to pay the rent on the villa across the cove, I was touched. I refused at first, but she insisted. Called it a loan. She'd seen my work and said I'd be paying her back in no time. I didn't like doing it, but by then I was falling in love with her. It gave her a place to stay when we were…together."

The answer sounded pat—rehearsed. I know rehearsed when I hear it. His story didn't quite ring true. And had he paid back the "loan?"

I needed more information. If he was pumping me about Mother, then I could do the same regarding Irene. "But the family saw it differently."

The waiter brought our food and for the next few minutes we ate. His grouper looked fabulous with the grill marks perfectly aligned. My crab salad was the freshest I'd ever tasted. Better than anything I'd had on Rodeo Drive.

The minutes ticked by, and we were almost finished when Ben rekindled the conversation.

"I remember the first time I ever met the family. Irene and I had been seeing each other about six months when one day she called to say Sir Geoffrey wanted to meet me."

I considered returning to the subject matter strange and, once again, rehearsed. Actors rehearse to get it right, make it believable. Was this his intention? I pretended to go along with his story.

"Ah, the royal summons."

"More or less. We met and I explained how much I loved Irene and that any money she'd given me was strictly a loan. Oddly enough, I think the old boy liked me. I let him ramble on about his ancestors and how important the Goodhue name was, yadda, yadda."

"Sounds to me like you listened." And maybe gleaned a crumb of how much the family, namely Irene, was worth?

He nodded. "But the die was cast. As far as the rest were concerned, I was a gigolo. It amused Irene, and since it amused her, it amused me. I was shocked when she turned down my proposal. Said she never wanted to marry again, but saw no reason why we couldn't keep the relationship as is. After that, things cooled off a bit. We were just getting back on track when she…died."

Irene's actions with Ben the night of the party hadn't suggested anything other than friendship. I continued to play along. I reached across the table and touched his hand as it clenched around the wine glass.

"I'm sorry no one thought to call you that day. I should have suggested it to Stephen."

He snorted and raised the glass to his lips. My hand fell away.

"Yeah, Stephen Albright. Supercilious bastard. He's not all he seems, Liza. Don't trust him too much."

Criticism of Stephen did not sit well with me. In the first throes of love, I didn't want to hear anything negative.

"He told me the same about you."

Ben ran his hand through his hair. "Stephen Albright has reason to see you not fulfill the terms of the will."

"And that is?"

"His firm handles all Goodhue business and if you're not around, then it's business as usual."

I sighed and wanted to choke him. "Exactly what is it you're trying to say?"

"Grand Britannia is like a fiefdom. Old families rule, including the Goodhues. They practice law, sit as magistrates, are heads of corporations and preside as chairmen on a lot of boards of directors. And every dollar raised or funded goes through Albright, Albright, and Swisher. Did you know that if you don't stay the full year, all the money goes to various charities?"

"Stephen told me. So what?"

"Well, did you also know that the Historical Society gets much of its funding through the Goodhue Foundation?"

"The Goodhue Foundation?"

"It was set up by Sir Geoffrey years ago. Same with the Mariner's Home, and a dozen other institutions. Money to charity is tax deductible here like in the States. And guess who sits on the boards of those places that stand to benefit if you go home. Goodhues. And I wonder how much of the money collected actually makes it into the coffers for which it's intended."

I drew in a breath. "Are you saying Stephen and his firm are embezzling?"

He shrugged. "Such a cozy relationship makes for a lot of temptation. And good old Richard is the estate manager—and I do mean estate, as in everything that goes to those charities, goes through him first."

And here I thought estate manager meant Bountiful. "How do you know all of this?"

"Irene told me ages ago. She was also relieved she didn't have to deal with Bountiful. And another side note—remember the conversation about Sir Geoffrey being murdered? Well, Mary Ellen specifically stated that at luncheon that last day, Sir Geoffrey said he *might* change his will." He leaned forward and lowered his voice. "Irene admitted to me weeks before that it was already a done deal. He'd told her privately."

So Irene had confided in Ben about the will change. His comments, especially concerning Stephen, disturbed me.

"Can you prove any of this?"

Ben sat back and sighed. "Not a bit. I can't offer proof of financial witchcraft. But all the same, if I were Evelyn, I'd keep my mouth shut."

I drank enough wine to moisten my dry throat. "Then you'll forgive me if I don't believe you."

"That's up to you. But think about this. If you stick it out, what's the first thing any sensible heir would do?"

"I don't know, ask how much money there is, I suppose."

"That's right. If it was me, I'd demand an independent audit."

"To see if there are any irregularities in the books. Forgive me, but Sir Geoffrey didn't sound like the kind to be hoodwinked."

"Sir Geoffrey was getting on in years, and he trusted his family. He might not have liked them, but he trusted them, especially his attorneys."

Thoroughly irritated with Ben, I snapped, "And what has family got to do with Albright, Albright, and Swisher?"

He stared at me, and then laughed softly. "You don't know, do you? You really don't know."

"Don't know what?"

"I can't believe Evelyn hasn't spilled the beans."

If he didn't quit this I was going to clock him one.

"Spit it out, Ben!"

"Stephen G. Albright—the G stands for *Goodhue*. He's one of them."

Chapter Eighteen

No acting class in the world had prepared me for this. I gasped in total shock. Stephen was *family*? Exactly how close?

"He…he never mentioned that!"

"Of course not. I can't imagine when the last audit was requested, but think of the massive conflict of interest. He can't even hand the accounts off to Swisher. He's married to Stephen's cousin, Veronica Goodhue."

"Is the whole goddamned island incestuous?"

Ben's eyebrows rose and an expression crossed his face that said he knew Stephen and I had made love.

I didn't care what he thought. My shock was rapidly turning into anger. Stephen lied! Even though it was a lie of omission, it was still in that gray area of not being truthful.

The son of a bitch!

"Exactly how is Stephen related?"

"His great-great-grandfather, Edgar, was Sir Geoffrey's younger brother. His grandmother married Norman Albright, hence the name change."

I didn't like the self-satisfied smirk on his face, but right now I was angrier with Stephen.

"So, that makes us cousins how many times removed?"

"I have no idea. Irene could have told you." He signaled the waiter and asked for the check before turning back to me. "I just hope you weren't lulled into some kind of relationship with him. Someone should have come clean."

"Damned right they should have, and I'm not in a relationship. We just had dinner a couple of times." I wasn't about to admit to Ben I'd slept with a relative. It gave me the creeps, no matter how far removed.

"Ben, are you going to the funeral tomorrow?"

"I would if I knew where and when."

"It's at noon in the West End church with burial at the local cemetery. Would you like to drive me?"

"Of course."

"Oh, and there's some kind of gathering at Bountiful afterward. You're invited to that, too."

I don't know why I suggested this—other than the fact I was pissed as hell. And hurt. I wanted a little revenge on Stephen. The waiter brought the check. Ben paid in cash, looked at me and grinned as we rose to leave.

"Something tells me the family will not be pleased."

"The Goodhue family can go to hell. I own Bountiful now and will invite whomever I please. As for Stephen *Goodhue* Albright...I can see it now—a couple of dinners, a little hand holding, pleasant conversation, and then the suggestion island living isn't compatible to my lifestyle, so why don't I go home. I'm sure he'd handle everything."

"I'm sure he would, including a nice settlement for your time and trouble. Probably even figure out a way to keep Bountiful in the family and not in the hands of the Historical Society."

"God, these people are more devious than an alcoholic director and a cheapskate producer."

"That I wouldn't know about. Do you still want to go to Irene's?"

"Don't see why not. Suddenly, I'm a lot more interested in my grandparents. I just hope Irene had something useful."

"Knowing Irene, she may have just kept a lot of the research materials. Oh, she'd return them sooner or later, but with so many Goodhues around, it made sense for her to have them at her fingertips. Another branch of the family might have wanted to investigate their genealogy."

"If nothing else, I'm sure she'd have made copies, especially of newspaper articles from way back when. Was there an obituary for Irene?"

He hesitated and drew in a deep breath, but kept his eyes focused on the road.

"Yes. No mention of murder was made, of course. The family would see to that after the obit for Sir Geoffrey."

We skirted the south coast back toward Cutlass Bay. Some of my anger had gone, but I still had a bad case of the "I've-been-betrayed" blues. Was I right? Was Stephen keeping me off balance with a little hugging, kissing, and friendly boinking so I wouldn't ask important questions dealing with the estate?

It came close to working. I even made a will with him as the executor.

My spine stiffened as a sudden thought seared through my mind. *If I were to fall down the stairs and break my neck, he'd have control. Mother would mourn, but follow his advice. She hates dealing with lawyers. She'd sit in LA and let Stephen Albright handle everything.*

I made the decision to e-mail her what I'd done when I got back to Bountiful. I'd have to warn her about possible conflict of interest without mentioning Irene's death.

Ben slowed and turned. The narrow paved road twisted up a hillside. He pulled into a driveway and we swept up in front of a charming villa. The stucco construction was painted a warm yellow with white trim. Cranberry shutters and door made a lovely contrast. The terra cotta tiled roof completed the tropical exterior.

"How lovely!"

Ben parked the car, got out, came around, opened my door, and helped me from my seat. "Irene had excellent taste. I often wondered why she didn't give interior decorating a whirl. Wait'll you see the back yard. It's got a sweeping view of the bay and at the foot of the stairs there's a private beach. I often dived on the reef just offshore."

We mounted the three steps to the porch, which ran the width of the house. Ben inserted a key into the lock and opened the door.

I stepped into a cool foyer covered with Mexican tiles. Straight back, I spied a terrace through a set of French doors.

Ben moved around me and headed down the hallway. "Let's take a look at the den first. She did a lot of her work in there. The view is fabulous and…"

He stopped abruptly both verbally and physically when he came to the doorway. "What the hell is this?"

I peeked over his shoulder. The room was in disarray. Books and papers littered the floor along with the cushions from the rattan furniture. The drawers of the desk stood open gaping like yawning mouths. Someone had given the place a good going over.

Ben whipped out his cell phone and dialed. "Don't touch anything, Liza. Hello? Get me the Cutlass Bay Police." He waited a couple of seconds, and then said, "Hello, I need you to send a squad car to 473 Cutlass Bay Drive. There's been a break in…Yes, Irene Goodhue's place…Benjamin Collier. I'm a friend…Thank you."

"I wonder what they took," I said. A tremor made my legs wobble. This was my second crime scene since coming to the island. Three if I counted the car business with Stephen.

He brushed by me and headed down a side corridor where he ducked into a room. I followed. If this was Irene's bedroom, then it, too, looked like a storm had hit. The thieves had been more aggressive in here. The mattress was askew, the covers ripped back. Dresser drawers were overturned and open. Clothes lay strewn on the floor.

The closet contents fared no better. The shelves had been cleared as if swept by a giant hand. He then checked the open drawer of a large vanity.

"Got her jewelry, at least some of it. Son of a bitch!" His voice was tight with anger.

I placed my hand on his arm. "Maybe we should wait for the police in the foyer or on the front porch."

He ran a hand through his hair and heaved a sigh. "Yeah, I guess that makes sense."

We only had to wait a few minutes before the local

sheriff, or whatever it's called on Grand Britannia, arrived. Two impeccably uniformed men emerged from a car.

"Are you the gentleman that called, sir?" the first man asked while the second man entered the house.

"Yes, I'm Ben Collier, a friend of the late Ms. Goodhue. This is Liza Channing."

I nodded. "This is very upsetting."

"Yes, I can imagine. Are you a friend of Ms. Goodhue's, too?"

"She was a relative."

"Channing, Channing, the new owner of Bountiful?"

"Yes." Word had traveled to every corner of the island.

The second officer returned with a cell phone clapped against his ear. "Yes, sir, the place is pretty well ransacked. I suggest sending a team of forensics out here…Through the back door. The glass is broken…Yes, sir, will do."

He hung up and looked at us while the first policeman filled him in on who we were.

"I heard about Ms. Goodhue's tragic death. My condolences. I'm Constable Liggett. This is Constable Ambrose. Could you tell us if anything is missing?"

"I noticed her jewelry case was missing from the vanity," Ben answered. "I didn't think to check if the TV and stereo were still around. Too shocked, I guess."

"The TV, stereo, and DVR are still in place. In fact, the living room seems to be untouched."

"Odd. Why not take those items?" I asked.

Constable Liggett raised his eyebrows. "Too big and bulky perhaps? Looks like they went for what was easy to conceal. Besides, it isn't easy fencing the big stuff. And why are you here? How did you get in?"

Ben shot me a glance. "I was showing Ms. Channing the sights and realized we were close to Irene's. When we stopped, we noticed the front door was ajar. Naturally, I investigated, found the mess, and called you."

I refrained from sending a glance toward Ben at his little white lie.

"Did you touch anything inside?" Constable Liggett asked.

"No, at least, I don't think so. But then my prints would show up. I was here a few weeks ago."

Constable Ambrose wrote everything in a small notebook. "You will need to come to headquarters for fingerprinting—just to eliminate yours."

Ben shrugged. "No problem."

"You were friendly with Ms. Goodhue?"

"Yes, we saw each other often. Sometimes at my place, sometimes here."

The constable turned to me. "Ms. Channing, why did you want to see Bayview?"

"Bayview? Oh, this place. I didn't know it had a name." Of course it had a name. All Goodhues named their homes. "Irene had told me about it at a party last week. It sounded lovely, so when Ben suggested we drop by, I couldn't refuse."

"I don't suppose you saw anyone about?" he asked.

"No. Everything looked fine until we got on the porch and saw the door." I still didn't look at Ben. It was just a little lie, but a lie nonetheless. Why did I go along with his explanation? I was now an accomplice in lying to the police. I should have ratted him out, but it was too late.

"But why go in? Why not call us immediately?"

Ben ran an agitated hand through his hair. "Constable…Liggett, is it…I was just checking to make sure the place was okay. If it had been, I'd have assumed Irene had been in a hurry and forgotten to latch the door properly, in which case I would have done so and been on my way. As it was, we found the joint a mess and I called."

His voice had turned testy and the other constable gave him a keen look.

I placed my hand on Ben's arm. "Officer, are we free to go? You said something about fingerprinting. Will it take long? We have to return to Bountiful. Ms. Goodhue's funeral is tomorrow."

"Fingerprinting won't take long and of course, we'll need statements from both of you," Constable Ambrose said.

"Yes, of course. Sorry if I sounded irritable, but as Ms. Channing said, this has been upsetting. I assume you will notify Ms. Goodhue's children, Wyatt and Isabelle. They're currently staying at Bountiful," Ben replied.

"That would be Mr. Harding and Mrs. Ramirez?" He turned to me. "I'll notify the local constabulary in West End as soon as we return to the station. I'm sure they'll call."

The forensics team arrived, and we followed the first two officers back to Cutlass Bay. Two hours later, we were on the road home.

"Why did you tell them the door was open?" I asked.

"To avoid complications. No one knows I have a

key. Irene never asked for it back after we broke up and I didn't offer. I'd hoped we'd reconcile."

"Who could have done this?"

He shrugged. "Kids maybe? A quick smash and grab and a trip to the local pawn shop. I'm sure the police will run a check on recently pawned jewelry. You won't say anything about the key to the family, will you? It might make things awkward for me."

I saw his point. Evelyn would no doubt come up with a dozen different theories regarding it. I could only imagine Mary Ellen's reaction.

"I won't say anything. It's none of their business who had keys to the place."

He smiled, reached for my hand and brought it to his lips. "Bless you."

I pulled my hand away already regretting my decision about having Ben escort me to the funeral.

We arrived back at Bountiful an hour later where he stopped at the foot of the front steps.

"I won't come in. I've had enough drama for the day. I'll pick you up tomorrow at eleven-thirty, if that's all right."

"Fine." I waved as he drove away, and then entered the lion's den. According to my watch, I had another hour before the cocktail ritual. I wasn't looking forward to it.

For once no one was about, so I scooted up the stairs to my room. I needed a hot bath and time to think.

Violet wasn't anywhere to be seen, so I turned on the taps and let the water gush into the tub. I quickly shed my clothes and stepped into the calming warmth. I rested my head against the rim and sighed. *What a day.*

Stephen popped into my mind, and the anger from

earlier returned—this time directed at me.

I was the one to blame. Since coming here, I'd broken my cardinal rule of men—get to know them before hitting the bed. I'd known Stephen Albright less than a week and hopped right into the sack. His charm had floored me and if I'd been on my home turf in LA, it would never have happened. But I was in his ballpark, and uncertain about the family, needed a friend.

Some friend. A liar, a possible thief, and a lawyer to boot. A master manipulator who's a better actor than me. How could I have been so stupid? From now on Stephen Albright will be relegated to the position of attorney for my late great-grandfather's estate. Nothing more.

What disturbed me the most was the fact I had made love with a relative. I wondered if there was some kind of law about kinship and marriage here in the islands. I knew the States had one, but no idea how close the two parties could be before it was allowed.

The water had cooled. I washed quickly, dried off, and rummaged through my closet for something to wear. My hand closed on a pair of dark wash jeans. Why not? I was tired of playing dress up. Richard had said everything in the islands was casual—although, his and Mary Ellen's idea of casual wasn't mine.

I grabbed a simple yellow t-shirt adorned with sequins, and shoved my feet into a pair of thong sandals. I'd wear this to any decent restaurant in LA, so it was good enough for Bountiful.

In this defiant mood, I descended the staircase and entered the drawing room. Mary Ellen, Isabelle, Evelyn, and Giles had preceded me. Richard and Wyatt had not yet arrived. Without the gong, I had no idea of the time. The clock on the mantel read seven-forty. I wouldn't be surprised if Sir Geoffrey's frowning ghost was in the room.

Seated on the sofa, Mary Ellen and Evelyn gazed at me and my attire with raised eyebrows. I ignored them.

"Giles, would you mind getting me a rum punch? It's been a hell of a day."

"Yes, of course."

Isabelle stood near the fireplace, a glass of wine in her hand. She blotted her eyes with a tissue.

"Liza, I just can't tell you how upset I am."

"I take it the Cutlass Bay police told you of the break-in."

She nodded. "The constabulary in West End called a while ago. Wyatt and Richard are in the study talking to the men in Cutlass Bay. Who on earth would do such a thing?"

"Some low-life who saw an opportunity," Mary Ellen replied. "What were you doing at Irene's?"

I gave them the same story we had the police. Giles handed me a tall frosted glass swimming with rum—a lot of rum. I drank a large portion. I needed it. During my explanation, Richard and Wyatt entered and poured straight scotch for themselves.

"The door was open? That's crazy," Wyatt said. "Mother always locked up when she was gone. She was very security conscious."

"The thieves probably exited that way. And she obviously didn't have an alarm system," I replied.

"How do you know?" Evelyn challenged.

"If she had, then it would have gone off when the thieves broke in."

"It was still a despicable thing to do," Isabelle sniffed.

"But not unheard of," Richard said in a calm tone.

"Happens all the time in the States," I added. "Thieves read the obituaries, look up the addresses, and break in during the funeral."

"I can see that happening in the States," Mary Ellen said. "But this is Grand Britannia. We have higher standards."

"Not necessarily. Just fewer people," I snapped back. I took another long drink to squelch my rising temper. I'd had it with her subtle and not so subtle put downs.

"Isabelle and I will be leaving as soon as the funeral is over. I understand only the den and her bedroom were vandalized."

"Yes, according to Ben they got some jewelry, but didn't know what else. I suppose you'll have to take an inventory. Looks like what we call in the States, a smash and grab. Break in, grab what's available and easy to conceal, then leave."

Evelyn leaned forward. "And other than the break in, how was your date with Ben."

"I wouldn't categorize it as a date. He invited me and I accepted. We saw some sights, had a nice lunch, and that was it."

"Yet you stumbled into another crime scene," Evelyn said.

"I've got to stop doing that. I've been on this island for a week and have been involved in more crime than thirty years of living in Los Angeles, a city with twenty times the population of Grand Britannia." I turned to Mary Ellen and said in a snide tone. "I guess Grand

Britannia has more crime per capita than I imagined."

Her nostrils flared, but before she could answer Willie announced dinner was served.

I sat in my usual seat and placed the napkin on my lap as Violet set yet another cold soup in front of me. I was in a combative mood and didn't care who knew it.

"Violet, you may take this back." She removed the offensive bowl. "What is it with you people and cold soups?"

Mary Ellen raised her eyebrows, a shocked expression on her face.

"I beg your pardon?"

"I like soup, but prefer it hot."

She stiffened. "Any time you wish to take on the job of menu planning, let me know. It's quite an arduous task."

"Fine. I'll meet with Georgette after tomorrow's gathering and take a crack at it."

Silence settled in the room as everyone looked at each other in surprise.

Wyatt winked and chuckled. "Let me know when it's burger and fries night. I'll be sure to stop by."

"Consider it done. I love a good burger and fries."

Richard stared at his wife who looked as if she'd been slapped. Evelyn smirked. Isabelle had a confused expression on her face. Giles spooned soup into his mouth.

"Jolly good soup, Mary Ellen," he said as if not hearing the conversation of the past couple of minutes.

Evelyn shot him a glance. "Oh really, Giles!"

Wyatt's laughter boomed.

I had finally taken charge.

Chapter Nineteen

I descended the stairs the next morning at eleven-fifteen. My wardrobe did not include funeral duds, so I made do with a light blue skirt with a crisp white cotton blouse. A chestnut colored belt cinched in my waist. Since the silver ballet flats hadn't survived their dip in Stephen's pool, I settled on a pair of low heeled, tan escadrilles. Voices from the drawing room told me at least some of the family was waiting. After last night's run in, I didn't think Mary Ellen would be pleased to see me. So what? I was beyond caring.

Isabelle, Evelyn, and Giles sat on various pieces of furniture.

"Good morning," I said in an even tone.

"Good morning," Isabelle replied. She wore a black suit with a cream colored blouse underneath.

"Morning, Liza," Giles said in his normal booming voice. "Missed you at breakfast."

Since his face was usually buried in his food, I was surprised he noticed. Both he and his wife wore dark clothing.

"Yes, I ate in my room. Not much appetite."

"After last night, I can understand that. What will your first menu be, dear," Evelyn said. Her tone was neutral, but her eyes showed a gleam of pure cussedness.

"I haven't decided yet. And I referred to yesterday's unfortunate findings at Irene's, not the dinner."

Evelyn patted her hair. "Of course. That's what I meant."

Wyatt, wearing a light gray suit, entered and headed straight for the liquor cart where he poured a shot of scotch. He raised the bottle. "Anyone else?"

We all shook our heads.

Richard and Mary Ellen swept in. Richard bore a grim expression while his wife looked under control. Both wore black. Mary Ellen even managed a wide-brimmed hat with a veil. Her gaze swept over me from head to foot and her eyes turned frosty. "Couldn't you have found something a bit more appropriate, Liza? I have a black dress I'm sure will fit."

"I wasn't expecting to attend a funeral, and besides, Irene didn't strike me as the kind to sheath herself in black just because it was expected of her."

Wyatt knocked back his scotch in one swallow. "Right you are! Mother hated pretension and never did what others expected. Did you know she showed up at the old boy's funeral in a pair of black slacks and a jacket with a Chinese dragon on it? All red, yellow, and gold."

"It was inappropriate and I told her so," Mary Ellen said.

"And what did she say?" he came back with a grin.

She stared at the empty glass in Wyatt's had as if yearning for a stiff belt. "It doesn't matter!"

The front door opened, and then closed. A few seconds later, Stephen walked in.

"Hullo everybody. Glad I'm not late." He smiled at

me.

I didn't return the favor. Instead, I swung away and strolled to the front windows. In spite of all my training, I wasn't sure I could keep my conflicting feelings from showing.

He looked good enough to eat in the navy blue suit with the light blue shirt and maroon tie. Angry with him or not, my heart thudded when he'd walked into the room. If I hadn't known the truth, I'd have rushed to him like a simpering nincompoop. *How long does it take for an attraction to end?*

"You're right on time, Stephen," Richard said. "Myron should be coming along in a minute."

Stephen walked over to me. "You can ride with me, Liza."

I finally turned to face him. "No thank you. I have a ride. Ben offered and I accepted."

"Ben!"

"Yes. Since no one mentioned transportation to me, I had no idea how to get there."

Richard frowned. "But I just assumed you understood you were included in the limo."

I shrugged. "A miscommunication, obviously. It's a good thing I was with him yesterday. He had no idea of the time or place of the funeral."

"As you said, a miscommunication," Richard replied.

"Liza, may I speak with you in the foyer for a moment?" Stephen asked.

Shrugging again I led the way out of the room and paused in front of a large mirror where I ostensibly checked my hair and make-up. I refused to look at him.

"Liza, is something wrong—other than what

happened yesterday? Richard phoned me this morning about the break in."

"Wrong? What could be wrong? Yesterday was upsetting, of course, but had nothing to do with me."

"You sound angry about something. What is it? What happened?"

"I do? Can't think why."

"Has Ben been giving you a sob story about how much the family hates him? He didn't love Irene. He loved her money. Don't let him lead you astray or play on your emotions."

"Let *him* play on my emotions? That's a good one."

The limo rolled up in front of the house closely followed by Ben's car.

"What do you mean by that?"

"Excuse me, my ride is here. See you in church."

With my chin held high, I breezed from the room in my best queen of the realm role.

Outside, Ben opened the car door and I slid inside. Within minutes the rest of the family assembled. Richard, Mary Ellen, Wyatt and Isabelle entered the limo. Stephen stared at me through the car window as he walked to his car. I ignored him. Giles and Evelyn hurried down the driveway to their car. Then an unsettling thought hit me.

Giles had been in Bristol, a stone's throw from Irene's house. Giles—quiet, plodding, boring Giles. Could he have searched Bayview to find the diaries? What could have been his motive?

And his car was a light tan. A light-colored car had run Stephen and me off the road. I bit my lip as Ben's words about a family member being the killer came home to roost.

****

Ben and I arrived after the others and entered the quaint church. Multihued light sifted through the stained glass windows and old-fashioned chandeliers hung from exposed rafters, the wood dark with age.

The Goodhues paraded down the center aisle to the family pew. Beatrice and the rest of the servants sat directly behind. I stopped, Ben brought up the rear. Only one space remained to sit. I stared at Mary Ellen who stared back with a cold expression.

"We need more room," I said.

"This pew is for family," she hissed.

My glance swept down to Stephen sitting toward the far end.

"Well, Stephen's here." Would she have an explanation for that?

Her nostrils flared and her gazed shifted to Ben, then back to me. She nudged Richard who moved allowing us to squeeze in.

Once seated, I fussed with the collar of my blouse. Ben leaned in to whisper in my ear.

"I don't know who's more likely to bust a gut first—Mary Ellen or Stephen."

"I don't really care."

I focused my attention to the front of the church. A closed white casket draped with a blanket of red roses stood alone and lonely. A two by three foot enlarged photo of Irene perched on an easel next to the casket.

"I'm surprised there was no viewing at a funeral home," I said to Ben.

"Here in the islands they tend to bury quickly. Besides, these old families like a big turnout in the church. More respectful, or something."

Organ music swelled from behind me and the minister emerged from a door near the altar. He spoke of resurrection and life everlasting. I even listened for much of it. My mind, however, tended to drift, especially during the numerous eulogies.

Other than my new suspicions concerning Giles, something about Irene's house bugged me. I understood the concept of smash and grab. I was from LA where it was an art form among petty thieves—assuming that's who had done it. Trashing the bedroom for jewelry, I could see, but why bother with her office? Her laptop was at Bountiful, and for the life of me I couldn't see what riches the robbers expected from that room.

I shifted on the hard wooden pew. At the moment, Wyatt was delivering a few words praising his mother.

"She enjoyed helping others. Genealogy was her passion, and she loved digging into the past. No stone was left unturned in her quests. I think that's what I admired most about Mother…"

Digging into the past. Holy crap! What if we've got this backwards? What if the thieves stole the jewelry as a cover for something in the office?

What if Irene did have the Goodhue diaries? What if there was something—a family secret—a present day relative didn't want revealed?

Would Irene keep such valuable journals in her house? Why did she only bring the manifest to Bountiful? Had this been where she'd found it in the beginning? Had she intended to return it? And what about those journals? The Goodhue family tree had been written a few years ago. What new information could come to light?

Unless, Sir Geoffrey withheld sensitive information from Irene.

I straightened with the revelation. It wasn't in print, but still existed in a diary—there for anyone to see. Information so sensitive a person was willing to kill to preserve it. Giles? *Oh my God, maybe a family member did kill Irene.*

Was Evelyn right about Sir Geoffrey? Had he also been eliminated for reasons not pertaining to his will?

****

The service ended and most of the mourners departed. A short walk to the cemetery elicited another brief Biblical allusion, and then it was over.

Without mentioning Giles, I tackled Ben with my theory on the drive back to Bountiful.

"You may have hit on something, Liza. Irene liked to finish her night with the occasional bottle of champagne. I think you're right. Someone in the family followed her out onto the overlook. They argued, Irene was clobbered, and the killer heaves her over the rail then kicks it down to make everything look like an accident. But which family member did it?"

"I have no idea. I still don't understand why she brought the manifest to Bountiful."

"What manifest?"

I hadn't meant to say anything about what I'd found in Irene's suitcase. But now that I had, I told him—minus the information about the floor plans. I wanted to look at those by myself first.

"Wow. You mean he listed all the booty?"

"Right down to every crucifix. And this being Spanish booty, there were a lot of crucifixes."

"Did he say where he hid the stuff?"

"No, nothing like that. In fact it was pretty boring. The last entry listed ill-gotten gains from some ship called *Hacienda Mar* or something like that."

"Is the manifest dated?"

"I think it began in 1667 and ended in 1670."

"According to legend, about the time *The Marauder* sank in a storm. Would you mind if I read it?"

"No, I guess not."

We followed the limo to the front steps and exited. Already the front lawn was lined with parked cars. The vultures had arrived.

"A lovely service, Richard," Ben said. "I'm sure Irene would have liked it."

"Thank you. My sister was a special person." He climbed the steps and entered the house.

What else could he say? At least, it was civil. No one else had bothered to say hello.

Inside the house, the dining room table and sideboard were loaded with plates of sandwiches, desserts and huge urns of coffee and tea. Servants I didn't recognize circulated among the gathering crowd with heaping trays. For a group this size, Beatrice must have hired outside help.

"Will you excuse me for a moment, Liza? I want to talk to Beatrice. She and Irene were very close."

They were? Other than the red-rimmed eyes the day Irene died, the housekeeper had remained almost invisible. Ben made his way into the drawing room where Beatrice stood near the French doors giving instructions to one of the servers. He placed his arm around her shoulders and led her onto the side veranda.

Near the liquor cart, a bartender poured drinks. I

headed in that direction and asked for rum punch.

As I sipped and turned I ran straight into Stephen.

"Liza, what's wrong?"

"Can we discuss this at another time?"

"No, I want to discuss it now—privately. Come with me. The study should be free."

He cupped my elbow with his hand. I twisted out of his light grip.

"And I said, no. Not now."

Before he could insist, Evelyn walked up.

"Really, Liza, having Ben sit with the family was insulting. I'm sure Mary Ellen and Richard were mortified."

"Don't be silly. What did it matter? And since when did you care? Besides, Stephen was there, too."

"It mattered because the family doesn't like or trust Collier," Stephen said in a clipped voice, making no comment on my observation. "He should have been in another pew."

A stranger came up offering condolences. Stephen introduced us. While they chatted, I wormed my way out of the group and toward Isabelle and Wyatt standing near the door.

"I thought you were leaving from the cemetery."

Wyatt smiled and picked up a sandwich from the plate in his hand. "We were, but decided to get something to eat first."

"I'm sure Ben's presence in the family pew upset Mary Ellen, but Mother would have approved," Isabelle said also nibbling on a small cake. "I may not like him much, but she did and that's what counts."

"I'm taking heat for including him."

"I'll just bet you are," Wyatt replied.

"Have a safe trip home and let me know what develops with the break in."

"We will," Isabelle promised.

I moved on to another group of people that included the minister—or was he referred to as the Vicar? I introduced myself, chatted for a moment or two, before moving on again. Along the way I managed to finish my rum punch, get another, and eat several sandwiches. Ben also circulated, but we didn't meet. The crowded room bubbled with conversations.

I finally found myself in a circle of family members, including Stephen. A man introduced himself as a magistrate. His wife stood next to him.

"So, Miss Channing, do you have any plans for Bountiful? It's a lovely old home. Don't see many of the old plantation houses so well-preserved," she said.

Since I was in an ornery mood, I decided to give the family a major league shock.

"I've been thinking about it. There's just so much wasted space for so few people. But the grounds are spectacular thanks to Mary Ellen."

Mary Ellen nodded acceptance of her due.

"However, I may not want to live here on a full time basis. I'm sure I'll return to the States when my year is up."

Family members looked between each other and smiled. All except Stephen who frowned.

"Now, don't quote me on this yet, but I'm thinking of turning it into a bed and breakfast."

As an actress, I had to love the reaction.

Richard's eyes popped wide, Evelyn's jaw dropped, Giles looked from one to the other in astonishment. Stephen stared, shock written all over his face. Mary Ellen drained her almost full wine glass and grabbed another from a passing waiter.

She gulped a generous amount before asking in a tight voice, "You've…you've…is this a joke?"

"Not at all."

"How very interesting," the magistrate said.

"It would certainly pay the taxes," his wife added.

I nodded. "That's what I thought, too. The third floor can be converted into larger rooms and the baths updated. A swimming pool and tennis courts near the garage will make a nice addition. It has everything needed to be a success."

"And where would we live? Certainly not with the paying clients," Mary Ellen said in an outraged tone.

"Of course not. Since I'd be displacing you, I'd kick in a few bucks so you could buy something in West End or the local village."

"We can afford our own home," Richard said through tight lips.

"Strangers sleeping in Sir Geoffrey's room?" Evelyn squeaked.

"Can't say as I approve of this," Giles said.

"You never mentioned any of this to me," Stephen declared giving me a strange look.

I shrugged. "I wanted to think it through. You, yourself, told me Bountiful required a lot of upkeep. It might as well pay for itself in one way or another."

"I'd rather see it go to the Historical Society," Mary Ellen spat out.

"You need to re-think this," Richard said.

"I have thought about it, and this makes the most sense. Grand Britannia is a major tourist destination. During season, hotel rooms are expensive. Bountiful is a lovely place. Why not let tourists stay here at a reasonable price? That way we can stay full up through the spring months. And with the right marketing, might even attract customers in the summer." I finished my drink. "Maybe I could fix up that little boathouse and the jetty, and then get a few small sailboats or some personal watercrafts to rent."

"You're insane," Evelyn said with a gasp.

"Just practical." Ben beckoned to me from the doorway. "Excuse me for a moment."

"Liza! Wait! We need to talk," Stephen began.

"You certainly do," Mary Ellen said. "This is all your fault, Stephen."

I weaved my way through the thinning crowd.

"Looks like you were in the lion's den," Ben said.

"I was. Sorry, I haven't talked much to you."

"No problem. I'm about to leave anyway. Just wanted to thank you for everything and ask if you'd like to go snorkeling later this week. I need to take care of some business tomorrow, but I'm free the next day."

Still in a mood to show Stephen Albright who was boss, I accepted. "That sounds lovely. Do you know I haven't been in the water since I got here?"

"That's a sin. I'll call you tomorrow."

He leaned down, kissed my cheek, and straightened with a wink. "That was for Mr. Albright's benefit. He's glaring from about twenty feet away."

He chuckled and left. As a few nights ago, I wiped my cheek.

Stephen materialized beside me. Once again cupping my elbow, he said, "We need to talk. Now!"

He marched me down the foyer and into the study, closing the door behind us.

"Now, what is this all about? Where did you get the idea for a bed and breakfast?"

"As I said, it makes the most sense. In this day and age even rich people can't afford to be burdened by the upkeep on an estate. You pointed that out to me."

"Yes, yes, I know. Mary Ellen reminded me of that a few minutes ago. But why not let the Historical Society deal with it? And what's this about you not staying?"

"I left a career to fulfill my great-grandfather's whim. When my year is up, I'll make arrangements for renovations, and then head home."

"Being an absentee land owner is difficult. Who will deal with the everyday running of the business? Who'll be in charge? I'm not sure Richard will have the time to devote to a Bountiful bed and breakfast."

"I'm sure his family duties are pressing and time consuming. I'd bring in an outsider, of course. It's about time."

Stephen stared. "You have been making veiled comments all day. Am I supposed to understand what you're talking about?" His eyes narrowed. "What has Collier been telling you? Whatever it is, it's nonsense. The family doesn't like him because he always mocked them. Irene got a kick out of needling Mary Ellen and let him get away with it."

"Leave Ben out of this."

"No, I won't! Something happened yesterday besides Irene's house being burglarized."

"What's the matter? Pissed off because I find another man attractive? Where does it say, I'm at your beck and call? Maybe I'm having buyer's remorse. I should never have slept with you. I'm very choosy about my partners and can't think of why I let you woo me into bed on such short acquaintance."

He scowled, muttered something under his breath, and then yanked me into his arms.

"Maybe this will tell you."

His lips crushed mine in a searing kiss. The action caught me off guard, and my treacherous body responded with a throb deep in my core. Unable to stop myself, I parted my lips allowing our tongues to tangle and explore. He tightened his grip and my arms snaked around his neck. My body quivered with desire.

His hands roamed to my derriere and pulled my hips against him, his erection pressing into my abdomen.

My heart pounded and the blood roared in my ears. My hormones screamed, yes. My mind was too far gone to think coherently. His lips did all the talking.

He broke from my mouth and trailed kisses up to my ear where he nibbled, and then said, "God, Liza! I want you so bad."

I opened my eyes and stared at a portrait of some ancestor above the fireplace. Then I remembered Stephen Albright was a liar—and a relative.

I pushed him away and retreated a few steps.

"I don't care how attractive you are or how much you turn me on. I will not make it again with a liar."

His chest heaved, but whether in anger or passion I wasn't sure.

"What the hell are you talking about? When did I lie to you?"

"When didn't you?"

"Liza! Make sense!"

I took a deep breath. I should quit pretending. I

wasn't that good an actress.

"Stephen G. Albright. The G stands for *Goodhue*. Kinda forgot to tell me you were family, didn't you?"

He looked like I'd hit him with a two by four. He rolled his eyes and ran a distracted hand through his hair.

"Collier. The son of a bitch. I wasn't aware he knew."

"It really doesn't matter, does it? The important part is *I* know. The next time we talk, it will be in your office."

I lifted my chin, strode to the door, opened it and walked through but not before slamming it behind me.

I paused in the hallway for a moment to gather my wits.

Damn, that felt good!

Chapter Twenty

I'd taken two steps down the hall when the door reopened.

"Liza, wait!" Stephen said.

I ignored him determined to make it to my bedroom where I could unload the tears threatening to choke me.

"Liza, please, I can explain."

I swallowed hard and blinked the moisture from my eyes, then whirled to face him.

"Oh, I'll just bet you can. And if I wasn't so disgusted, I might even listen."

Voices from the drawing room carried into the foyer and down the corridor. Stephen put his arm around my shoulders and steered me back into the study.

"Let's discuss this in private," he said.

I jerked away from his touch and deliberately chose a chair to sit in.

"Okay, discuss."

"It's quite true my grandmother was a Goodhue. Her grandfather was Sir Geoffrey's brother."

"Yes, the genealogy was explained to me. Tell me, did we do something the other night that was both illegal and morally corrupt?"

"Of course not. What kind of a man do you take

me for?"

"You tell me!"

"We're something like third cousins once removed, or maybe it's twice removed, I don't know, but it's far enough down the generational line not to be a problem."

"Did you check with Irene before you put the moves on me?"

"No. I never meant for things to develop between us." He ran an agitated hand through his hair. "I suppose that's how Ben found out—through Irene. And I never lied to you."

"Oh yes, you did. A lie of omission is still a lie. You're a lawyer, you should know. And while we're on the subject, how can you represent all the charities the Goodhue money goes to if I don't fulfill the terms of the will *and* uphold those terms at the same time?"

I wasn't sure that made total sense, but he seemed to understand.

"I warned Sir Geoffrey my involvement and that of the firm could be construed as conflict of interest, but he refused to hire different solicitors. Said it was family business and should be administered by family."

"And when was the last time everything was audited?"

"The charities are audited every year. The family businesses every two or three years."

"And the Goodhue Foundation?"

"It was established by Sir Geoffrey to consolidate all donations so they could be distributed easier."

"Who does the audits?"

"A local accounting firm. Collier's really got you asking questions, hasn't he? He's as much a meddler as

Evelyn," he said in a tight voice.

I ignored his reference to Ben. "And this local accounting firm wouldn't happen to have the name of Goodhue in it somewhere, would it?"

He bit his lip and looked uncomfortable. "The head of the firm is Giles's second or third cousin, and yes, he is further related to the Goodhues through marriage, but don't ask me the lineage."

"Oh, brother!" I rose and walked to the door. "I want an audit by someone not affiliated with the family. If I have to go off the island to find that firm, I'll do so."

"Liza, may I remind you that legally you are not yet in a position to do that. Since you haven't officially inherited, you can't demand an audit. I can, however, ask for one to prove there's been no funny business with the books anywhere."

"I'm sure the name Goodhue will be buried in the genealogy of that accounting firm, too. I'm sorry, Stephen, I don't trust you. Not anymore."

He closed his eyes and drew a deep breath. "I told Richard keeping this to ourselves was a mistake."

I paused with my hand on the doorknob. "I can just hear that discussion now. 'Keep her off balance with kisses and intimate dinners. She'll trust you and we can go on like nothing's happened.'"

"Liza, that isn't true. We wanted to see if you had staying power. If you couldn't complete the terms of the will, then what did the relationships matter? You'd leave, and Richard and I would deal with the consequences. I didn't expect to find you so…so…"

"Gullible?" I finished.

"No, dammit, so attractive. I was drawn to you the

minute you got in the car that day at the airport."

My shoulders slumped. "Don't compound your sins. If you'll excuse me, I've had enough of family, both dead and alive. I'm going upstairs. I'm sure you need to report to the rest. And tell them for me, that I possess tremendous staying power. I have every intention of remaining the full year and of turning this place into a paying concern. If they don't like it, they know where they can shove it."

I swept from the room. This time no footsteps or calls to wait were issued. I hurried upstairs to my room, threw myself on the bed, and let the tears flow.

Damn, damn, damn! How could a man I had hoped was Mr. Right have turned out to be so wrong? He had me addlepated to the point of idiocy, I might have done anything the man suggested.

I dried my tears, washed the traces from my cheeks, and stared into the bathroom mirror. A woman with red-rimmed eyes and a pink nose stared back. Now the conversation I'd overheard that first day here made sense. Stephen and Richard had been discussing the lie.

I lifted my chin. "Get ready, Goodhues, because Liza Channing is about to become the mistress of Bountiful."

****

I walked downstairs the next morning with a determined air. After my confrontation with Stephen, I'd been too keyed up to bother with dinner. Now, however, I was ravenous.

Richard, Giles, and Evelyn were in the dining room. Mary Ellen, of course, was not. Just as well. I didn't feel like enduring her snubs anyway.

"Morning, Liza," Giles said, a forkful of scrambled

eggs poised to enter his mouth.

"Liza! Hope you had a good night's sleep," Evelyn chimed in with a smile.

Richard said nothing, but nodded. His disapproving expression said it all.

"Good morning, and yes, I had a wonderful night's rest." I didn't add it had been artificially induced by a sleeping pill.

Making my way to the sideboard, I filled a plate that could rival Giles's, grabbed a cup of coffee, and sat in my usual place at the table.

"Are you and Giles staying longer?" I asked her.

"Giles is going back as soon as he's finished eating, but I have an idea."

"What's that?" I replied before crunching into a slice of bacon.

"I thought about what you said last night regarding Bountiful and decided you may be right." She shot a glance at Richard who refused to make eye contact. "If you'd like, I'd be willing to stay an extra day or two and give you my input."

"Good idea," Giles intoned. "Evelyn has a flair for decorating and seeing how things work in rooms."

The offer surprised me. I bit into my toast and chewed thoughtfully. Evelyn might be a troublemaking pain in the ass, but another viewpoint couldn't hurt. I suspected she suggested this as a way to needle Mary Ellen. Plus, the thought of being alone in the house with the supercilious lush and her now silent husband didn't appeal.

"Thank you, Evelyn. I'd like that. I'm sure you must remember the former decorating styles of the house."

"Oh, yes," she said, an eager look on her face. "I wonder if there's any furniture from long ago in the attic. Do you know, Richard?"

Richard gave her a frosty look, finished his tea, and stood. "I really have no idea. If you'll excuse me, I have work to do. The Goodhue Foundation takes up a lot of time."

On that verbal jab, he left the room.

"Guess somebody's nose is still out of joint," Evelyn said, chuckling. "Stephen told us you found out he's related, too."

"Yes, I thought the omission unethical and told him so."

"He was extremely upset. I almost told you one day."

I remembered that morning. She'd been interrupted. If I'd pursued it, I could have saved myself a lot of heartache.

Giles cleaned his plate and gulped the last of his coffee. "Don't know why they didn't tell you right off."

He glanced out the window. I followed his gaze. Low clouds scudded across the sky.

Giles rose. "Looks like rain. I'm all packed, so I'll be off. I'd like to get going before the weather turns. Call me when you're ready to come home, dear. Goodbye, Liza. Happy planning."

He kissed his wife's cheek, waved at me, and left. I stared at the empty doorway. With my emotions more under control, I decided my suspicions about Giles were silly. Or were they? I shook my head. He was exactly what he seemed—dull, boring, and slightly oblivious.

Violet entered the room from the butler's pantry.

"Miss Channing, when you're finished, Beatrice and Georgette would like a word with you in the kitchen."

"Thank you, Violet. Tell them I'll be down in a few minutes."

She did that little semi-curtsy thing and departed.

"Oh that's right. You'll be planning the meals from now on. Mary Ellen will probably refuse to eat and die of starvation."

"Nonsense. She can still do the majority of planning. I just want a few things I like on the menu, too."

"Knowing her, she'll abdicate out of pure spite."

I finished my breakfast and rose. "I'd better see how this works."

Evelyn also stood. "I'll be in the rooms down here getting a new perspective. See you in a while."

I made my way into the kitchen. Beatrice and Georgette sat at the large farm table drinking coffee. Both rose when I entered.

Pulling out a chair, I motioned them to sit. "I assume this is in regards to the menu."

Beatrice nodded. "Mrs. Goodhue told us last night that you would be doing the meals from now on."

"I only wanted to suggest a few items more to my liking."

"Oh, she was quite specific," Georgette replied.

Evelyn had this one nailed. "All right then, how does this work?"

"Once a week, usually on Saturday, Mrs. Goodhue and I pull various recipes, and then check them against menus used in the last month. She doesn't like servings to become repetitive."

"And do you also have input, Beatrice?"

"When her tray is taken up in the morning, she gives me by way of Gladys the number of people expected for lunch or dinner and I relay that to Georgette."

"Georgette, I have no complaints with your cooking. It's fabulous, but I don't like cold soups. However, I see no reason why others who enjoy them should be deprived. Perhaps on days cold soup is served, you could serve me a fruit cup or a glass of tomato juice. If Mrs. Goodhue no longer wishes to do the menu planning, then I suggest you choose what to serve and simply run it by me. Is that acceptable?"

Georgette smiled. "Yes, Miss Channing. I have a lot of recipes that haven't been used in years. I'd like to update them."

"Wonderful. Keep this week's menu intact, and we'll begin fresh on Saturday morning. Is there anything else?"

"Yes," Beatrice replied. "I'd like to take tomorrow off if that's all right with you. I want to go to the Historical Society in Port Elizabeth and see if they have any information on my ancestors."

"Oh that's right, Irene was doing work for you. She mentioned it the night of the party. Take all the time you need. I know it's important to you."

She nodded. "Thank you, miss."

"It was a lovely service yesterday."

Her eyes clouded over. "It brought me peace. I still feel guilty. I should never have allowed her to leave with that half-empty bottle of champagne."

I stared as goose bumps broke out on my arms. "Champagne? She brought the champagne with her to your place?"

"Yes, she wanted to celebrate. I'd given her my family journals, letters, and other documents a few months before. She returned them that evening saying she found the information invaluable in establishing Elijah Taylor's place in my family."

I stood to leave, and then remembered something. "Beatrice, did Irene also bring champagne flutes with her?"

"Yes, she did—one for each of us."

"I see."

This explained why the police had found the remains of a champagne bottle and a glass with the body.

"Oh, and miss, if I may…Mr. Stephen is quite trustworthy. He'd never cheat anyone."

"I see news travels fast. Who told you? Ben? I saw you together at the reception."

She smiled for the first time since we'd met. "No, he offered condolences and asked about the work Ms. Goodhue was doing for me. I overheard Mr. Stephen talking with the rest of the family last night. He is not a devious person, miss. Please believe me."

"Thank you, Beatrice. By the way, what are your thoughts on turning Bountiful into a bed and breakfast? I'm sure you've heard about that, too."

She smiled again. "One of the maids heard you in the drawing room. I think it's a wonderful idea. Better a commercial establishment than a museum."

"I agree."

I left the kitchen and sought out Evelyn finally finding her in the library.

"You know, Liza, I think the smart thing to do with the downstairs is to leave it the way it is. The layout would provide guests with several options."

"Yes, I can see that. Reading here in the library, small conversational clusters in the drawing room would work. And keep the cocktail hour. What do you think of small tables in the dining room as opposed to one large one?"

"By all means go with smaller tables. The study could either remain an office or be a business center. And the smaller rooms could be converted to viewing TV or watching movies. Perhaps a game room for when it's raining. Something along those lines."

We progressed to the second floor and viewed the rooms with the exception of Richard and Mary Ellen's. We stopped in the master bedroom last.

"If I were you, Liza, I'd keep this as the owner's suite. Don't rent it out. You might want to stay for a protracted period. It's lovely what with the fireplace and all the French doors. But I would turn Richard and Mary Ellen's room back into two, don't you think? Or perhaps keep it as is. A suite would demand a higher price."

She strolled over to the open French door, gazed at the fountain, and then turned back to me.

"I know I often say outrageous things, but please believe me when I say I'm glad Sir Geoffrey did what he did. About the will, I mean."

"Because of Mary Ellen?" I asked.

She laughed lightly. "Mostly."

Death—sudden death—was on my mind. "Evelyn, what room were you and Giles in when Sir Geoffrey died?"

"The one on the far end that overlooks the lawn and garage. Why?"

I shrugged. "Why do you think Sir Geoffrey was murdered? If your room was so far away…" I let the sentence end unfinished.

"We had about ten minutes until the gong went off. I was already dressed and Giles was still in the bathroom when I thought I heard a cry followed by a series of thumps and thuds. I opened the door and stuck my head out to listen. A few seconds later, someone screamed. I rounded the corner, ran to the head of the staircase, and found Mary Ellen standing there. Then everyone came out of their rooms."

"Everyone?"

She shrugged. "Irene, Isabelle, Richard and Mary Ellen's boys, our two. It was a full house."

"And you suspect Mary Ellen pushed him?"

Evelyn grimaced and rubbed her forehead as if in pain. "Not really, but I love to twist her tail." She glanced at her watch. "Shall we go on?"

Evelyn saw potential in the third floor. A wall out here and there along with extra bathrooms and updating the present ones wouldn't cost a fortune. I recalled a snippet of conversation from this morning.

"Evelyn, this morning you asked Richard about furniture in the attic. What attic? I assumed this had been the attic."

"Oh no, this floor was always designed for servants. The real attic is over here."

She led me to a narrow door at the end of the hallway next to a bathroom and opened it. Even narrower stairs rose in a steep pitch. I flipped the light switch at the bottom of the steps. Nothing happened.

"Bulb must have blown," I said. "I'll check it out later."

We returned downstairs where Evelyn rubbed her head again. "I have a nasty headache coming on. I think I'll lie down until lunch."

"I've neglected my e-mail and blog the last few days. I'll see you later."

She slipped off down the hall. I entered my room and rooted out the floor plans I'd found in Irene's suitcase. *Who knows? I might find a secret passageway after all.*

I'm not a whiz at floor plans, but these looked pretty straightforward. Unfortunately, nothing showed hidden passageways or rooms. All I saw were walls, doors, and windows.

I wonder if any renovation plans existed. Perhaps something secret was added later.

I abandoned the plans and fired up my laptop. I Googled "secret passageways in houses." Thousands of sites popped up, so I modified the search to Caribbean islands. The information was general, but satisfied my curiosity.

Some old houses had secret rooms and passageways built as panic rooms for safety or a means of escape. Slavery was an on ongoing enterprise when Bountiful had been built and rebellions occurred from time to time. I found it odd Jonathon Goodhue hadn't followed the safe route.

Of course, being a pirate had its advantages. He knew how to defend himself and his family.

I logged off the site, wrote a short blog for the newspaper and e-mailed Mother. I still hadn't told her about Irene's death. I could ask her to come down. Her company was a damned sight better than Richard or Mary Ellen's. Stephen and I were no longer on speaking terms. That left Ben. In spite of using him to bug Stephen and the family, I didn't see unloading my angst on him. A knock on the door brought me out of my thoughts. I opened it.

"Luncheon is served, miss," Violet said.

"Thank you. I'll be down in a moment."

I washed my hands, combed my hair, and descended the steps, then into the dining room. Richard and Evelyn were already seated. Lunch today was buffet style with sandwiches, salads, and one cold and one hot soup selection. To my surprise, Mary Ellen stood at the sideboard pouring a cup of coffee from an urn.

She politely ignored me. Richard sat at the head of the table. Mary Ellen sat next to him with Evelyn beside her. My place was set on the other side next to Richard. I was being isolated. The desire to see my Mother increased.

"How's the headache?" I asked Evelyn.

"Still there. I took a couple of aspirin before I came down. Maybe food will help. Thank you for asking." She rose and sauntered to the sideboard. I joined her.

"This looks good," she said, filling a small bowl with hot tomato soup.

I did the same. I'd come back for a sandwich and salad later. Mary Ellen and Richard defiantly ate the cold soup.

When seated again, Mary Ellen murmured, "I prefer hot lunches."

"Mary Ellen, I told Georgette this morning to follow the menu selections for the rest of this week. The buffet was your idea."

She glared at me. Okay, so the politeness was

superficial. Mother was so getting a call.

Evelyn, never one to pass up an opportunity, smiled. "Liza has some wonderful ideas for turning the house into a bed and breakfast."

Mary Ellen's soup spoon clattered into the bowl. "Must we discuss turning our home into a hotel? Sir Geoffrey would rather have seen it burn to the ground. So would I. I can't imagine strangers—*tourists*—living here."

"Now, now, dear, don't get upset," her husband soothed. "We have a year before anything can be implemented."

"And perhaps Liza will leave before then," Evelyn added.

I stared straight across the table at her. "I have no intention of leaving Bountiful."

"Good," she replied.

Mary Ellen and Richard ate quickly and left.

Evelyn chuckled. "She's mad enough to spit nails."

"I don't know why you brought the subject up in the first place. Needling Mary Ellen doesn't help. I have to live here with them, you know."

She yawned. "I'm sorry, Liza, but I've had to put up with her snide remarks and condescending attitude for years. I consider needling her a form of entertainment. Good heavens, I'm tired. I didn't sleep well last night. Maybe that's why I can't shake this headache. I think it's time for the medication."

"You didn't take it before?"

"The stuff's so strong, it leaves me groggy. I'm only supposed to take one every twelve hours. I prefer taking it at night to help me sleep. What are you going to do?"

"Maybe investigate the attic."

She yawned again. "Have fun. I'll see you later."

She rose and, wobbling slightly, departed. I lingered, finished my iced water, and then went to the kitchen where I requested a flashlight.

Violet found one and handed it to me. "Here you are, miss. Whatever do you need a flashlight for?"

"Violet, it is not your place to question why Miss Channing needs a flashlight," Beatrice scolded.

"Oh, I am sorry, miss."

"No problem. Evelyn and I couldn't explore the attic this morning. The bulb is burned out, hence the flashlight. Is there anything of interest up there, Beatrice?"

"Not that I can remember. Some old furniture, a trunk or two."

"Oh well, can't hurt to look."

I made my way to the third floor. Someone had opened several windows allowing the freshening breeze to air the place. Leaving the door open behind me, I climbed the narrow stairs and turned on the flashlight. The place was stuffy and smelled of dust.

Beatrice was right. There wasn't much to see. I peeked under dust sheets to view a few pieces of furniture, probably antique and of possible use in the third floor rooms. Four large trunks lay scattered about. I was tempted to lift the lids and investigate, but feared what I might find. My imagination conjured up dead bodies. My practical side suggested moldering clothes. At least one of the trunks looked to be a couple of hundred years old. The wood appeared intact along with the iron bands. I ran my finger along one and squinted at the result. Rust. This trunk wouldn't last much longer.

Suddenly from downstairs, a door slammed. It took me a moment to realize it was the attic door I'd left open.

I fumbled my way down the narrow steps and turned the doorknob.

It didn't budge.

I was locked in.

Chapter Twenty-One

I'm not subject to things that go bump in the night. No real fear of the dark. And I'd never had that rush of apprehension about closed in places. But now, the adrenaline kicked in and my heart pounded with unexpected fear.

I rattled the knob and banged on the door.

"Hey! Let me out! Open the door!"

I listened. No hurried footsteps approached. I hammered on the wood again with the same results. No one came to my rescue.

Breathing hard, I sat on the lowest step and tried to control my nerves. Surely, someone would hear me. I rose and used the end of the flashlight to beat long and loud on the panels.

"Hey, dammit! I'm locked in! Someone let me out!"

Nothing. I sat again and wiped the beading sweat from my hairline. Perhaps someone was playing a joke and would release me in a few minutes. And when they did, I'd kick their ass from here to the States. This wasn't funny.

I employed a few deep breathing exercises until I calmed down.

Okay, I won't be here long. Beatrice and Georgette knew where I was going. When I don't show up for the cocktail hour, they'll tell Richard or someone. It's not like they'll find my skeleton twenty years from now.

Since I was stuck here, I figured I might as well make the best of it. I remounted the steps and headed for one of the trunks. I knew enough to recognize trunk number one with its humped lid dated from the mid-1800s.

I opened the lid and discovered books—lots and lots of moldy books. The musty smell made me back up, but not before I sneezed several times in succession. I slammed the lid back down and moved on to trunk number two.

This was a steamer trunk and by the destination stickers plastered all over it, deduced it had found its way to the attic in the late fifties. It was empty. I peeked in the drawers anyway finding nothing until reaching the bottom. There sat a small book. Curious, I lifted it and scanned the cover. The lock on the side told me I'd discovered a diary. Whose I had no idea. Setting the flashlight on the floor, I fiddled with the lock, but years of humidity had corroded it shut. No matter. I'd mess with it later. I shoved it into my slacks pocket and continued my search.

Trunks three and four held various items wrapped in tissue paper including vases, pitchers, along with other things Mother would term dust catchers. I peeled back the covering of one and read "Limoges" on the bottom. If Bountiful needed renovations to become a bed and breakfast, then perhaps these things could help pay the bill. Antique lovers would pay a nice penny for them.

During my explorations, I'd occasionally go down to bang on the door and shout. No one came. I had no idea how long I'd been locked in, but a sudden peal of thunder sent me scurrying like a frightened mouse. Like the first night of my arrival, the heavens opened with little warning. Rain pounded on the roof so close over my head.

I rushed down the steps, banged on the door and hollered. The door opened. A dark figure was silhouetted in the doorway. I gasped in sudden fright.

"Miss?"

I let my breath out in relief. "Violet! Am I ever glad to see you!"

Her mouth gaped in surprise. "My goodness, miss, whatever happened?"

I stepped into the hallway, free at last.

"I was looking at stuff in the attic when someone locked me in."

"Are you sure, miss?" Her voice held a tone of disbelief.

I didn't blame her. Now that I was out, it sounded melodramatic. "I can't think of any other reason. How did you unlock it? Was the key left in the lock?"

"Oh no, miss. This is an old door with a spring catch."

"Well, that's dangerous." I put changing the lock on my mental list of things to do.

"There's a button in the doorknob you can push to open it from the other side. I don't ever remember this door being locked."

I inspected the attic side of the door and saw what she meant. In the darkness, I'd overlooked it and perhaps in my panic, had reactivated the locking mechanism.

"How did you unlock it?"

"I pushed the button on this side, miss."

Beatrice emerged from one of the rooms. "Are you still up here?"

"She was locked in and couldn't figure out how to open the door," Violet informed her.

Astonishment showed on her face. "Locked in? Thank goodness we came up to close the windows. You might not have been discovered until dinner. Are you all right?"

I nodded. "I'm fine, but when I get a hold of the practical joker who did this, there'll be hell to pay."

"Practical joker? I don't think anyone would do something so silly. The wind must have caught the door and blown it shut. I don't understand how it got locked," Beatrice said.

I suppose it could have happened that way. "I may have accidentally locked it. At least you found me. What time is it?"

"Almost four-thirty, miss," Violet said.

My unintended incarceration had lasted a little over two hours.

"I think a hot bath is in order."

We walked down the hallway to the staircase. In my room, Violet ran a bath. The tropical rain slanted in horizontal sheets blown by a strong wind. I placed the diary on the nightstand. It might make good nighttime reading.

I wasn't sure I bought the explanation of being locked in the attic as an accident of nature. Anyone could have done it. Activate the lock by pushing the button in and slam the door shut. The question was who? Mary Ellen was my first choice, closely followed by her maid, Gladys. I didn't see Richard in the role of vindictive joker. And what about Evelyn? Did she really have a headache? I dismissed that notion. Why lock me in after helping with the bed and breakfast plans?

Knock it off, Channing. You're becoming paranoid.

I soaked for an hour, dressed in clean clothes, and made my way downstairs to the drawing room. It was too early for cocktails, but found both Mary Ellen and Richard with glasses in their hands. Outside, the storm continued booming and flashing, although in a less violent manner.

"Wow, this is some storm," I said.

"It seems to have stalled out right over us," Richard informed me. "Happens this time of year."

I looked around. "Where's Evelyn? I'd think she'd be down here, too."

"I'm sure she'll be along," Mary Ellen said.

"Maybe she's still napping, although how anyone could sleep through this storm is a wonder," I murmured.

As I said the words a chill swept over me. No one *could* sleep over the thunder booming and the rain pounding.

"Maybe we should go check on her," I suggested.

"I'll go," Mary Ellen offered. She placed her glass on the end table and left.

"She wasn't ill or anything, was she?" Richard said.

I shook my head. "She thought she had a nasty headache coming on and wanted to lie down for a while."

I rose and poured a glass of wine. Being absent from the crowd was out of character for the world's biggest busybody and troublemaker. Uneasiness prickled my scalp. A crackling flash of lightning followed immediately by a huge crack of thunder made me scream. The lights flickered, and then went out.

"Damn," Richard said setting his glass on the mantel. "I'd better make sure the generator kicks in."

Before he could leave another scream sounded from the top of the staircase.

"Richard! Richard! Come quick!" Mary Ellen's voice throbbed with fear.

We both rushed from the room. In the gloom of the upper hallway, Mary Ellen stood grasping the banister.

"Help me! I can't wake her!" she cried.

"What!" I shouted.

Richard didn't waste words, but bounded up the steps with me right behind. We entered the bedroom just as the lights blazed on again.

Evelyn lay sleeping on her side. Richard leaned over and grasped her wrist. I put my hand on her chest.

"She's got a pulse, though it's very weak."

"Her breathing's shallow and slow," I said. "Call an ambulance."

Mary Ellen rushed to the phone on the desk and punched a button while Richard and I pulled the comatose woman upright.

"Evelyn! Evelyn! Wake up!" I shouted, slapping her cheeks for emphasis. Her head lolled and snapped. I repeated my actions. "Come on, dammit! Wake up!"

"Beatrice is calling," Mary Ellen said, her eyes wide with fear. "Get her up. Walk her around."

"She's unconscious," Richard snapped.

I slapped her again and shook her hard. Evelyn moaned.

"Oh, thank goodness, she's coming around. I'll cancel the ambulance," Mary Ellen said.

"You'll do nothing of the kind," I replied. "She needs medical attention."

Evelyn moaned again and finally moved on her own, able to hold her head upright. Her eyelids fluttered.

"Wass wrong?" she muttered, slurring the words.

"Come on, Evelyn, can you stand?" Richard asked.

"Huh?"

"Can you stand?" he repeated in a loud voice.

I rubbed her wrists. "Swing your legs over the side."

She moaned again. "Just let me sleep. I'm so tired."

"No, you're going to wake up." I pulled her legs to the side while Richard jerked her back straight. "Be careful."

Beatrice ran into the room. "Is she all right? What happened?"

"We have no idea," Mary Ellen answered. "Perhaps she's had a stroke."

"Are the paramedics on the way?" I asked.

"Para…oh, the ambulance. Yes, it's coming."

Evelyn sagged to the right in an effort to lie down.

"Oh no, you don't," I muttered. "Come on, open your eyes and look at me."

Miraculously, she obeyed. "Wha…what's going on?"

"Do you feel any pain?" Richard inquired. "Any tingling sensations in your arms or legs?"

"Left arm. Can't move it."

She'd been lying on her left side when we entered.

Perhaps the nerve had been pinched. I rubbed it vigorously.

"Does that help?"

"Little bit." She opened her eyes wider and looked at us all. "What…what's going on? Why are you all here?"

Her speech was still slurred, but her focus seemed to have improved.

"Can you try walking, Evelyn?" I asked.

"Don't know." Her shoulders slumped again. "I'm so tired."

"I'll make some tea and coffee," Beatrice said.

"I'll go with you," Mary Ellen replied.

They left while Richard and I hauled Evelyn to her feet, one of us on each side to support the wobbly woman.

"Come on, baby steps. You can do it," I encouraged.

She walked with a stumbling gait around the room.

"If she's had a stroke, should we be doing this?" Richard asked.

"I have no idea, but it's better than letting her go unconscious again. Come on, honey. One foot in front of the other."

Footsteps sounded in the hall. Seconds later Mary Ellen and the paramedics entered. Rather than give her the temptation of the bed, Richard and I eased her semi-limp body into a chair. The medical personnel surrounded her, slapped an oxygen mask on her face and took vital signs. They called out the results to each other.

Her blood pressure, heart rate, and respirations were low. I stood to the side, chewing my bottom lip. A few minutes later, new readings showed slight improvement. I breathed easier.

"Is it a stroke?" Mary Ellen asked the men. "Will you be taking her to the hospital?"

"Don't know yet, ma'am, but yes she's going to the hospital as soon as we can stabilize her," one of them answered.

"Ma'am, ma'am," another paramedic said to Evelyn in a loud voice. "Have you had anything to drink today? Taken any drugs?"

"Cer…certainly not," she responded. The mask muffled her words, but to me they sounded less slurred.

A gurney was brought in and they led Evelyn to it.

"Don't need this," she protested.

"Just do as they ask, okay?" I said.

The men carried her downstairs and out the front door to the ambulance. In the distance, thunder rumbled, but the rain had slackened to a few sprinkles. The storm had finally moved on.

"Shouldn't somebody go with her?" I asked.

"I will," Richard said. "I can deal with the doctors."

"Should we contact Giles?" Mary Ellen said.

Richard hesitated. "Not yet. Let's see what the doctors have to say first." He leaned over and kissed his wife's cheek. "I'll be back as soon as I can.

The ambulance left with lights flashing, but no siren. We re-entered the house as Richard walked toward the garage.

"I need a drink," Mary Ellen said heading for the drawing room.

For once I agreed with her. A good, stiff belt sounded like a damned fine idea. She poured scotch. I chose wine.

"Good Lord, what a week," she said bolting the contents of her glass in one swift motion, and then poured a refill.

I also took a generous gulp from my glass. "I hope Evelyn's going to be all right. I thought her color looked better once they got the oxygen mask on. It's a good thing you went to check on her."

"I'm sure she'll be fine. Strokes are funny things. My mother had one. One minute she was fine, and the next she fell over. Her entire right side went numb. Rehabilitation took months."

Beatrice entered the room. "Georgette wants to know about dinner. The Chicken Cordon Bleu is half cooked."

Mary Ellen heaved a sigh. "I'm sure food is the last thing on our minds, but tell her to go ahead and serve. Perhaps Richard will be back by then with news."

Beatrice nodded and left. Mary Ellen cleaned her glass again in two gulps and added another refill before sinking into a corner of the sofa. I chose one of the chairs.

I didn't want to think or talk about Evelyn. I sipped my wine and glanced at the other woman. She stared into the contents of her glass, a fearful expression on her face.

"I understand you're originally from England. How did you and Richard meet?"

"In Port Elizabeth. I was here on holiday. We sat next to each other at the theatre. During one of the intermissions, he offered to buy me a glass of champagne. I accepted, and found myself agreeing to dinner after the show." She stopped and drank half the contents of the glass.

"Sounds very romantic." I sipped my wine.

"Yes, I suppose it was," she said softly.

I had the impression the romance had long since faded.

"Moving to Grand Britannia must have been culture shock."

She shrugged. "I found other ex-pats in Port Elizabeth, and later in West End. We'd gather for luncheon or tea a couple of times a week."

"Ah, a little of merry old in the colonies."

She looked at me directly for the first time in a long while.

"I know it must seem strange clinging to the old ways, but I missed England terribly. The weather here is always summer. I wanted snow at Christmas and to feel a nip in the air once in a while."

"I can understand that. Yet, I'm sure your friends in England envied you living in paradise."

She snorted inelegantly. "What did they know? My mother-in-law was a whining hypochondriac. My father-in-law doted on her. When he died, that old devil, Sir Geoffrey, anointed Richard to take his place as estate manager. My mother-in-law had a miraculous recovery from the ailment of the month when Sir Geoffrey informed her he wouldn't put up with what he called 'women's nonsense'. She eventually remarried and lived out the rest of her life in sunny Spain."

"And you moved from your home in the village to Bountiful then?" I glanced at my watch. How much longer until we had news?

"No, that came later."

"I understand my great-grandmother's name was

Evangeline. What a lovely name."

"I didn't know her very well. She died shortly after Richard and I married." She finished her drink and rose. Please forgive me, Liza, but I'm not in the mood for polite conversation. I don't feel very well. The funeral and this business with Evelyn, not to mention other matters, have been upsetting, I think I'll have a tray in my room. Good evening."

"Yes, of course," I murmured to her retreating back. I sighed, finished my wine, and rose to pour another glass. A few minutes later, Willie announced dinner was served.

I ate the excellent Chicken Cordon Bleu quickly. Funny how eating speeds up when there's no conversation. I was done by eight-thirty and wandered back into the drawing room. Now, what the hell am I going to do for the rest of the evening and why hasn't Richard called?

Then I remembered the diary on my nightstand. Now seemed like a good time to read it.

I ran upstairs, grabbed the small book from the table and returned to the drawing room. I jiggled and pressed the lock to no avail. A letter opener from the study along with a few jabs and twists soon sprung the mechanism. I curled up on the loveseat and opened the cover.

Evangeline Mercer Goodhue, June 1952-September 1954, #10. Good heavens—my great grandmother. *Mercer. My grandfather's name.* And the years were slightly prior to my mother's birth.

I turned the page. The ink had survived the test of time with very little fading, and the slanted penmanship showed an elegance not often seen today. As with the family history, I resisted the urge to skip ahead to find what might concern me.

Having never written a diary, I wasn't sure what to expect. The opening pages were dated and the contents a mix of social and household duties. I read about bridge games, garden clubs, and her grief at having to put her Scottish terrier, Peaches, to sleep. She described the utter boredom of the island social scene, but attended the parties and dinners for the sake of her husband's budding career and political ambitions.

I glanced at my watch—nine o'clock. Where was Richard? Was Evelyn all right? I sighed and returned to my reading.

The household problems piqued my interest more than the social obligations. In August of 1952, my great-grandmother dismissed a maid for being "in the family way without benefit of wedlock."

I wondered what Evangeline would have to say about today's women giving birth outside of marriage.

Not all entries in the diary were on a daily basis. Days, sometimes a week would go by before she wrote the next passage. A few were only a sentence or two, while others covered as many as six pages. Most I could skim. Her discussion with the gardener about where to place the hibiscus ranked right up there with Jonathon Goodhue's manifest, and her indignation when a bridge club member was caught cheating told me she had a strong moral streak.

My interest picked up, however, in February of 1954.

Oh, what excitement! Mercer has just announced his engagement to Pamela Sykes, the Governor's daughter. The union could be very beneficial to the

Goodhue's, especially Geoffrey.

At last, something concrete. Mercer must have been no more than twenty or so.

Then in April, another entry caught my attention. *I leave for New York next week for some shopping before boarding an ocean liner for a trip to England. I wish Geoffrey could accompany me, but he's so tied up with business at the moment, I rarely see him. In fact, he's sending Mercer to New Orleans to investigate the possibility of expanding the company to the States.*

She didn't say which company. Then the timing hit me. Mother was born in late February, 1955. The dates matched. Tires crunching on the gravel outside broke my concentration. Richard was back.

The front door opened and closed. He entered the room and headed straight for the liquor cart where he poured a large quantity of scotch into a tumbler.

"Richard? Is everything all right? How's Evelyn?"

He drank a sizable portion before answering. "Evelyn is going to be fine, but I'm not sure everything's all right."

Chapter Twenty-Two

The grim look on his face puzzled me. "I don't understand. You said Evelyn's on the mend."

He sighed. "They're keeping her overnight for observation and will perform some neurological tests in the morning."

"Did she have a stroke?"

He shook his head. "It's a precaution against one of those mini-strokes that can come and go quickly. They let me see her before I left. She was walking and talking with no problem."

"Walking?" So soon after we had practically dragged her around the bedroom?

He nodded. "She had an IV, of course, but was arguing with the doctors about staying. To show she was fine, she got out of bed and walked."

"So what is it you're not telling me?"

He finished his drink and picked up the bottle to refill the glass, then stared before putting both back onto the cart.

"The doctor's think she took an overdose of migraine medication."

"How did she do that? She told me the pills are pretty strong stuff. They tend to knock her out."

He shrugged and sipped his drink. "Evelyn told me she laid down to see if the headache would go away on its own. It didn't, so she took two aspirin before she came down to luncheon."

"In the hopes food might help." My friend in L. A. drank caffeinated soda daily on the theory it helped soothe any migraine coming her way.

Richard nodded. "It didn't, so when she returned upstairs, she took her migraine med. The doctors think she may have taken the migraine medication earlier by mistake."

"Are the pills similar?"

"I have no idea. Of course, if she was in pain, she might not notice the mistake—confuse one bottle for the other."

I remembered Evelyn yawning after Mary Ellen had left the table.

"She complained of being sleepy after lunch. What does Evelyn say?"

"She denies being that stupid, but admits the pills are side by side on the bathroom vanity."

"So, it was a simple error. Has anyone let Giles know?"

"I called him from the hospital. He's leaving right away and will go straight there to spend the night with Evelyn. If you'll excuse me, Liza, I need to see Mary Ellen. If she's still awake she'll want a progress report."

"Of course. Goodnight, Richard."

He left the room.

Thank God, we found her when we did. She could have died.

Then I remembered a play I'd once been in—a murder mystery with a plot twist. Evelyn's possible overdose and the victim in the play had a chillingly similar MO. I shook my head. *Don't be silly. Who'd want to harm Evelyn?* But then who'd want to harm Irene? I glanced at the diary in my hand. I'd read further once in bed, but first I had to check something out.

I hurried upstairs and turned toward Evelyn's room. Light glowed from under the closed door to Richard and Mary Ellen's domain. The wood muffled the sound of raised voices. Good. Their altercation guaranteed I wouldn't be disturbed.

Making my way down the hall, I entered Evelyn's brightly lit chamber. The mess left by the paramedics was still on the floor. I ignored it and headed for the bathroom. The light was on in here, too. I made a beeline for the vanity. Sure enough, two bottles of pills sat next to each other, but at least five inches separated them. Even in pain, would Evelyn accidentally take the wrong one?

I reached for the migraine medication first. The information on the label showed the dosage as one in a twelve hour period. It had been filled two weeks ago. I opened the bottle and shook one into my hand. It looked similar to aspirin.

I recapped the bottle and opened the aspirin, shaking a couple into my hand. One of the pills was slightly smaller and more yellowish in appearance— just like the migraine medication.

A door slamming down the hall made me jump. I replaced the pills in the aspirin bottle and hurried to the door. Richard turned the corner and headed straight for Evelyn's room. I didn't want to be caught here, especially with my suspicions as to what had occurred. Where could I hide? This old house had few closets. My gaze darted around the room. An armoire stood near the corner. I rushed over and squeezed between its side and the wall. Richard entered a moment later.

I inhaled a deep breath and tried to hold it. Surely he could hear my pounding heart. I exhaled softly when he went straight to the bathroom. Unable to resist, I poked my head around the corner of the armoire, but saw nothing. The bath was not in my line of sight. I pulled back and waited. An eternity passed until Richard came out and left the room.

I eased from my hiding place with a sigh of relief, and then hustled into the bath. The pill bottles were now side by side with little space between them. I opened the aspirin again. No smaller, yellowish pill was there.

Standing in the hallway, I wondered when the substitution had taken place. A lot of people had been in the house during the funeral.

Anyone could have done it. I was rationalizing and knew it. The alternative wasn't pleasant.

I tiptoed downstairs to retrieve the diary. Back in my room, I locked the door for the first time since arriving. Evelyn was a pain in the ass, but that wasn't a motive for murder.

Mary Ellen was the obvious suspect. My stomach churned at the thought. Was that what the argument was about? Had Mary Ellen tampered with the pills? Or had Richard? Was he covering for his wife, or himself?

I replaced the diary on the nightstand and got ready for bed. I was tired of reading, tired of thinking, and just plain tired.

Curled up under the sheet, I shivered with fear.

I sucked in a ragged breath wishing with all my heart Stephen was here. In spite of my anger, I missed him. I wanted his strong arms around me, and his confident voice telling me everything would be all right.

Unfortunately, it wasn't.

****

I tossed and turned most of the night not falling asleep until after three o'clock. As a result, I was late for breakfast. Richard was already gone, presumably to the study and whatever it was he did there.

I picked at my food, not really hungry, but needing to eat. Violet entered the room and stood near the sideboard.

"Will you be having more eggs and bacon, miss?"

"No, you can take everything away. I'm not too hungry this morning."

She hesitated. "Please don't think it forward of me, but how is Mrs. Harrison?"

"It's not forward, and Mrs. Harrison is fine. She's going to have a few tests, and should be back soon."

"Oh, I'm so glad, miss." She picked up the chafing dish with the eggs and headed for the butler's pantry.

"Violet, do you know what's being served for lunch and dinner today?"

"I believe Georgette has poached salmon for luncheon and beef Wellington for dinner."

"I see. Thank you." Poached salmon wasn't my favorite, but the Wellington sounded good. I contemplated another cup of coffee when one of the household maids entered.

"You have a phone call, miss. You can take it in the library."

"Thank you," I said, rising.

As I hurried down the hall, I hoped Stephen was

calling. After the events of yesterday, I desperately wanted—no needed—to talk to him. I'd reacted with anger on the day of the funeral without giving him a real chance to explain. In spite of the cousin thing, I couldn't squash my feelings for him. Somewhere along the line, I had slipped from attracted to involved to serious.

I shut the library door behind me and picked up the extension.

"Hello?" My voice had a breathless, hopeful sound.

"Good morning, gorgeous," Ben said. "How goes it this fine day?"

My shoulders sagged. "Oh, good morning, Ben."

"That didn't sound too enthusiastic."

"Sorry, but I didn't sleep well last night."

"Suppose I make up for that this afternoon? I have a few things to do, but how about I pick you up after lunch and give you a guided tour of the island from the sea? My boat's docked at the Marina in West End."

His invitation sounded interesting, but with Evelyn due home I wanted to be here when she arrived.

"Ben, could I take a rain check? Evelyn had to go to the hospital last night and should be home this afternoon. I'd like to be around when she gets released."

"Hospital? Why, for pity's sake?"

I wanted to talk to someone about last night, but Ben wasn't the person. I wasn't ready to share family problems of this extent with him.

"Oh, she had a bad reaction to some medication. Nothing terribly serious."

Silence hung on the line for a moment. "I see. I kind of thought they'd be gone by now."

"Giles left, but Evelyn stayed behind. She gave me some nice tips on my plans for Bountiful."

"Which are?"

"I'm thinking a bed and breakfast. Upkeep is a lot on this house, and it needs to pay its own way. Evelyn offered her opinions."

"I'll just bet she did. Probably did it to bug Mary Ellen."

"Perhaps."

"Tell you what. Let's make a date for tomorrow. I'll pick you up around ten, and we can have lunch at this great little spot I know on the south coast."

I hesitated, not really wanting to go, but not willing to stay here, either. Stephen's face flashed in front of my eyes. *What? You gonna sit around and wait until he calls? Since when did you ever do that?*

"That sounds lovely, Ben. I'll see you tomorrow."

"Good. Have a nice day. Hope Evelyn's better."

He hung up, and I waited a split second before doing the same. A soft click told me someone had listened. I replaced the receiver wondering who was spying on me, and why.

****

I had no idea what Mary Ellen did with her days and didn't care, so I was surprised to find her in the foyer dressed in a powder blue suit, heels, and pulling on a pair of gloves. Other than onstage, I'd never seen anyone wear gloves, but watching her smooth the white fabric over her hands seemed natural.

She looked up with a calm expression. "Oh, good morning, Liza. Please tell Georgette I won't be in for luncheon. Neither will Richard. We're going into West End for the day. We'll see you tonight at dinner."

288

I thought about last night and wondered what they were up to. "Have you heard any news about Evelyn?"

"Not yet. I imagine Giles will call when he knows something."

Richard descended the staircase. "Ah, there you are, Liza. I'm afraid you're on your own for a while. Won't be too long. Just thought Mary Ellen needed to get out and about for a change. It's been a long week."

"Yes, it has. I'll be fine. Have a nice time."

Mary Ellen nodded regally and swept from the foyer to the limo parked out front. Richard followed. Myron held the door and, a few moments later, the car glided down the drive.

I hustled to the kitchen. No sense letting good salmon go to waste. I found Georgette and several others finishing the breakfast remains.

"There's no need to go to so much trouble for me," I said after giving her the news. "I'll be happy with a simple salad."

She frowned for a moment. "I'll go ahead and make the salmon, but use it in a cold salad. If you don't mind, I can serve it to the staff, too."

"That's fine with me. Did Beatrice leave already for Port Elizabeth?"

"I suppose so, ma'am. She has family in the city and wanted to spend some time with them. She'll be back tomorrow morning."

I returned upstairs and stood in the foyer. I didn't have a damned thing to do until lunch, so went up to grab the diary I'd discarded last night.

Settled in the drawing room, I re-opened the book where I'd left off. It wasn't all that interesting. Evangeline described the voyage over to England and her time there in excruciating detail. I skipped over several pages, not fascinated with who wore what where. I was nearing the end of the diary when the date June 6, 1954, leaped out at me.

Mercer has returned unexpectedly from New Orleans with devastating news. He met some waitress and says he's fallen in love. He actually wants to marry her! Geoffrey is livid. Oh, I can't even describe the argument that ensued. I had to leave the room.

June 1954. My mother was born in February of 1955, which meant the deed had been done. The question was did my grandfather know his girlfriend was pregnant? The entry continued the following day.

I cannot believe Mercer has chosen now to grow a spine. Unbeknownst to us, he saw Pamela this morning and broke off the engagement! I was worried I'd have to call the doctor for Geoffrey. My son seems bound and determined to marry this...this person. However, knowing my husband, he has a plan for making things right.

I wondered what "growing a spine" meant. That my grandfather was under Sir Geoffrey's thumb like the rest of the family? What kind of tactics did my great-grandfather use to have my grandfather abandon his love?

The diary entries for the next two weeks alternated between anger and high anxiety. Evangeline ranted and ripped everyone concerned, with language that bordered on insane. This was one pissed off woman. The next entry left me cold with disgust.

Leave it to Geoffrey to find the solution to our little problem. Under the guise of understanding, I talked to Mercer and managed to discover the girl's name—

Cassandra—who ever heard of a waitress named Cassandra—and the restaurant where she works. My husband immediately sent an emissary to the States to deal with the little gold digger. I later learned a hefty sum of money was offered. I knew the little witch had a price. They all do. A letter from the girl arrived for my son a week later, breaking off their romance. Geoffrey has sent Mercer off to the shipping offices in Trinidad for a few months. Now, if only we can repair the damage done with Pamela.

That was the last entry.

Yeah, only Pamela probably told them all to take a hike. I closed the diary. What a sordid bunch of snobs! Evangeline's name may have been lovely, but she and Mary Ellen would have been the best of chums.

Cassandra. I now had a name. Had my grandmother taken money to end the affair? Had she done so knowing she was pregnant? What kind of pressure had my great-grandfather exerted for her to accept? Or hadn't any pressure been necessary?

I didn't like my biological grandparents—wimpy and greedy—any better than my great-grandparents—snobbish and controlling. *Thank goodness Mother was adopted by people with strong morals.*

Violet entered the room. "Mr. Harrison is on the phone for you, miss."

I took the call in the study. "Hello, Giles. How's Evelyn?"

"Much better. We're awaiting the results of the last tests. Should be home in time for dinner. We'll stay the night and then go home first thing in the morning."

"I'm so glad."

"Uh, Liza, is Richard there by any chance?"

"No, he and Mary Ellen left for West End a while ago."

He paused. "I see. Never mind. I'll get a hold of him on his cell. See you later."

Giles rang off. I returned to the drawing room, picked up the diary, and went upstairs where I tossed it into the desk drawer.

So Cassandra, probably called Cassie or Sandy, had lived in New Orleans in 1954. Was she a native of the Crescent City? And what did Mercer do with his life after the break-up?

How hard would it be to find a birth certificate from February 26, 1955? Especially with the mother's name listed as Cassandra? Could my grandmother still be alive?

I had no idea how to go about looking for her. *And do I really want to? What would Mother say? Knowing Mother, she probably doesn't give a damn.*

If I wanted to institute a search, I needed the help of professionals, and who more professional than my stateside attorney?

I e-mailed Adam Wyles with the information at hand and authorized him to hire someone experienced in finding lost relatives.

So far, the family wasn't forthcoming with information concerning my grandfather. *But I'll bet Stephen could find what I need to know.*

****

After a solitary lunch of salmon salad with refreshing cucumber vinaigrette, I found myself at loose ends. The weather was cloudy and warm, but the sea breeze kept heat and humidity at comfortable levels. I wandered outside and made my way through the maze to the overlook. A temporary barricade was wedged against the missing rail and supports. Averting my gaze, I opted for the steps heading down to the beach. At the bottom, I removed my sandals and wiggled my toes in the sand. The aqua water of the cove lapped gently at the shore fifteen yards away. I moved closer stepping over a small ring of shells marking the high tide level and allowed the cool water to caress my feet and ankles.

Bliss, sheer bliss. This will be such a selling point for a bed and breakfast.

I swiveled my head to the left. The old stone jetty stuck out into the water like an obscene finger. No reason why it couldn't be renovated. In my mind's eye, I imagined sailboats bobbing along side. My gaze traveled on to the boat storage house. *What a wonderful place for a beachside bar. Major reconstruction will be needed, maybe even a total tear-down, but the payoff's worth it.*

To the right, the beach narrowed. I turned and walked that way. I wasn't sure how far my section of the beach ran or who owned the land next to Bountiful. I'd have to ask around. Perhaps the owners would lease me the property. Nature trails through the woods would appeal to hikers. And of course, an expanded beach could be cordoned off for sporting endeavors like volleyball.

Retracing my steps, I sat on a rock and stared at the water, my mind racing.

I can do this. With the proper marketing and promotion, Bountiful could turn a profit. Keep the limo for pickups at the airport and the port. How classy would that be—a limo ride to your destination in the package price. For the first time since arriving, I was optimistic.

I'd been so engrossed in my thoughts I didn't hear anyone approach behind me.

"Hello, Liza." Stephen's voice lifted my heart.

I rose, turned to face him, and stared into those blue-green eyes, so close to the eyes in the portrait of our ancestor. Longing and desire sent a stream of hot blood straight to my core. Relationships be damned. A lot of generations had passed.

Standing here with sandy feet and the wind mussing my hair, I acknowledged I was in love.

Chapter Twenty-Three

"Hello, Stephen." My heart pounded, yet I resisted running to him.

"Can we talk?"

Still exhilarated by my knowledge, I nodded. He walked toward me carrying a pair of deck shoes in his hand. Today, he wore shorts and a polo shirt.

I gestured to where I'd been sitting. "Pull up a rock and join me."

He smiled, and we sat side by side. "Liza, I want to apologize for everything. You were absolutely right. We should never have kept my family connection a secret. At the time, however, it seemed sensible. Please forgive me."

I inhaled a shaky breath. "There's nothing to forgive. I was hurt and angry, but looking back on it I can see where you might not think it mattered, especially if I didn't stay out the year." I turned to look at his profile, chiseled against the background of rock and sand. "And the cousinship is rather distant, isn't it?"

He turned his head and the smile widened. "Yes. Nothing scandalous happened, although I can tell you there are a couple of cases of first cousins marrying, but that was ten or more generations ago."

I laughed lightly. "So, where does that leave us?"

He took my hand and brought the back of it to his lips.

"I'm not sure, but I need to repair the trust I betrayed. For starters, I've instigated an audit of all Goodhue holdings by an independent accounting firm out of Port Elizabeth. Not a Goodhue to be found." He frowned and dropped my hand. "Think I told you this, but I warned Sir Geoffrey that having Albright, Albright, and Swisher plus Mark's accounting firm do all the work would be a conflict of interest, but the old boy refused to listen. He wanted everything to remain with the family."

"Why? Are there hidden skeletons?"

"Probably, although I don't know of any personally."

"Sure you do. Me. My mother and I are major league skeletons."

"But you aren't hidden."

"Not anymore."

"I'm also in the process of transferring oversight of the charities to another solicitor. Should have been done a long time ago."

"Won't that put a dent in your firm's bottom line?"

"Yes, but we'll survive."

"Does Richard know?" I asked, thrilled he was trying to make things right.

"I told him yesterday. He wasn't happy, but had to go along with it."

"I can send some work your way." I told him about finding Evangeline's diary and its contents. "So, anything you can dig up on my grandfather would be appreciated."

"Given the time frame of fifty—almost sixty—

years ago, Dad wouldn't have been involved, but my grandfather might have. He was head of the firm then."

"The old boy also must have searched and found Mother after Mercer died. That's when the letters started coming, which means he must have known about her."

He nodded. "Sir Geoffrey may have used a private investigation firm. I'll ask Dad if he knows anything about it."

I also brought him up to date on my plans for Bountiful.

"I was shocked at first, but it's brilliant and makes sense. I'll help however I can."

"That's what Evelyn said, too. You do know what happened last night, don't you?"

He nodded. "Richard called and told me this morning. Is she all right?"

"I talked to Giles a while ago. He said she'll be released soon, and they expect to be here in time for dinner, to which you are invited, by the way."

He grinned and dropped a kiss on my forehead. "Invitation accepted. Now, suppose we go take a look at this boat house and the jetty. See how much work it'll take to renovate."

We walked along the sand, hand in hand toward the pier.

"It can use a good cleaning to get rid of the algae buildup and needs reinforcement, but all in all, it's not in bad shape considering its age," he said.

"How old is it?" I asked, scraping with a rock at a clump of dried greenish glop.

"Maybe Gentleman Jack built the jetty and the boathouse. Being a sailor, he probably kept a pleasure boat." He looked up and down the structure. "I'd say you could dock maybe three or four small sailboats with no problem. Of course, you'd have to make sure they didn't go out of the cove. Inexperienced sailors, a small boat, and an open sea are lawsuits waiting to happen. You'll need good liability insurance."

"Let me guess—Goodhue Casualty?"

He laughed. "This time it's a good thing. Cheap family rates."

We checked out the boat house next. No more than a twenty-by-fifteen foot rectangle, the door was on the shorter end. The long side nestled against the cliff face.

I expected the hinges to be corroded, so was surprised when the door opened smoothly. The interior was dark, the only light source coming from the two water facing windows. The place was divided into two rooms. Shelves full of boating equipment lined the walls in the first room. The smaller second room had been set up as a work area. Dust motes danced in the light from another window. A pick-ax stood against the workbench.

"That's odd," Stephen said inspecting the tool. "What's a pickax doing in a boat house?"

"What's any of this crap doing in here?"

He fingered one of the points. "This has been used recently."

"And the hinges didn't make any noise when we opened the door."

Stephen crouched and peered under the bench. "Liza, look at this."

I stooped and followed his gaze. Someone had chopped a large hole in the back wall. The debris littered the floor off to the side.

"Why did they stop?"

He felt along the edges of the hole and beyond. "Because they hit the base of the cliff. The cliff must have originally been the back wall. Eventually, someone added the supporting stone, probably due to water damage. The rain would slide down the cliff and into the house."

"Let's get out of here. I don't like that someone is sneaking around the property."

"Kids, maybe. Coming to search for Gentleman Jack's buried treasure. They motor in at night, dig, hit the cliff and give up. They go home, forgetting the pick, and talk about their big adventure."

It made as much sense as any other explanation. "I'll post no trespassing signs."

We made our way back along the beach, stopping at the foot of the steps to replace our shoes. I hesitated, and then decided trust was a two-way street.

"Stephen, there's something I'd like you to know." I told him about the pills and Richard's appearance in Evelyn's room last night. "I assume Richard is covering for Mary Ellen."

He stared with an astonished look on his face. "Are you sure?"

I nodded. "Do you think Mary Ellen is…unstable?"

"I don't have that close a contact with her. Beatrice would know."

"Beatrice isn't here today. She went into Port Elizabeth to see if she could get more information about her ancestor." I sighed. "Mary Ellen had no way of knowing Evelyn would take aspirin before coming down to lunch. This is so like a play I was once in."

"What play?"

"God, I can't remember, it was six or seven years ago and closed after three performances. The plot dealt with the killer substituting a capsule containing poison or something in regular meds. Eventually, the wrong one would be taken."

"Giving the killer an alibi." He frowned. "Liza, I don't like you staying in the house."

"I locked the door last night, but the veranda gives easy access. I've upset Mary Ellen with my bed and breakfast plans. Will she come after me with the hedge clippers tonight?"

"I'll have a talk with Richard before dinner." He cast a keen look in my direction. "I don't want anything to happen to you."

We climbed the steps back to the overlook and gazed out over the water.

I glanced at the rocks and beach below. "It seems incredible that…"

"I know," he said when I couldn't finish. "I spoke with Chief Inspector Bradshaw yesterday. The investigation has stalled."

"Not surprising. I don't think anyone will admit to being up here with Irene."

He placed both hands on my shoulders and turned me to face him. "Promise you'll be careful. Don't go wandering off alone."

"I won't, at least not at night. Maybe I should say something about making a will."

"That might not be a bad idea."

He smiled and pulled me into his arms. The heat of his embrace made my knees go weak, and when his lips covered mine, a burning fire erupted in the pit of my stomach. I snaked my arms around his neck and lost myself in the warm sensations that raged through my body like surf pounding the shore during a storm. He was back, and that's all that mattered.

He broke contact and trailed his lips to my temple.

"Oh God, Liza, it's been a long couple of days. I can't get you out of my thoughts. You're always beckoning. I've never had this reaction to a woman before. You're damned important to me. I never saw it coming."

"I know," I whispered. His words sent a shot of pure desire shooting along my nerves. "I feel the same way. I didn't expect this to happen when I got off the plane."

Stephen threaded his hands through my hair and kissed me lightly.

"We'll talk later. Right now, I have a few things to do at home. I'll be back early tonight and talk to Richard."

I drew in a shaky breath and nodded, then grasped his hand and walked with him across the lawn to the house.

The hole in my heart of the last few days was once again filled.

****

I waved goodbye to Stephen from the front porch and strolled up the stairs, my head in the clouds. I'd only said "I love you" once before to a man. I was in college and thought I'd meant it. Six months later, I realized I hadn't.

But this was different. It was more than just physical. Something twisted deep in my soul, telling me not to let him get away.

It was almost five and I wondered when Evelyn

would be home. Had Richard and Mary Ellen returned from West End yet? I called down to the kitchen, but no messages from anybody had come through.

I showered quickly, changed clothes, and was halfway downstairs when the front door opened. Richard and Mary Ellen walked in.

"Hello," I greeted. "Did you enjoy your day of freedom?"

"What do you mean by that?" she asked.

Her sharp tone took me by surprise. "Uh, I meant did you have a nice lunch and a good time?"

Richard answered quickly. "Yes, thank you, Liza, we had a lovely lunch and enjoyed walking about."

His wife licked her lips and glanced toward the drawing room. "Yes, it was nice to get out."

I had descended into the foyer and got a good look at the couple. Both were pale, but Mary Ellen's gaze darted from place to place. Her hands clenched and unclenched around her purse. Body language suggested she *hadn't* had a good time.

She inhaled a shaky breath. "If you'll excuse me, I think I'll go lie down for a while before dinner. All that exercise…" She brushed past me and hurried upstairs.

"Of course, I under…"

She was gone before I finished my sentence.

"If you'll excuse me, too, Liza, I have some things to do in the study."

"No problem."

He walked away and into his office, closing the door behind him.

Wandering into the drawing room, I poured a glass of wine and settled into one of the chairs. I stared at the portrait of Jonathon and saluted him with my glass before taking a sip.

"So, Jonathon, read any good books lately?"

He didn't answer, but neither did his almost four hundred-year-old smile waver.

The word book took me back to the luncheon conversation from last week. We'd all tried so hard not to wallow in grief that the talk had turned to the first Goodhue and his treasure. Someone had brought up the possibility of a diary. Surely Irene would have mentioned reading one. Did that mean a journal didn't exist or merely that she didn't say anything about it?

Sir Geoffrey popped into my mind. Being such a control freak, had he demanded the journal—if it existed—be returned to him? He'd make sure the family was shown in the best light. Whatever had made its way to the Historical Society would be the purest linen in the islands.

But where would he have kept the family secrets? Did Richard know about any diary? Up until last night, I'd have said no. But covering up a possible pill substitution now suggested otherwise.

In plays and books, the quiet ones are always the killers. Yet I couldn't see him whacking his own sister over the head with a champagne bottle and pushing her off the overlook.

The doorbell rang, and one of the maids answered. I heard Stephen's voice and rose hurrying to the foyer.

He leaned down and kissed me. "I called Giles when I got home. He and Evelyn should be here shortly. Now, I need to have a chat with Cousin Richard."

He walked to the study, knocked, and then entered. I made my way back to the drawing room. A few moments later, tires crunched in the driveway. I hurried to open the door to a grim-faced Giles and a pale, nervous Evelyn.

"Evelyn! How are you feeling?" I asked, hugging her.

"As good as can be expected."

"Why don't you go lie down for a while, dear," her husband said.

She brushed his idea aside. "No, I have no intention of being left alone anywhere in this house with that woman. What I want is a glass of wine."

She strode into the drawing room and headed straight for the liquor cart. Giles sighed and followed, pouring a shot of scotch.

Once seated on the loveseat, she stared at me. "Mary Ellen suggesting I don't know the difference between aspirin and migraine pills is infuriating. I did not confuse my medications."

"Perhaps you had a reaction to the aspirin and the migraine pills."

She gulped a generous portion from her glass. "That's the theory, but I've done it before with no problems. I took two aspirin before coming down to lunch. That's all. I think someone messed with them. And I know who—Mary Ellen."

Evelyn having the same theory as me was scary. "But why?"

"Because she was angry I offered to help with the bed and breakfast thing. If it hadn't been for you, I'd be dead. Giles and I will leave first thing in the morning. I will never again stay in this house overnight with her."

"We have no proof of anything," Giles said sipping his drink.

"I don't care," his wife insisted. "She's always hated me. I think she's on the verge of a breakdown or something."

"If it's any consolation to you, Mary Ellen was truly concerned for you last night," I said.

"What scared her was that I didn't die."

"But, Evelyn, for all we knew you'd had a stroke."

She snorted. "Stroke my ass. That woman's unhinged."

I crossed and then re-crossed my legs while sipping wine. Evelyn's comment about Mary Ellen echoed my concerns about her mental status I'd voiced to Stephen earlier.

"Maybe Mary Ellen needs a change of scenery," I speculated.

"Good idea, Liza," Giles said. "A trip to see her family in England or a nice cruise somewhere."

"Only if Richard shoves her overboard!" Evelyn drained her glass, rose and refilled it. "Liza, you'd better watch your back, too. She wasn't happy with the conditions of Sir Geoffrey's will."

"I don't feel threatened." *Or do I?* I remembered the creaking veranda floorboard, my room being searched, the watcher in the window, and the attic door.

Stephen entered the room and poured himself a shot of scotch.

Evelyn glanced at us and smiled. "Patched things up?"

"Yes. I overreacted to the news Stephen is one of the family. I can see now, it doesn't make any difference."

She waved her hand. "Of course it doesn't. The relationship isn't that close. Your children won't turn out to be idiots or homicidal maniacs."

I choked on my wine.

Stephen laughed. "Things haven't progressed to that point yet, Evelyn." He sobered and looked at me. "By the way, Richard would like to see you in the study."

I set my glass on the side table and rose. "I'll just be a moment."

The study door was closed, so I knocked and then opened it. Richard sat behind the desk.

"Come in, Liza." He stood and motioned me toward the leather sofa. "Let's have a seat."

I sat looking him straight in the eye. He took his seat on the other end of the sofa, bit his lip, and ran a hand through his hair. Deep lines grooved his face as if he'd not slept in several nights. I almost felt sorry for him.

"Liza, I want you to know that you are perfectly safe in this house. Evelyn's illness was a horrible accident. And I want to apologize for Mary Ellen's behavior the last few days. This whole situation with Sir Geoffrey's will and your plans for Bountiful have been very upsetting. She's under a great deal of stress."

"Richard, has it occurred to you your wife needs professional help?"

He rose and paced. "I took her to the doctor today. Her drinking is not as yet out of control, but sounding off to a psychiatrist may help her deal with events. I certainly hope so."

I also stood. "Therapy is always a good idea. I hope the doctors help her." I hesitated. "Why don't you get her off the island? A nice vacation somewhere she's never been before. A change of pace and scenery can do wonders. Helps a person cope."

"The doctor suggested just that. She's always wanted to tour Italy." He stopped wearing a path in the carpet and faced me. "Starting tonight I'll be taking dinner and breakfast with her in our room."

"Sounds like a good idea."

He walked me to the door. "Please make my excuses to the others."

I opened the door and stepped through. "Good evening, Richard."

He smiled a weary smile and nodded. Neither of us had mentioned the pills.

Making my way back to the drawing room, I had to hand it to him. He hadn't admitted a damned thing, yet had been put on notice both Stephen and I had questions. If Mary Ellen had switched those pills then she needed to get away for her own and everyone else's safety.

****

I sent the latest installment of my blog and stretched. The morning had flown by. Evelyn and Giles had departed soon after breakfast. Richard had both meals with Mary Ellen in their suite.

Dinner last night had been a quiet, awkward affair with Evelyn eyeing and sniffing each morsel of food before eating it. Not until they went upstairs did Stephen and I have a chance to talk.

"Richard didn't confess anything," he said after I'd told about my conversation.

"And I couldn't very well tell him I played hide and seek."

"You're right. A change of scenery is long overdue. He also agrees now about the changes I want to make in how the businesses are run."

I snaked my arms around his neck. "Any other changes you'd like to make?"

He laughed and kissed the breath out of me. "Yes, but we'll talk about it later. I have a full court docket tomorrow in Port Elizabeth and probably won't be home until late. Think you can amuse yourself until the next day?"

"Ben's asked me to take a ride in his boat."

He'd pinched my bottom. "Little devil! Don't you dare throw Collier in my face."

I laughed. "I accepted, although I'd much rather be with you."

We'd talked a bit longer before he gave me a kiss that lit up my night and left.

A knock on my door brought me out of my pleasant recollections. "Come in."

Violet appeared. "Mr. Collier is calling, miss. You can take the call in here if you like."

"Thank you."

She left and I lifted the receiver and pressed the transfer button. I hated this phone system. The main line in the servant's hall was the only one that rang. The rest of the phones only did when the extension was dialed in. Yet they were all interconnected allowing anyone to pick up and listen. Only the study had a separate private line.

"Good morning, Ben."

"And a good morning to you, too. I'm going to be about an hour late picking you up. I have to make a stateside call at ten. Is eleven all right?"

"It's fine. I'll see you in a couple of hours."

I hung up and strolled onto the veranda. The breeze

had freshened and the salt air filled me with a need to be outside.

I exited the front door and breathed deeply. Where to go? I chose the driveway. Perhaps I'd explore one of those trails.

A movement from the side of the house caught my eye. One of the maids was also walking down the driveway. I called out for her to wait.

She stopped and smiled as I approached.

"Good morning, Miss Channing."

"Good morning. I don't think we've met."

"No, miss. I work in the kitchen. My name is Helen."

We resumed walking. "So, Helen, are you taking a breath of sea air, too?"

"Oh no, miss. Georgette sent me to see if Beatrice is all right."

"All right?"

"Yes, miss. She didn't come to work this morning and doesn't answer the phone. Very unusual."

"Well, she went to Port Elizabeth yesterday. Perhaps she got back late and decided to sleep in."

The gravel crunched beneath our feet as she shook her head. "It's just not like her to do that. I do hope she's not ill."

A wave of uneasiness slipped over my skin. It was odd. Beatrice struck me as the sort to get off her deathbed to fulfill her duties. I quickened my pace, and then turned into the narrow drive leading to her cottage. My anxiety eased at the sight of the Mini-Cooper parked off to the side.

"Look, there's her car. She's home. Just taking it easy. Perhaps she discussed an extra day off with Mrs.

Goodhue who neglected to tell the staff."

This made sense in view of the pill incident.

Helen smiled. "You're right, miss. If anyone deserves to take a morning off, it's Beatrice. She works long hours."

She hurried on as I turned to continue my stroll down the drive. I saw no trails, but lots of underbrush.

Another thing that needs changing. Clear this mess out, and tear down that stupid wall or at least, replace it with something less intimidating and institutional.

For reasons unknown, a sudden chill rippled up my spine. My heart accelerated.

Then a scream ripped through the air.

Chapter Twenty-Four

I ran. The gravel flew from under my feet as the scream sounded again from the direction of Beatrice's. My heart pounded and my breaths came in choking gasps.

Helen stood on the small porch, her hands over her ears and her mouth wide open, the screams coming non-stop. I skidded to a halt, grabbed her shoulders and shook her hard. Her eyes bugged out. The screams continued. As a last resort, I slapped her.

The screaming ceased. She gulped, clutched at the porch support, and slid to the floor. Mute, she pointed with shaking finger toward the door.

I went inside, knowing what I'd find. The tiny living room had been ransacked reminding me of Irene's place a few days previously. Beatrice lay in the middle of the floor, the back of her head a gory mess. A brass candlestick lay next to her.

I clapped a hand over my mouth fighting nausea and exited. I helped Helen to her feet and led her to a wicker chair at the far end of the porch.

"Sit here, Helen. You're all right. We need to call the police."

"There...there's...a...a phone inside," she said through chattering teeth.

I returned inside, and stepping around the crime

311

scene as carefully as I could, made my way to the kitchen. This, too, had been tossed. *Who the hell ransacks a kitchen?*

I found the phone and dialed the operator telling her to send the police immediately. Then I called Richard.

"Richard, get down here now," I said in a shaking voice. "Beatrice is dead—murdered."

He didn't ask questions, but hung up. A few minutes later, he, Myron, and Willie arrived. I was back on the porch with a wailing Helen.

"In there," I said, pointing. "I called the cops already."

The men disappeared inside and reappeared within moments.

"Myron, inform the guard so the police can get in. Girl, get a grip," he said to Helen. "The constable will want to question you."

The maid gulped and nodded.

I stared at Richard. "My God, who could have done this?"

He ran a shaking hand through his hair. "I have no idea. It looks like she may have interrupted a burglar."

"How did he get past the gate?"

"I told Sir Geoffrey that wall was useless. Any determined thief could scale it."

"But why rob Beatrice? Why not come to the main house?"

"Because this was convenient. Maybe he figured to make off with small stuff on the theory the big house was secure."

I glanced at Helen who made choking noises, and then back at Richard. "Does Bountiful have an alarm system?"

He shook his head. "Grandfather refused to put one in. Said he'd never remember the code, and that's why we had a guard at the gatehouse during the day."

"Only during the day?"

"I know, it sounds silly, but it made sense to Sir Geoffrey."

"So, how do people get in at night?"

"Our cars are equipped with a transponder. Guests push a button and a servant activates the gate. Sometimes they even remember to close it again, too," he replied in an angry tone.

I remembered how after the accident, the police car had entered through an open gate. I also recalled the night Stephen and I had returned from Port Elizabeth. We'd entered without a guard present. Stephen probably had a remote for easy access. The whole thing sounded useless. Anyone could get in.

Two police cars pulled into Beatrice's driveway. Helen and I were questioned.

"Why were you walking down the driveway, Miss Channing?"

"I wanted some fresh air and exercise."

"And you met up with the maid?"

"Yes, she came from the direction of the kitchen. I strolled with her until we got to the cottage."

I told him of leaving Helen there, continuing on, and how I'd run back when she had screamed.

"So, you walked through the crime scene to call us," the first constable asked.

"Yes, I'm sorry. I tried to do as little damage as possible, but Helen was hysterical. I used the closest phone."

"I'm sure we can sort it out."

"How long has she been dead?"

"At least twenty-four hours."

He left me and walked over to a whimpering Helen.

Beatrice had never left for Port Elizabeth and the Historical Society. Twenty-four hours. Could the killer have taken advantage of the confusion over Evelyn's overdose to slip through the gate? The ambulance had come and gone along with Richard's car. It was a possibility, especially with the so-called security set-up.

And later that night after things had calmed down, Beatrice walked in on a robbery in progress.

On the other hand, could someone have scaled the wall in the daylight hours expecting Beatrice to be at the main house only to find her home and in the process of leaving for Port Elizabeth? I'd assumed someone had told her Evelyn was out of danger and that she'd gone on to Port Elizabeth.

The image of Irene's house was still fresh in my mind. The similarities were hard to ignore. But what could Beatrice and Irene have in common that someone was willing to kill for? The answer eluded me. Then Helen's voice cut through my thoughts.

"Oh, yes, sir, she was dismissed."

"I see. When?"

"I'm not sure, but it was before dinner. I only know because Beatrice told me I'd have to do laundry chores until a replacement could be found."

"Wait a minute. One of the maids has been dismissed?" I interrupted.

"Yes, miss. Gladys."

"But why?"

"I don't know, miss."

"Who dismissed her? Beatrice?"

"I don't know. Maybe."

"And where does this Gladys live?" the constable asked.

"In the village, sir. She lives with her father and three brothers."

I walked over to Richard who huddled with Chief Inspector Bradshaw. The latter nodded at my approach.

"Miss Channing. I see you've discovered another body. Is this a habit of yours in the States?"

I injected a bit of frost into my voice. "Technically, I didn't find Beatrice. Helen did. I was just along for the ride this time."

"I assume Constable Wainwright has interviewed you," he said in a neutral tone.

"Yes, he has. Am I free to return to the house?"

"You are."

"Richard, when you get back, could I speak with you privately?"

"Of course, Liza. I'll be along shortly."

I made my way to the house. Why had Gladys been dismissed? And if Beatrice had done it, it had to have been with the approval of Mary Ellen. What had the woman done to warrant firing?

And could Gladys or one of her brothers have come back seeking revenge?

****

Richard's idea of shortly and mine differed. I was left tapping my foot for an hour. When he finally appeared, I tackled him about Gladys.

"Who fired Gladys, and why?"

"Let's discuss this in the study." He led the way to

his office. I followed closing the door behind me. "This is a terrible situation. Beatrice was like a family member. The staff is very upset."

"Of course they are. I am, too. I didn't know her that well, but two deaths in two weeks are a little much. What did the head honcho of cops have to say?"

His eyebrows rose. "The head hon…oh, you mean the Chief Inspector. It certainly looks like she interrupted a robbery."

"Yes, but what could Beatrice possibly have that would interest a burglar?"

"I have no idea, and keep in mind that Grand Britannia is like any other country. Drugs are not unheard of, and crime follows the tourist trade."

I took a deep breath. "Why was this maid dismissed?"

He steepled his fingers under his chin. "I'm not at liberty to say at the moment."

"What the hell kind of an answer is that?"

"It's the only one I can give for now."

"Look, Richard, even if she and Beatrice had a major league tiff, Mary Ellen or you would still have to okay the dismissal. So, what did she do that was so awful?"

"Liza, just leave it alone."

I bit back a sharp reply, my frustration levels rising with every second. I tried another tack.

"If Beatrice did the actual firing, then Gladys might have a motive. Was she the sole support of her family in the village?"

"I have no idea. And the Chief Inspector knows the details of the dismissal." He reached for a sheaf of papers. "Is that all? I have a lot of work to do."

Richard wasn't going to answer any of my questions. Was this payback for the bed and breakfast thing? He had effectively left me on the cold side of the door. Whirling, I strode from the room and headed into the kitchen. Maybe the staff would be more forthcoming.

"Georgette, my condolences on the loss of Beatrice. It was a horrible shock."

She wiped tears from her eyes. "It's awful. I can't imagine who'd want to hurt her."

"I also understand a maid was dismissed. Do you know why?"

"Not really. Beatrice spoke to her after luncheon day before last. The dishes were done, and I was just tidying up, when Gladys came storming out, saying she wanted to talk to Mrs. Goodhue. Beatrice said Mrs. Goodhue concurred and there was nothing to be done."

"And you have no idea what they were talking about?"

She shook her head. "None, miss, although just between you and me, Gladys wasn't above copping a little knickknack here and there. No one could ever prove it, mind you, but Beatrice counted the silverware every couple of nights. And Gladys was sneaky, too. Eavesdropped a lot."

I could relate to that. Eavesdropping was sneaky, but sometimes highly informative.

"Uh, miss, what should I do about meals today?"

"Mrs. Goodhue isn't feeling well, so keep both lunch and dinner simple."

I left and entered the drawing room. So, Gladys may have been a petty thief. If true, Mary Ellen would see the maid found the unemployment line fast. Gladys or one of her family had better have one hell of a good alibi.

And Georgette said Gladys eavesdropped—as in listening in on telephone conversations? Or creeping around outside doors or on verandas? And did she do so at Mary Ellen's bidding?

I glanced through the windows as Ben's Mercedes skidded to a stop in front of the steps. He bounded out and trotted up the steps. No bothering to wait for a servant to answer the bell, I opened the door myself.

"Good God, what's going on down at Beatrice's?" He demanded, stepping inside.

"Nothing good, I'm afraid." I delivered the bad news, sticking to an interrupted burglary theory, but refrained mentioning my involvement.

"Good Lord! Any idea who did it?"

"Not yet," I said leading the way into the drawing room. "As you can imagine, things are chaotic at the moment."

"I suppose you want to cancel the boat ride, but maybe you'd rather just get out of the house."

Suddenly, I couldn't stand the sight of Bountiful. As insensitive as it sounded, I had to get out or go crazy. "Getting out of here sounds wonderful. And I'd love a tour of the island by boat. Let me inform the others I won't be in for lunch."

I called the news down to Georgette. Richard, I ignored. Let him find out on his own.

Seated next to Ben, I averted my eyes from Beatrice's cottage as we passed. Several police cars were still there.

"So, who found her?" Ben asked as he turned out of the driveway.

"One of the maids. We'd been walking together just before. Can we talk about something else? I just can't deal with this now. Tell me about your boat."

"It's a thirty-five foot Sea King with two staterooms, a galley, and a head. All the comforts of home. It's docked at the North Bay Marina just outside of West End."

"Not at the house?"

"I don't have the luxury of a private dock or boat house. I just have a little slip where I can tie up a dinghy if I want to motor around the cove."

He told me the finer points of the boat while he drove. I let him chatter since it kept my mind occupied until he finished.

To keep the conversation going, I said, "Oh, this will amuse you. I found the floor plans to Bountiful."

The car swerved ever so slightly. "You what? When?"

"A few days ago."

"And?"

"And nothing. The plans are the same now as they were then."

"Where did you find them?"

I told him about going through Irene's things before the funeral.

"Irene. Funny," he said almost to himself. "Discover anything else?"

"No, but Stephen and I explored the boathouse. Someone had damaged one of the walls. What they were looking for was anybody's guess."

"Treasure, of course. But I doubt the old pirate hid anything in the wall of a boathouse. You should have called me." The last sentence had a sharper tone.

"Why?"

He shrugged. "I'm worried about your safety. If someone's snooping in the boathouse, then they have direct access to the house and grounds."

"It was probably kids, who gave up when they got tired of digging."

After parking at the marina, we ambled down the concrete docks, passing a restaurant along the way.

"How about take out?" I suggested.

He grinned. "You mean as in a burger, fries, and a shake?"

"Do they run to that here?"

"No, but they do a nice fish and chips, and I'm sure we can scare up a beer or two out of the fridge on the boat."

Minutes later, he helped me aboard complete with food. I admired the sleek lines of the blue and white boat. "She looks fast."

"She is," he replied when I asked. "Come below, we'll eat in the salon."

The interior was plush with a sizable seating area and galley. In the forward cabin I caught a glimpse of photographic equipment.

"Here we go," he said hauling two beers out of the fridge.

"Are those underwater cameras?" I asked, accepting the frosty brew and unscrewing the top, then tilting the bottle to my lips. The beer slid down my throat. I checked the label—an island brand. It was damned good.

"Yes. I also keep my snorkeling stuff on board. If I'm going deep, I rent scuba gear. Can't afford to own."

"What about the boat? Do you own this?"

I crunched into a hunk of breaded fish. Not bad for cod. The chips were thick cut and perfectly fried.

Ben grinned. "Sure do. That's why I can't afford the scuba gear. I wouldn't go out on the open water in anything less than thirty-five feet. You're from L. A., do much boating?"

"Some. Never owned one though. Marina fees in Southern California are killer. Did you grow up around boats?"

"Hell, no. I'm from Kansas. Remember? I learned about boats when I was in the Keys. If you'd like, I can take us to the reef where I've been working lately. Do a little snorkeling. I think there's a swim suit around here somewhere. Irene always kept one on board."

I liked the idea. An afternoon on the water with a bit of snorkeling on the side. While Ben fired up the boat, I found the swim suit—a bikini—in the main aft cabin, changed, and went topside.

Ben sent an appreciative glance down my body. "Looks better on you, than it did on Irene. Can you go forward and cast off the bow line?"

Not sure I appreciated the comment, I made my way up front and disengaged the line from the dock cleat. We backed slowly from the slip. Once clear, Ben moved the throttle forward, and we set off at a sedate pace through the marina to the sea.

There we zipped along, over slightly rolling water under a sunny sky. The wind whipped my hair back and I breathed deeply of the clean salt air. Ten minutes later, Ben tied up to an anchor buoy just off the reef. After assuring him I knew how to use the gear, I positioned my facemask and eased off the swim platform. I took a few minutes to adjust my breathing with the snorkel, and then plunged fifteen feet below to the reef. Ben joined me, camera in hand.

Grasses and fan coral waved in the current while sea creatures peeked out from their rocky hidey-holes. A manta ray bolted from the sandy bottom and swam away with graceful moves.

Taking frequent trips to the surface to breathe, I found the experience just what I needed. Already, the sight of Beatrice's body had dimmed in my mind. I was at one with the sea—at least for a while.

On my final journey, I stopped a few feet above the reef. From out of nowhere dozens of brightly colored fish surrounded me. Yellow, orange, blue, all the colors made me feel part of a rainbow. Then something flashed scattering the fish.

I looked over at Ben with his camera. He jerked his thumb upward and I nodded. With a powerful thrust of my swim fins, I surfaced and swam toward the boat where I tossed my equipment on the platform before climbing back on board. Ben followed.

"Hope you don't mind the picture," he said. "But it was one of those Kodak moments I couldn't pass up."

I laughed as I toweled off. "Not at all. Just hope you got my good side, that's all."

Ben leaned over and gave me a quick kiss on the lips. "All your sides a good."

Surprised by his action, I backed off and to cover my confusion bent to dry my legs. Why the kiss? Was this some kind of come on because he thought Stephen and I were through? Disgust welled in my chest.

Smarmy—that's the word. Ben is smarmy and probably a con man. Does he expect me to take up with him and pay his way like Irene?

Ben, however, didn't appear to notice my reaction. Whistling, he entered the cabin.

"You want a beer?" he called up from below.

"Uh, no thanks. What time is it?"

"A little after three. You ready to head for home or would you like to see more of the island?"

"I think we'd better go back." From now on, I'd limit any time spent with him. For some reason, I didn't trust him.

He returned to the cockpit, a cold soda in hand. "No problem. Why don't you change while we're still anchored? I'll stow the gear."

Fifteen minutes later we were underway. A short time after that, we entered the marina and docked. In the car, I leaned my head against the headrest. If nothing else, at least I could be gracious. "Thank you for a wonderful afternoon, Ben. The water was cool enough to be refreshing, and I'll never forget the sights."

He'd maneuvered the car from the parking lot and turned onto the road. With a casual gesture, he picked up my hand and carried it to his lips.

"And don't forget the company. I found the company beautiful and charming. You were much too good for Stephen Albright."

Creeped out, I pulled my hand free and sat upright. Stephen! Oh my God. I'd forgotten to call Stephen about Beatrice. How could I?

"Something wrong?"

"Stephen! I forgot to tell him about Beatrice."

"So what? Richard probably notified him, although why he'd be interested in the housekeeper is beyond me. He's as much a snob as the rest of them."

"He is not!" I snapped with heat turning to stare.

Ben's jaw muscles clenched. "I take that to mean he's no longer on your list of liars and swindlers."

Given my feelings for Stephen, I didn't like Ben's accusatory tone.

"He dropped by yesterday, and we ironed out the problems."

"In other words, he turned on the charm and sweet talked you."

I inhaled a deep breath to bring my rising temper under control.

"No, he told me he agreed with my concerns and is in the process of removing himself and his law firm from many of the Goodhue charities and such."

"And you believed him? How gullible are you? Once a liar, always a liar."

I curled my fingers into fists, my nails digging into my palms, and counted to ten.

"His explanation satisfied me, and I really don't see how any of it is your business."

He shot me a contrite look. "Liza, forgive me, but I'm worried about you. First Irene. Now Beatrice. You're in that house surrounded by people who'd be happy if you were the next victim. I'd make sure the house had an alarm system installed, and only authorized visitors are allowed in after hours."

"You forget I don't officially own Bountiful. In fact, I'm not sure who does."

"My guess it's being held in trust for you—by Albright, Albright, and Swisher."

"Then if I feel unsafe, I'm sure I can request more security."

"Which I'm sure will be turned down. You *need* it,

Liza. First someone takes a pick to the wall. Then some thief sneaks in to rob the first house he sees, which happens to be Beatrice's and bashes her head in. I'm scared for you. One of the Goodhue's is up to no good. And that includes Stephen Albright."

I'd had it with Ben and his suspicions. Anger clogged my chest. I was tempted to have him drop me off at the nearest wide spot in the road. If nothing else, this conversation had hammered home the fact how much I loved Stephen Albright.

Mother always said when I fell it would be hard and fast. Boy, was she ever right.

"Ben, I have no intention of discussing this with you any further. Stephen and I have come to an agreement. I like him—a lot. I understand your animosity toward the family, but I'm sure your attitude is partly responsible. I think you enjoy saying and doing things you know will raise eyebrows. Like it or not, this is my family, and I want to get along with them, so knock it off. Okay?"

He didn't answer, merely drew a sharp breath and pressed his foot on the accelerator. We rocketed down the road, the speedometer needle edging to fifty. He took a turn and drifted into the other lane. An oncoming truck swerved to avoid sideswiping us.

I clutched at the armrest, my heart pounding in my ears. "Are you nuts? Slow down!"

He did immediately. I clenched my teeth against the angry, frightened words bubbling in my throat.

"I'm sorry, Liza. Please forgive me," he said in a low voice.

I breathed a sigh of relief when we turned into Bountiful's driveway. The guard emerged from the little hut, nodded, and opened the gate. We swept through and on to the house.

As soon as the car stopped, I wrenched the door open.

Ben reached over and put a hand on my arm. "Liza, I truly am sorry. I loved Irene and wanted her family to like me. When they didn't, I did exactly as you say." He ran a hand through his hair. "If Stephen Albright is in your future, then I wish you good luck. But remember, if you ever need me, I'm here. Just call—day or night. I'll come. I promise."

"Thank you, Ben." I glanced at the house. "I'd better get inside. See if anything new has turned up on Beatrice."

I slid out of the car and closed the door. Ben was an opportunist on the make. The supposed love of his life, Irene, was dead, yet he had no problem coming on to me. I didn't believe a goddamned word he'd said.

He leaned over and called out the open window. "Keep me in the loop. Please? I liked Beatrice, too."

I nodded and climbed the steps to my home.

Chapter Twenty-Five

After entering the foyer, I headed straight for the study where Richard informed me there was nothing new on Beatrice's death.

"We don't know if anything was taken from the house," he said. "I can't imagine what a thief would expect to find. Beatrice didn't have expensive jewelry or antiques."

"Thieves with a drug habit rob for damned near nothing. As long as they can hustle a couple of bucks out of it they don't care. I had a friend who was mugged for a bunch of costume jewelry worth maybe twenty dollars. Did you let Stephen know about Beatrice?"

"Yes, I left a message with his secretary. He's in court today in Port Elizabeth. He called back during a recess. Shocked, of course." He sent me a sly glance. "I told him you were with Ben."

My irritation level rose, but I kept my voice even. "Ben took me snorkeling. It was wonderful. All those fish and in such lovely colors. Do you snorkel?"

"Good Lord, no. I never understood the fascination with holding one's breath and staring at a bunch of fish. By the way, I invited Stephen for dinner."

"Good. Perhaps he'll have some suggestions about security at Bountiful. After all, if I turn this into a bed and breakfast, extra security will be needed."

With that little dig, I turned and walked toward the door. I didn't see his expression. I really didn't care. I'd made up my mind. Bountiful would pay its own way, and a bed and breakfast sounded like a good idea.

Upstairs, I ran into Violet in the upper hallway. Her eyes were red and puffy.

"Oh, good afternoon, miss. Can I help you with anything?"

"No, thank you. I'm fine. I'm so sorry about Beatrice. Were you and she close?"

"Not close, but I liked her. She was fair. She expected you to do the work and do it properly. Handing out praise wasn't her style, but she let you know if you didn't measure up. It's awful what happened. Do the police know who did it yet?"

"Not to my knowledge. Uh, Violet, what's this about Gladys being dismissed?"

"Oh yes, it happened day before yesterday. I'm not sure exactly why."

I feigned surprise. "Goodness, I wonder what she did to warrant being let go. Did she pinch something?"

Violet frowned. "It's possible. Helen said small things had a habit of disappearing." She paused. "Are you sure I can't run a bath or set out your clothes for the evening?"

I waved my hand. "No, no, don't bother. I have no idea what to wear and I'll grab a quick shower."

She nodded and resumed her steps down the hallway as I entered my room. I showered and rummaged in the armoire for something simple, finally deciding on a pair of white slacks and a sleeveless amethyst blouse. I glanced at my watch. I had a good thirty minutes before the cocktail hour commenced. I lounged on the chaise in the corner and let my thoughts wonder.

Why would thieves bother to come to the rural areas to commit a robbery? Much better pickings in the towns or city. And why rob what was obviously a cottage or guesthouse? And why kill Beatrice? Unless, the thieves were local, and she could identify them. In which case, they must have known she lived in the cottage. Nothing made sense.

Something lurked in the corner of my mind. Something I heard or saw. I thought about the night of Irene's death. I know I heard her scream, but had I also heard the sound of a boat? Or had I merely tuned into a car on the road?

And Irene had been at Beatrice's that night. Are the two deaths connected? I waved a mental hand. *How? What did Irene and Beatrice have in common that would lead to murder?*

A new thought occurred. Suppose I *had* heard a boat. Could Irene have come across an intruder on the overlook? That didn't make any sense either. Who'd come by water to break into a fully occupied house? I sighed in frustration. Let the police handle it.

My gaze wandered to the portrait of Evangeline over the fireplace. Her lovely face looked back with a haughty expression. Given her words in the diary, I no longer found her so beautiful. Tomorrow, I'd request the painting be removed and replaced with something else—a landscape, a still life, anything.

A Janelle Madison original might be nice. I'm sure Mother would ship something.

The conversation about floor plans and diaries

popped into my mind. I'd found the floor plans and a diary, but nothing written by Jonathon Goodhue. I stared at Evangeline's portrait. In books and the movies, portraits often masked the presence of a safe. *No way. Could it?*

The logical place for a safe would be the study, yet the master bedroom might conceal items of a more personal nature.

I rose and hurried to the fireplace. The portrait was huge measuring close to five by four feet. The gilded frame surrounded the canvas by a good eight inches. I pulled the bottom corner away from the wall a fraction. It moved but not by much, so if it hid anything the opening wasn't hinged. Still unable to see, I dragged the heavy steps by the bed to the fireplace and mounted them. Taking a deep breath, I grasped the sides and lifted. The painting disconnected from the hangar.

The damned thing weighed a ton, and I overbalanced. I cried out and tumbled down the two steps landing on the floor with a loud thump, my great-grandmother on top of me. I heaved the picture aside and scrambled to my feet. The wall over the fireplace was an unblemished, brighter shade of white.

Well, so much for that idea. At least I got the old girl down.

Footsteps rushed along the veranda. A second later, Richard burst through the French doors.

"Good Lord, Liza, are you all right? What happened?"

"I'm fine. I was checking for a wall safe."

"Not in here. The only safe is in the study. Sir Geoffrey installed one when he had the place remodeled. Are you sure you're all right? That portrait is heavy."

I reassured him again.

"I'll have Willie re-hang it immediately."

"No, don't bother. Evangeline staring down at me is more than I can take. Perhaps Mary Ellen knows where to put it. I'll replace it with one of my mother's paintings."

"Well, if you're sure you're all right, I'll see you downstairs in a few minutes."

I leaned the painting against the wall, replaced the steps by the bed, and swept the dust from my slacks with a clothes brush. A quick wash in the bathroom removed any dirt from my hands. A knock sounded on my door.

"Mr. Albright is here, miss," Violet informed me when I opened it.

I thanked her, smoothed a stand of wayward hair, and descended the staircase to meet Stephen.

He stood by the bar cart pouring a scotch as I entered the drawing room. He looked up and smiled.

"Can I get you something to drink?"

"Sherry will be fine."

I took a seat in one of the chairs. Stephen brought me the glass, and placing his finger under my chin raised my head for a light kiss.

"I'm sorry about Beatrice."

"Oh God, it was awful. Who would want to harm her?"

"I don't know," he replied, his mouth set in a grim line. "Who'd want to harm Irene or Evelyn? What I do know is you aren't safe. Come to Land's End with me."

I shook my head. "I'm all right. If someone wanted to kill me, they'd have taken a crack at it by now."

He sighed and took a seat on the sofa. "Maybe, maybe not. I have the oddest feeling we're missing something."

"Like what?"

"Like a connection between the murders. I just can't believe they were random."

"The only connection, besides having known each other for years, was the genealogical research Irene was doing for Beatrice, and I can't see how that matters."

"What can't you see as mattering?" Richard asked from the doorway. He crossed the room and poured himself a glass of sherry.

"We were just talking about how Irene was checking on Beatrice's ancestry," I said.

He waved a hand and sat in the chair next to me. "Something about Beatrice being related to Jonathon Goodhue's first mate, wasn't it?"

"Yes," Stephen said. "And Irene *did* dine with Beatrice before she died."

"I can't see how my sister's research would be a motive for murder."

"Unless, the research involved not the first mate, but the captain," I said slowly.

"What are you suggesting?" Stephen asked with raised eyebrows. "That Beatrice is in some way related to the Goodhues?"

"Nonsense," Richard replied sharply. "Beatrice's ancestry is obviously from the island."

"Wouldn't be the first time a captain amused himself with an island woman while in port," I said. "For all we know, Beatrice had Caucasian blood and over the years, her ancestors intermarried with former slaves."

Richard bolted his drink and then rose to pour another. "Rubbish."

Willie appeared in the doorway to announce dinner.

Seated at the table, Stephen placed his napkin in his lap and smiled. "I understand you went snorkeling today. How was it?"

"Lovely." I didn't enlighten either of them about the argument or Ben's concerns about Stephen and the rest of the family.

"Then he knows about Beatrice," Stephen said. "What was his reaction?"

"Shocked, of course. He thinks Bountiful needs more security."

"Well, it's not in the budget at the moment. Besides, how do you prevent someone from trespassing on the sea side of the estate?" Richard said, his tone peevish.

I shrugged. "I have no idea, but something has to be done." A movement at the doorway caught my attention. "Mary Ellen!"

Richard rose and hurried to his wife's side. "My dear, I didn't know you were coming down. Are you feeling better?"

She smiled a thin smile. "Yes, a bit. I shouldn't have told you to come down for dinner. I got lonely upstairs."

With her husband's help, Mary Ellen walked to her place at the table on shaky legs. I wondered if the hesitant gait was due to wine or true illness.

As she sat, Richard pulled an old-fashioned bell-pull next to the fireplace then resumed his chair. Willie appeared promptly.

"Willie, Mrs. Goodhue has decided to join us tonight."

Willie nodded and left. Within minutes, one of the maids had the place setting and the first course in front of her mistress.

"When I entered the room, I heard Liza say something had to be done. What has to be done?" She dipped her spoon into the lobster bisque.

"Security," Stephen answered.

The spoon hovered just short of her mouth before finding its destination. She swallowed.

"I'm not sure the added expense is necessary. Besides, whoever killed Beatrice will be apprehended soon."

"And Irene?" I asked.

The spoon made its shaky way back to the soup bowl.

"I'm sure the constabulary will solve both cases," Stephen said.

"I suggest we talk about something else," Richard said. "Murder is not conducive to good digestion."

Pompous ass. "Maybe we should discuss my plans for a bed and breakfast," I replied, waiting for the reaction.

Stephen stifled a smile by spooning lobster bisque into his mouth. Mary Ellen drew in a hissing breath, while Richard glared.

Mary Ellen recovered first. "I find that subject distasteful, too." She paused to send me a tight smile and shot a quick glance at Stephen before turning her malicious gaze back to me. "I understand you went snorkeling with Ben today. Seems rather an odd endeavor, considering Beatrice was dead on her living room floor."

I could always count on Mary Ellen for snide remarks disguised as casual conversation. I swallowed another spoonful of soup before answering.

"Yes, I suppose it does, but I didn't know Beatrice well, and felt in the way, so I jumped at the chance."

"Where did you go?" Stephen asked.

"Some reef not far from the marina where he keeps his boat. I needed the distraction. The water was warm and the scenery lovely."

Stephen nodded. "I know that area. It's very popular with the tourists. If you do turn this into a hotel, you might consider striking a deal with one of the dive boat captains. I'm sure four or five guaranteed customers a week can result in a discount."

I suppressed the laughter bubbling in my chest. Stephen had turned the tables on both Richard and Mary Ellen by mentioning my plans and not taking the bait concerning Ben.

"What a wonderful idea."

Mary Ellen's spoon clanked against the rim of the soup bowl. "Yes, I'm sure Stephen has many suggestions concerning Bountiful."

I had no idea what she meant, but assumed she'd just tossed a dig at him. *Time to put her on the hot seat.*

"By the way, I heard you dismissed Gladys the other day. What did she do to warrant getting chopped?"

Mary Ellen stared into her almost empty bowl. "I prefer not to discuss it."

"Well, if she was pinching the silver, I think I have a right to know," I replied.

"She was not pinching the silver as you suggest,"

Richard said in a tight voice. "It was a matter between mistress of the house and staff."

I don't like being dissed by supercilious bozos, but before I could comment, Mary Ellen spoke.

"If you must know, Gladys gossiped. When Beatrice caught her listening on the telephone extension and found out she'd made observations about the family to other staff, she came to me. If the woman was gossiping with staff, then she was also probably doing the same off the property."

Willie entered the room with a wine bottle, deftly uncorked it and poured a bit into a glass by Richard's plate while one of the maids whisked our bowls away. At Richard's nod, we were all served wine. Simultaneously, the salad arrived.

When the servants left, I resumed my questioning. "So Gladys gossiped. So what? All servants gossip about their employers. I watched enough *Upstairs, Downstairs* to know that. What made this so heinous?"

Richard's jaw clenched, but Mary Ellen speared a piece of lettuce.

"When I told her it was not her place to discuss what occurred in the house, she got sassy. I refuse to accept insubordination. After luncheon, I told Beatrice to dismiss her. Does that satisfy you?"

No, it didn't, but her crisp tone told me I wouldn't learn any more.

"Yes, I suppose so."

"Liza, you will find that here on the island there is a distinct line between master and servant," Richard said.

Double pompous ass. What a snob. I sipped my wine to cool my temper.

"There's also a distinct line between snobbery and treating others with respect," I said. "When this turns into a bed and breakfast, I will *employ* people, not have servants."

We finished the salad course in silence. A small throb tapped in my temple. How was I going to stand being around these two for a year? I would need lots of time away in order to avoid being overwhelmed.

The main course, a local fish of some sort with a delicate cream sauce, was brought in along with rice and asparagus. It was delicious, but with a headache forming, I had little enjoyment.

After dinner, Mary Ellen retreated to her room sans wine for a change, while the rest of us trooped into the drawing room. Richard poured two glasses of Drambuie.

"Please excuse me, but I want to make sure Mary Ellen is all right. She really shouldn't have come down tonight."

Without another word, he left with both glasses. I looked at Stephen and shrugged.

"Guess the dinner conversation was subpar," I said.

Stephen poured us each a glass of the liqueur, handing me one.

"It's odd how Mary Ellen seems to have cut herself off from family contact. When did this staying in her room begin?" he asked.

"Shortly before Irene died. I was on the veranda one day and overheard her telling Richard she couldn't take any more of Evelyn. I don't know her that well, so I can't tell if her behavior is normal."

Stephen frowned and then sipped his drink. "Mary Ellen is the type to adhere to tradition at all costs."

"Image is everything," I replied, also sipping.

"This is very much out of character. It's almost like she's hiding."

"My decision to stay and turn Bountiful into a paying concern has upset her. I can't believe Sir Geoffrey's will couldn't be overturned."

"Neither could she. It was the only time I've ever seen her anything but calm and cool. She was so angry, she looked ready to kill."

At his words, a tremor radiated from the pit of my stomach to the tips of my fingers. "Kill?"

He waved a hand. "I don't mean literally. Can you really see Mary Ellen bashing Irene over the head and shoving her off the overlook?"

"Maybe it does all stem from Sir Geoffrey changing his will." I swept a hand through my hair. "I don't know what to think any more. We have two murders and a possible attempted murder with Evelyn's pill incident. If the family was so upset at the old boy's will, why hasn't someone tried to nail me?"

Stephen bolted the rest of the Drambuie down his throat and set the glass on the end table.

"I don't know, but I'm worried. Please come to Land's End with me."

I shook my head. "No, this is where I belong. And to be honest, it may be the safest house on the island. Another incident would raise a lot of police eyebrows."

He pulled me to my feet and into his arms. "I just know I don't want anything to happen to you. Promise me you won't go off on your own. Stick to the house for a while."

I kissed the tip of his chin. "I'd go stir crazy. Don't worry. I'll be careful. I promise."

His sea green eyes turned to emerald as his head descended. His lips found mine in a scorching kiss. Delicious heat flowed through my veins. I fisted my hands in the front of his polo shirt.

He finally broke contact and feathered light kisses across my forehead.

"I'm tied up in court tomorrow, but should be home by six. Would you like to go to Gentleman Jack's for dinner?"

"I'd love it."

I walked him into the foyer where we indulged in another searing kiss before he left. As I slowly climbed upstairs, I wondered if my future had already been settled. I suspected Grand Britannia might be home for the rest of my life.

Chapter Twenty-Six

I tossed my book aside unhappy with the ending. The killer was exactly who I thought. The bedside clock read almost two and still sleep refused to come. I'd come upstairs shortly after Stephen left, determined to get a good night's rest. But determination and reality are two separate things. In desperation, I'd picked up the mystery I'd begun several nights earlier.

Outside, the chirping insects, burbling fountain, and palm fronds rustling in the light breeze got on my nerves. Jittery and jumpy, I put off turning out the bedside light. Could Beatrice's killer still be lurking in the woods?

Get a grip, Channing. Whoever robbed and killed Beatrice is long gone, the chemical high from the proceeds of what little he stole over.

I heaved a sigh and stared at the lighter colored rectangle on the wall above the fireplace. Evangeline's portrait was gone, whisked away during dinner by one of the staff as I'd requested. I couldn't decide which was more unnerving—her portrait or that blank space.

My gaze swept down to the mantel. I assumed it was original to the house and was glad that no one had thought to paint it. The dark, ornately carved chunk of wood had character. I thought about all the Goodhues who had placed keepsakes on it throughout the centuries.

The fireplace itself didn't appear to have been renovated either. The wide firebox was faced with an antique fire screen and andirons that looked mid-Victorian. Soot blackened the first few rows of bricks above the opening. I still had no idea why a fire was needed in the tropics.

I couldn't stop staring at that blank space. Okay, so there was no safe. But this was the master bedroom, at least as far as Sir Geoffrey was concerned. Had Jonathon Goodhue also occupied the room? I wondered if anybody really knew.

Then a thought occurred making me sit up abruptly. *A safe would be obvious, but how about a hiding place within the fireplace? Happens all the time in the movies.*

I scrambled from the bed, switched on the overhead light, and stood gazing at the mantel. The carvings were both recessed and in relief. *In theory, the heroine presses or pulls something, and a door springs open revealing a hiding place.*

I pressed and pulled, but nothing happened. The mantel remained solid and unyielding. I fingered the supports and the surround along the perimeter. Still nothing.

Backing up, I stood at the foot of the bed with my hands fisted on my hips and stared. Maybe it's nothing so clichéd and obvious. What about the bricks?

I ran my hands over the brickwork testing for a loose one that could be removed with little trouble. Zilch. The damned things had been cemented in for almost four hundred years.

My gaze settled on the wide slate hearth. It sat

flush with the floor, the dark gray color interspersed with shades of blue and deep rust suggested this was not original, but most likely a renovation. The randomly shaped stones had been grouted in with a dark mortar, except for one near the right andiron.

Curious, I knelt and ran my finger over the line. The grout moved enough to tell me it wasn't grout. More like a heavy sand. *The kind of thing that can be removed and replaced with little fuss or notice.*

I scraped the grit from between the stones, but my fingers wouldn't fit in the crack. I rose and scurried to the vanity rummaging in my cosmetic bag until finding a nail file. I wedged it into the crack and pushed. The file snapped.

Dammit! What the hell else did I have to get this stone up? I ran into the bathroom. Nothing there. I then checked the armoire. A belt buckle? A high heel? One was too small and the other too big. *Maybe I'll find something that's just right.* I suppressed a giggle at the Goldilocks allusion.

Come on, Liza! Think! Then I stared at the fireplace implement stand on the left side of the hearth. It contained the usual poker, brush, tongs, and shovel. The shovel! Maybe it would work.

I grabbed it from the stand and tried inserting the edge into the crack. The side lips were too big. I replaced it and snatched the tongs. I fit one into the seam and pushed. The stone rose an inch or so. Excited, I heaved again, then standing on the handle, wedged my fingers underneath and pulled. To my surprise it moved.

I knelt, removed it, and reached into the space. My fingers made contact with a metal box. My heart pounded in anticipation. What did it contain? Jewels?

Papers? Money? I pulled the box from the hiding space, set it on the floor, then flipped down the clasp, opened it, and stared at two ledgers—one large, quite old and bound in leather, the other more recent—the kind found in any bookstore. Nestled in the corner was a leather drawstring bag.

Not knowing the age of the bag, I opened it with gentle fingers and emptied the contents onto the rug.

Jewelry tumbled out in a brilliant display of ruby red, emerald green, deep blue, and clear, clear diamonds, all set in gold or silver. In awe, I untangled necklaces, rings, bracelets, and earrings. They were very old, but who had hidden them?

I'd ask Stephen what to do with them tomorrow. I didn't care all that much for jewelry, but something inside of me didn't want to sell them. Maybe a spark of Goodhue family pride was kindling.

I replaced the items and turned my attention to the ledgers. Were these the diaries everyone assumed didn't exist? Natural curiosity made me reach for the oldest first.

The spidery, cramped writing had faded to the point of near invisibility. I would need a magnifying glass and strong light to decipher any of it. The entries were dated with a day and month, but no year. Nor was there anything as helpful as an inscription stating, *Diary of Jonathon Goodhue,* yet the handwriting was reminiscent of that in the manifest. On the other hand, it could have been written by anyone, even his wife Isabelle. Perhaps the jewelry had belonged to her.

I also returned this piece of history to the box. Maybe Stephen would know someone who could deal with it.

That left the newer diary, but before reading it, I needed a place to hide the box, finally settling for the armoire. I shoved it into the far corner on the bottom and hid it with a couple of pairs of shoes.

After replacing the stone and loose sand from the hearth, I crawled back in bed, opened the smaller diary, and recognized the handwriting from the letters sent to Mother. Sir Geoffrey had written this. He had provided dates which helped set the timeline. My ancestors had been possessed with a keen sense of self-importance.

I wiggled my shoulders into a more comfortable position against the pillows and read.

February 6, 1950—Bountiful contains a lot of secrets. My father told me about the boathouse years ago and how his great-grandfather had taken care of the problem, but today offered a surprise from within the house itself. While working on replacing the hearth in our bedroom, one of the workmen unearthed a cache of jewelry and an old diary wrapped in burlap from a hidden space under the bricks.

The mention of the boathouse intrigued me. Did it mask the entrance to a treasure cave like the legend inferred? I'd have to check on that.

The jewelry belonged to Isabelle. She's wearing some of it in the portrait. Rumor has always said Jonathon Goodhue kept a diary. I suspect this is it. I can't wait to read it.

The next entry skipped ahead to March.

March 16, 1950—I should burn Jonathon's journal, but can't bring myself to turn a part of Grand Britannia's and the Goodhue heritage into ashes. I instructed the workman to leave the space intact and tile over it. The items can go back to be found by someone else. Maybe by then it won't matter. Besides, it's all lies.

What kind of a lie did the Goodhue family live? It had to be a whopper if my great-grandfather was willing to cover it up for all eternity. Everybody knew Jonathon was a pirate—okay, a privateer—so that couldn't be the secret. I read on hoping he explained further.

Jonathon Goodhue was a thief and a scoundrel. I can only hope no descendants of Elijah Taylor exist anymore or, if they do, are unaware of the connection. The man died three years after The Marauder *sank. Could someone at this late date arise to wreck what generations of Goodhues have worked to preserve? Thank goodness Evangeline is in Paris. I'll take care of everything. She'll never know.*

This morning I chiseled the grout from the slate covering the hidden hole and replaced the jewels and the journal along with this diary. I made a paste of sand, glue, and ink to replace the grout. Unless someone looks hard, no one will know. The secret will remain buried until the next renovation. By then I'll be dead. Perhaps it won't matter.

Well, this was a freaking cop out. He gave no details at all. What the hell was in that journal? I was tempted to scrounge up a strong flashlight and a magnifying glass immediately, but held off. The journal of Jonathon Goodhue was old, the paper near crumbling, and should be handled by experts.

I set the diary on the nightstand and turned out the light. I needed to pay another visit to the Historical Society in Port Elizabeth. I had to know more about Jonathon Goodhue, Elijah Taylor, and the fate of *The*

Marauder.

****

Myron dropped me off at the Historical Society a little after ten the next morning. He would run errands while I did research.

The woman at the front desk escorted me to the document reading room.

"You understand that all materials must remain here, don't you?" she said.

"Yes, I know."

She handed me a pair of thin latex gloves. "Please use these when handling the items. The oil and fluids from our skin can damage delicate paper. We haven't as yet completed all the necessary protection."

I slipped the gloves on as she left the room. She returned a few minutes later with several large books and placed them on the table before me.

"This is the early history of Grand Britannia," she said, indicating a dark brown leather covered journal. "It covers the years from fifteen-seventy to sixteen-eighty-five and was compiled by a number of Crown-appointed Governors."

A second journal similar to the first was placed to my right.

"This is a census done in sixteen-eighty. It's quite thorough. I think you'll find your ancestors listed." The third book found a spot to my left. "This is another history of Grand Britannia done in the mid-eighteenth century. It goes into more detail regarding the citizenry and how they came to the island. Don't hesitate to call if you need anything else."

I thanked her and opened the first journal. History had never been my strong suit unless it had to do with researching a character or setting in a play. Now, I hoped it would help me understand more about the family I'd never known. And secrets have a way of emerging sooner or later. Especially those we'd rather keep hidden.

The first journal proved disappointing. I wouldn't have called it a history, but more of a list. The authors had archived damned near every dollar taken in for the crown. People, taverns, whorehouses, merchants were taxed to the nines. If someone set foot on the island, they got nailed.

Grand Britannia was also the clearinghouse for British privateers. The booty was brought in, divvied up between the Government and the captains, and then sent back to England on legitimate merchantmen.

Could this be what Sir Geoffrey meant by Jonathon Goodhue being a thief? Had he skimmed some of the ill-gotten gains for himself and buried it before entering port and the customs house? If so, pirate treasure legend was more about tax evasion.

And I'm sure the authorities knew. Probably looked the other way for a fee.

Gentleman Jack's ship, *The Marauder*, was mentioned several times with a detailed list of the contents. After 1670, it disappeared from the rolls, about the time family history claimed it had sunk.

I closed the book and turned to the one containing the census. The binding crackled as I opened it. I skimmed most of the pages until finally finding the Goodhue family. The writing, while faded was legible.

The property known as Bountiful.
Owner Jonathon Goodhue, age 40, sugar
cane grower, distiller of rum, sole proprietor

of Goodhue Shipping Company in Port Elizabeth.

> *Other residents, wife Isabelle, age 30.*
> *Son, Jonathon, age 8.*
> *Daughter, Belinda, age 7.*
> *Daughter, Carina, age 6.*
> *Son, Bradford, age 4.*
> *Servants, 4 male, 5 female.*

So, Jonathon had married a woman who had produced three kids right off the bat. If I remembered correctly, the sarcophagus in the crypt had shown Isabelle dying in 1684. I wondered if the odds on surviving childbirth in those days had caught up with her.

Apparently, the servants' names didn't matter. Sir Geoffrey's diary had mentioned the first mate dying three years after the ship sank. I reread the listings in search of Elijah Taylor, but found nothing. He either didn't own property or was no longer on the island and had died elsewhere. Yet Beatrice had claimed him as an ancestor.

What was it someone said? That he died in some kind of brawl? And what was the secret that had so upset my great-grandfather? Had Jonathon stolen from his first mate? But what? His share of the treasure?

Hmm. Now that was a thought. But if Elijah Taylor felt wronged by his captain, wouldn't he do something about it?

Good grief! Maybe he did. Could the good captain have killed the first mate either deliberately or in self-defense?

I shook my head and opened the final journal. The title, *A History of Grand Britannia and Inhabitants*, was cumbersome, but said it all. This one was easier to read even though some of the spelling was a bit hard to follow.

I breezed through most of the book until finding Jonathon Goodhue's name and contribution to the island. And there was what I sought in old-fashioned black and white.

The Goodhues have been established on Grand Britannia since 1672 when Jonathon settled on a piece of land granted to him from King Charles II for service to his country.

I read that to mean, thanks for pillaging, here's your reward.

He was, however, no stranger to the island, having often seen port with his ship the Marauder and its crew. Unfortunately, the ship sank off Pirate's Point near Cutlass Bay in October 1670 during a storm. He and his first mate were the only survivors. He built the house known as Bountiful in 1673. His bride, Isabelle De Santos, was the daughter of the governor of Cuba. Jonathon Goodhue grew sugar cane, distilled molasses into an excellent rum, and owned Goodhue Shipping. He died in 1705.

That was pretty much it on Jonathon Goodhue. The family didn't come to prominence until later generations. But the part about his ship sinking so near to where Irene lived was ironic to say the least. Or maybe not. A ship sinking in a storm off an island with reefs galore wasn't unusual. Had Irene known? Probably. If I'd found this, then she must have seen it, too.

I glanced at my watch. I'd been occupied with family history for close to three hours. I assumed Myron's errands had been run and he patiently awaited my arrival at the front doors.

I left the books on the table, peeled off the gloves, and departed, pausing to thank the woman at the desk again before emerging into the bright sunshine. Myron waited beside the limo.

On the ride home, I realized I'd come up with more questions than answers.

My next trip would be to the boathouse. Someone had taken a pick to the back wall. I wanted to know why.

Chapter Twenty-Seven

After returning to Bountiful, I had Violet bring a sandwich and some soup to my room, along with a flashlight and a magnifying glass. If my maid had any curious questions about the latter two items, she kept them to herself.

"Violet, I don't wish to be disturbed until dinner," I said when she removed the tray an hour later.

"Yes, miss. Is there anything I can get for you?"

"No, thank you. Did Mr. or Mrs. Goodhue say anything about my absence at lunch?"

"Not that I know of, miss. Mr. Goodhue said he had work to do, and Mrs. Goodhue retired to the library to make phone calls."

"I see. Thank you, Violet. You can go."

It sounded as though Mary Ellen was beginning to come out of hiding. Perhaps she was contacting cruise lines for information.

I didn't want anyone to see me leaving for the boathouse. By five o'clock, the servants would be in the kitchen preparing for the dinner service. Richard and Mary Ellen would be upstairs relaxing and dressing for the cocktail hour. All I'd need was a flashlight and an hour to look around. The cave of legend had to be there.

To kill the three hours until five, I unearthed what I assumed was Jonathon Goodhue's diary from the box in the bottom of my armoire and placed it on my desk. I carefully opened the cover.

The first page was almost illegible. The years under the hearth hadn't done it any good. I turned on the flashlight and used the magnifying glass. No good. I was only able to decipher a few words here and there.

The same held true for the next ten pages. The faded ink, cramped writing, and the four hundred year old spelling and speech patterns, made little sense.

Toward the center of the journal, the ink was less faded, and I managed several paragraphs describing his early years on the island. *So this* is *the long-lost diary.*

I was surprised to learn that Jonathon Goodhue had lived in a small house on the property erected during the construction of Bountiful. The description came close to that of Beatrice's place.

I read on as far as I could before the ink once again faded. Leaning back, I rubbed my eyes and massaged the crick in my neck. I'd made out the name Elijah on several pages, but couldn't read the rest. Nor could I see where Sir Geoffrey got that our ancestor was a thief. *Unless the writing had been more legible then or he'd done other research.*

I returned the journal to the armoire and glanced at the clock. It was only four-thirty, but I needed to change from my town clothes to something suitable for the beach. I also needed to call Stephen.

I got his voice mail and left a detailed message. I tossed the phone onto the desk and changed into a pair of shorts and my running shoes. I picked up the flashlight and cracked the bedroom door open an inch or so. Voices drifted up from the foyer. Then someone came up the stairs. Richard paused on the last step and stared at the runner, a frown on his face. He bent over and ran his hand along the edge.

Come on, come on, get ready for dinner!

He finally moved on. I heard the sound of a door closing, and then scuttled down the stairs. I paused for a moment to listen. All was quiet. With Richard and Mary Ellen's windows facing the front of the house, I turned toward the terrace entrance. Without looking back, I hustled through the maze and across the lawn to the overlook.

I supposed Stephen would have a fit if he knew what I had in mind, but no one was about. Nor did I have that creepy feeling of being watched. Besides, I'd only be gone a few minutes.

I hurried down the steps to the beach and trotted through the sand to the boathouse. I jerked the door open, entered the gloomy room, and switched on the flashlight.

According to the legend, Gentleman Jack had hidden the treasure in a cave. I had seen no possible entrance to a cave along Bountiful's section of beach. The possibility of the pirate stashing the goodies on another part of the island didn't make sense. Why build Bountiful miles away from your main source of income? No, the cave had to be here, behind the boathouse. It was the only answer.

I entered the smaller room where the trespasser had used the pickax. Someone had been looking for the cave, and it wasn't kids. A cursory inspection of the wall next to the cliff convinced me the entrance wasn't here. That left the front room.

Returning, I scanned the back wall. Bags of sails, cans of motor oil, lanterns, and numerous coils of rope jammed the shelves. I had no idea where to begin, so I started in the middle, pulling items from places, not sure what I sought.

Each set of shelves ran about six feet between vertical supports, except for the unit in the far corner. Those shelves were narrower in width as well as depth. I took a closer look. Sure enough, this unit was set back several inches. Cans of paint and old solvent filled the spaces. I removed a couple. My heart rate increased. The other units were true shelves with the stone wall behind. Here I touched wood, wood similar to that of the wine cellar door, thick and hard as the rock of the cliff.

Excited, I emptied the shelves, and then pulled on the unit. It moved a few inches, opening like a door with unrevealed hinges screeching in protest. Encouraged, I tried again. Another six inches. Panting, I drew in a deep breath and yanked, putting all my leverage behind it. With one final shriek, it opened a full three feet. Dank air rushed out to smother me. I recoiled and took a few breaths to clear my lungs, and then shone the flashlight on my find—a fissure some 6 feet high.

The opening could easily accommodate my body, and I slid through into a narrow passageway, inspecting small patches of damp on the walls as I walked. I paused at an ell in the corridor. Curiosity forced me to make that turn.

A large, circular room stood before me, hollowed out by millennia of dripping rainwater percolating through the soil and rock. Perhaps it still did from time to time, but at the moment the sand beneath my feet was dry. Stalagmites hovered overhead. The chamber was empty. If Gentleman Jack had hidden his treasure here, it was long gone. The atmosphere was dank and stifling. I'd discovered the cave—there was just nothing in it.

"So, you found it," a voice said from behind me, the sound echoing strangely.

I screamed and whirled. "Ben! You scared the hell out of me! What are you doing here?"

"I was fishing and saw you run in here. When you didn't come out, I decided to make sure you were okay." He gazed around the cavern. "So, where's the treasure?"

"Gone. Assuming there was ever one to begin with."

"But it existed—still does. I know it. The Goodhue's stole it."

"How can you steal what's yours to begin with?"

"Not all of it," he said in a low voice. "Old Jonathon Goodhue was a common thief."

Funny he should echo the words in Sir Geoffrey's journal.

"How do you know that?"

He made a dismissive gesture. "Irene told me. And not even the Goodhues could cash in all the loot at once. My guess is they moved it to the house at some point in time."

"Ben, that makes no sense. Everyone knew Jonathon Goodhue's roots as a privateer. Face it, there is no treasure. It doesn't exist."

"Yes, it does! She told me it did!"

His rising voice bounced off the walls. "She, who?"

He turned his dark gaze toward me. "Irene, of

course. Who else?"

Ben was giving me the creeps. A long rolling shiver slithered up my spine. I had done exactly what Stephen had warned me not to do. I just hadn't expected to see Ben. It dawned on me that maybe I should get out of here.

"Let's go back to the house. Would you like to stay for dinner?" While speaking, I swept the light along the walls and floor of the cave. It looked as undisturbed as the day my pirate ancestor had found it. Then, off to the side, something gleamed in the light. I moved toward it.

Pain exploded in my head. Brilliant flashes of light blinded me from the inside. Then my world went dark.

****

I awoke with a throbbing headache and rolled onto my back. Something hard jabbed me in the shoulder. I groaned and struggled to sit up, trying to remember what happened.

I discovered the cave. Then what? Ben! Has he been attacked, too?

My flashlight still shone. I grabbed it and swung it around the cave. I was alone.

Ben? Ben hit me?

I staggered to my feet, wincing as pain slashed through my head. I moved the flashlight along the floor again. The beam shone on a length of pipe lying in the sand near where Ben had stood. In the semi-darkness, I'd never noticed. He'd probably held it close to his side.

The item I'd seen when struck, and had poked my shoulder, stuck up a couple of inches from the sand. I knelt and pulled it free—a gold crucifix still shiny after all these years and encrusted with rubies and pearls fit into the palm of my hand. *The last piece of Gentleman Jack's treasure?*

My mind was still fuzzy from the blow, but suddenly a lot of things that had puzzled me now made sense. His angry reaction to my discovery of the floor plans. He'd also been put out that Stephen and I had gotten back together. Plus he'd given me a strange look when I told him about the boathouse wall being damaged. What was it he'd said?

"You need better security, Liza. First someone takes a pick to the wall. Then some thief sneaks in to rob the first house he sees, which happens to be Beatrice's. She catches him and bashes her head in. I'm scared for you. One of the Goodhues is up to no good. And that includes Stephen Albright."

I'd been angry at his comment about Stephen. No woman likes to hear from anybody that the man she loves is a louse.

And while I had told Ben about the wall being damaged, I couldn't remember if I'd mentioned the pickax. But I knew without a doubt I had never told anyone that Beatrice had been bludgeoned. Only the police, Helen, Richard, and I knew that. I supposed by now the family also knew, but no way in hell would they share that information with an outsider, especially Ben Collier. And the maid had gone home to her family in the village immediately, so Ben wasn't likely to have talked to her. The question was why? Why did he kill Beatrice? Had he also killed Irene? Attempted to kill Evelyn? And what about Sir Geoffrey? My head spun and my stomach clenched. *Why didn't he finish me off?*

I grabbed the flashlight and hurried back to the passageway. I didn't expect the door to be open and I was correct. He'd shut it on the way out. I pushed, but it didn't budge. I didn't waste time wondering how he'd locked it. It wouldn't take much to jam one of the hinges. He hadn't needed to kill me outright. Three days in here, and I'd be dead from dehydration. Or maybe he thought the blow had killed me. Even though it was useless, I pounded on the door.

"Help! Help! Let me out of here! Can anybody hear me?"

Of course they couldn't, but when facing certain death, you try anything.

I retraced my steps to the cavern. How long would my flashlight last before the batteries died plunging me into total darkness? Would anyone think to look for me in the boat house?

Stephen will. I left him a message, but will he look for the hidden entrance to the cave? Maybe the movement of the shelves had left a mark on the floor. And if he does find me, will I still be alive?

Stephen! I patted my pocket searching for my cell and then remembered tossing it onto the desk. What a time to be without it! On the other hand, I was encased in solid rock. No way would service get through.

I sat on the sand, clutching the crucifix, and cried. Thoughts of Mother, Stephen, even Richard and Mary Ellen flashed through my mind. Then I remembered the damp patches on the passageway. Air circulated. Air that caused condensation. And even a tiny opening somewhere in this cliff would give me a voice to the outside. *And Stephen will search for me.*

I scrambled to my feet and probed the walls in the torchlight. Here and there, more thin fingers of damp revealed themselves. Even a hole in the roof would allow me to shine the light to the outside world. However, I found no obvious hole in the roof or anywhere else.

About to give up, the light caught darkness against the stone wall at the rear of the cave. The closer I got, the harder my heart pounded. I ended up running to the spot.

Another fissure, narrower than the one in the cliff face, but a fissure nonetheless. Could I get through?

I turned sideways and edged my way in. The opening widened after a few feet. A few feet further the passageway gave way to a small room no more than five feet in diameter. To my astonishment, an iron ladder was bolted to the wall. I had no idea where it led, but anything was better than where I was now.

I jammed the crucifix into the waistband of my shorts, and holding the flashlight in my hand, climbed.

The rungs were spaced farther apart than normal ladders making my progress slow. Rust crumbled at my touch. The sea air had corroded, but not yet destroyed. I cried out and clutched the sides when one of the rungs snapped causing my legs to momentarily dangle in space. I scrambled to regain a foothold and continued climbing. Near the top, I shone the light upwards. The ladder ended ten feet above my head against a ceiling—not the ceiling of a cave, but a manmade structure.

My head hurt like hell, and my thought processes were a bit murky. I had no idea where I was or what was above me. The ceiling had to be the floor of something else, but how on earth did I get out of here? Could I get out? The ladder was here for a reason.

I finished my climb and probed the area at the top of the ladder. Wood. I traced the cracks into a two foot square. Just the right size for a man to shimmy through if necessary, but where in the house did it come out?

I pushed and almost lost my balance. I grasped the side of the ladder, the gritty rust flaking in my hand. Not a good time to fall. I was at least sixty feet above the cave floor. The flashlight joined the crucifix in my shorts. With the beam pointing overhead, I held tight with one hand and pushed again. Something moved, but not enough to open. The crack along the left side had widened enough to jam my fingertips in. This time I tried sliding it to the right. The heavy square moved another inch.

"Help! Can anyone hear me?"

No one answered. I hooked my leg around the side support and heaved again. Four inches gapped. Fresh air bathed my face. I breathed deeply and gathered my determination for another try. Licking my lips, I gritted my teeth and pushed. The square made a scraping noise. Another six inches. I repeated the process a few more times until I could wiggle my way through the gap.

I grabbed the flashlight and shone it on my new surroundings. A large object stood next to my head. A wall rose ten feet away. It took me a moment to realize I was in the crypt. The wooden square I had moved was covered with stone, and had slid under the sarcophagus of Isabelle Goodhue.

I climbed out of the hole both laughing and crying with relief. Isabelle had died young. What better way to hide any remaining treasure than to build a final resting place over the entrance.

Neither the tears nor the laughter lasted. I needed to call Stephen and the police. Ben was still out there!

Chapter Twenty-Eight

During my captivity, darkness had fallen. I hesitated to turn on the flashlight. What if Ben was still around? I had no desire to tangle with him again. *He might finish what he started.*

I made my way slowly down the path from the crypt to the garage. Clearing the trees, I ran across the lawn and through the maze, entering the house from the terrace. I paused inside the doors to catch my breath.

I needed to find Richard and tell him to call the police. *And Stephen. I want Stephen.* I needed those strong arms around me and his voice telling me he'd never let go—that I was safe.

I moved down the hall when loud voices coming from the drawing room made me stop.

"Dammit! Where is she?" Stephen demanded.

"And I told you, I don't know," Ben's voice replied.

A chill skittered down my arms. Ben! They'd captured Ben. The doors to the drawing room were partially open. I crept forward to listen.

"She left a voice mail earlier saying she found an old journal and was going to check out the boathouse. Then lo, and behold, security finds you coming out of the boathouse. What were you doing there?"

"How many times do I have to tell you? I was out

in the dingy when I came down this side of the cove and saw the boathouse door open. I went in to investigate, found nothing and left. I was about to dingy back to the villa when your rent-a-cops here grabbed me. They checked the damned place and found nothing, too. Now, if you'll excuse me, I'm going home."

Rent-a-cops? As in security guards? Where did they come from?

"Not just yet, Mr. Collier," another voice said. It sounded like the Chief Inspector. "I'd like to ask you a few questions concerning Miss Irene Goodhue."

"Oh, for crissakes, will you give it a rest. I didn't kill Irene."

"Of course, you did," Mary Ellen said with loathing in her voice. "You also killed Beatrice. And have probably killed Liza, too."

"You're crazy. Or drunk. Or both."

"Now see here, Collier…" Richard began.

"You have neither proof, nor motive," Ben answered in a surly tone. "At least, Liza had the sense to hire more security for this place."

"Liza had nothing to do with it," Richard replied, his voice cool and composed. "Stephen and I talked it over this morning and decided it was a prudent move."

"Let's get back to Liza, damn you! Where is she, Collier?" Stephen's voice had risen to a shout.

"Albright, I have no idea and really don't give a damn. I haven't seen her since yesterday and that's the truth!"

Oh my God, it was the cue of a lifetime! I grasped the doors, slid them open, and lifting my chin paused for the dramatic moment.

Directors around the world would have salivated.

Mary Ellen, seated by the fireplace gasped, and then emptied her almost full wine glass. Richard, standing next to her, stared with raised eyebrows. The top cop and his two constables jerked their heads toward the door. Stephen whirled with a look of total relief on his face.

My attention, however, focused on Ben who stood with the constables near the French doors. I've heard the expression "turning white as a sheet", but had never before seen the reality. I had now. Ben literally paled to the point of elementary school paste.

"Hullo, Ben. Nice to see you again so soon. Bet you're surprised to see me."

"Liza!" Stephen, standing in back of one of the chairs near the fireplace, took a step toward me. In doing so, he placed himself in front of Ben and the policemen.

Ben shoved Stephen into a constable. They stumbled into each other and the chair. Mary Ellen screamed. Richard, the Chief Inspector, and the other cop moved to help. I rushed forward adding to the mayhem. In the confusion, Ben bolted out the French doors and into the night.

Stephen wrapped me in his arms and kissed my forehead. "Are you all right? What happened?"

"I'm fine, but no thanks to Ben. He tried to kill me. Hit me with a pipe of some sort. I found the cave. And he was lying. He told me he was fishing when he saw me enter the boathouse. And then I found my way out through the crypt."

Reaction to the entire last couple of hours set in and I made no sense. How could I with my heart pounding away at ramming speed and my knees ready to buckle? Stephen didn't seem to mind. He tightened his arms and kissed the top of my head.

When I caught my breath, I raised my face from his chest. The policemen were still standing in the room, Chief Inspector Bradshaw on his cell.

"What are you waiting for? He's getting away!" I cried.

He ended his call and smiled. "Miss Channing, it's an island. He has nowhere to go. Airports have been alerted."

"But he has a boat at the West End Marina!"

"Constables are on their way to secure the area along with the main port in Port Elizabeth. It won't take long. He's trapped. If you're feeling up to it, I'd like you to come to headquarters and make a statement."

For the next several hours, I sat on a hard plastic chair, drank innumerable cups of coffee, told my story, and answered questions.

"And you never suspected Mr. Collier?" the inspector asked.

"Not until he hit me. Did you find the cave and the pipe?"

Stephen sat next to me holding my hand. "The constables are going over the boathouse now. All this time and no one knew about the hidden door. Amazing."

"I think Sir Geoffrey knew. He left a diary that mentioned the boathouse." I'd told everyone about finding the journals and my trip to the Historical Society. "I'm sure Ben killed Irene and Beatrice, but have no clue as to motive."

"We'll soon be searching the villa and his boat. Perhaps we'll find one."

I set the coffee cup down with a shaking hand.

"Inspector, if you're finished, can I take Miss Channing home? It's been a long night."

Inspector Bradshaw closed the file folder and smiled. "Yes, by all means. And don't worry, we'll find Mr. Collier."

Stephen and I were silent as he drove out of West End toward Bountiful.

"So, how long do you think it'll be before they catch up with Ben?" I asked breaking the quiet.

"He's extremely resourceful. I wouldn't put it past him to bribe a fisherman to take him to St. Georges, but if I know the Chief Inspector, he'll have already alerted authorities on the surrounding islands. Now, tell me more about those journals."

I spent the rest of the drive describing in greater detail what I'd found, and why I'd gone to the boathouse.

"I'll take the old journal to the historical society first thing in the morning. They'll know what to do with it." He turned into the driveway at Bountiful and paused by the guardhouse. A man inside nodded. A moment later the gates swung open.

"So, you and Richard decided to hire more security?"

"We talked early this morning and were both worried, especially about the beach access. As a precaution, we added more men to patrol the woods and beach. That's how they caught Collier. He was just crawling into the dingy. Another two minutes and he'd have been in the middle of the cove."

"Wonder how they missed seeing me enter."

"They couldn't be everywhere." He stopped in

front of the house, and then turned to face me. "I don't care what anyone says, I'm staying the night. Collier is still out there. I want you safe."

"With you, I'll always feel safe."

It was after midnight. I was exhausted and hungry as hell. After a quick trip to the kitchen and a sandwich, we headed upstairs.

Stephen paused at the door to my room. "Do we observe propriety by me taking a guest room?"

"Screw propriety."

I opened the door and pulled him inside.

****

There's nothing like a brush with death followed by some serious sex to make a girl sleep soundly. I never cracked an eyelid until after nine. And the only reason I did then was because Stephen's cell phone rang. I nestled my head further into the pillow and listened to his end of the conversation.

"Yes…You did? Where?…That was close. Doesn't surprise me…Yes, ten-thirty at Bountiful will be fine…Thank you for calling. Have you informed the others?…Good. See you soon."

"Who was that?" I mumbled.

"Chief Inspector Bradshaw. They caught Collier about two this morning trying to steal a boat from a small marina in Cutlass Bay."

The news poked me into full awareness. "Cutlass Bay? How did he get all the way over there?"

"Stole a car. I don't have many details. All I know is he's been under interrogation ever since."

I sat up as he swung his legs out of bed. "Does Richard know?"

"Yes. He was informed a little while ago. The

Deadly Inheritance

Chief Inspector wants to meet with us here at ten-thirty."

"Doesn't give us much time. I wonder if breakfast is still laid out."

We dressed and hurried downstairs to the dining room. To my surprise, both Richard and Mary Ellen were seated at the table. Her eyebrows rose and her spine stiffened when we entered.

"You spent the night, Stephen?" she asked.

"Yes, he did," I replied giving her a look that dared her to make a remark.

For once, she took the hint. We ate with a minimum of conversation, refilled our coffee cups and waited for the Chief Inspector in the drawing room. He entered promptly at the appointed time.

"Inspector Bradshaw, please be seated," Richard said. "What have you got to tell us?"

"We apprehended Mr. Collier attempting to steal a boat from the Cutlass Bay Marina around two this morning. He put up quite a fight, but the night watchman is big and strong as the proverbial ox."

"What did he have to say?" I asked.

"Began by claiming Miss Channing's version of what happened in the boathouse is sheer fantasy. Said insanity must run in the family. He kept to that line until we discovered a lot of very interesting material in his villa and on his boat."

"Such as?" Stephen said.

"Letters, diaries, and genealogical papers dealing with Elijah Taylor."

"Jonathon Goodhue's first mate?" Richard asked.

The Chief Inspector nodded. "We're testing them for fingerprints, but I'm sure we'll find Ms. Goodhue's

367

and Ms. Hawthorne's on them. Also found several pieces of jewelry likely belonging to Ms. Goodhue."

"So, he killed Irene and Beatrice," Mary Ellen said. "I always said he did it."

"But why? What does Elijah Taylor have to do with Collier? And why did he kill over a genealogy?" Richard exclaimed.

"Sir Geoffrey's diary," I said slowly.

"What diary?" Mary Ellen asked.

"I found a diary he wrote, along with another journal from Jonathon Goodhue. Sir Geoffrey made a comment about his ancestor being a thief and how he hopes no descendants of Elijah Taylor ever get wind of it. Something tells me the good Captain swindled the first mate out of his share of booty. Beatrice might not be the only one to claim the Taylor lineage."

"Ben?" Mary Ellen said, gasping.

"What else? Remember all the questions he asked about the house and treasure? He must be related. Somehow, somewhere, he heard about the treasure and came to make a claim."

"First of all, he tries to do it through Irene," Stephen surmised. "But when she turns down his marriage proposal, he turns to plan B, which is remaining friends. He can still pump her for information and probably search for *The Marauder*. He did a lot of snorkeling and diving on these reefs."

"But why kill Irene?" Richard said. "She was his conduit to the family."

I took a deep breath. "Because she began researching Elijah Taylor. And Irene was good at her job. Even if she didn't discover the connection to Ben, she would unmask a lot of information."

"And my sister was closed-mouthed about her clients," Richard added. "I can see it now. He meets her after her dinner with Beatrice, demands information, and when Irene tells him no, he loses control and hits her with the bottle hard enough to kill her. Then he tosses her off the overlook, making it look accidental."

A lot of things clicked in my mind. Things, that at the time, I never suspected. "He came by way of the beach. That's why I thought I heard the sound of a motor. He used the dingy to get home. Afterward, he drove to Irene's, ransacked the place, found her research, and used me to help him discover the break-in."

"But why kill Beatrice?" Stephen asked. "That was taking a huge chance."

"Because Beatrice told us Irene had dropped off information that night," I offered. I thought for a moment. "You know, the legend says that Elijah Taylor died three years after the ship sank. I wonder how many other descendants are on Grand Britannia. Obviously some migrated to the States."

"Did he expect to eliminate all of them in order to inherit what he assumed was his part of the treasure?" Richard said.

"Was the man insane?" Mary Ellen asked.

"If he found any remaining treasure, he'd toss it onto his boat and take off," Stephen replied.

"Sounds crazy to me," I added.

The Chief Inspector had been silent during our speculations. Now, he spoke up. "I'm going to have to have a look at those journals."

"Jonathon Goodhue's is in delicate shape. I'm sure the authorities can work with the Historical Society," I said. "I'll go get them."

I ran upstairs and fetched the box from my wardrobe. I turned both diaries over to him, but not before shoving the jewelry into my dresser drawer. I wanted an appraisal before deciding its future.

With the journals in hand, the Chief Inspector left. Richard drifted toward the study to call Wyatt and Isabelle with the news their mother's murderer had been caught. Mary Ellen murmured something about attending the rose garden and also departed, leaving Stephen and I alone.

"Do you suppose he planned to actually claim the first mate's share of the treasure? Or was it something as simple as blackmailing Sir Geoffrey?" I wondered.

"I guess we'll never know completely what went through Ben's mind," he said. He smiled and pulled me into his arms before planting a hard kiss on my lips. "We need to talk."

I wound my arms around his neck. "About what?"

"You know perfectly well what about. Us." He took a deep breath. "How serious are you about this bed and breakfast thing? Or do you plan to give up on being Bountiful's owner and deed it over to the Historical Society?"

I leaned back in his arms. "I'm serious. This is a wonderful house. I think I fell in love with it the first time I saw it. And I plan to fulfill the terms of that old scoundrel's will. Maybe turning it into a paying concern is my way of getting even with him."

"What about your acting career?"

His words struck a nerve. What about my career? Two months ago, I'd been on a slow track to a probable nowhere. Did I want to return? And what about

Stephen? I loved him. I knew that with a certainty that left me breathless. It was time for an honest assessment of my life.

"Stephen, when your letter came about Sir Geoffrey, I hadn't worked in several months. The only reason I said yes was because I'd washed out on several auditions. But something about this place tugs at me, and I have no regrets giving up acting to remain on the island." I shot him a keen glance. "Provided, of course, I had the proper incentive to do so."

He smiled, ran a finger down my cheek to my chin, and lifted gently. "Incentive?"

"Yes, you know, something compelling me to stay."

"Something or someone?"

"Gonna make me say it first, aren't you? All right, Stephen Goodhue Albright, I love you. There! Are you ready to run in the opposite direction?" My heart hammered fearing that's exactly what he'd do.

"The only direction I'd run is to you. I love you, too. I didn't expect this, never saw it coming. But when we met at the airport, I knew I had a problem. I tried to ignore you, but you're not the kind of woman a man can ignore. When you went missing last night, I thought my life had ended. Then you appeared, and I knew I never wanted to let you out of my sight again."

I ran my finger across his lips. "Does this conversation end with something a bit more substantial?"

"Like what?" His eyes held a teasing look.

I pretended to be angry. "Humph! I said 'I love you' first. I'll be damned if I propose, too."

He laughed and kissed me again. "Elizabeth Marie

Channing, will you marry me?"

Any doubts about giving up my career vanished. "You betcha!"

He pulled me tighter and kissed me harder until we had to come up for air.

"Do you suppose my great-grandfather saw this coming?"

Stephen chuckled. "That wouldn't surprise me at all. Closer family ties."

"For once, I'm glad the old devil meddled in my life."

"So am I."

He pulled me close and kissed me again. The future began now.

Chapter Twenty-Nine

Ben cracked several days after being arrested and confessed to killing both Irene and Beatrice. He swore Irene was an accident. No one believed it. How do you accidentally hit someone over the head with a champagne bottle? For Beatrice, however, he had no such excuse.

Stephen brought me, Richard, and Mary Ellen up to date at lunch.

"Most of what he'd told us about his background was a lie. He grew up in the South Bronx and had a history with the police department."

"The South Bronx? That's a rough area and certainly isn't Kansas," I replied. "How did he learn about Jonathon Goodhue?"

"His grandmother raised him on stories about how the family had been swindled out of a huge inheritance by a pirate captain named Goodhue, complete with details on how important the family now was on Grand Britannia."

"Sounds like someone on the Collier side of the fence did a little research," Richard said.

"Most of it was anecdotal, but it wasn't hard to trace the names Goodhue and Taylor to the island. I also have the report from the Historical Society. Jonathon Goodhue's diary substantiated some of the accusation. The captain and first mate decided to wait a couple of years before splitting up the treasure."

I nodded. "No reason to show a sudden influx of gold, silver, and other plunder. Get rid of it bit by bit. Only Elijah Taylor died before the distribution."

"Eight months after his death, a woman showed up on Jonathon's doorstep with a newborn, claiming to be Taylor's wife."

"Let me guess—she demanded her share of the first mate's loot."

"Jonathon refused to give her anything. There were no marriage records, and the woman was a known prostitute from Port Elizabeth. He sent her packing. She, in turn, harassed him for several years with demands. Eventually, she landed herself in trouble with the constabulary. Jonathon Goodhue talked the magistrate into kicking her off the island."

"Gets rid of a nuisance and covers his ass on the treasure," I said. "At some point in time, descendants migrated back to Grand Britannia and to the United States, along with the family history."

"That's about it. As far as we know, Collier is the only one to actually attempt to get his share."

Mary Ellen, silent until now, spoke in a fierce tone. "I always knew he was no good, and Jonathon Goodhue was right to refuse that woman anything. Was Beatrice planning to claim a piece of the pie, too?"

Stephen shrugged. "I doubt it. Not at this late date. I think she just wanted to know more about her ancestor." He glanced at his watch. "Have to run. I have a client due in West End soon."

He rose from the table and I followed him into the foyer. "Any idea when you'll be home?"

A quick kiss on my lips sent my heart racing.

"Around seven, I suppose. Has Mary Ellen said anything about me moving in?"

"No, but she's not a happy person at the moment."

He kissed me again. "She'll get over it. See you later."

We had announced our engagement to the family. Richard congratulated us, and while his wife said the proper words, her eyes told me she was angry. I also reinforced my intentions concerning Bountiful. Once again, the chance to play mistress of the manor had slipped from her grasp.

I went upstairs for some downtime. Richard had adjusted to the new order, declaring he wouldn't miss the stress of dealing with the house. He would still manage the trust and the rest of the properties.

By this time, Mother knew what was what. I'd called the day after accepting Stephen's proposal.

"And you've know this man, how long?" she said.

"Long enough. If I'm not mistaken, your husband number five was rather a whirlwind courtship."

"And if I'm not mistaken, the marriage lasted a whole ten months. Ah well, at least I can give you the name of a good divorce lawyer."

"Thanks, but no thanks. Won't be needing one."

"Famous last words." She sighed. "I always said when you fell, it would be hard and forever."

Mother wasn't as cavalier about Ben.

"Two people murdered and you didn't tell me? Plus you were consorting with the killer? Liza!"

"I didn't want to worry you. Besides, you couldn't have done anything. And I didn't know he was a killer."

"I should have been there, which is exactly what

I'm planning to do. I want to meet this Stephen Albright."

We agreed Christmas was a good time to introduce Mother to the rest of the family.

I blogged, messed around on Facebook and Twitter, and then laid on the bed, making plans in my head for the renovation of Bountiful and for my wedding. Stephen and I decided April was the perfect month to say, "I do." And of course, the perfect setting was the back lawn of Bountiful with its panoramic view of the cove.

I dozed for a while before finally getting up. Stephen would be here soon. The knowledge brought peace to my mind. He'd moved in last weekend.

Dressed in a simple skirt and top, I stood at the vanity searching my jewelry box for a pair of earrings when the creaking veranda board announced someone was outside my room. A moment later, Mary Ellen walked in.

"Liza, I need to talk to you."

I slid the earrings into my ears and reached for a bracelet. "What about?"

"Bountiful. Are you still obsessed with turning it into a hotel?"

"Mary Ellen, we've been over this a hundred times. Yes! It's the only way to cover the expenses of such a huge place. Even Richard agrees with me now."

Her eyebrows drew together. "Richard doesn't understand. He never did. This house is mine!"

I heaved an irritated sigh and turned toward the door. "No, it isn't. In a less than a year, it will be mine. Richard told me a couple of days ago that he has an offer in on a lovely home near West End. He thinks you'll be happy there near your friends."

"I will not be happy any place except here!"

I ignored her rising voice and stepped into the hall. Over the last several days, Mary Ellen had become aggressive regarding my plans. Richard, Stephen, and I had decided it best if she left.

I was almost to the staircase when strong fingers grasped my shoulder and spun me around. I gazed into her furious face. Her eyes had narrowed and her lips pulled back from her teeth in a snarl. A muscle in her cheek twitched.

An uneasy feeling of *déjà vu* swept over me, which was strange since Mary Ellen had never been anything except icily polite to me. I'd never felt threatened— until now.

"Don't you dare walk away from me!" Her voice had risen to a shout. "I won't have it!"

My heart accelerated and my breath caught in my throat as I twisted away.

"Get your hands off of me! I was willing to let you and Richard stay here indefinitely, but it's time you two made other living arrangements."

I turned back toward the stairs.

"No!" she screamed.

A split second later a hard shove in the small of my back sent me hurtling toward the top step. I made a frantic clutch for the newel post. My fingers curled around it just as my foot slipped on the edge. I twisted and fell still clinging to the post.

Sir Geoffrey! Oh my God, this was how he died! The thought ran through my mind as she came at me again.

"Dammit, you will not inherit this house. I told that

miserable old man the same thing."

With superhuman strength, she ripped my fingers from their tenuous hold and grasping my wrists, shoved again.

I screamed and tumbled halfway down before grasping a balustrade to stop my descent. My ribs hurt like hell. I saw stars when my head made contact with at least one step.

Mary Ellen followed, her voice now shrieking, "No, no, no! This house is mine!"

Richard's voice boomed from the top of the staircase.

"Mary Ellen! Stop!"

She twisted to face her husband, lost her balance, and made a grab for the railing. She missed and fell over me. With a scream, she hurtled down bouncing all the way to the bottom complete with cracks and thumps where her head made contact with the steps. I gazed down at her crumpled, unmoving body. Richard rushed past me.

I shakily regained my feet and limped toward them. He held her in his arms, sobbing her name over and over. Her eyes stared at the ceiling, yet saw nothing. Even I knew she was dead. I sank down onto a step, buried my face in my hands, and cried.

A moment later, Stephen entered. I ran to him. His warm comforting arms held me. There was no need for words.

****

Four days later, after the funeral, Richard, Giles, Evelyn, Stephen, and I gathered in the drawing room. Everyone else had left.

The constable who answered Stephen's emergency

call had bought the story we all told.

"A terrible accident," Stephen said. "Mrs. Goodhue and Miss Channing were coming downstairs for cocktails when Mrs. Goodhue caught her heel on the tread and fell. Miss Channing attempted to catch hold of her, but fell herself."

Now, seated with drinks in our hands, Evelyn stared at Richard. "What really happened?"

I didn't answer, but wondered about that eerie *déjà vu* episode on the steps. "Did she kill Sir Geoffrey?"

Richard walked to the window and stared out at the grounds.

"That whole day was awful," he said in a subdued tone. "Mary Ellen and Irene were sniping at each other all through luncheon until Grandfather banged his fist on the table and said, 'You people are all useless human beings. Mary Ellen, you're a snob. Irene can't seem to find a man of substance.' At that point he rose and tossed his napkin onto the table. 'I have an announcement. I'm changing my will. I'll find someone more deserving than the lot of you.' With that, he left the room."

"Only he had already changed it and had told Irene of his decision weeks before," Stephen said.

"It looks that way. Irene never wanted the responsibility of Bountiful," Richard declared firmly.

"And Sir Geoffrey knew that, which was why he left it to her in the first place," I ventured. "Until he got the bright idea of tangling me in the family net."

Stephen shook his head. "When he handed me the will *he'd* written, I advised him not to do this, but the old boy was adamant. The long-lost granddaughter of his favorite son would inherit everything not already in trust. He didn't cut his family off completely, but just enough to show who was boss."

Giles sipped his scotch. He nodded again. "Evelyn and I were surprised. Irene was unusually calm, but that's to be expected since she apparently knew it was already a done deal."

Richard sighed. "I was shocked by his threat, but Mary Ellen was livid. She ran up to our room. I followed. For the next ten minutes she screamed, cursed, and threw things—books, magazines, hair brushes before collapsing onto the bed. I gave her a sedative, waited until she fell asleep, and then went downstairs to have it out with Grandfather. Only he wasn't there. He'd had Myron drive him into West End. I assumed he just wanted to get the hell out of the house."

Richard left the window and sat in a chair. He closed his eyes. "I did estate work in the study before coming upstairs to bathe and dress for dinner. I figured I'd let tempers die down and talk to him later.

"Mary Ellen was already dressed when I entered the room. I asked if she was feeling better and she said no, but decided Sir Geoffrey wasn't serious. I went into the bathroom. While the tub filled, I ran the shaver over my face. The noises masked Mary Ellen leaving the room. She went to talk to Grandfather. He was on his way down to the drawing room. They met at the head of the stairs."

"And they argued," I said, shivering with remembrance.

"She said he told her Bountiful was his and he'd do with it as he pleased. She begged him to reconsider. Reminded him of how much she and I had sacrificed.

He called her a fool, then turned to go down the steps." He heaved a shaky sigh. "Mary Ellen swore it was an accident. Claimed she grabbed his arm. He twisted away, lost his balance and fell."

"Did you believe her?" Stephen asked in a low tone.

"I don't know. I honestly don't know. It sounded plausible, but at the same time I can see her pushing him."

"Just like with me," I replied. "It was even the same time of day."

He nodded. "Eerie coincidence. The room was empty when I came out of the bathroom. I thought she'd gone on down, so started to change clothes. Then I heard you scream. I rushed out to find…" he didn't continue.

"Did Mary Ellen also switch out Evelyn's pills?" Stephen asked.

Richard looked up at Evelyn and drew in a ragged breath. "Yes. I switched them back later."

"I knew it, I knew it," Evelyn muttered. "Why?"

"You threw out that nonsense at the dinner party about Sir Geoffrey being murdered. Everyone at the table knew you were accusing Mary Ellen. You didn't say it, but the implication was there," Stephen answered.

Richard shook his head. "The plans for a bed and breakfast coupled with Evelyn offering to help sent her over the edge. While you were touring the house with Evelyn, Mary Ellen sneaked into the bedroom and switched the pills. She swore she only wanted to make you a little sick. When she realized what happened, she was terrified."

I wanted to tell him that was a crock, but held my tongue. What good would it do now?

"She didn't know you'd take aspirin before lunch and the migraine medication later," I said.

Evelyn downed her wine in a swift gulp. "I suppose."

Her expression said she didn't believe it either.

Giles finished his drink and rose. "Are you ready, dear? I'd like to make it home before dark."

"You're welcome to stay," I said.

He shook his head. "No, maybe another time, when we've had time to recover from this."

Evelyn also stood. "Giles is right. Let me know when you're ready to renovate. I'd enjoy helping."

They left and drove off.

Richard got to his feet. "It's time I left, too."

I rose and laid my hand on his arm. "You don't have to, you know. You're welcome to stay here as long as you want."

He smiled and looked at Stephen. "I don't think you need a stuffy old third wheel hanging around. I'll be in town, staying with Roger until the new house is available. Perhaps fresh surroundings will erase the memories. I'll come back for my personal items in a day, or two."

The front door closed behind him leaving Stephen and me alone. He took my hand.

"Come on, let's get some fresh air."

We wandered onto the terrace and into the rose garden maze. I touched one of the fragrant blooms with my finger. Did rose bushes in the tropics bloom year round? I had no idea.

"Guess the gardener will have to keep everything

looking good." I sniffed the heady blossom. "Mary Ellen loved this. She was so proud the day she showed me around."

Stephen squeezed my hand. "It was all she had. That and the dream of one day being mistress of Bountiful."

We continued on, then across the lawn to the repaired overlook. I looked out onto the calm turquoise waters and shivered.

"I still can't believe all that's happened. Ben, Mary Ellen, the killings. It sounds like something I'd act out in a play."

From behind, Stephen encircled me in his arms and kissed the top of my head.

Earlier he'd told me Ben, enraged at the thought of another roadblock to romancing Bountiful into his hands, had also confessed to running us off the road. And while I couldn't prove it, I believe Mary Ellen had locked me in the attic.

"I warned Sir Geoffrey he was playing with fire. I put off contacting you until the last legality for breaking the will was done." He turned me to face him. "On the other hand, it brought you to me."

"Where are we going to live?"

"I'll build you a new house in Port Elizabeth. One that's easier to maintain, but with room to grow. Perhaps one day we can live at Lands End."

"Room to grow? As in children?"

"Lots and lots of children." He smiled and kissed me.

"You have a deal, Mr. Albright, provided not a one of them is named Jonathon or Geoffrey!"

He laughed. "Deal!"

We swung around to watch the last rays of the setting sun sparkle off the water. Bountiful was beautiful. I loved it, but we needed a place to call our own.

A new home, a new beginning, a new life. As long as Stephen was with me, all would be well.

A word about the author...

Suzanne was born and raised in Indianapolis, Indiana, but has had the pleasure of living in several states throughout her adult life.

During her college years at Ball State University she majored in History, and was the only student in the dorm who actually enjoyed writing term papers.

She has two grown sons and is blessed with five grandchildren, three boys and two girls.

Currently, she and her husband live in Ft. Lauderdale, Florida along with dogs, Lucky and Liza, taking advantage of year-round warm weather, the beach, and all that goes with it.

She loves sharing her fantasies with readers and looks forward to meeting her fans.